"STEP OUT

Blancanales listened for signs of a possible hidden gunman. He had a prisoner, at least for the moment, but one mistake and his brains could be spilled on the street with the would-be killers he'd just dispatched.

The prisoner followed Pol's instructions.

"Lie down on your stomach and lace your fingers behind your head," Blancanales barked. The guy, obviously in a mood to survive this encounter, did as he was told. His breath came in rapid gulps, anxiety too real to be faked.

"Anyone else get away?"

"Yeah," the man answered. "He ran…"

Toward the front of the van, the Able Team warrior concluded, as a shadow flickered in the windshield of the vehicle, disappearing around the corner. There were no abandoned weapons on the sidewalk, so there was a good chance the escaped ambusher was packing some serious firepower.

Blancanales dropped to a kneeling position at the sound of footfalls on the asphalt on the other side of the van. The gunman intended to flank him, but Blancanales was ready, front sight on the spot where a head would appear.

DON PENDLETON'S

STONY

AMERICA'S ULTRA-COVERT INTELLIGENCE AGENCY

MAN®

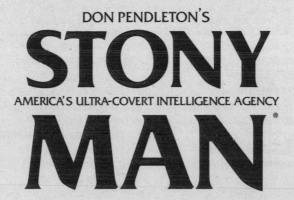

EXIT STRATEGY

A GOLD EAGLE BOOK FROM

WORLDWIDE®

TORONTO • NEW YORK • LONDON
AMSTERDAM • PARIS • SYDNEY • HAMBURG
STOCKHOLM • ATHENS • TOKYO • MILAN
MADRID • WARSAW • BUDAPEST • AUCKLAND

Recycling programs
for this product may
not exist in your area.

First edition December 2015

ISBN-13: 978-0-373-80454-2

Exit Strategy

Special thanks and acknowledgment to
Douglas P. Wojtowicz for his contribution to this work.

EXIT STRATEGY

CHAPTER ONE

Few things were ever truly worthwhile on these witness protection jobs, but Domingo Perez did find this family to be actually worth a damn. Sadly, Justice never really had much for "innocents" who were in the line of fire; their deals went to scumbags who had their hands painted red with blood up to their elbows. This case was different and Perez had known there was something of worth in this security detail when he'd gotten word that the operation involved blacksuits. Seeing Harold Brognola at the briefing for the mission had been the icing on the cake. The big Fed was known as someone who was well connected to even the highest-level covert ops.

The Castillos were a fine family. There was the father, formerly a crusading journalist in Mexico. Joaquin Castillo had stirred the hornet's nest of government and law enforcement corruption plenty of times over the years, and Perez was fully aware that anyone the reporter had targeted was well and truly bent. His wife, Amanda, was herself in the journalism business; practically the other half of the investigative team that peeled back layers of grimy corruption by carving through the tumorous hide of the diseased beast that was south-of-the-border law enforcement.

Perez had worked with more than enough of them to realize that while the rank and file were good and honest, the higher in rank you rose, the more stink you had to roll around in, rutting in it like a pig in mud. Up high, you either had to be a saint with the reflexes of a cockroach or practically dance in the laps of the cartels.

Donald Burnett, the marshal in charge, had given Perez the three Castillo children to place in protection. The oldest was a fourteen-year-old boy, also named Domingo. Then there were his younger sisters, Pequita and Annette, born at two-year intervals after Domingo.

At fourteen, Domingo Castillo had already lived in two different countries and was as fluent in English as he was in Spanish to the point where he'd only have an accent if he wished to. His hair was a light brown, a "gift" from his grandfather by his mother, Amanda, strong currents of Spaniard blood coursing through that side of the family. His eyes were hazel and mercurial, flashing at times bright green or smoldering into a dark brown, which often reflected the young man's moods.

Pequita, at twelve, was already growing into a young beauty. She had her father's black hair and her mother's cool blue eyes. Whenever Perez was in the room, Pequita seemed to never look away from him. He remembered when he was twelve and how girls his age had never showed the slightest interest in him, not when there were older boys or men around.

Perez was flattered at the attention, but at the same time he thought of all the poor twelve-year-old boys of the world who were just starting to form an interest in girls. Twenty years ago, Perez would definitely have been agog over Pequita, and at the same time be halted by crippling shyness that such a cute girl would have had on him.

Grin and bear it, Dom, he told himself.

Annette was just as tall as her older sister, but more round-faced and bespectacled. That pure Spaniard blood showed in how her cheeks freckled instead of tanning evenly, the glimmering yellow highlights in her hair and the flash of blue in her eyes.

The safe house in Arizona was one that was large and comfortable enough for the Castillo clan and the eight agents assigned to protection. The security wall around the estate was twelve feet in height and equipped with some of the best and latest sensors available. This, Perez thought, also likely thanks to the top people at Justice.

It was a good setup, at least in terms of technology. The members of the witness protection team themselves were equipped for a war if necessary. Except for Burnett, every member of the team was armed with a Glock 21 .45 ACP autoloading pistol. With fourteen rounds on tap and thirteen in subsequent reloads, Perez couldn't have asked for more firepower that he could hide under an untucked shirt.

Perez, watching over the kids as they enjoyed a swim day in the roasting Arizona heat at a pond on the property, had a Mossberg 930 SPX not far away in the Jeep. Using the lessons learned from the earlier Mossberg Jungle Gun made for the United States Marine Corps in the nineties, Perez knew his semiautomatic 12-gauge shotgun was designed for combat. Nine rounds of 12-gauge were in that piece with more shells in a sidesaddle on the stock of the big blaster. He liked the interchanging of buckshot and slugs because there was no telling at what range he'd encounter an attacker.

There were M4 SOPMOD rifles and actual M16s back at the villa, as well, but Perez was a Chicago boy and in his heart and mind being a cop meant using a shotgun.

Domingo Castillo swung on a branch out over the glassy surface of the pond and let go. The boy's slender limbs flailed for a moment as he hung in the air before splashing down. Pequita and Annette laughed at his "air dance" and Domingo burst up through the surface with an ear-to-ear grin.

"Did you see that?" Annette called out. The bespectacled youngest sister had been shy around all the strange new adults, even the female marshals, Lewis and Moore, but as Perez was their primary "sitter" the girl was comfortable with him.

Perez nodded and smiled. As he did so, he saw her cheeks redden and he realized that Pequita wasn't the only one who had an interest in older men.

¡Dios! Perez prayed for strength. Ignore it and move on, Dom. And pray to hell this doesn't cause any trouble for you in the future.

As if at the very thought of trouble, the rumble of distant helicopters wafted to Perez's ears. Nothing appeared to be flying in this direction, but he lunged into the cab of the pickup to grab the set of binoculars he'd left on the dash.

There were three helicopters hovering over the compound. Dull black metal, not even reflecting sunlight off their skins, dark-tinted windows and strange tail booms told him that these were not normal aircraft. Their rotor-slap was only suddenly heard not because of their approach but because they no longer were operating under minimal noise profile. Perez loved helicopters and noticed that one had the little dolphin nose of a Bell Ranger but the same round, squat body of the AH-6 "Little Birds" of US Special Operations fame.

It took a moment for him to recognize one of the helicopters as the Bell MD-900 Explorer. The normal Explorer was a bird that could carry six passengers alongside its pilot and copilot and had a range of nearly three hundred miles on internal tanks. Through the zoom of his binoculars he saw drop tanks, as well, which could easily double its flight time, and he knew it could cruise at 154 miles an hour with its turbo Pratt & Whitney engines.

One stayed in the air, side door open, an odd strobe flickering off the side. Perez swept the binoculars down to the other Explorers that had landed and disgorged men. A dozen of them, dressed in black, with helmets, heavily laden vests and assault rifles rushed toward the compound

As soon as gunfire crackled in the distance, Perez let the binoculars drop into the seat well. He looked back at the children by the pond.

"Get in the truck," Perez ordered. "Now!"

Domingo Castillo's pupils were tight, his normally tanned cheeks flushed and damp with sweat as he guided his younger sisters toward the marshal's service vehicle.

Perez heard the violent faraway roar of something big. Guns sounded a lot louder, much more dangerous than they did on television, but this wasn't new information for him. Had he the time to contemplate, he'd show some regret at living so close to violence that he knew the true sounds of gunfire. His parents had tried to keep him and his sisters safe from the ravages and the corruption of everyday life in Mexico.

The girls, to their credit and to the shame that they had learned this so young in life, knew what was wrong, what was happening. Perez had the passenger-side door open for the kids, Glock .45 in his fist ready to go.

Violence seethed up at the villa and though his every instinct was to rush up there and assist his fellow marshals, he knew that bringing three preteens into the middle of a gunfight was the worst possible thing that he could do. In the choice between helping his friends and saving the lives of the Castillo children, his orders were to run like a scared little girl.

Cursing, he moved around to the driver's side, got in and fired up the engine. If someone pursued, and so far he saw nothing in the rearview mirror, his job was to evade hostiles and to defend the kids if cornered. The fight he could put up with his shotgun and pistol would be long and loud. And, hopefully, be more than enough to keep this precious cargo secure.

Pedal to the metal, he put distance between the children and the conflict at the main house.

"Stay down, girls!" Perez shouted. "Stay down!"

Keep going faster and faster. Pull away before they hear—

The rear windshield cracked as something hit it. It wasn't a pebble. Not with the force of the impact. But it was also not a bullet that retained enough energy to punch through safety glass.

Perez stomped on the gas harder, building up speed.

AMANDA CASTILLO'S LIFE was never considered to be one of caution and comfort. She was born into privilege in Mexico, with enough European Spanish blood in her to allow her natural blond highlights and the glimmer of blue eyes. Though the differences between her and other Mexicans weren't that apparent, especially given the richness of her sunburned skin, her father's wealth was something that had kept her in undeniable comfort. His kind of money meant that he didn't have to worry about the legalities of protecting her from the "lower classes."

What had started as rebellion as a teenager had turned into something much different. She'd hung with Joaquin, an idealistic, young wannabe revolutionary in the slums of Mexico City, and her youthful aimlessness had evolved into a crusade for justice. Joaquin Castillo had turned from Marxist idealist into someone who saw the truths of corruption, both right- and left-wing. Amanda Moran conveyed her good looks and connections into a place where she could strip bare the hypocrisy and corruption in an anchor's chair.

They'd married, but Amanda Moran Castillo was part of a one-two punch. Joaquin dug deep into the secrets behind the camera and Amanda laid them raw and unfiltered on nationwide TV. It was dangerous, risky, and Amanda was reminded of that every day when she looked in the mirror at the scars on her hips and stomach. The end of her two-piece-bikini days was a small price to pay, however, for the cause of truth and justice.

Now, however, as she watched a US Marshal apply emergency first aid to Joaquin, she realized that some prices were just too high to pay.

"*¡Mi corazon!*" she breathed as Marshal Burnett put his arm across her chest, holding her back from the scene.

Amanda wanted to tear loose from the old lawman with his Southern drawl, but she became all too aware of the need for his restraint. The wooden floor between her and her wounded husband was shredded, splinters and sawdust erupting as a wave of heavy automatic fire rained down.

"Gettin' yourself killed ain't gonna help your man!" Burnett growled. He tugged her farther back from the damaged wall, keeping himself and his big silver hand-gun between Amanda and any incoming harm. Burnett, no stranger to Southern law enforcement given his twang, walked the line with a big old 10 mm STI Executive.

Amanda, who'd spent enough time around firearms thanks to her rich family, was impressed at the beast of a gun. Everything from its gleaming, mirror-polished slide and black polymer frame screamed "fear me." The Executive was essentially what happened when a Texan decided that the Colt 45 just didn't have enough punch or enough rounds in the magazine. The basic design of the 1911 had been preserved, but the polymer frame had a hole in the grip to handle a double-stack magazine. Burnett said he had twenty rounds in each of the fat magazines on his belt. The 10 mm round carried as much punch at 100 yards as the .45 ACP had at the muzzle, and Burnett wasn't using the down-loaded FBI rounds that had eventually given birth to the .40 Short and Weak, as he called it.

The house had gone from silent to a maelstrom of thunder and disintegrating objects in the space of heartbeats. With Joaquin down, but seemingly miles away on the other side of a deadly firefight, Amanda's thoughts quickly turned toward her children. They were out of the house…

Out in the open!

Burnett kept her still, edging them farther along the interior of the house, avoiding clear fields of view from the windows.

"The kids!" Amanda shouted.

"Out on the edge of the estate," Burnett growled. There was a motion caught out of the corner of Amanda's eye, and Burnett reacted, firing that big silver gun through the naked windowpane. The Executive roared loudly enough to make the crackle of gunfire outside disappear for a moment. Apparently, Burnett's first shot didn't have an effect. He shifted his aim and fired through the wall. Massive chunks blew out and in less than a moment the figure of a toppling man appeared for a brief instant in the window.

"We have ground attackers! Side three!" Burnett shouted over his hands-free mike. Whether any of the other lawmen around the compound could hear a thing was highly in doubt. But even as Burnett barked his observation, bigger guns cut loose from inside, blasting more chunks through walls, tearing into those laying siege to the house.

Amanda knew that, unfortunately, that vulgar display of firepower made them targets. Something turned the ceiling of the house to shredded remnants of terra cotta, tar paper and ceiling struts raining down in the wake of a blaze of automatic gunfire. The silhouettes of gunmen disappeared in the rain of burning lead.

The next thing she knew, her voice was raw from screaming over the loss of two of her defenders. Hell clattered all around her and Burnett forcibly pushed and pulled her to her feet. She stumbled, but Burnett's hand never allowed her to trip. He was a steady guide, a protector.

Amanda glanced back and the room where she'd left Joaquin was obscured by collapsed ceiling and walls. Her stomach twisted. Joaquin's injuries already horrific, he was now either buried in rubble or chewed to ribbons by the torrent of fire and death hurled by their assailants.

If death hadn't already claimed her husband from his gunshot wounds, it was closing its grasp on his life tighter and tighter.

Her eyes stung, throat constricted.

"Make sure that Perez got away with the kids," Amanda shouted over the din.

"He had his orders," Burnett growled. "He'll get them as far away as possible. Or die trying."

Amanda's eyes widened with horror at that thought.

"They're hammering this house from all sides. I doubt they brought enough aircraft to do that and chase down Perez in his truck," Burnett emphasized. "But those kids need their mother. That means we keep on the move!"

Thunder and lightning seemed to blast Amanda's world to splinters, her vision and hearing fading out. She could feel the dull thud of the floor against her cheek and shoulder, and even through the wail of ringing in her ears, Burnett's big bad gun cracked through the mayhem of her sensory deprivation.

Rough hands suddenly yanked her to her feet, pushed her along. This time her feet snarled against each other, her knees cracking against clutter. These were the hands of a thug hauling her around like a piece of meat, not the hands of a protector.

Time had little meaning, but she felt her feet bash and stumble against each other what felt like a thousand times.

Just when she was tired of tripping on her own feet, her vision cleared enough to see that she was outside in the Arizona sun.

She only caught a brief glimpse of the blue sky before she toppled face-first into the dry grass of the yard. Spitting and coughing blades from between her lips, she heard the grumbles of two men talking. Explosions and gunfire left her ears too muddled to make out their conversation, but when one bound her wrists behind her back, it didn't leave much doubt.

From witness in federal protection to widow and prisoner.

With the aircraft and sheer firepower on hand, Amanda quickly put together that this was one of the many enemies she had made. Undoubtedly this was a cartel, since few others could afford helicopter gunships and trained troops, and only the most insane of Mexican government agencies would dream of murdering US Marshals on American soil.

Then again, Accion Obrar was a branch of the *federales* known for its gleeful willingness to break the rules. Harold Brognola of the US Justice Department had brought the Castillos to Arizona to protect them from AO, and if these men were cartel, they were only once removed from the paramilitary, unsanctioned vigilante force that she and Joaquin had gathered so much dirt on.

And now they owned her. The nylon cable ties bit her wrists cruelly, and her shoulders burned in protest as a captor hauled her to her feet.

"On the chopper, *puta*" came the order. Amanda struggled to stay upright despite the force of the thug's shove, and she did enter the helicopter, but only after banging her knees and thighs against the bottom of the opened side door. The bare metal flooring chilled her cheek, and more hands snagged her ankles and lower legs, levering her up and into the cabin. She wanted to turn over, but a forest of combat boots surrounded her. They penned her in; she couldn't move. She wanted to spit and curse them all, but more than one of them planted a sole on her back. The weight of their feet immobilized her, informed her that she was only meat for them; a trophy deer brought back from a successful hunt.

She only lived at their whim. One mistake and they crushed her underfoot, without qualm, without mercy.

Though, if their intent was to keep her, then she knew there was only one destination ahead for her.

El Calabozo sin Piedad.

These were Los Lictors, a group of merciless yet utterly precise commandos whose skills relegated the similar Los Zetas to second best. Assault rifles, special operations tactics, brutal accuracy and violence of action made them the elite champions of the cartel wars.

El Calabozo sin Piedad.

The Dungeon without Pity.

In her decades of covering corruption among Mexican law enforcement, no other prison in the world harbored such a grim, soul-chilling reputation. Not even the Black Dolphin prison in the former Soviet Union had such a reputation for violence and level of security.

People went in there, and the only reason they came out again was that they'd only been put there for "a vacation." Accion Obrar used it to keep their favorite gun thugs and smugglers out of the view of the law. It was a place where demons were allowed to indulge their tastes for mayhem and abuse against rival cartels and political dissidents.

Amanda Moran Castillo was such a political dissident in the eyes of Accion Obrar.

And in the space of a day's travel, she would be handed over to the worst inmates at the darkest, deadliest asylum on the planet.

No, Amanda didn't live at the whim of these kidnappers. They wanted her to live.

For she was on the fast track to hell, and death was a mercy she'd soon beg for.

CHAPTER TWO

The assembly of all the members of the Stony Man Farm's teams—Able Team, Phoenix Force, as well as the cybernetic squad—was not a good portent. With all hands on deck, this either had to be a national emergency or a direct threat to the Sensitive Operations Group itself. Without the presence of the founder of Stony Man—the Executioner, Mack Bolan—the covert agency still thrived, undimmed by the privation of the legendary soldier. The lone warrior had his own missions out in the world; things that fell through the cracks that even a top secret government-sanctioned antiterrorism agency could not attend to.

Carl Lyons, brawny, blond and grim-faced, and his colleague in arms, David McCarter, bracketed Harold Brognola at the head of the table. In contrast to the square-jawed, all-American football hero Lyons, McCarter was lean and fox-faced. His build was no less defined than Lyons's, but he was more panther than king of the jungle. They were the respective leaders of their teams; Lyons commanding the urban warriors known as Able Team and McCarter being the leader of Stony Man's foreign ops unit named Phoenix Force.

Though Able Team consisted of only three commandos, it was just as effective as the five-man army that was Phoenix Force. There was a spirited competition between the two groups, but each saw the other as an equal. The eight of them together were quite brilliant in a diversity of fields ranging from emergency medical treatment thanks to former SEAL and Navy corpsman Calvin James of the Force, to Able Team's electronics genius Hermann Schwarz. When Brognola and Bolan had vetted the teams, they'd looked for smart, capable, quick-to-learn men who were straight shooters and athletic combatants.

The cyber team leader, Aaron "the Bear" Kurtzman, may not have been low in body fat, but with his thick shag of beard and furry, heavily muscled forearms, he was no weakling. Despite being confined to a wheelchair by a gunshot wound to the spine, Kurtzman's upper body was slabbed over in thick muscle from exercise and the constant maneuvering of his manual chair. As strong as his arms and chest were, though, his mind was equally powerful as the creator and coordinator of the incredible computerized data collection and intelligence system that made the Farm's missions possible.

"What's the deal, Hal?" McCarter spoke up first. Though McCarter's antic energy had been tamed greatly by the role of leadership of his team, the British SAS veteran still was not given to idling when there were things to do. "What's the crisis du jour?"

"I just got news from Arizona," Brognola answered. "We lost a lot of blacksuits serving as a security detail."

An older bulldog of a man who had been with the Farm since the very beginning, Brognola had been an FBI agent assigned to capture or kill Mack Bolan a lifetime ago, back when the Executioner had waged his unsanctioned vigilante actions against organized crime on US soil. Rather than ultimately eliminate Bolan, Brognola had set up a situation where his lethal fighting skills could be more readily used to protect the United States. Since then, the big Fed had expanded the Sensitive Operations Group's reach by creating the blacksuit program.

The blacksuits were cultivated from the best and brightest of the military and law enforcement, well-trained and honest men and women who didn't quite have the clearance or lack of ties that would make them perfect for the covert agency. They came to the Farm in the shadow of the old Stony Man of the Blue Ridge Mountains, where they received continuing education and refresh training. They were also tapped for intel that didn't make it into top secret databases immediately. Often, it was the men of Able or Phoenix who educated these warriors, so the loss of one was the loss of a friend as well as a student.

"How many?" Lyons asked, his voice a low rumble like thunder across the plains.

"Seven confirmed dead, five wounded. Don Burnett is missing, as well as one of the packages they were protecting," Brognola advised regrettably. "Another principal was killed."

"How many were they protecting?" McCarter quizzed.

Brognola took a deep breath. "Five. A man and his wife. Three children. The man, Joaquin Castillo, was killed. The children were out at a swimming hole. Their protection detail pulled them out when the attackers struck."

Brognola handed out packets for the two action teams to read. The cybernetic crew had already gone over the information and grisly imagery in preparing the briefing packages.

"Son of a bitch," Calvin James growled. James was the first American member of Phoenix Force. Despite the kind of discipline it took to be a medical corpsman and a SEAL, and later a member of San Francisco SWAT, James was still a little quick with a curse. Tall, black and lanky, he was passionate about his position. "You don't need to ask me twice to put boot to ass against the bastards behind this."

"I'll have to," Brognola returned. "That's Mexican *federale* equipment at the scene of the crime. That means this is an international incident. One that the State Department wants to keep under wraps."

"Excuse me?" Rosario Blancanales, the elder of Lyons's two Able Team partners, asked. Five foot eleven, with silver hair and a face wizened beyond his years, his lithe, spry frame belied the appearance of his age. Where Lyons was a police officer and undercover FBI agent who had allied with Bolan often, Blancanales had served in Bolan's unit during his military career and later assisted him in his private war against organized crime. Blancanales's first team-up with Bolan post desertion had ended with him in jail, one of only two survivors of the Executioner's death squad. His entry into Able Team had cleared those records. His elite Ranger training and natural diplomacy, which had earned him the nickname "the Politician," made Blancanales an invaluable member of Stony Man. "The government is going to downplay the slaughter of US Marshals?"

"It's being kept under a tight lid," Carmen Delahunt interjected. Delahunt, one of the members of Kurtzman's cybernetics team, had investigative and tech skills that easily translated into search algorithms that helped keep the Stony Man teams up-to-date on enemy action. "State Department and the White House don't want the public to get a word of this," she added.

"*Federales* involved? No doubt," Gary Manning added. Manning, a Canadian, was a barrel-chested polymath, tall and strong, and he was also a genius with explosives. His restless intellect, however, had kept him moving from field to field. He had proved to be an expert woodsman and hunter, served with the military in Southeast Asian operations, owned his own import-export firm and was an officer in the Royal Canadian Mounted Police, where he'd cross-trained with German antiterrorism agencies.

This depth and breadth of experience had made him a steady hand and wise counsel to Phoenix Force leader McCarter, while his hunting talents had translated into his being a lethal sniper and his engineering had made him a master of demolitions. He, like McCarter, was an original Phoenix Force operator and was not surprised by an act of cross-border violence being held in secret to avert the possibility of war between two nations. Too often, Phoenix's five had been sent in to defang and defuse conflicts instigated by outside parties looking to profit from war and chaos. "Given that Joaquin and Amanda Castillo *are* considered enemies of the state in Mexico, the legitimacy of this strike force could be fairly solid."

"You know about these two?" Hawkins asked. The youngest and newest member of Phoenix, T. J. Hawkins, was the other American who'd diluted the original mission description of Mack Bolan's foreign legion.

Hawkins, who had grown up on the South Side of Chicago, was a veteran of the US Army Rangers and Delta Force. He had a history of going outside the rules to protect innocent lives to do what was right, politics be damned. He was a prime candidate to fill in the ranks after McCarter replaced their retired original commander.

"The last time we were in Mexico, I managed to catch a newscast about Accion Obrar. The similarities to Stony Man made me curious enough to delve further," Manning noted.

Hawkins frowned. "Being a Texas boy, I looked into Accion Obrar because they were allegedly behind unseating paramilitary gangs operating on both sides of the border. Just in case we had to deal with Los Sigmas or Los Omegas or some group like that."

"The new hotness is Los Lictors." Hermann Schwarz spoke up. Schwarz was Blancanales's longtime friend and a fellow survivor of Bolan's death squad. Balancing electrical engineering and Ranger training made Schwarz, nicknamed "Gadgets," one of the top ten fighting elite in the country alongside his fellow Able Team warriors. "For those of us on Able Team who aren't fluent in Spanish, that's 'the officers' or 'the magistrates.'"

Lyons met Schwarz's gaze at his friend's usual razzing. "How illuminating."

"He's up to five-syllable words, Gadgets! Cheese it!" Blancanales stage-whispered across the table. The humor, so close in the wake of the loss of several blacksuits, was meant to distract from the pain. These men were law enforcement professionals and gallows humor was a means to keep laughing instead of crying. For that, Lyons was glad for his friends' antics, though it didn't ameliorate the anger he felt for the murderers of the blacksuit marshals.

"This is particularly disturbing in that we have little idea who could have betrayed the location of the Castillos," Huntington Wethers, the third member of the Farm's cyber crew, noted. A tall African American who looked born to be a college professor, complete with corduroy jacket and pipe, Wethers was a mathematical genius and a man who was meticulous in seeking out information on the web. This didn't mean that he was slow; indeed, he was able to process raw data in bulk, but he was thorough. "The setup arranged by Hal, utilizing 'in-house' resources, was kept away from agency heads specifically."

"The potential for a mole to intercept was minimized, but there's never a sure thing where more than one person is involved," Brognola grumbled. "So, we have a list of who could have let slip about their security."

"A list we're going through with a fine-tooth comb," Akira Tokaido said. No irony was lost that the young Japanese American's spiky punk hairstyle only saw a comb to further splay and launch it toward the ceiling. Where Wethers was meticulous, Tokaido was punk rock and thrash metal, making wild leaps of deductive logic, though his mathematical and coding capabilities were not haphazard.

Where speed and intuition were required, Tokaido was an F-22 Raptor pulling 9 Gs to outmaneuver his opponents. Wethers was more the aircraft carrier sailing along at 35 knots but with eyes and ears everywhere. Delahunt was the bridge between the two, using her own investigative instincts to seek handholds of information to scale impregnable fortresses of mystery.

"I pity your quarry, mates," McCarter quipped.

"Eventually they become yours," Delahunt said. "And when they do, that's when things get…satisfying."

Gary Manning raised an eyebrow at Delahunt's breathless final word. The red-haired ex-cop was a beautiful woman, regardless of age, and even her toughness never marginalized her feminine allure.

Manning turned toward the big Fed, hoping to keep his mind clear. "You don't think that it's a direct link to the government, do you, Hal?"

"No," Brognola returned. "The crew has been digging deep and hard, looking for threads that might have exposed the blacksuit witness security detail, and those assignments are showing up in the system. It's not an actual mole inside WITSEC, either."

"More like a worm in the computer systems," Tokaido acknowledged. "I'm picking up the damage left behind and Hunt and I are trying to locate and end it."

"As well as to perform some forensic work on the worm so we can learn where it came from," Wethers added. "Its elusive nature confirms that a genius put it together, or even a team of geniuses."

"Say, the best hackers a Mexican covert agency could put together?" Lyons asked.

Wethers nodded in affirmation.

"Accion Obrar is a fairly blunt name for a so-called top secret government op," McCarter said.

Lyons tilted his head. "It seems more like a terrorist

group. In fact, I think some French commies could sue for stealing the title 'Action Directe.'"

"It'd make targeting them easier," McCarter mused.

Lyons smirked. He turned back to Brognola. "We'll be babysitting the kids? Because you know that they'll still be a target."

"That, and I know you want a crack at the thugs who killed so many of our blacksuits," Brognola confirmed. "Weapons free. No rules. No referee."

"Using the kids as bait is going to be tough." Blancanales spoke up. "But, sadly, this wouldn't be the first time we've had to do it."

"And we haven't lost one of our protectees yet," Schwarz interjected. "We won't let them down."

"You said the father was killed and the mother is missing," McCarter said. "She might be on her way back to Mexico?"

Brognola indicated the Briton was right with a nod. "The most likely place they'll put her is El Calabozo sin Piedad. So, right now, our priority is for Phoenix to head to Mexico to get her out of there."

Rafael Encizo grumbled, drawing McCarter's attention. "I've heard rumors about that place. It's on a scale of the Cuban prison I was kept in as a teenager."

In his youth, Encizo, the last of the original founders of Phoenix Force, had fought against the Communist dictatorship in his native Cuba. Only by breaking his jailer's neck and stealing a boat did he escape to the United States. One of the few members of Stony Man's action teams not a military veteran, Encizo's lifetime of work as a salvage diver and as a special consultant for the US Drug Enforcement Administration in Florida had forged him into a highly capable combatant. Officially the oldest of Phoenix Force, he was a swarthy and incredibly strong man for his diminutive height of five-eight. Not the most muscular member of Phoenix—that was Manning—his strength was still considerable, as were his skills with knives. "The worst part is that this is a prison in a *friendly* nation to ours."

"Cuba's on the friendly list now, after all this time," James offered. He was Encizo's closest friend on the team, the two spending long stretches of off time scuba diving as well as practicing sparring with their chosen knives. "But, yeah, Mexico is supposed to be a democracy."

"If Mexico were working so well as a democracy," Hawkins interrupted, "people wouldn't be flooding across the border illegally to escape poverty, corrupt governments and the cartel wars."

The Texan didn't often offer his opinion on a crisis unless he felt strongly about it. Raised in a border state, Hawkins had a lifetime's worth of perspective on illegal immigration, and could tell the difference between the criminals who exploited desperation and those seeking escape from turmoil in Mexico or other Central American nations. He caught a knowing nod from the three members of Able Team who had engaged in their own operations against corruption in El Salvador, Guatemala and some of the harsher Mexican states.

Then again, the people of Stony Man were in a position of experience and education, having intimate familiarity with the forces of corruption that trampled humans with their clumsy steps.

"Since we'll be breaking into an official Mexican prison, I don't think we'll be able to head across the border with our arsenal in diplomatic luggage," McCarter said to Brognola.

"Sadly, no. You'll be working without a net," the big Fed agreed. "Unless you happen to have some contacts down there. We'll arrange a HALO jump for you, if necessary."

"The day the five of us can't skirt border security without a parachute insertion is the day we're retiring as a team," McCarter countered. "Sorry, T.J."

Hawkins shrugged. As the team's jump master, he was usually the one who prepped them for such intrusions, the same as James and Encizo took the bulk of the preparation work for underwater operations. "No skin off my nose on how we get there, boss. We just need to get there before Amanda Castillo is irreparably damaged."

"We are on the clock," Brognola said.

"Is that why Barb's not here?" McCarter asked. "Burning up the phone lines looking for alternate approaches?"

"Making use of every asset we can." Brognola affirmed the mission controller's absence. "I don't have to tell you that this is going to be one of the stickiest things we've had to deal with in a while. One wrong move and we could have a war flare-up on our border."

"We're never called in when the options are clear and easy," Schwarz said. "That's why they call it the Sensitive Operations Group."

Brognola's scowl didn't bode well for the continuing discussion.

"Something else amiss?" Manning asked.

Brognola nodded. "Somewhere in the mix, the attackers on the Arizona safe house left a trail of breadcrumbs that ties the blacksuits to the Farm and this operation. So far, we're still an unsubstantiated rumor, but a Congressional Oversight Committee is being assembled for the express purpose of finding out who created this enormous screwup."

"The blacksuit training program and you are out in the open and vulnerable on this," Lyons said. "And considering the kind of political infighting that's been wrecking Congress over the past five or so years, if they learn that you have the ear of the President…"

"They will come down on us. They'll use it to crush

him and weaken the nation even further in international eyes," Brognola confirmed. "It's not me that I'm worried about, but our sudden vulnerability is too coincidental with the Castillo situation for it not to be a direct attack."

"People have come at the Farm with armed force before," McCarter observed. He glanced over to Lyons, remembering one instance where virtual reality hypnosis had turned Able Team into one such assault force. "But this time they're going after our underbelly."

Lyons narrowed his eyes. "We've been making more than enough enemies and ruining more conspiracies. And the one that has the deepest-digging fingers is the Arrangement."

"White supremacists and Mexican drug gangs?" Tokaido asked.

"You remember the Fascist International in our files," Lyons offered. "There are plenty of pure-blooded Mexican and other Central American 'whites.' More than enough to keep us steadily busy all this time. Our last outing with them was more than enough to cause them a lot of pain and discomfort in the media."

"The loss of Stewart Crowmass," Blancanales added.

"Well, apparently he'd lost enough iterations of the Aryan Right Coalition to have an idea who or what we are," Brognola said. "That's another thing that Carmen and Aaron are working on. We're trying to erase the trails and the crumbs that would expose the President and the Justice Department."

"So even if we bring down Accion Obrar, there's still a chance that you'll be made to fall on your sword? After all we've done for the country?" McCarter asked.

"Face it. We've done a lot more than just water-boarding and drone strikes," Lyons said. "The Democrats will go nuts over civil rights violations of our targets, especially someone not proven guilty like Crowmass. The Republicans will just stamp us as another out-of-control government program and a symbol of big government picking on the innocent."

"Crowmass was good at whipping up each party, hitting their particular hot buttons," Schwarz added. "Even dead, he's giving us shit."

"Not just Stony Man," Encizo added. "The whole country. Because if things degrade to the point where we might go to war with Mexico, the groundwork he laid might just spark a civil war."

The Stony Man operatives got up from the meeting table. As of now, they were on the clock and more than just one life was at stake. Just as it always was. They wouldn't have it any other way.

CHAPTER THREE

When David McCarter mentioned being able to circumvent the law in getting them into Mexico without outside assistance, he'd exaggerated some. During the flight to Yuma, Arizona, where the surviving blacksuit had retreated with the Castillo children, McCarter had Rafael Encizo and Calvin James calling in favors with their friends. In addition to the blacksuits trained by Phoenix Force, James had friends in both California and Nevada police agencies from his time as a member of San Francisco SWAT, and Encizo had similar brothers in arms in the Drug Enforcement Administration.

Deputy Marshal Domingo Perez had driven south from the safe house, moving closer to the Mexican border instead of farther away. But that was a good thing; it provided a major city and airport hub. The Yuma PD, the county sheriff's office and local FBI and USMS were present and on alert, keeping watch over the still-free family. Yuma sat only fourteen miles and change from the Mexican border, and with the Gila River and all manner of county roads webbed across the countryside, there was plenty of above-ground activity to keep an eye on.

What McCarter sought was the underground smugglers' routes, all the way from Andrade, California, on Interstate 8 to Douglas, Arizona, on 191. Over the years, nearly one hundred covertly built tunnels had been discovered; routes by which the cartels could get between the Sonora State in Mexico to Arizona. Heroin, cocaine, guns and money flowed freely through those tunnels, and there were likely many more that hadn't been unearthed by American and Mexican law enforcement. Both Phoenix Force and Able Team had experience with the subterranean trespasses over several missions, and McCarter was certain of one thing: if they found one end of such a tunnel, they'd be set for supplies.

Considering the state of tunnel politics, they would be going full clandestine. Sure, each member of the Force was equipped with sanitized versions of their preferred sidearms, but having access to cartel weaponry and money would be a boost of support that McCarter could truly appreciate. After all, one way that Stony Man was able to keep its chunk of the US government's black budget so small was thanks to rules of engagement that stated the blood money assembled by drug dealers and terrorists would be well spent turned back against them. Over the years Stony Man kept a minimal footprint despite its government sanctions, having adopted Mack Bolan's rule of robbing the robbers.

Hitting the end of a smuggler pipeline would not be anything new for the team.

Encizo's nodding increased in frequency, his expressions growing more excited as he spoke in rapid Spanish to the person on the other end of his call. McCarter smiled, snapping his fingers to get the attention of the others, none of which showing signs of a solid lead.

While Encizo had his cell phone to his left ear, his right hand was busy scribbling down notes. He was on to a very hot lead, which was exactly what McCarter wanted. Everything was written down in pencil, because McCarter watched the eraser bob and wag with each new bit of info.

After a seeming eternity, Encizo was finally off the phone.

"Whatcha got?"

Encizo grinned at McCarter. "Nogales, Arizona. Here're the notes."

McCarter took the pad, reading up and down.

In essence, the Nogales site was one that was heavily suspected, thanks to weeks of surveillance, but both Mexican and American judges were dragging their feet. It was, little doubt, due to pressure from one of many cartels. In years past, the cartels had carried out assassinations and other attempted murders on both sides of the line, irrespective of the tourist draw of the small cities and, according to the local DEA, Los Lictors had picked up the slack.

That the enforcer gang seemed to be doing a lot of cleanup of rival cartels, while drugs still flowed across the border, was a sign that Mexican *federales* and military were working in collusion with "the Magistrates." In particular, the report claimed the government was helping the Caballeros de Durango Cartel to take control of the Juarez Valley area and destroy other cartels.

Joaquin and Amanda Castillo had personally interviewed dozens of officials and ordinary people for their investigation. One report quoted a former Juarez police commander who claimed the entire department was working for the Knights of Durango Cartel and helping it to fight other groups. He'd also asserted that the cartel had bribed the military. Also quoted was a Mexican reporter who'd stated hearing numerous times from the public that the military had been involved in murders.

Further evidence appeared in the US trial of an ex-Juarez police captain who admitted to working for the cartel. He asserted that the Durango Cartel influenced the Mexican government and military in order to gain control of the region. A US DEA agent in the same trial alleged that the bent cop had contacts with a Mexican military officer. The report also stated, with support from an anthropologist who studied drug trafficking, that data on the low arrest rate of Durango Cartel members was evidence of favoritism on the part of the authorities. A Mexican official denied the allegation of favoritism, and a DEA agent and a political scientist also had alternate explanations for the arrest data. Another report detailed numerous indications of cartel corruption and influence within the Mexican government.

The ties between Los Lictors and the Knights of Durango Cartel were strong and apparent, but the Castillos, in uncovering those ties to the Mexican *federales* and the armed forces, had drawn down enormous heat. Their evidence threatened a lot of powerful people south of the border.

That the tunnel was owned by the Knights of Durango was icing on Phoenix Force's cake.

"That's a lot of good intel," Hawkins said. "Damned shame that Mexican judges and American Feds are afraid to take the dive into shutting down such a sewer."

"No shame at all, brother T.J." James spoke up. "With this pipeline still open, it gives us a walk through an unlocked back door."

McCarter nodded. "Hey, up front, can you drop us off at Nogales?" he asked their pilots.

"Not a problem" came the response. Jack Grimaldi and Charlie Mott served as the flight crew of the Stony Man Gulfstream jet. Outfitted with top-of-the-line avionics, storage facilities that could hide an armory, and double the normal range of a standard private jet, the aircraft would have little problem stopping at one airport or another. With Grimaldi and Mott at the controls, the plane could be set down on the shortest of municipal runways if necessary. Stealth electronics would also help it land inside an enemy nation without notice if need be.

Carl Lyons agreed with the air crew's assessment. "Currently, Deputy Perez and the kids are surrounded by a ring of armed lawmen."

"A bigger one than the last protection team, at least," Schwarz amended.

"As brazen as the assault on the Arizona safe house, it still was less blatant than an incident at a federal building in Yuma," Blancanales added. "We can spare a half hour to drop you off."

"Thanks," McCarter returned. "It'll save us the stress of driving and prepping for an assault across country."

"You're not the only one planning in the cabin, David," Lyons said.

McCarter smirked. "How's your work going?" he asked Schwarz.

"Well, since we have the enemy wanting to come to us, we'll just figure out the best place to draw them in. Lines of fire, dirty tricks to even the odds, all manner of shenanigans," Schwarz added. "Like at Gary's place. Remember when the Russians took a run at you in Montana?"

Manning's lips curled into a slight smile. When elements of the Russian espionage machine had grown tired of Phoenix Force's interference in their operations, they'd launched an all-out effort to exterminate the group. Two hundred men, from the Spetsnaz and various wet-works agencies, were thrown at Phoenix. The first few skirmishes were not much, but Manning and the others had let the Russians know where to find them in the remote cabin in the Rockies.

There, Phoenix Force had sniper rifles, booby traps and explosive mines set up to turn the assault force into carrion for scavengers. The team survived, and those who'd believed in the old Soviet corruption ways had been taught a very expensive lesson.

"Knowing what battlefield you'll be facing your enemy

on goes a long way toward evening the odds," Manning observed.

"Evening the odds?" Blancanales asked. "We want every unfair advantage in the book."

"Truth spoken," McCarter agreed. "Whoever said cheaters never win hasn't studied his military history."

"Any particular gear you bringing on this mission?" Lyons asked.

"I'm missing my old MAC-10, and Rafe loves his Heckler & Kochs, so we decided to split the difference and pack the MP-7. We've got suppressors and proper ammo for quiet hits as well as loud," McCarter explained.

"Yeah, got to love the old tried-and-true T-grip style," Schwarz added.

Lyons wrinkled his nose. "I'm barely comfortable with the .22s that come out of an M16. But 4.6 mm? That's only .18 caliber."

"Well, that's the thing, Carl. Rafe and I actually know how to shoot," McCarter answered with a wink. "Plus, everyone we've hit with those little .18-caliber bullets has been suitably impressed and hasn't complained."

Lyons chuckled.

"Since Cal and I are AR guys, we're rolling out with these stubbies based on the DPMS PDWs," T. J. Hawkins added. "Seven-inch heavy barrel AR-15s and a nice little name."

James smirked. "Technically, it's not called the Kitty Kat anymore in that configuration."

"If our founder could have his Big Thunder, then I'm entitled to my Kitty," Hawkins returned.

Blancanales nodded toward Manning and the weapon he was checking in its case. "Chopped-down Fabrique Nationale FAL?"

"No," Manning answered. "I'd love to have my favorite battle rifle, but the Mexican army still issues the G-3 in 7.62 mm NATO. Kissinger made a version for me with a thirteen-inch barrel and collapsing buttstock I can fit it into a tennis racket case, yet still have 500 yards of reach for precision shooting. Cowboy made this up from a 'clean' Heckler & Koch, like he did with the sanitized Kitty ARs that Cal and T.J. are rocking. No chances of jamming with any of these guns."

"Nor with the M203 compact he made for my Kitty," James said. He affected a sneer. "Say hello to my little kitty!"

Encizo rolled his eyes. "And here I thought that world was mine."

"What happens when you run out of ammo for David and Rafe's BB guns?" Lyons asked.

McCarter smirked. "The Caballeros Cartel actually has been working with MP-7s or, rather, Brazilian-built copies, complete with ammunition designed for it. And since the ammo and guns are built to spec on cartel money..."

"You can scrounge reloads from the drug runners' own security forces," Lyons surmised.

"Bingo," McCarter said. "That, along with the M16s and G-3s, which already use the ammo for the rest of our teams' guns."

"Shrewd," Blancanales noted.

"We've showed you our toys for this trip. What about you?" McCarter asked.

"Well, you know Carl's feelings on the 5.56 mm NATO that the rest of us haven't had a problem with," Schwarz said. "We're not going to be trying to bust into any smuggling tunnels, or penetrating into a prison, so we can operate with our rifles having longer barrels."

"Also, a stubby 7-incher isn't going to put out much murder at five hundred yards like a proper rifle barrel would," Blancanales said.

"We're rolling with .300 Blackout rounds in our M16s.

We'd have gone with .458 SOCOM, but then we'd be limited to only nine rounds in a magazine," Lyons added. "And we also want some reach with our rifles."

"Ever since you had that custom AK made for you on that Lebanon mission, you've been wanting an AK-caliber M16 for yourself," Blancanales pointed out. "And the Blackout was designed to provide that kind of horsepower per bullet, while still being usable in an accurate rifle."

Lyons nodded in agreement. "Going for punch and lots of punches for everyone sent at us."

He opened his case. "And my particular Blackout has a box-fed shotgun attachment. Because sometimes you just need the kind of attitude only provided by a 12-gauge load of buckshot or slugs."

"Doesn't the M26 just make it too heavy?" Gary Manning asked.

Lyons laughed.

"Sorry… I forgot who I was talking with," Manning returned. "The second strongest of the Stony Men."

"Second, eh?" Lyons challenged.

Manning winked, knowing any rivalry or competition between members was in good fun.

"I see you're jumping on my bandwagon, too, with the revolver," Lyons noted, catching sight of the handle of Manning's big Python Plus handgun.

"This hog leg?" the Canadian asked. "I've had an 8-shot .357 Magnum for a long time. The trouble is Cowboy can't seem to hold on to any of his Colt Anaconda frames and clean cylinders long enough to sanitize one for my field-work."

"Glad you finally have one for yourself," Lyons said with a laugh. "Sorry for hogging them all."

"You have two with you, right now?" Manning asked.

Lyons nodded. He pulled them both out; one from a shoulder holster, one from behind his hip. One was a big matte-stainless machine with a four-inch under-lugged barrel. The other was a stubbier snub-nosed revolver cast in a dark Parkerized finish. Both had fat cylinders, each holding eight rounds of .357 Magnums, one to be hidden more completely than the other. Though they had the polish and action similar to Lyons's old .357 Magnum Colt Python, they were converted .44 Magnum Anacondas, cylinders altered to hold an extra two rounds in the larger design. Kissinger and Lyons dubbed it the "Python Plus."

Manning's, on the other hand, was a long, sleek, camouflage-gray revolver with a six-inch barrel and weights. It looked as if, somewhere in its family tree, an ancestor'd had relations with a Desert Eagle, with flat, high-tech angles and facets along the barrel's length.

"Nice coloring on yours," Lyons said, admiring the big gun. Naturally, the Canadian woodsman would have preferred a hunting-size revolver. All the horsepower of a Magnum bullet meant nothing if you couldn't hit with it. "I usually don't have problem with my four-inch revolvers, but, man, the only sucker who could miss with this puppy is the one with the bread to afford it."

Manning chuckled. "I also like a little bit of reach with my weapons. You're good out to a hundred, a hundred and fifty yards with yours. This, I've hit steel ram targets at three hundred yards."

"Okay…that's impressive," Lyons admitted. He didn't have to try out the trigger pull on the big .357. It was hand built by John "Cowboy" Kissinger, Stony Man's armorer, an artist of steel and springs. His personal revolvers were slick and smooth, parts gliding across each other as if ice skating. They were also coated and treated against even the harshest of elements, further protecting their inner workings from hitches and imperfections that would ruin accuracy or speed of shooting.

"Just be careful out there," Lyons said, trading Manning's hog leg back for his pair.

The brawny Canadian nodded in return. "Careful? Or just do it as we've always done it? Because, pardon my linguistic torture, careful don't do the job."

"Yeah," Schwarz admitted, interjecting. "We tend to err on the side of wild-ass hijinks. But this time, we've got the Farm under attack from an outside source. One we just can't shoot up."

"Well, we could, but then we'd be on the run for blowing a renegade congressman in two," Hawkins added.

"It worked for Mack," James offered. "On the run… convicted of a crime—they pretty much pulled—they operate in the Los Angeles underworld. If you have a prob—"

"Please. We got enough of that when the movie remake came out," Blancanales groaned. Even so, he got a smile out of James.

"I'm not going to lie and say we don't each have our own exit strategies." McCarter spoke somberly. "But right now the only way out we need to concentrate on is getting Amanda Castillo back together with her children."

"Don't worry. We've never let a kid down," Schwarz said. "And you five are pretty damn good yourselves. You'll free her."

"First things first," Encizo added. "We bust down the doors of a Caballeros Cartel smuggling tunnel and get into Mexico the hard way."

"Always with the negative vibes, Rafe," Blancanales quipped. "To us, it'd be the fun way."

"We'd also like to not level half of Nogales, Arizona, though," Encizo countered.

"Don't worry about that," McCarter calmly assured. "We've got Gary. Even if we go with a nuclear option, he'll make sure no bystanders are hurt."

"Just Los Lictors and the Caballeros de Durango," Manning added with emphasis.

"And in this case, since I'm better with Mexican-dialect Spanish, I'll take the lead," Hawkins, the Texan, said. He continued in the language he indicated, "Or don't you think I'll be convincing?"

"You know, Gadgets, I think we've been coveting the wrong member of Phoenix for Carl's replacement on Able," Blancanales joked.

Schwarz grinned. "We'd be golden even with a member of the Lollipop Guild if we wanted."

Lyons scratched his head with his middle finger, extended as a beacon to his two wisecracking buddies.

"If any cartel is going to have a light, Caucasian-looking gent, no matter how well tanned, it'll be the Durango mob," Encizo admitted. "Especially with their ties to Accion Obrar."

"Those bastards smell awful familiar," Lyons said. "Like our old sparring partners. Remember Miguel Unomundo?"

"The Fascist International had a minor resurgence a while back. Remember the Ankylosaur robots?" Hawkins asked.

"Ankylosaur combat drones," Manning corrected.

"Something tells me that with the involvement with Stewart Crowmass, the Fascist International has a brand-new title."

"The Arrangement," McCarter concluded.

Lyons nodded. "We thought that taking him down during the Japanese whaling crisis would have ended all of his problems, but that shrewd bastard already had a set of fail-safes in place. It's why Hal's got his neck on the line back in Wonderland and we're busy pretending to be target practice for paramilitary cartel enforcers."

"Are you certain it was merely Crowmass?" Manning inquired. "He was not alone in all of this. According to

Carmen, he had allies in Central and South America *and* the Middle East."

"Do you have any specific names?" Blancanales asked.

Manning quickly wrote down several notes on a page, tore it out and handed it over. "If, while you're playing the Judas Goat, you happen to run across someone in Texas or California, you might want to bring the trouble to their very own front door."

Blancanales looked over the sheet, face torn between a frown of concern and a mirthless grin of malice. "Him? You sure?"

"It's only rumors at this point," Manning stated.

Lyons took a peek at Manning's notes and sighed. "Even when he shot a lawyer in the face, he was still a goddamn hero. No wonder this wasn't a part of the official briefing."

"Hal and the Sensitive Operations Group are on thin ice as it is. Going after this guy, with his hooks in the US government and overseas, it'd take a hell of a lot of brass," Manning stated.

Lyons ejected a shell from his rifle's under-barrel shotgun. It gleamed from base of round to the tip. "Brass? I've never been accused of being short of that."

Grim silence enveloped the cabin as the two teams returned their gear to their cases.

Nothing less than full-on warfare was going to occupy their thoughts for the next several days.

CHAPTER FOUR

From his position operating a small tamale cart near the refrigerated warehouse run by the Caballeros de Durango Cartel, Pedro Guzman was easily able to keep an eye on the US side of the smuggling tunnel and any who'd dare approach it. If something strange showed up on his personal radar, he was in direct walkie-talkie contact with his brethren. So far, his tour of duty as security for the tunnel had been uneventful.

Few lawmen would ever want to take on Los Lictors, and he and his brothers in arms had dealt with Los Sigmas, the last group of hard-core paramilitary cartel muscle that had obtained control of Nogales and the border crossings into and out of Arizona. Competition and the authorities were set to rout, and anyone who still maintained an interest was left impotent, thanks to friends in high places who had handles on judges and ranking law enforcement officials.

So, when he saw the two men walking toward the Durango "icehouse," Guzman's instincts suddenly went into overdrive. Both wore dark sunglasses and carried the bronzed skin of those who lived in the unflinching sun on the border. He gave a tap of the send button on his communicator; a sort of heads-up that hissed inside the warehouse.

If this turned out to be trouble, he'd be on the line immediately, but so far the two didn't appear to be hostile. Both wore oversize button-down shirts as light jackets, nothing out of the ordinary since this was technically winter in Arizona. Even so, Guzman's gaze was locked on the smaller of the men.

He was darker than the other, but he walked with a hard authority, arms swinging, ending in fists that swayed to and fro like idling wrecking balls on a gale-force day. The tall man was younger and moved much more casually, arms and legs undulating as if he were straight out of a cartoon. Both looked like legitimate gangsters, though Guzman hadn't seen them around here before.

They were making for the icehouse as if they were arrows aimed and fired. The little guy had purpose and a scowl bowing his lips down. He gave Guzman a glare that was hard even through opaque sunglass lenses.

"We expect any business today?" Guzman asked over his hands-free radio, speaking loud enough for only the walkie-talkie to hear him.

"Nope" came the response.

Guzman continued watching the pair. "Well, they look like they're here on business. And like they don't give a damn who knows they're here."

"Yeah, we're watching now. Damned odd," his partner, Zacco, replied. "But we start shooting, who knows what kind of heat we'll call in."

"So far, things are quiet. Maybe get them inside. You'll have them outnumbered and outgunned, even if they are strapped," Guzman noted.

Zacco chortled. "We kinda figured that plan out already. Just keep watch, in case they've got backup."

"Keep me posted," Guzman returned.

RAFAEL ENCIZO WAS hardly a tall man, but his shoulders were broad and powerful, his torso bulky yet tapering to a slender waist. Thanks to this build, the Cuban Phoenix veteran was able to conceal the sleek and compact Heckler & Koch

MP-7 machine pistol under his jacket. As backup, the stocky, swarthy professional had his P-30 9 mm autoloader from the same manufacturer as the machine pistol.

T. J. Hawkins, on the other hand, was not blessed with shoulders or a torso that could snug a foot-long automatic weapon underneath a jacket. The best he could do was a matching pair of Beretta Brigadiers in 9 mm Parabellum. The former Ranger and Delta Force veteran had developed an appreciation for the sleek Beretta handguns in his service, despite the fact that Delta tended to operate with .45s rather than 9s. His time with Phoenix Force and Calvin James had merely reinforced his appreciation for the Italian design, now entering its fourth decade of service with the US Armed Forces.

The Beretta he wore in his shoulder holster had a stubby suppressor and a rail-mounted gun light, both accessories taking the already negligent recoil of the sleek pistol and turning it into nothing short of a laser beam in his hands. Hawkins's other Brigadier was clean, meant to operate as a backup should the first somehow jam or get lost in the fury of conflict.

Behind the two of them, McCarter, Manning and James followed as stealthy ghosts shadowing and guarding them. At this moment McCarter was a whisper in their earbuds.

"Tamale cart. He's noticed you and is giving you the hairy eyeball," the Briton warned.

"We made him immediately," Encizo murmured into the hands-free microphone at his collar. "Any response from the icehouse?"

"Negative," Manning informed them. "The windows are covered, but my infrared has picked up bodies behind the glass. Normal movement for now."

"Awesome," Hawkins returned. "That means they're still paranoid."

"It's only paranoia if no one's out to get them," Encizo stated. "And since we *are* out to get 'em…"

The corner of Hawkins's mouth turned up in a smirk. "Cartel goons didn't get to be rich by hiring lazy or inattentive soldiers. This'll be a bit tricky."

"Well, you're the one taking the lead. Granted, I can't hide much of myself behind your skinny Texas ass, but I'll still be alive long enough to say 'I told you so,'" Encizo replied.

"How about you use that time to shoot back?" Hawkins asked.

"That's a good idea. For a moment I thought I was a cable news pundit," Encizo grunted.

"Preferring to being 'proven' right than to actually solving the damn problem?" Hawkins said.

"Exactly," Encizo returned. "Don't worry, my foolishness has swiftly passed."

Manning interrupted the two. "We've got two in the window, looking down on you. Both have big dark voids where their hands should be."

"Gunmen," Encizo extrapolated.

Hawkins cut in. "They aiming at us?"

"No, they just look curious about why two guys are walking up to their warehouse. Weapons are at low 'not quite ready,'" Manning answered.

"Thank goodness for some laziness in this crowd," Hawkins said.

McCarter's gruff voice broke in on the hands-free communicators. "Maybe they just feel like they can handle you. Overconfidence, especially since they've likely got rifles and such inside the warehouse."

"We can work with overconfidence, *esse*," Hawkins returned, settling verbally into his role and flow. His walk already was smoother, rolling, his head bobbing to an internal beat. It could have been seen as a stereotype, but the truth was that he'd seen far too many boys from the barrio who affected the gait and rhythm he copied. Just because it was a cultural cliché did not mean that it wasn't real.

Encizo, on the other hand, stomped along, shoulders swiveling, fists rocking back and forth. Not tall, his strut would take up an entire sidewalk, if only by force of his demeanor, not counting his wide shoulders and brawny arms. This was the confidence and weight of a veteran of the streets. No gang member or cartel representative could look at him and *not* think that he'd been representing *la raza* out on the front lines. Even without seeing the scar tissue he'd incurred over the years on Phoenix Force, observers would see a longtime warrior. That, plus his mode of dress and his demeanor, made him not merely an enforcer, but *the* enforcer.

The two of them were indeed strapped to the teeth. Encizo had his two HK pistols, plus his favorite Walther PPK in its ankle holster, and a pair of Tanto-styled fighting knives, one in a sheath hidden on the calf opposite his Walther, the other hanging from a leather thong around his neck. Hawkins had additional weaponry, too, including a push knife inside his gaudy-looking belt buckle, and a snub-nosed .357 Magnum—a tiny five-shot in comparison to Manning's and Lyons's handguns. The trouble for the cartel's watchman and the other observers was that they had no idea that these two were ready for all-out war, or that the other three members of Phoenix Force were poised and ready to give them a hail of blazing cover fire on a moment's notice.

The two of them also had extra surprises to grant them an advantage. Their electronic ear buds, low-profile and hard to notice without a high-powered telescopic lens, provided not only communications with their allies, but also hearing protection, electronically filtering out ear-damaging booms the likes of indoor handgun fire, or even better, flash-bang grens, which the two of them were also equipped with.

Curiosity would be the bait for the cartel gun thugs to allow them into the icehouse. Security and thorough procedure would make them shut the sound-proofed doors before they even considered firing the first shot to eliminate the two intruders. And in the moments between, Encizo's plan was to buy them precious extra minutes and the element of surprise by popping off a distraction device at 140 decibels and blazing bright. That was what the sunglasses were for, given the flash-bangs went off at an intensity of 600 thousand lumens, more than enough to leave an opponent seeing stars and blotches of afterglow for a long time.

It wasn't a sure thing; nothing ever was. But anything that gave them at least one second's worth of surprise was worth another second of life in the middle of a firefight. Each extra second alive was one where they could find another opportunity, another means of cheating death. Those instances were supported by Encizo and Hawkins wearing undershirt body armor, advance intel based on ground-facing satellite radar and infrared, and Gary Manning's sniper-rifle-mounted thermal vision, which could peer though even the tinted windows of the icehouse to see gunmen looking down upon them.

This was a plan burned into their brains in the past half hour, and all of that after an hour of study of the options, approaches and possibilities. The five men of Phoenix Force were trained professionals, and they were bringing with them the best technology ever assembled for combat and espionage. Their minds combined were the worth of any combat computer, let alone the paranoid security measures of the Caballeros Cartel.

Hawkins rapped on the door. *"¡Abrir, esse!"*

Encizo was impressed enough with Hawkins's facility

with the tone and dialect to think that they might have a chance at getting in the front door.

A panel opened up. "What makes you think we're interested in what you're selling?"

"We're not selling anything," Hawkins returned in rapid street Spanish. "Unless it's your own asses."

Wary, suspicious eyes burned through the door panel.

"It's only the two of us. What are we going to do?" Encizo growled, every inch the veteran gang-banger. "What's coming on our heels is much worse."

Hawkins gave the door another thump, right under the aperture the guard glared through. "Come on. Tamale Boy knows there's nothin' coming with us. But we wait out here five more minutes, ICE is going to be rolling up with tanks!"

The reference to Immigration and Customs Enforcement widened the eyes of the doorman. "Rolling up in tanks?"

The door opened only slightly. A submachine gun muzzle poked through the crack. "Keep your hands where we can see them at all times."

Hawkins rolled his eyes and interlaced his fingers at the back of his head. "This good, homie?"

Encizo did likewise. The door opened farther, hands snatching at their shirts and tugging them into the foyer. As soon as they were inside, Hawkins was able to count the welcoming committee: four men, including the guy standing at the door. He'd been standing there with an MP-7 leveled at Hawkins's midsection and was continuing to follow him.

Encizo's flannel shirt dropped open and the assembled Durango gun thugs recognized the hardware hanging in a shoulder harness.

There was a brief instant of confusion.

"Are you from—" one began to ask.

Unfortunately the moment the doorman started to close the door, Encizo's interlaced fingers released the tension on the flash-bang grenade he was holding at the back of his neck. He'd thumbed out the pin when it looked as if he was surrendering, but the canister dropped to the floor, the safety spoon clanging away middrop.

The ensuing thunderbolt detonation at his feet was so hard that Encizo felt it like a punch to his chest. That was while wearing eye and ear protection. To the unprepared cartel guards, it was an assault on the senses.

In a flash of movement, Encizo drew his Cold Steel Tanto and drove it into the belly of the man holding an MP-7 at Hawkins's navel. Six inches of chisel-tipped, razor-sharp steel plunged through muscle and viscera, severing the Caballero doorman's aorta. Such a vicious arterial wound would kill in under a minute. Encizo sped up the process to prevent his suffering, driving the point upward and impaling the cartel guard's heart.

Hawkins also opted for a non-gunshot first strike. He had out his punch dagger in the space of an instant and leaned into a hard jab to the neck of a second of the sentries. The wide arrowhead-shaped blade parted flesh and muscle, severing arteries and nerve clusters in its passage through the Mexican's throat. With a twist, he presented the blunt back edge of the knife and pulled out with all of his strength. Any blood vessels or muscles not neatly slashed were now corkscrewed and bluntly ripped on the exit path. The sentry's blinded eyes rolled up into his head as he toppled backward in a boneless mass.

Encizo gave a powerful kick to the third of their welcoming committee. The point of the Cuban's boot was steel-tipped, and when he connected with the hip of that man, the force of the impact dislodged the femur from his pelvis. There was a numbed wail of horror, but it was cut off as Encizo clawed his free hand's fingers into the

Mexican's face. The Tanto knife came up and punched through the relatively weak bone of the caballero's temple. Bone splintered and large chunks of brain lacerated with brutal efficiency, Encizo ended this man much more swiftly than the other.

Hawkins snatched the submachine gun in the fist of the fourth and last of the group in the foyer. Blinded and deafened, the caballero barely had a grasp on the machine pistol before Hawkins spun it around. The Texan triggered a 3-round burst under his enemy's chin, putting him out of commission in the blink of an eye.

The rest of Phoenix Force was at work now, as they heard the toppling form of one man hit a pallet from the catwalk by the icehouse's windows. Gary Manning's work with the G-3 was dead-on, taking out at least one of the gunmen in the windows. In the same instant, dock doors around the back exploded off of their hinges with the aid of a Manning-designed breaching charge.

Hawkins and Encizo tossed another flash-bang. On the detonation, they exited the foyer, machine pistols tracking.

There'd been another pair of men poised to act in case something happened, but the sudden crash of one of their partners from the catwalk caught their attention. A moment later they were the recipients of a flash-bang detonation and, in that next instant, streams of 4.6 mm autofire that slashed through their internal organs.

From the back, McCarter and James were blazing away with their own weapons. The Briton with his MP-7, James with his Kitty carbine that, despite a suppressor, still produced a vigorous clatter as high-velocity 5.56 mm tore through the air at nearly 2,500 feet per second. Cartel gunmen twisted and writhed as swift bursts chopped through their flesh.

Another body toppled over a railing above. His arrival on the warehouse floor was punctuated with the thun-

der of splintering wood and a mist of spraying blood as
bones on the way to the concrete split flesh between like
ersatz scissors. Hawkins paused long enough to see who
else Manning had engaged from a distance. He saw another three bodies sprawled on the wire mesh flooring of
the catwalks, each lying with limbs twisted to impossible
angles. He saw that there were another two gunmen up
there and was about to aim at one, but Manning's marksmanship was demonstrated again. The man's face burst
into a cloud of dark gore, skull cored by 7.62 mm NATO
jacketed lead.

The last of the gunmen threw his weapon away, holding his hands up in an effort to keep the invisible god of
death from taking his life.

The others on the icehouse floor were still in the mood
to fight, no sudden thunderbolts of doom whispering out of
nowhere to execute them. Hawkins hurled a flash-bang at
a clot of Mexican cartel gunners, letting his empty MP-7
crash to the floor. The distraction device struck one of the
caballeros and bounced skyward before it detonated, raining earsplitting thunder and eye-burning light.

With the crash of the grenade, Hawkins transitioned
to the light-equipped Beretta, drawing it up and firing.
As in practice with the barrel given extra weight from the
mounted torch, recoil was nonexistent. A stream of 9 mm
bullets barked out of the five-inch barrel of the M9, connecting with Durango soldiers and punching through upper
chests and heads with laser precision. For ten shots, four
men were down and dead, Hawkins so fast on the trigger
that he punched them twice or three times before gravity
caught up with the suddenness of their demise.

Encizo had the stock extended on the MP-7, braced
against his shoulder. From this position he was able to
move and pivot with speed and grace, and yet, every time
he had a clear view of an enemy, he also had the machine

pistol on target. High-velocity projectiles exited the barrel so swiftly, their mass so minor, that recoil wasn't a factor in putting rounds on target, either. A flurry of 4.6 mm hornets zipped through skin and cartwheeled through muscle, lodging in bone once they struck fluid mass.

Though adrenaline and the fog of combat made the fight seem to stretch out longer, in truth, it was barely closing in on a minute since Encizo had dropped the first flash-bang to start the battle. Moving with trained precision, and making certain they were in cover, the four men of Phoenix Force inside the icehouse exercised brutal efficiency at crushing any opposition.

A minute and five seconds after the flash-bang started festivities, an eerie silence enveloped the icehouse

"Gary, how loud was it out there?" McCarter's voice rang over their hands-free communicators.

"Except for the tamale cart, nobody even noticed it. He crashed just inside the foyer when I took him," Manning returned.

"Right. Get down here," McCarter ordered. "Good breach, T.J., Rafe."

"Thanks," Hawkins answered. Even though they were engaged in radio chatter, none of the five commandos were letting their attention wander from the tasks at hand. For the four inside, it was making certain no one was up and fighting. For Manning, it was removing himself from his hide and joining the others.

So far, they'd only secured one end of the Nogales icehouse smuggling tunnel.

There was still three hundred feet to trek underground and security at the other end to deal with.

CHAPTER FIVE

Perez took another sip of his energy drink, his eyes feeling full of sand and grit. He wasn't sure when the last time was that he'd blinked. Nerves buzzed throughout his body, but all that really mattered was the Castillo children. The two girls slept. Pequita with her arms around the younger, shorter Annette, protecting her. The two kids drew strength from their contact and he hadn't allowed their minds to wander to the fates of their parents.

Domingo Castillo, however, stayed mostly awake, or only partially asleep. Young Dom was classically nodding off, pulling himself awake only as he dipped into slumber.

Perez sucked back another sip. A knock at the door startled him and he nearly choked on his drink.

His hand fell to the big .45 on his hip.

"Friends coming in," growled a voice from the other side.

Dom jerked fully awake but his sisters remained wound together in sleep.

In walked three men, newcomers Perez hadn't seen around the offices before. He'd been told to expect them. While he recognized them, he didn't know any names. He knew the trio was usually referred to by code names. He also knew these guys weren't supposed to exist, and the things they did when not teaching cops and soldiers were to stay secret until the end of time, according to the nondisclosure agreement Perez had been made to sign during training ops.

"I don't know if you're a sight for sore eyes or if I'm gonna regret dragging you guys into this mess," Perez said.

Carl Lyons strode forward, holding out his hand to the deputy marshal.

Though Perez initially worried that these three men might be hurt, the handshake waylaid any fears that the man introduced as Ironman was fragile.

The man Perez knew as Politician seemed only two-thirds the size of Ironman by muscle mass, and yet the gray-haired warrior's grip and arm were no less tightly muscled and firm. There was a wary alertness in his eyes, and though his hair had gone prematurely light, he still possessed a limber ease of movement that accompanied that strength.

The last was called Gadgets, and though he didn't have the same muscle tone and cut of build as the other two men, he didn't lack for a good grip in his handshake. It just seemed as if everything the genius did required very little physical or mental effort; that he glided with the flow rather than struggle unnecessarily. That Zen mentality had showed its true nature when he'd watched the man win a bench-press competition among the blacksuits without a grunt of exertion.

"We're not going to talk about too many details in front of the kids," Lyons warned. "By the way, I'm Karl Stone, he's Pol Rosa, and Gadgets is Hermann Black."

"Nice to meet you again," Perez replied.

Schwarz walked over to Domingo Castillo carrying a small pack. He unzipped it and pulled out a small bottle of orange soda, handing it to him. "You doing okay?"

The boy nodded. He glanced over at Perez, as if to ask if it were okay to drink this. Perez gave a nod of assent, and Dom pulled off the top and took a thirsty sip. He approached his sisters and whispered to them, "Pequita, Annette!"

The girls' eyes opened. Schwarz watched them, reminding Perez of a loyal family dog, one that would die for them before allowing harm to strike.

Sadly, tragedy had already struck.

"Orange soda and candy bars. Dentists might hate him, but he knows how to raise a kid's spirits," Blancanales said to Perez. "How about you?"

"I'm pretty certain my urine will be glow-in-the-dark neon green next time I piss," Perez said, tapping the side of his can. "But the jokes aren't true. I can't smell colors yet."

Lyons plucked the can from the blacksuit marshal. "You'll get some sleep before we go anywhere. I need you in good operational condition."

"You think I *want* to sleep?" Perez asked.

Lyons sat him down. "We'll give you an hour. Don't worry. We've got your back."

"I don't…" Perez began. His eyes grew heavier.

He realized that Pol was tapping rhythmically on his shoulder. The steady, soothing beat hypnotized him. Slumber came quickly.

"Nice trick," Lyons said.

"Learned it from an old guy when I was stationed in Korea," Blancanales replied.

Lyons smirked. "Think he'd teach it to me?"

Blancanales shook his head. "Nah. You're too much of a pale sow's ear."

Lyons rolled his eyes. "Take a look at the kids while Gadgets has them filling up on sugar."

Blancanales did so. In the meantime, the Able Team leader took Perez's cell phone and checked it. He didn't expect there to be anything on it, but maybe someone had sent messages to Perez. Lyons found some alerts on his phone, but they were simple emails and social media garbage. That didn't mean there weren't clues inside the phone that someone else would find useful.

"Done looking at the magic picture box?" Schwarz asked.

"All yours, wizard," Lyons returned. "Grog not understand intricacies of electronic communications within it."

Schwarz smiled and pulled out his Combat PDA. He connected a wire between the two devices then let the microcomputer dive into the phone, checking for the sort of trace programs and outré technology that would turn a cell phone into a weapon. "Bang."

"Find something?" Lyons asked.

"This phone's riddled with worms," Schwarz explained. "I'm running through the diagnostics and there's little wonder how the safe house was found. And it's still transmitting."

Lyons nodded. "That means we can expect shadows."

Schwarz locked eyes with his friend and partner. "Expect them? I never figured you for a passive host waiting for guests."

Lyons looked over at Blancanales, who had finished his initial evaluation of the kids. Though they hadn't come to physical harm in the escape to Yuma, they were frightened, and very likely had a feeling that their parents were either dead or in fatal danger. Blancanales's expression evidenced that those worries dogged the children, though they each managed to maintain a brave face.

"I'll only be in passive mode until you give me something to shoot at, Gadgets," Lyons announced. "So how fast can you give that to me?"

"That's the Ironman I remember," Schwarz returned. "Call it fifteen minutes?"

Lyons narrowed his eyes. "Make it ten."

Blancanales gave his report on the mood and emotional status of the Castillo youngsters quickly and succinctly.

"I hate dragging them around as bait," Lyons grumbled. "But I also don't want to abandon them. If this thing is an attempt to ramp up tensions between the US and Mexico, leaving them here makes the federal building a target."

Blancanales rested his hand on the younger man's shoulder. "We've handled babysitting-style assignments before. If anything, with us, they not only have a group of the best defenders in the world, but also folks who can handle the trauma the kids have experienced."

Lyons nodded. "We already went over this at the Farm and on the plane. It's the least of all possible evils, and it's something I can live with."

Blancanales returned to Dom and his sisters while Lyons took a mental inventory. Utilizing the resources of the Farm, as well as the skills and strengths of his partners, there was little doubt that Able Team could bring the hammer down on Los Lictors or whomever the Durango Caballeros were using as their enforcers on this side of the border.

Their plan to have Deputy Marshal Perez on their side, continuing his role as caretaker for the kids and as a fourth gunner, allowed them some wriggle room, but he was glad for Schwarz's additional suggestion. Out in Los Angeles, where Able Team had a lot of friends and contacts, they had a woman who could also supply her own brain and firepower to the mix.

Lao Ti and her business partner, May Ling Fu, had aided the Stony Man trio on previous occasions and were now on their way to assist once again. As they were not a federal law enforcement agency, although Dr. Lao Ti's electronics and computer firm was a government contractor, there was a better possibility that holes in Brognola's agency security would be averted. If not, then there was another angle with which to see how the Mexican agency and their pet cartel were penetrating US government security.

He got on his assigned phone. "Barb, it looks like some-one loaded some tracking software into the phones of the blacksuits. Gadgets says he's going to see if any trackers are in the area."

Price sounded skeptical. "We're skating on the edge here. Maybe this was just the thing necessary to draw all of you out into the open."

"A trap. Something from the legacy of Crowmass and the Arrangement," Lyons mused aloud, giving in to grudg-ing agreement.

"They've resurrected the Aryan Right Coalition enough times to figure out who you are and why you're their num-ber-one target," the mission controller added. "You as in Able and Phoenix."

"And we're going in expecting them to want to trap us," Lyons answered. "Just look back on all of those am-bushes we've been through. We fight our way out. It's what we do."

"But sooner or later that string of luck is going to fail," Price countered. She sounded worried, and Lyons knew that his bluster and bravado wouldn't do anything to soothe her nerves. There were facts and knowledge, prior exam-ple, but there was also the knowledge that for all their tal-ent and strength, the warriors of Stony Man Farm were still human, still fallible. Mistakes and a run of bad luck could be the end of any or all of the Stony Man warriors. Lyons had watched too many comrades fall, too many lov-ers in his life cut down by vengeful thugs.

"Luck isn't a string. It's a wave you ride. And in be-tween the waves, a good surfer knows how to stay afloat and position himself for another swell," Lyons added. "There's so much more than just chance working for us."

"Gadgets should be getting the telemetry necessary to home in on your shadows," Price said. "And he and you were right. They're waiting to ambush…at least ambush Perez and the kids if they leave."

Lyons looked at his Combat PDA, which displayed the presence of three vans on a satellite view of the federal building. He tapped one of the van blips and could see heat sources from downward-looking infrared.

"They're on the same channels…I think," Price said. "Bear and Gadgets have the proper terminology of how these traces go. And those vans don't look like they're sitting waiting for rush hour to take advantage of the car-pool lane."

Lyons, phone tucked between his ear and shoulder, scanned the vans that had been marked as targets. Every one of them was loaded with men and all were huddling, ready to explode into action. Lyons had seen that kind of ready-to-roll-out tension before, back when he was on the LAPD and the FBI. He'd been on enough SWAT raids to understand that preparedness, to know the coiled energy waiting for an opportunity to burst. He'd felt that tension in his own bones, so he knew what he was looking at, even through a thermal camera in low orbit over Yuma, Arizona.

He put the PDA away. "We'll take care of the vans. After all, there's only one vanload for each of us. We've practically got them outnumbered."

"Pride goes before the fall," Price noted.

Lyons snorted. "But to really bowl 'em over, you need 12-gauge."

Price managed a laugh and disconnected.

"You got it all in five minutes," Lyons said to Schwarz. "You were yanking me on needing fifteen to do the job."

Schwarz grinned. "What makes you think that?"

"Because you're trying to impress me, inflating the haggling price so that when you finish in a third of the time, I'm surprised," Lyons answered, giving Schwarz a gentle pop on the shoulder.

"Curses...foiled!" Schwarz answered. "We're leaving Perez to snooze?"

Lyons nodded. "Saddle up, Pol. We got people to do and things to see."

Blancanales held his tongue for the sake of the kids, at least until he bid them so long. Outside the safe room, the eldest member of Able Team was brought up to speed on the situation and layout of the ambushers.

"One per van?" Blancanales asked. "We hit them simultaneously. Are we looking for prisoners?"

"That would be a bonus, but considering that these creeps are looking to kidnap kids and murder more federal agents and local cops, I don't see a lot of need to be gentle. Just leave enough for dental or fingerprint identification," Lyons explained.

The three men went to a locker room that had been set aside for them. They'd left their gear bags within and now quickly went to work changing.

"What's the plan, Ironman?" Schwarz asked. "I mean, beyond kill 'em all and let God sort 'em out?"

"We don't want them to see us coming until it's too late," Lyons returned. "I'll be a hiker."

Lyons stripped out of his suit and pulled on a pair of cargo shorts. He laid and tucked his body armor, complete with trauma plates, over his bare, muscular torso, which he covered with a loose-fitting T-shirt. The cargo shorts were held up with a full two-inch belt. He clipped an inside-the-waistband holster and an outside pancake holster, for the snub-nosed and full-size Python Plus respectively, to that belt. The oversize T-shirt fell over the two weapons, disguising them against his waist.

He reconfigured his war bag into a hiking pack, throwing the carry loops over his shoulders. There was a sheath into which he could reach, drawing a compact, folding-stock version of the Mossberg 930 SPX. *Compact* wasn't really a true term for it. The scattergun still had a full 24-inch barrel and an under-barrel tube magazine that held eight 3-inch Magnum shells or nine standard 12- gauge rounds. With the folded stock, however, it disappeared inside the backpack. Pulled out, the stock would snap instantly into place, braced against Lyons's shoulder to control recoil and direct the fistfuls of pellets with deadly precision.

With an extra in the chamber, Lyons was happy with having ten hefty blasts of 00 Buck from regular 12-gauge shells. He also had sixteen rounds of .357 Magnum ready to go with just a quick draw. The semiautomatic Mossberg didn't need to be pumped to lay out its payload of rage against a group of targets.

Schwarz shrugged into a windbreaker and sunglasses, but only after he put on a shoulder harness for a Brügger & Thomet MP-9 submachine gun. This, too, had a folding stock and condensed itself to the length of a standard handgun, yet had a shoulder stock and a vertical handgrip for the same kind of precision Lyons got out of his shotgun. With a 15-round flush-fitting magazine to start off the festivities and spare 30-round sticks, Schwarz wasn't undergunned, either. Especially when it spat out 9 mm rounds at 900 in a minute.

"I'll just be another Fed going out in an unmarked car," Schwarz announced. "What about you, Pol?"

"Hate to say it, but I don't think these guys are going to pay much attention to a Hispanic in coveralls with a tool chest," Blancanales responded as he changed into his gear. "The toolbox is going to be a nice little knock-knock joke."

With that, the Politician set a stand-alone M203 grenade launcher in the toolbox. He also had an MP-9 subgun, which tucked under his loose coveralls nicely. A name tag and a battered old ball cap rounded out to make him look like a maintenance man coming off duty or going to some other appointment.

"How do I look?" Blancanales asked.

"Like I should give you a tip so you can get your cousin to clean my pool," Lyons grunted.

"Be careful, man. Someone might think you're trying to be ironic and politically correct," Schwarz chided.

"Perish the thought," Lyons returned.

"He'll get a little more than an hour of nap if we don't wake him." Blancanales motioned toward the safe room where the deputy marshal and the children were being kept under guard.

"Just as well. You saw how exhausted he was," Lyons said. "We're fresh, and we're ready to give some payback."

With that the Able Team trio split up to take their separate exits.

Phoenix Force had their opening shots in this war, but it was time for the Able Team warriors to make their entrance.

CHAPTER SIX

Under Nogales, Arizona, specifically under the icehouse utilized by the Caballeros de Durango Cartel, the five members of Phoenix Force were busy at various tasks.

Gary Manning checked out the systems of the smuggling tunnel, impressed with both the tunnel's professional construction and with the powered cart-and-track combination that ferried goods across in bulk. Each cart could convey up to 250 kilograms on a pallet, and there were two sets of tracks, each with trains composed of four such cars. Both were on the Arizona side, docked in, as the train meant to travel down to Mexican Nogales was partially loaded. There were crates for rifles and other weaponry, as well as stacks of ammunition for those weapons in the process of being loaded. The attack by Phoenix Force had interrupted the shipment.

The crates were being examined by McCarter and Encizo, each assessing the types of armaments destined for warfare to the south of the border. Judging by the small arms and ammunition amounts involved, some form of security force was being reequipped. Lack of rocket launchers or other antiarmor weaponry indicated this shipment wasn't going to a guerrilla force somewhere in the vicinity of Central America or the northern part of South America, where FARC and similar antigovernment troops needed that kind of firepower to take on military forces. This gear looked like the stuff necessary to give a small paramilitary force the edge it needed to overwhelm and slaughter police officers in the streets of a major Mexican metropolis or to even the odds against a rival cartel.

Encizo confirmed it with a shipment of knockoffs of their MP-7 submachine guns. A close examination and he could tell that these weapons were built in the People's Republic of China, which also produced an unauthorized copy of the SIG Sauer P228. That knockoff ended up as the sidearm of many a clandestine operation for both sides of the Bamboo Curtain. Encizo looked carefully at the ammunition.

"These look like just the right kind of hardware for an executive protection team," the Cuban said.

McCarter nodded. "Or some blokes who might want to go through a temporarily powered-down metal detector."

Encizo frowned. He'd heard plenty of stories of the audacity of Mexican cartels, but the Durango faction and their caballeros had earned their notoriety from walking through seemingly airtight security to make their kills. "Well, it'd be a shame to let them fall into the wrong hands."

"Don't worry, we'll keep a nice stash of spares handy," McCarter said. "Gary can booby-trap the rest."

"No traps," Manning countered. "Just need to make certain they're unusable. Remember, the police are going to be here."

"Right, I forgot," McCarter said. "The last thing we need to do is hurt the blokes who are on our side."

Calvin James and T. J. Hawkins returned from their reconnaissance sortie down the tunnel, both men moving swiftly.

"We got within a hundred feet of the other end and heard activity ramp up," James reported. "No cameras sighted us, but T.J. was watching a scanner and the airwaves were busy down there."

"They know that this side of the border has been compromised," Hawkins added.

"And they're counting down to their side being hit. Through the tunnel."

"That explains the lack of rockets or grenades," Manning mused. "They didn't want us to roll a cart down to that end with sufficient explosives to take out a mob of defenders."

McCarter looked around.

"What are you thinking, David?" Encizo asked.

McCarter looked at the carts and their supplies. "Barb said she would contact me if the Nogales authorities were coming. I'm going to call them and make certain that things are still quiet. In the meantime, bring down kilos of coke."

Encizo grinned. "We going to have a Hollywood party?"

"No, but the air will be thick with booger sugar on the other end," McCarter said. "Can you make charges that can disperse it in a large cloud?"

"Give me ten minutes," Manning answered. "How high do you want them and how far away?"

"Blurred to the gills," McCarter ordered. "And as large a cloud as we can assemble. Just don't have all of Nogales get hooked on cocaine."

Manning nodded and then he, Hawkins and Encizo, the three strongest members of the team, went back into the icehouse for the supplies for McCarter's plan.

"Cal, you're with me. We're going to see if the caballeros have any wheels for what we need," McCarter instructed.

The lanky team medic nodded but paused to pick up bags of ammunition and spare magazines. "Why make one extra trip? Besides, we might need some of this free ammo."

McCarter smirked. "Good idea."

The Phoenix commander also grabbed some of the contraband munitions in a pair of bags. Together, the Stony

Man warriors climbed into the icehouse. As they moved toward the warehouse parking lot, they saw Manning carrying an oxygen tank. Neither of them had to doubt the purpose of that huge metal bottle. McCarter wanted to produce a wide-spreading cloud, and the oxygen inside the tank was under tremendous pressure. A good charge of explosives would crack the bottle and the ensuing burst of the tank would be catastrophic.

Just the sort of element that a David McCarter plan usually hinged upon.

"What are we looking for?" James asked.

"At least a Ford F-350," McCarter said. "Enough room for all of us in the cab, plus the horsepower to help us ram through the fence. If possible, something a bit smaller to help flanking maneuvers and avoid bunching all of us together in a fight or chase."

James indicated that he understood with a curt nod and split from McCarter.

The British commando found the burly pickup he sought, little doubt that he would as Arizona and off-road-capable working trucks went hand in hand. He muttered over the throat mike to James, "It's not shiny or new, but neither is it a rusted-out hulk. It should hold together, even under enemy fire."

"They do tend to be good at busting down blockades," James returned.

McCarter circled the truck before climbing inside. It had seen months since its last washing, but opening the door and hot wiring it showed that it had a full tank, a good battery, and its massive V-8 engine had a healthy roar.

Across the lot, he heard James start the car he'd found.

James spoke over the com set. "Got a Toyota RAV 4, not really a load-hauling engine of business, but it's off-road capable. More of a SUV than the pickup you chose.

Both vehicles can hold the full complement of the team, as well as weapons and other gear."

McCarter grunted in response. "The brute Ford will be first through the border fence and the Toyota would use its maneuverability to back it up. That way, we can flank and fake them out."

They parked the two side-by-side at the icehouse's loading dock door.

By the time they had gotten out, Encizo and Hawkins were there with more sacks full of loot and seized equipment.

"We're taking two trucks?" Encizo asked. He put his gear into the back of the Toyota.

"Two is one and one is none," Hawkins interjected. "Always good to have an extra."

"I can't argue with that," Encizo answered.

"I also intend to have you be Cal's gunner, just in case," McCarter told Encizo. "T.J., you'll be with me and Gary. Fit your carbine with a grenade launcher."

Hawkins gave an understated salute to the commander and left to retrieve his stubby assault rifle.

McCarter then connected with the Farm. It was time to find out what Kurtzman's cyber wizards had picked up as a response to Phoenix Force's incursion into Mexico.

"Price, here," the Stony Man mission controller answered. "I take it you saw the response waiting for you in Nogales."

McCarter grinned. "We know there is some. And they're ready for us to come through. I'd like specifics."

"I'm having Bear send satellite infrared and radar to your PDAs," Price told him. "You doing a direct border breach?"

"Like my countrymen sang back in the '80s, 'it's so fun being an illegal alien,'" McCarter answered.

"The lyrics were 'it's *no* fun,'" Price corrected.

McCarter's smirk deepened. "Well, they play their tunes, I'll play mine. The boys and I are going to ambush our ambushers. No chance that our border people will accidentally stumble into it?"

"The Caballeros Cartel seems to have cleared everything on its side of the fence, as we've done for you. This isn't a smuggling tunnel. It's an arena," Price explained. "You're supposed to be the Christians and they are the lions."

"We've sold our cloaks for swords in that event," McCarter said. "Granted, they're in 4.6 mm, 5.56 mm and 7.62 mm, but they are swords."

"I'd prefer you had some 40 mm," Price returned.

"Cal and T.J. are fitting their M203s," McCarter told her. "No grenades to replenish the supplies on the Arizona side, but we'll see what we can scavenge over there."

"In that case, happy hunting," Price concluded.

McCarter could tell that Barbara Price wasn't excited about the means by which Phoenix Force intended to circumvent the cartel's ambush. The plan was going to involve a lot of explosions and a ton of gunfire.

Even so, this was the bed the Caballeros de Durango had made for itself. McCarter, anticipating the possibility, had had Blancanales, Encizo and Hawkins, using Arizona and Texas Spanish accents, record messages while on the plane. The plan was simple. If the cartel and Accion Obrar hoped to make Stony Man look bad with a front-page splash of violence and terrorism on the border, the agency would throw up a smoke screen. The three Spanish-fluent Stony Man commandos would be portrayed as *reconquistas*: radical Mexican insurgents who wanted the southern border states added to their own.

"We didn't cross the border, the border crossed us!" and *"¡Viva la raza!"* peppered the recordings. There was also condemnation of the criminally complacent Mexican government and law enforcement.

It was a simple ruse, but intricate enough to obfuscate the presence of the American covert agency in this mission. Just as the packets of cocaine and the oxygen bottle would provide a blinding haze, so would the messages to news agencies. The press, however, would receive their high from the juicy weight of the incident.

HUNDREDS OF MILES AWAY, on the streets of Yuma, Arizona, Rosario Blancanales maneuvered into position with his toolbox full of warfare. The earbud, hands-free communicator he wore was invisible, and even if it were noticed, his salt-and-pepper hair was light enough to allow him to get away with appearing to need a hearing aid.

The real concern he had was that he'd betray the presence of the arsenal under the loose folds of his coveralls, but so far, no one had noticed. Arizona was a state that allowed for open carry, but a shoulder-holstered submachine gun, a full-auto converted Para-Ordnance P14 "Franken-Colt Mark II" and a grenade launcher would stretch the limits of even the state's relatively lax gun laws.

He found the van and confirmed that it was his target. Part of his disarming appearance, aside from the work clothes and toolbox, was the bag lunch he'd brought with him. Blancanales took a spot on a bench, set the red metal case beside him and pulled out a sandwich and a bottle of cola. A bag of chips to complete the lunch-break illusion, and he was armed to the teeth, yet invisible in plain sight.

Blancanales waited for his partners to set up on their targets.

"Ready." Lyons's voice crackled in his ear.

"In position," Schwarz confirmed.

Blancanales set down his lunch and opened the big red toolbox. Inside, he had his stand-alone M203. He kept the grenade launcher hidden until he thumbed a buckshot round into the breech of the mighty weapon. The 40 mm barrel was twice the diameter of even the heaviest over-the-counter shotguns. That doubling of bore meant that the buckshot "grenade" held eight times the payload of a 12-gauge shell, turning the launcher into a brutal anti-personnel device. He closed the breech then swung it out of the toolbox, aiming at the driver's-side door of the van and firing.

The range was fifty feet, which gave the swarm of projectiles Blancanales triggered the room to spread out to a four-foot-diameter circle. Each pellet, a third of an inch in span, perforated sheet metal and glass. The driver of the van and his steering column were ravaged brutally, bearings finding flesh, bone, plastic and wiring equally fragile. With a single blast, the Able Team warrior had eliminated the ambusher's ability to escape the counterattack.

With smooth, practiced precision, Blancanales ejected the empty shell and pushed a second one home, aiming toward the rear of the van. Its back doors started to swing open, which confirmed that there were gunmen bunched up and ready to burst out onto the street.

The same sheet metal that provided so little protection for the driver buckled under the onslaught of another four-foot-wide swarm. The buckshot might not have had enough energy to punch through the skin of the van and an entire human body, but the second salvo of flying copper and lead meant that corpses tumbled out onto the street, not active, angry shooters.

The double burst of doom provided more than sufficient staggering horror to keep the gunners still inside the van stunned and indecisive as Blancanales put the grenade launcher back in its box and ripped his MP-9 from its harness. The shoulder stock clicked into place and Blancanales moved forward, selector on full-auto.

One of the enemy decided valor was the better part of discretion and leaped from the rear doors, weapon in hand. Before he could land, Blancanales tracked him and ripped off a burst of four 9 mm slugs. All four rounds were on target and instead of landing on his feet like a hero, the charging assassin toppled and crashed into a bloodied mess on the asphalt.

Cries in Spanish and English rattled from inside the van. Blancanales heard the jangle and roll of a side panel on the opposite side of the vehicle. Those unhurt, or at least able to beat a retreat, had decided to keep the bulk of the van between them and whatever avenging force was bearing down upon them.

However, sheet metal was as ineffective against a 9 mm submachine gun as it was to the 40 mm buckshot payload. Blancanales knew where the side door on the van would be; he aimed at the right spot and triggered two more short bursts. Slugs chopped into the thin skin of the van and a cry of agony split the air. To say that Blancanales felt bad about literally shooting fish in a barrel would be a lie.

These men were stationed, watching a federal building, and in wait to attack and either kidnap or kill a US deputy marshal and three terrified children.

No, mercy was not in the cards for these armed thugs, and as Blancanales swung around the rear of the van, keeping his eyes on the open doors, he was primed to continue blazing out 9 mm retribution as long as someone was there with a gun in his hand.

Cutting the pie to not expose himself to enemy fire, he spotted another cartel soldier standing in the rear doors. He was splattered in wet pink clothing, white shirt and linen jacket soaked through to the skin where his partners had bled all over him. He still had a rifle in both hands and the sight of Blancanales startled him.

Blancanales, on the other hand, had expected someone

to be there and he stroked the trigger on the MP-9. At 900 rounds per minute, he emptied the last of the 15-round magazine into the blood-drenched ambusher. Blancanales destroyed his face and upper chest with that extended burst. In a heartbeat, he ejected the spent box and pushed home a fresh stack of thirty 9 mm slugs.

The last man in the van, the last living body at least, was huddled behind the driver's seat, hands up and fingers splayed wide. "I'm not armed! Don't shoot!"

Blancanales kept the muzzle of the machine pistol leveled at the man, but scanned the area. There could be one more gunman, possibly crouched around the front of the vehicle. This guy might be a legitimate surrender, or he could simply be a distraction. Either way, Blancanales refused to lock into tunnel vision on him.

In the distance the heavy booms of a shotgun and another machine pistol crackled in the midafternoon streets of Yuma.

"Step out of the van through the panel door," Blancanales ordered. He listened for other signs of a possible hidden gunman. He had a prisoner, at least for the moment, but one mistake and his brains could be spilled on the street with the would-be killers he'd just dispatched.

The prisoner followed Blancanales's instructions.

"Lay down on your stomach and lace your fingers behind your head," Blancanales barked. He wanted this man as far out of position to start a fight as possible. The guy, obviously in a mood to survive this encounter, did as he was told. He intertwined his fingers and lay down, eyes shut. His breath came in rapid gulps, anxiety too real to be faked.

"Anyone else get away?" Blancanales asked.

"Yeah," the man lying on the sidewalk answered. "He ran—"

Toward the front of the van, the veteran Able Team warrior concluded as a shadow flickered in the windshield of the vehicle, disappearing around the corner. There were no abandoned weapons on the sidewalk, so there was a good chance that the escaped ambusher was packing some serious firepower. Judging from what he'd seen in the hands of the dead sprawled in the back of the van, they had submachine guns, too.

Blancanales dropped to a kneeling position, making himself a smaller target as footsteps sounded on the asphalt on the other side of the van. The gunman intended to flank him, but the wily veteran was ready, front sight on the spot where a head would appear.

The cartel gunman burst into view, firing from the hip. That stream of bullets would have torn through Blancanales's face had he remained standing, but instead, slugs merely sparked against a stone wall and lost their energy. Deformed bullets tinkled to the concrete like metallic turds.

In the meantime Blancanales fired from the shoulder, controlling his trigger pull and maintaining his front sight on his target.

The last violent ambusher died as Blancanales shredded him from crotch to throat with two tribursts of autofire in quick succession. Groin, spine and heart were all defiled by the brutal swathe of 9 mm rounds Blancanales threw at them, and with that, in the space of a few moments, the gunfight was over.

He looked to the man on the sidewalk.

"Stay right there. Make a move and you'll be in hell before you untangle your fingers," Blancanales warned him.

"Yes, sir."

Blancanales wasted little time securing his wrists with a nylon cable tie.

"Carl, we've got our prisoner," Blancanales said over the com.

"Good," Lyons returned. "Because nothing's left of my target."

Blancanales could tell by the gruff tone of his partner's voice that he'd found something particularly nasty in his attack.

Whatever it was, it was too important to broadcast even over the secure communication frequencies Able Team used in the field.

And if Lyons was worried, then Blancanales was in a hurry to know why.

CHAPTER SEVEN

Carl Lyons heard the thunder of Rosario Blancanales's grenade launcher and got to work. He ambled up to the rear of the van, the bill of his battered ball cap shading his features to make him look less intimidating. His loose hiking gear also kept his broad shoulders and biceps on full display. The shotgun between his shoulder blades and obscured by his hiking pack was ready to draw and blaze away. He got to the sidewalk-side panel door and turned, giving it a vigorous kick.

The man in the front passenger seat, ironically called the shotgun seat, threw open his door and stepped out, a pistol in hand.

"What the hell do you think you're doing?" the man shouted even as Lyons whipped out his brutal Mossberg semiauto. The shoulder stock extended and as soon as the gun was at eye level, the Able Team commander pulled the trigger. A fist-size knot of 00 Buck struck the gunman in the face, obliterating his features in an instant. The gunner's corpse crashed against the passenger-side door, and it held him up for a few brief moments.

Lyons charged to get into the seat that his first target had vacated. He seized the door frame with his left hand and pushed the shotgun into the front seat ahead of him. As soon as the muzzle touched the chest of the ambushers' driver, who was busy starting the vehicle, he pulled the trigger. At contact range, Lyons unleashed a firestorm inside the driver's torso. Ribs disintegrated into splinters, and the burning jet of force that hurled projectiles faster than the speed of sound added to the unfettered devastation that nine copper-jacketed balls a third of an inch across could tear through flesh.

Rather than attempt to maneuver the barrel of the shotgun over the front seats, Lyons backed out immediately. With two strides, he was in the middle of the sidewalk and aiming at the area he'd just vacated. He saw an arm swing into view and blew it off with a well-aimed blast. He didn't completely sever the limb, but the bones of the forearm were stripped of large chunks of muscle and artery. Blood squirted from the mangled limb.

With a slight pivot, Lyons hammered out three more shotgun blasts at close range. The van's sheet metal proved little hindrance to the concentrated salvos of pellets, and the gunmen inside the vehicle released grunts of pain and dying breath as they caught the deformed slugs in vital areas. The panel door unlatched and swung open, but Lyons caught the first one there with a volcanic boom.

In the second time in seemingly as many seconds, the thug's skull was excavated, face and brains stripped out of the crushed bowl that used to be his head. A figure was just over the nearly decapitated man's shoulder and Lyons pivoted and pulled the trigger. The Able Team commander killed that gunman with a flourish of gore, the shotgun spraying the interior of the van with spongy clots of shredded human and splintered skeleton. This was full-on slaughter, the eye for an eye writ large, as Lyons considered a fellow lawman worth a dozen dead gun thugs.

The Mossberg locked empty and he tore one of the .357s from its concealed holster.

Ten shots, cruiser-loaded, was more than enough for the vanful. Ninety projectiles packed into ten shells had chopped apart the eight killers within. The floor of the van was now a spongy, squishy swamp of gore-soaked carpeting. Lyons leaned in and pushed bodies around, looking for means of identification. He wanted to know the source of this army of killers. He hung the shotgun sling on one of his shoulders and used the camera on his CPDA, scanning the charnel-house interior.

Lyons focused on one figure sprawled on the ground. His complexion was more olive than tan, which piqued the ex-cop's instincts. He sifted through the mess and pulled his right hand. There was a gun in it and the olive-skinned man's fingers were in a death grip. Prying the claws away, Lyons took several good fingerprints. A quick set of photos and he sent them off to Stony Man Farm.

A fast pat down showed that none of the gunmen had any identification, and the weapons he examined had had their serial numbers eradicated.

The CPDA beeped an alert that Price had information for him. He switched off the camera mode and put it on phone.

"Carl, those fingerprints you sent came back with a hit," Price answered.

Lyons grunted. "That was why I sent them in."

"They belong to a 'terp who went AWOL," she concluded.

'Terp, he knew, was Price's short for *interpreter*. Given the swarthy appearance of the corpse, Lyons figured he was from one or another Middle Eastern country. Lyons looked at the screen as the information on the corpse rolled in.

He was not an official 'terp who'd been assigned to US forces in either Afghanistan or Iraq. He was from somewhere in between, and he was disavowed in official circles. Ethnically Iranian, he'd been born in the United States—Arizona to be exact—and had been raised in the Truth of Pinchas ministry.

Lyons immediately recognized the Pincharites. The

ministry was named for a zealous grandson of the Hebrew Aaron, who'd taken the initiative to murder a Hebrew who laid with a Midianite woman. Because of the interbreeding with idol worshipers, Pinchas believed that the Hebrew God inflicted a plague upon the tribe of Israel. Only by the cold-blooded murder of two consenting adults was this "plague" ended. The Truthers of Pinchas were notorious for violent bank robberies, bombings of abortion clinics, the attempted murder of FBI agents and attacks on same-sex-marriage rallies.

"And because this sack of shit converted, he was given enough of a vetting to be associated with these goons," Lyons murmured. "And US foreign policy."

"Carl, we've got our prisoner," Blancanales said over the com.

"Good," Lyons returned. "Because nothing's left of my target."

Lyons continued retrieving fingerprints, using an unfolded piece of white paper and bloody fingertips. He wanted to see if others were from a similar organization. That would give even more weight to Price's worries about the conspiracy that had kidnapped Amanda Castillo not being merely an old sparring partner for Able Team but actually an agency fully aware of the existence of the SOG.

There were times in the early years of the Farm when Able Team found itself continually butting heads with renegade factions of the CIA. The first attack on the Farm was an effort by one such faction to eliminate the threat of Mack Bolan's identity as Colonel John Phoenix, the agency's chief officer.

And then there were also the KGB hard-liners who still hung on to the Cold War. Lyons had heard enough of rumors of a long-term sleeper plan, where the old Soviet Union would pretend reforms, all the while rebuilding itself from the economic suicide it committed in the 1980s.

It was called the Long Con and of late, with the Russian government making moves in the Ukraine, as well as other behavior akin to an eight-hundred-pound gorilla, Lyons couldn't dismiss thoughts of Phoenix Force's old enemies hard at work.

The Able Team commander had another recollection that easily could tie Russian involvement with fascist fanatics in the Americas. A KGB agent under the name of Colonel Gunther had managed to infiltrate and gain a high rank in Miguel Unomundo's Fascist International. Some of those renegade CIA groups had ties with Unomundo's group, and the one who launched the attack was supported by old Kremlin hard-liners. Again, Lyons was reminded of the Russian attempt to assassinate Phoenix Force culminating with an army of two hundred operatives attacking them on a mountainside in Montana.

There were plenty of old foes still out there, and new ones kept rising every day, either from "allied" nations such as Pakistan and Iraq or from economic competitors such as Venezuela.

Lyons mentally backtracked to go over the facts.

The dead 'terp had CIA ties.

The dead 'terp was also part of a violent, fanatic Christian identity group.

This group of killers was also aligned with the group that had attacked a Justice Department safe house.

The targets were investigating the ties between a Mexican agency known as Accion Obrar and the Caballeros de Durango Cartel, and the Durango group claimed ties to the Knights Templars.

When Blancanales and Schwarz showed up with their two living prisoners, Lyons felt a little bit of relief, though he looked down at his CPDA, searching for more data on the corpses he'd assembled.

"Let's haul these turds inside where we can shake some answers loose," Lyons growled.

Schwarz and Blancanales shared a look. Able Team had encountered more than enough fanatics who believed in some form of racial or religious superiority. The ones who might have ties to the hated Fascist International were especially onerous, but any "true believer" with a willingness to spill blood for the cause all got the same mercy from Lyons that they provided others.

"You guys are in some serious shit now," Schwarz informed one of the gunmen. "Because if you stiff that bad boy on anything, and you've got the slightest affiliation with some neo-Nazi gang, he'll tear your intestines out. And after it's hurt for a few hours, then he'll let you die."

"What're you talking about?" Schwarz's prisoner snarled. "You and this spic attacked *us*." The gunman spit his distaste to the ground.

Lyons turned and locked his gaze upon the fool who'd thrown the racist term. "You and me. No Miranda rights. Not even the restrictions at Camp X-Ray. You'll cry. You'll bleed. You'll mess your pants. And then you'll beg me for death."

The prisoner froze. Lyons didn't need a mirror to realize that he resembled nothing more than a devil at this moment. Crawling among the dead, corpses slaughtered and blown to chunks by a shotgun, he was drenched in blood up to his shoulders, and his eyes had a hard, deadly glint. His lips were peeled back from his teeth and his cheeks hurt from a combination of hateful grimace and grin in anticipation of future horrors.

"They said you were some kind of federal agents. You're not allowed to do…" The other gunman spoke up, trailing off as Lyons turned toward him.

"Tell me what I'm not allowed to do, punk," Lyons snarled. Inside, his rage writhed and twisted, a lion pacing back and forth in anticipation of fresh blood, the tearing of meat and the shattering of bones. His annihilation of a group of gunmen was one thing, but the Able Team leader's dark side seethed at the notion of unleashing close, personal vengeance upon those who cost him friends.

Lyons grabbed Blancanales's prisoner by the back of his head and steered him to the open side panel of the van he'd turned into an abattoir. The stench of blood and burst organs reeked through the interior and the captive ambusher's face turned green with nausea. Lyons pushed a little harder, leaning him farther into the mess. He picked up the target of a shotgun blast whose skull had been carved into a bowl. Lyons held that rancid mess right under the prisoner's nose.

"Look down there and tell me what I'm not allowed to do!" Lyons roared. "You're not under arrest! You're alive for as long as you tell me information I can use! In fact, the faster you educate me about your bosses, the quicker I let you die!"

Blancanales wrenched the prisoner away from his friend. "We need answers, not panic babble."

Carl Lyons, to a stranger and from the outside, looked as if he were teetering on the edge of mass murder, ready to spill far more blood. But Blancanales and Schwarz knew full well that their friend and partner was still a man of ethics, no matter how enraged he was. Torture was the absolute last resort, and then, only against the most hated of enemies in an instance where seconds counted. Lyons knew that the more effective means of breaking a recalcitrant prisoner was through fear and imagination.

He also knew that there were times when he looked as if he were carved from pure nightmare. Right now was one of those moments, especially with the bugged eyes poking through the terrified faces of their prisoners.

"Let's go. Maybe we can find a way for you to have an open-casket funeral," Schwarz promised one of them.

The cartel gunmen accompanied the two Able Team warriors without a hint of resistance.

Now there was only the hope that they could get something useful out of them. If not, then Lyons resigned himself to remaining a target for whatever maniacs the Caballeros de Durango Cartel or their government counterparts unleashed.

Of course, when Able Team was the target, the shooters ended up dead.

DAVID MCCARTER LOOKED over the two vehicles, ready to take on their roles as personnel carriers. Or rather, that was what he was hoping any observers would think. There was a small army across the border in Mexico waiting for Phoenix Force to make its way across the smuggling tunnel between the two Nogales sites.

Undoubtedly there was someone on this side, other than those manning the icehouse, keeping tabs on the group that had just destroyed the illicit warehouse's security. The actual gear dragged out to the pickup and the SUV was simply ammunition that wouldn't be used in their guns. Their conversations were for the sake of anyone spying upon them with shotgun microphones or hidden surveillance bugs within the icehouse.

Phoenix Force wasn't going into this mission blindly. They'd already known that there was likely to be heavy security on both sides of the border. The confirmation from the Yuma federal building that it was surrounded by ambushers had merely been icing on the cake.

McCarter checked the Combat PDA, where he had a live satellite feed of a group of well-armed men approaching. They were in formation; a familiar Special Forces–style "conga line" meant to provide minimal profile for an approaching team with little chance of tripping each other up. Phoenix Force had trained with that method of approaching a target, as well, but there was a major weakness in that one shot from the right angle could put a bullet through everyone in that line.

This team, however, knew enough to stagger the line. Now it'd take three shots to take down the approaching group, and only if it were from three snipers simultaneously. Their vulnerability compensation proved that these were professionals.

These were Mexican soldiers and cops who had left the "losing side" of the drug wars, turning their talents and knowledge to assisting their cartel employers.

McCarter signaled the others, who ferried the hand signal to Manning in the drug tunnel.

Down there, Gary Manning would hit the controls on the automated trams, sending their surprises to the other side.

McCarter continued observing the approaching force. They stacked up, hemming in the appropriated vehicles.

The Phoenix Force commander flipped the safety cover off the remote detonator for the four packs placed in the parked vehicles. It had taken more than a few minutes for Manning to improvise a couple of crates' worth of small-arms ammunition into a deadly reception for the assault teams.

Barbara Price had indicated that these men were not with Arizona law enforcement, nor were they Immigration and Customs Enforcement. That meant they were fair game.

The gunmen closed and McCarter depressed the trigger on the detonator.

The icehouse shuddered under the wave of overpressure slamming into the docking bay wall with the force of a hurricane. The Toyota SUV and the Ford pickup each split apart, their sheet-metal skins rupturing as gunpowder and other combustibles erupted. Bullets placed in the backpacks became shrapnel and the kill radius was at least twenty-five yards.

Manning launched himself up into the icehouse moments before a second detonation shook the ground. On the other side of the border, the reception committee received the exact present they would have heard being planned for them. What they wouldn't be prepared for was Manning's secondary gift.

Antipersonnel charges had been loaded into more illicit gun and ammunition crates, turning them into ersatz claymore mines, similar to the two SUVs in the loading dock. Manning's follow-up detonation would come much later. Already, he and the rest of Phoenix Force were in full gas masks, just as the gunmen on the other side of the border would be.

The first detonation would be the signal for the enemy to make their initial move.

"Down the bloody ladder!" McCarter ordered.

The Stony Man commandos descended into the smuggling tunnel. At this end, the choking, possibly numbing and blinding, cocaine clouds were much thinner than the smoke screen at the other end. However, any strike team worth its salt would move in on the bang of a distraction device blast.

McCarter and his partners were also moving on the bang, anticipating the amount of time necessary for the other force to begin its charge. The plan was such that they would have been able to pin Phoenix Force in with attacks from two fronts.

The trouble with working like a professional was that other professionals could figure out what your plan would likely be.

As soon as McCarter was on the platform, Manning hit the trigger for the antipersonnel charges on subsequent— and well hidden by the cocaine clouds—carts.

The rapid-fire cracks of multiple detonations split the air, signaling a wave of shrapnel and death unleashed hundreds of yards downrange. They'd discovered a large shipment of methamphetamine, coming from the super labs in Mexico, and meth's volatility was legendary. Manning managed to turn the clumps of meth and ammunition into a brutal, devastating weapon. The roar was proof of that effectiveness.

"That should bloody well soften them up," McCarter said aloud.

Now that they'd blasted hell into the faces of their opposition, there was little need to keep taciturn about the rest of their counter ambush.

McCarter brought a spare Heckler & Koch G-3 to his shoulder, the rifle having the actual range necessary to reach to the far end of the smugglers' tunnel. The others also had up-gunned where their weapons were more for close quarters. Only Manning hadn't needed to change his gear.

The five men knelt, firing on single shot, sweeping the corridor. Even on semiautomatic, five rifles with the 7.62 mm rounds were more than sufficient to make the length of the subterranean passage inhospitable to human life.

The NATO rounds from the G-3s were more than capable of producing through-and-through cavities. Without needing to see, they knew that there were enemy gunmen down there, armed thugs who had turned their backs on their oaths of duty, waging war against a lawfully elected government and supporting the transport of poison and slavery across the border. Every human stopping a slug downrange was a murderer or complicit in murders.

It was cold and brutal, but the team was in firing-squad mode. Gunfire crackled at the opposite end, but no bullets came their way. The weapons discharged in death grips, or they were firing to where they assumed standing enemies were, as opposed to the Phoenix professionals shooting from prone. There was merit to that as dust and pebbles torn from the wall behind them rained on McCarter's back.

The Briton emptied the G-3's magazine and quickly reloaded. Twenty more high-powered slugs ripped downrange from the battle rifle, seeking out enemy torsos.

Within a few moments of emptying that second magazine, he and the others stopped firing. This was where the sound-amplification apparatus of their hearing protection was vital.

Groans and death rattles sounded at the other end of the tunnel.

"Grenades," McCarter ordered.

James and Hawkins brought up their grenade launchers and pumped 40 mm shells to where the sounds of the wounded and dying emanated. Thunder clapped and fragmentation shells unleashed waves of cruel mercy to the cartel mercenaries three hundred yards distant.

By now the thick clouds of cocaine smoke had died down. McCarter swept the carnage at the other end of the tunnel with his binoculars. It was an abattoir, more than a hundred rounds of 7.62 mm NATO and a pair of fragmentation grenades providing the coda for Manning's deadly, improvised antipersonnel mines. Bodies lay ruptured with flesh slashed and organs steaming in the darkened tunnel.

The butcher's work was done.

"Let's move out," McCarter grimly pronounced.

Waiting around wasn't getting them closer to freeing Amanda Castillo.

CHAPTER EIGHT

Harold Brognola heard his tablet beep softly as he sat in on the Congressional Justice Department oversight hearing. As he was in the back of the gallery, only observing as political appointees were currently sitting on the grill, he was allowed the luxury to check to see what the message was about.

It was a series of preliminary reports of fireworks displays going off in downtown Yuma and Nogales, both cities in Arizona. The odd bit of news was a clear sign that the Stony Man cybernetics crew and Barbara Price were on top of the game, dispelling any thought that an actual shooting war had occurred on the border between the US and Mexico.

The fireworks were supposedly the work of an organization of activists calling for a dissolution of the border between the United States of America and Mexico, as their ancestors had lived without that imaginary line in the sand. At least, this particular batch of *reconquistas* believed that. Others, truly dangerous thugs, were more in line with Mexico taking back Texas, Arizona and New Mexico.

The people who made these announcements were actually members of the Stony Man Farm action teams, utilizing their fluency in Spanish and adept mastery of different accents to make it seem as if this was a peaceful protest as opposed to open warfare.

Two videos were also transmitted, live infrared feeds

from satellite cameras covering Able Team and Phoenix Force in their legs of the mission. Brognola quickly skimmed, watching as warm bodies flared then cooled with sudden death.

As there were no emergency texts, it was a given that the lives ending were those of Stony Man's enemies, not his operatives.

Of course, seeing the kind of opposition emplaced against the two teams informed Brognola that they were up against dangerous opposition who were fully aware of the Sensitive Operations Group's capabilities. Only cunning and audacious violence of action had overwhelmed the initial preparations of Accion Obrar and the Caballeros de Durango Cartel, but that was a temporary reprieve. Once that conspiracy figured out the kind of response they would receive from the covert agency, they would step up with even more and more gunmen.

Brognola could imagine Carl Lyons's response to that warning. The Able Team leader loved it when he was surrounded and outnumbered. It meant that he didn't have to worry about where he was shooting, because he wouldn't miss a bad guy.

It wasn't bravado on his part, nor for any of the members of his direct-action teams. Their job was specifically to go out, hunt down and destroy the very worst of humanity, exterminating those who would engage in wanton slaughter. Brognola had no little surge of pride that "his boys" were the ultimate in malware removal, destroying psychotics, terrorists and gangsters with precision and overwhelming force. This was also boosted by the fact that neither Able Team nor Phoenix Force allowed noncombatants or bystanders to fall as a result of their actions.

They may have failed to get to and stop a slaughter in time, but they worked extremely hard to keep the enemy fire focused on them if there were others present. First and foremost, the Stony Man teams were protectors, not wild-ass maniacs. Second, they were avengers of those harmed in the name of greed and politics.

"How is it that all of the marshals at the Arizona safe house were part of a single program?" Brognola heard a senator ask. That jerked his attention away from the update on his tablet.

"It's a continuing education camp in the Blue Ridge Mountains, isn't it?" the senator continued. This was a party whip, an older, distinguished man who'd been in his senate seat for as long as Brognola could remember. When the man directed his gaze directly toward the big Fed, Brognola's stomach turned.

It was no surprise that the Farm would be referenced in this oversight committee, but when the senator had enough knowledge to link Brognola to it, it was the sign of a breach in operational security. One that was exactly the kind of threat that could sink not just the SOG, but also the current administration, as well as all the others that Stony Man had fought under. Without an official sanction, the teams had invaded other nations and killed some criminals and terrorists without due process.

Such actions were wholly illegal, despite the necessity of eliminating mad dogs without endangering the rest of the country. Brognola knew from the very beginning that the Stony Man operation was on the razor's edge between vigilantism and out-of-control governmental authority. That was part of the reason why it had been built to be mostly self-sustaining. The blacksuit program was a means of paying back into the law enforcement community, as well as keeping a pool open for replacement operatives.

Or, as in the case of the slaughtered marshals and Joaquin Castillo, assembling trusted lawmen for a protection detail that could be leaked to less-than-scrupulous politicians.

Brognola entered the name of the senator into his tablet's on-screen keyboard, tagging him for in-depth investigation. The only politician that Brognola truly had a stomach for was Rosario Blancanales, whose nickname was due to his ability to handle almost everything with diplomacy. Blancanales, for all of his skills, was still more honest than any ten of the men in this chamber of government.

"Why should an elite federal training facility be your focus?" Brognola's nominal superior returned. The man was a political appointee, but at least he was a man the big Fed could work with. He wasn't a stranger to law enforcement, and he actually had a feeling for justice that matched his own.

"Because of the rumors that this training camp might be for something much darker than our founding fathers intended government to be," countered the senator's bipartisan counterpart. "The Constitution was not written to be discarded in cases where the law was inconvenient."

That senator, from the opposite side of the aisle, was also a longtime staple of Washington politics. Normally, the two senators were at each other's throats, demeaning their beliefs in a steadily disintegrating display of civility, keeping the pace with the downturn of thought in pundits' public discourse. Where once they were erudite, now they were nothing more than spoiled children engaged in schoolyard cries of "are not" and "are, too!"

To see them on the same page showed that they were either being played by some outside force or that their chicanery had been spread out over the course of decades to undermine the government to which they'd been elected.

Either way, Brognola entered the counterpart's name in the tablet.

He could almost feel the breeze of CPU fans in distant computers springing to life as their processing power heated up.

So far, at least for this hearing, things were being steered toward "the attack in Arizona was all the US's fault" on the part of the left and the right calling it all an overextension of constitutional rights and powers.

"Our Constitution does not outline the necessity to protect journalists from another nation," the right-wing senator offered.

"After all the damage we've done with economic oppression and the war on drugs, we're surprised that Mexican entities haven't attacked us with such force before," the leftist countered. Both sides, of course, were wrong, at least in terms of where the blame of the attack lay. That didn't keep them from pushing their agendas ahead, with Stony Man Farm's blacksuit program as the whipping boy with which they achieved their perverted climaxes.

"The war on drugs that you so vehemently disdain is nothing we started. There are maniacs across the border who think nothing of murdering judges, lawmen, lawmakers," the Justice Department appointee snapped. "We've learned that waging war and using unfair sentencing on our own streets has been a failure in controlling the problems of addiction and violence."

"So, you'd circumvent the Constitution?" the right's senator asked. "Like invading another country with that contingent of lawmen? Or just use this as an excuse to disarm Arizona's lawful citizens?"

Brognola grimaced. Whenever the public face of the Justice Department tried to introduce logic in one direction, the other side would pop up with some other vacuous comment, a broad lie that would make a good sound bite back home or among the rest of their political party. This had been the mayhem and chaos of government for far too long.

Senate hearings like this one only accomplished one thing: filling the air with more noise signifying nothing.

Except these grunts and hoots actually did provide some information.

The opposition turning Accion Obrar against the United States had senators in its pocket and had loosed them as ravenous wolves.

THE NIGHTMARE OF being blindfolded and bounced around for hours came to an end when the charter plane began its descent.

Amanda Castillo was glad that she still had a sense of hearing after being hurled into the back of a helicopter without hearing protection. The pilot had taken off from the estate and flown for what felt like an eternity. The heavy throb of the rotor kept her from concentrating enough to gauge how long she'd been in the air.

The back of some truck wasn't much help, either. With her eyes taped shut and her ears ringing from the long-term abuse put upon them by the helicopter flight, her dead reckoning of the trip by road wasn't much better. She did know that a big tarpaulin had been thrown over her, which was a relief from the direct burning rays of the sun, but became stifling as the daylight baked everything under it.

At least I'll die without permanent skin damage.

From the pickup truck bed, she was wound in the tarp and carried up some stairs. Here she'd sat, wrists handcuffed behind her, making sitting back and relaxing impossible. Just the slightest weight leaning back was unbearable leverage against her elbows and shoulders. Shrugging to make her joints not stretch like taffy allowed the rings of the handcuffs to sink and bite into her wrists painfully. It was a no-win situation.

At least when I die, my abs will be tight as a washboard.

Amanda grit her teeth. Those kinds of defeatist thoughts

were not what she needed right now. All the effort she'd attempted to count the moments of the trip were some way of seeking hope in a hopeless situation. Finding the positives as to the attractive corpse she'd leave, one without skin cancer and with a trim, muscular stomach, felt as if she were giving up.

What she did know was that she traveled alone. No children joined her on this arduous journey.

That was a good thing. She'd be alone in the Dungeon without Pity.

She'd say something out loud, but the heat of the trip and hours without water had left her mouth dry and cottony. Amanda worked her lips and felt them crack.

Finally the tape was torn from her eyes. She blinked, and the interior of the plane was too bright for the countless hours of darkness they'd simmered in. Her head ached.

"Welcome home, Mrs. Castillo," a deep voice conveyed.

Amanda waited for her vision to clear and she saw a man in a three-piece silk suit. He was somewhere around forty, in the prime of his life, with classically handsome features. The stranger was as white as white could be, with wavy blond hair and piercing blue eyes. He spoke in Castillian Spanish, very crisp and perfect.

"My home is with my family," Amanda croaked from between chapped lips and through a raw throat.

"You can join your family, then," the man said. "Make a choice…your husband in death or your children, hiding in a federal building in Yuma."

Amanda stiffened in shock and grief.

"Your children won't be free for long," the man said.

"Why? Who are you?"

Amanda's wrists were freed, but any hope of gathering the strength to grasp the man in the suit was gone. Her hands were beds of needles as blood flushed back into them, and her muscles felt stretched and worn-out.

Merely lifting her hands was an insurmountable task.

Hands crooked under her arms, helping her to wobbly feet. They buckled, rubbery from too much disuse. Stretching her torso also made her stomach muscles cramp up as effectively as if she'd been punched just below the navel.

"You'll come to miss these hours of confinement and solitude, Amanda," the man said, brushing her cheek gently.

Amanda's vision cleared enough for her to realize that the voice, the face…they were all familiar.

"Hector?" she asked.

"Cousin," he answered. He trapped her chin between his fingers and kissed her deeply. "You had to go and run off with that little mixed blood, didn't you?"

Amanda strained, twisted her neck to escape his grasp. "You sick animal…"

"As soon as your brats leave the federal building, my men will be on them," Hector Moran said softly. "See, we need to clean the family gene pool. And those half-brown babies just need to be thrown off the bridge like a sack full of kittens."

"I'll see you in hell," Amanda growled through clenched teeth.

"You first," Hector said, knotting her hair around his fingers and pressing her face to the window pit. "El Calabozo sin Piedad."

Amanda's stomach twisted as she saw it. She'd assumed that it had been some kind of shanty town, assembled from huts, surrounded by barbed wire. The stories of its horrors and corruption had been rampant enough to fill her with the illusion of it being a Third World slum repurposed. But what she saw proved that a lie.

It sat as a squat fortress, mirror glass and steel shining in the setting sun, surrounded by a security wall of unblemished, battleship-gray-painted stone. Atop the wall, barbed wire curled and writhed, twisting along the lengths between the steely armored turrets.

The turrets themselves were grim standing towers with more mirror glass. Guards stood on the balcony, holding M16 assault rifles at port arms, as if coming out for the welcome of their newest guest.

It was modern, clean and perfectly squared. High-tech and polish gleamed on the skin of the penitentiary, and she couldn't imagine an entire army penetrating its walls, let alone her being able to crawl out through a spoon-dug tunnel.

Huge metal doors rolled open, showing themselves to be at least two feet thick, and Amanda was dragged to the door of the airplane.

It looked like a corporate headquarters, one that handled top secret government contracts, necessitating airtight security.

Amanda felt Moran's hand smack between her shoulder blades, and she tumbled down the steps to the tarmac, bashing her face on the ground. Blood streamed from her nostrils and she cursed her arms as they failed to obey her mental commands. She managed two or three kicks, which only served to grind her cheek harder into the rough ground. Moran reached her, stooped then dragged her up to her knees by her hair.

"Freak," Amanda growled.

"Because I prefer pure-blooded sexual partners?" Moran asked. "You're the stupid *puta*, letting any old sack of shit stick their filthy parts into you."

That was the galvanizing moment. Her arm surged with enough strength to swing up and smash into his face. Her delicate fingers had much more sturdiness than she'd anticipated as her knuckles cracked on his teeth, his lips split and bloody in the wake of the impact.

Moran staggered back, stunned and surprised by the hit.

His guards, however, were upon her in moments, swinging the stocks of their weapons into her ribs.

Amanda coughed, glaring at the racist bastard who unfortunately was related to her by blood.

"Don't dent her too much," Moran said. "We want her fresh and pretty for the lads inside sin Piedad."

"I thought you wanted a clean gene pool," Amanda slurred. One benefit of the blood washing into her mouth was that she no longer had a dry tongue and cracked voice. She tasted copper, but now it gave her something to mess Moran's clean, cream-colored suit with. She prepared to spit, but the bodyguard pushed her onto her back and slapped her cheek. The bloody spit burst from her lips and dribbled down her chin and cheeks.

Moran dabbed his mouth with his handkerchief. He smiled, the cuts on his lips giving him very little trouble as he glared at her with icy blue eyes. "That was a nice punch. Apparently you can find something in your heart for those mixed-breed subhumans."

"There's one subhuman I know, and he's my cousin," Amanda snarled.

The bodyguards yanked her to her feet, dragging her along, twisting her arms behind her back painfully. Moran walked behind. The only thing he showed concern for was keeping his suit clean.

As she came through the huge iron gates of the perimeter wall, she could see that there were at least four guard towers with a clear line of sight to her. Men lounged around in one recreation yard, dressed comfortably, a large pool and addled-seeming women milling alongside them.

It was then that she noticed there was a second recreation yard, without the country-club atmosphere; no cool drinks being served, no poolside umbrellas or lounge chairs. A line of broken men walked in a circle, heads drooped, following each other to form a serpent devouring its own tail. They were naked, except for rags tied at their waists, and as she was pulled closer to the group, she saw the bright streaks of red and white where scar tissue closed and healed from torment.

The group wasn't just made of men, but women, as well. But all had been so burned from the sun and had been left filthy and hungry that telling their sexes apart was nearly impossible. Amanda immediately recalled the looks of prisoners at places such as Dachau and Auschwitz.

Amanda looked back to the women who were at poolside with those seemingly on vacation. They didn't look so badly beaten, but there was a blank, dull glaze in their expressions. Those women were slaves, and whatever had shattered them was not a whip, but left scars on the soul instead.

"I thought you didn't want your gene pool dirtied," Amanda rasped. "You're going to turn me into a whore for these animals?"

Moran smiled. "There are reasons why these men are treating sin Piedad as a vacation getaway, cousin. And then there're reasons why those animals are being treated to a death march."

Amanda glanced back and forth, and her shoulders sagged.

"They are part of the machine that will make the world a much better place," Moran said. "And you? As much as I'd love to see you abused until your brains leak out of your ears, you have a much more vital purpose."

Amanda frowned.

"You're bait," Moran continued. "You see, our Arrangement has been stymied over the past several years. There has been a group out there constantly getting in the way of our vision."

Moran smirked. "I figured why not kill two birds with one stone."

Amanda's eyes widened.

"You see, the man who arranged for your protection has proven to be in league with this group. So, your turd of a husband dies and then, when they come to get you, we destroy them," Moran said.

"They? They who?"

"We've heard rumors of names, but it doesn't really matter. All that does is that you will not walk out of this prison until they are dead," Moran said.

Amanda was dropped to her knees between the two "recreation yards."

"Meanwhile, pick your poison."

Amanda grit her teeth.

CHAPTER NINE

Carl Lyons allowed himself to cool down, getting dressed after interrogating the pair of prisoners and showering. The two men were members of the Truth of Pinchas ministry, just as the ethnically Iranian interpreter he'd killed. No, he hadn't needed to engage in torture. Part of the cues toward breaking a suspect had to do with having a pile of irrefutable proof that you were in total control. With the data mining of Stony Man Farm's hacker staff, Lyons and the others had come into that interrogation as intimate with the prisoners as their own mothers, sometimes even more so in some cases.

"I thought we were going in an hour," Deputy Marshal Domingo Perez stated.

"Something popped up in the interim," Lyons answered, choosing a shirt from his go bag.

"If we had left on time, we would have encountered a very nasty reception committee."

"More of the guys who attacked the safe house?" Perez asked.

Lyons nodded. He pulled on his concealed body-armor vest before pulling his polo shirt on over it. "Maybe not the actual assault team, but someone was sent here to make certain you didn't leave the building."

"Any idea who's coughing up the location of a witness protection detail?" Perez asked.

Lyons looked him over. "We did some asking around."

"From the sounds of things, you did a lot more than ask," Perez said.

Lyons smirked. "We're the definition of a strongly worded request."

"So, all those times the President was criticized for only writing a letter?"

"Not *all* those times. Just the ones that truly counted," Lyons answered.

Perez nodded. "But just the three of you? Or did you bring a bigger army?"

Lyons hooked into his shoulder holster and slipped on his paddle for both of his .357s. "Like the Texas Ranger said, you only got one riot, don't ya?"

"Isn't this a little bit of overkill, even to protect someone in WITSEC?" Perez continued.

"Witness security, in many cases, isn't worth much, as it's usually scumbags rolling over on other scumbags. In this case, however, we've got a pair of honest journalists and their kids being threatened by a corrupt government agency," Lyons said. "Honest journalists who actually verify their facts are rare enough to be considered an endangered species. Kids, in any case, deserve every ounce of firepower on hand to protect them. And corrupt government agencies—"

"Even if they're from another country?" Perez cut him off.

"Especially if they're from another country," Lyons said. "And they came to ours and killed cops. Nobody gets away with that. Not on my watch."

Perez folded his arms. "Can anybody saddle up with this posse?"

"We'd have to vet you," Lyons answered. "We have a very strict recruitment process."

"Just to blow away the scumbags who killed my brother deputies?" Perez asked.

Lyons straightened and held out his hand. "Congrats. You passed the test."

Perez didn't quite smile but he accepted the handshake.

"So what is the plan on keeping the kids safe?" he asked.

Lyons put an arm around Perez's shoulder. "We're going to be a big fat target. A literal stalking horse."

"And the only way to do that…is to have the kids with us," Perez conceded.

Lyons shook his head. "I don't want to see them hurt, but we have a genius among us. All the time that you were napping and we weren't putting boot to ass, my genius was hard at work."

"How?" Perez asked.

In the next moment, as if on cue, the laughter of children sounded on the other side of the door.

"Kids?" Perez asked. He opened the door and saw Hermann Schwarz standing there with a small device in hand. "Oh. But what about their being in actual view?"

"Pol," Lyons called.

In the next moment Perez saw what looked like three children huddled underneath a bomb blanket, being brought into the open. Blancanales stood by them, wearing his vest. Three sets of legs moved almost as one as he guided them across the hallway.

"A bomb blanket provides a lot of protection, but…"

Blancanales pulled the top of the blanket back, showing a small Asian woman, about Dom Castillo's height, between two marionette-like rigs that were attached to childlike legs. Her slender build and small stature made her a normally imperfect duplicate for the young man who'd been under Perez's charge, but with the blanket, and with the extra sets of legs, it looked as if Able Team was guarding the whole family.

"I told you. We're going to be a stalking horse. They

blow us to hell? Then the kids will still be protected," Lyons told him. "We have other blacksuits in the building."

"I recognized some of them," Perez answered.

"And they'll be kept, safe and sound, in the fallout shelter in the basement," Schwarz added.

"You just keep in the protection mind-set with her," Lyons added.

"Dr. Lao Ti." The Asian woman introduced herself.

Her hands, though delicate and slender in appearance, were tough and callused, much like those of Lyons and Perez himself. The deputy marshal realized that the tiny figure in front of him was a seasoned, hardened martial artist.

"Deputy Marshal Domingo Perez," he told her. He smiled.

"Ling Fu is going to be okay here?" Lyons asked her.

"She's ready for anything short of a nine-hundred-foot-tall octopus tearing the roof off the fallout shelter," Lao Ti answered.

"Does she want an M203?" Blancanales offered.

Lao Ti shook her head. "Nine hundred foot, not ninety foot."

"We'll see about putting a satellite overhead with kinetic dart capability," Schwarz promised her.

"Giant octopus?" Perez asked Lyons.

"Hyperbole. We haven't run into something *that* big yet."

Schwarz nodded. "At worst, it was a tenth of what Ling Fu is talking about."

Perez's eyes widened. "For real?"

"That was an interesting submarine ride" was the only explanation that Lyons provided.

"Next thing you'll be telling me, you've met aliens," Perez quipped.

"Nope. Not one of our shuttle trips," Schwarz offered. "You'd think so, wouldn't you?"

"We know our targets," Blancanales said, steering the conversation back toward sanity, as if a renegade Mexican covert agency were a symbol of what was normal and logical in the world.

Perez frowned at the thought that such a cruel and corrupt entity *was* something common and normal.

That one such top secret group was making an effort to murder three children, and another black ops agency was standing against them, was sadly not a surprising turn of events.

"We think that the family was actually hit to draw us out," Blancanales said. "Because we taught you, in the blacksuit program, we'd step up."

"This is still a trap for you. Why are you letting them come after you like that?" Perez asked.

"Because that's the best way to get them to stand up as targets for us to slaughter them," Lyons answered. "To the last man."

"We've got some information out of the morons we took prisoner," Schwarz confirmed. "And we're going to follow those leads up."

"The more they come at us, the more we'll learn about them. Dead or alive," Blancanales concluded.

The group set up Lao Ti with the bomb blanket and marionette legs once more. Everyone gathered their fighting gear, and Lyons assigned Perez a Mossberg 930 SPX and a new handgun to replace his old Glock.

"You're used to 1911s, so this shouldn't be too hard for you," the Able Team leader explained. "It's an update of an old favorite of the team. A high-capacity version of the 1911, based off of the Para-Ordnance frame. The grips are ultra-slim aluminum scales, so you're holding on to a fourteen-round box without an increase in trigger reach or grip size."

Perez saw that there was a folding lever under the barrel. "I thought this was a flashlight or a laser."

"No," Schwarz told him. "There's an IR beam inside the guide rod, used without night-vision goggles. That's for extra bracing when you go into 3-round-burst mode."

"This is a machine pistol," Perez mused.

"With extended mags, it holds 28 rounds," Lyons added. "And the barrel nut, of course, is for a suppressor on the nose."

"What did you call these things?" Perez asked.

"Back in the day they were 'Colt Frankensteins,'" Lyons noted. "Or FrankenColts."

Perez nodded. "But no Colt parts are in it anymore."

Schwarz shrugged. "What do you call a 1911, generally?"

"A Colt .45 auto   Oh," Perez answered.

"Enough nomenclature," Lao Ti grumbled from under the blanket. "Time to deploy."

With that, Domingo Perez accompanied Able Team and Dr. Lao Ti to the van.

All the while, he could feel enemy eyes following him.

ON THE OTHER side of the Nogales border, Phoenix Force's individual members had each stolen one of the vehicles left at the ambush warehouse, driving them hard and fast to a rendezvous outside the small city. There, in the desert, they immediately went quickly to work, looking for means of tracking, utilizing their personal copies of Schwarz's Combat PDA, looking for cell signals within.

GPS mounts had been immediately torn out in the warehouse parking lot, but the five men had chosen older-looking vehicles unlikely to be heavily laden with internal electronics. Work trucks and older sedans were their picks, and the radio receivers inside the PDAs easily determined whether there were tracking devices within. The CPDAs had built-in technology necessary to pick up and clone other cell phones as a means of eavesdropping on targets, but the same radio-signal sensors were also perfect for determining the location of bugs and other trackers.

Only one of the trucks, a more recent model, had the kind of technology within capable of being used to trace the members of the team. Hawkins and Manning had quickly torn into the dashboard to remove the offending device.

All of that had taken an hour after the multiple detonations and rain of gunfire that had roared in the Nogales cross-border smuggling tunnel. Five minutes for locating and stealing vehicles, fifteen minutes for scanning and removing anything to threaten OPSEC, and the remaining forty minutes driving far enough out of town in a convoy to make certain they weren't being followed.

Phoenix Force's members were each trained in driving to avoid enemy surveillance, but they were additionally supplemented by the belt-and-suspenders backup of Stony Man Farm's eyes in the sky. Relying only upon their own or upon the NSA surveillance satellites was not the way the Sensitive Operations Group had stayed out of the limelight all these years. Practical on-the-ground skills and computer hacking were meant to work hand in hand, enhancing each other to the point where there was very little chance of mistaken exposure.

Finally, they were back on their hands-free communicators.

"Any update on Amanda Castillo's location?" McCarter asked Price, who was listening in via encrypted radio signals.

"We're still trying to figure out how they got her out of the country," Price responded.

"Well, where would El Calabozo sin Piedad be? We should have information about its location, shouldn't we?" McCarter asked.

"We know its general coordinates, but it's in a satellite dead zone," Price answered. "We're trying to get a good view from the top, but it's akin to our setup here in the Blue Ridge."

"Someone is using their computer smarts to make a blind spot that even the NSA can't dent," McCarter surmised.

"That's the general consensus around here," Price agreed. "Any attempt to access Accion Obrar's database, or regular Mexican justice department records regarding the prison, gets met with an intense response."

"'Intense'?" McCarter repeated. "As in counterattacks?"

"We went on virus lockdown three times trying to circumvent the security net," Price advised. "However, my ears on the other side of the border are showing that when they go against us, their systems also glitch out."

"Please tell me you have some kind of hint for us to follow," McCarter said.

"We've been studying air traffic across the border, specifically heading down south. There've been a lot of eyes in the air tracking low-flying craft from Mexico, but not the other way around," Price told him. "We lost track of one charter jet leaving Phoenix for Acapulco. It went off the radar in the general area around Calabozo sin Piedad."

"'General area,'" McCarter repeated. He was already thinking of possible angles.

"One thing, though...we're going back in the archives to seek out potential areas with room for a landing strip for such an aircraft, as well as a place to hide a maximum-security prison," Price said. "I've sent a map to the team's PDAs that will put you in the neighborhood. The minute we have an exact location, we'll send it to you."

"On the other hand, we'll do our own investigation," McCarter promised. "Rumors might provide more information than satellite mapping."

"That's one hope we're counting on," Price told him. "Good hunting."

"We'll be in touch." McCarter signed off.

"Well, that's interesting," T. J. Hawkins said over the com set. "Mexico has a prison that is effectively as remote and hard to pin down as Groom Lake Testing."

"Complete with *los hombres en negros*," Rafael Encizo added, referring to the mysterious "men in black."

"Mexico itself is no stranger to unidentified aircraft sightings," Gary Manning offered. "And just as a good portion of United States incidents, complete with so-called MiBs, had to do with various Skunk Works development projects, there's also a strong indicator that Mexican UFO traffic might be along those lines."

"Yeah, but the stuff at Area 51 are drones and for military application," Calvin James countered. "Whereas in Mexico, a lot of these craft are developed under cartel supervision for smuggling. Area 51 or Groom Lake were testing grounds for Cold War super technologies, but the Dungeon without Pity and the border tunnels are the drug lords' means of outwitting US law enforcement."

"I'd say you were being a bit cynical about UFO and USO sightings, but considering that the Colombian cartels have their own submarine fleet, I'd be lying," McCarter mused aloud.

McCarter thought over the recent bout of conversation. "Okay, who's calling Barb to ask about UFO sightings over the past few months…in that general area around the prison?"

"I'm on it," Manning said. "Texted the Farm to check out potential UFOs. Like stealth helicopters delivering prisoners to Calabozo."

"Good. Because I'd hate like hell to talk about UFO crap," McCarter said.

"Like when you were teamed with Mack, Lyons and Gadgets?" Encizo chided.

"Another damned example of hiding government secrets behind the candy shell of junk science," McCarter confirmed. "Rotters in compression suits and helmet masks, skulking around in stealth craft."

"Akira *would* have a database devoted solely to unidentified flying objects," Manning said over the secure com network.

The five-car Phoenix Force convoy continued along at a steady speed of fifty miles an hour on the highway. "We're about four hundred miles from a mapped epicenter of UFO activity right in the region where Barb says that prison *might* be."

"And since we're gathering this information from nongovernment sources, using search parameters that don't involve military or law enforcement, no flags should be raised," McCarter added.

"Oh, we can pretty much drop the delusion that this isn't anything more than an open invitation for us to come into one of the most heavily defended bastions we've ever been sent to," Encizo interjected.

"Knowing it's a trap doesn't change the fact that an innocent woman and the mother of three, the only surviving parent of three, is being held against her will in a corrupt-as-hell facility," James said. "We get there, we find a way to bust her out and if anyone gets in our way, we kill them."

"No one's arguing against that plan of action. We're just six hours away from the prison," McCarter said.

"Six hours? Four hundred miles in six hours?" Encizo asked. "We'll need to stop for gas about halfway there. And why are we limiting ourselves to under seventy miles an hour?"

"To keep these boxes from overheating, mate. And to allow for ten-minute rest stops so we don't get there totally exhausted." McCarter put the pedal down. "Eighty."

"He's gettin' pretty good at math, isn't he?" Hawkins joked over the radio.

"I've always been good enough at math to know when I've been around longer than you, rookie," McCarter shot back.

"Hopefully, we'll be able to pick up more supplies on the way," Manning said. "Especially explosives."

"We'll figure something out," James said. "We did manage to pack some meth-cooking chemicals and plenty of ammunition into the vehicles."

"Those are good for improvised firebombs, but the walls we might have to breach will be a lot harder," Manning returned.

"We've got some missiles on hand," Hawkins said. "If we can find enough fertilizer to mix with the meth cook…"

"That's what I was thinking, as well," Manning responded. "Good planning ahead."

"Planning ahead," McCarter stressed. "If we'd really had the chance to plan ahead, we might have found some better accommodations than used cars."

"You're overestimating the opposition," Encizo said. "Or underestimating their view of us. I mean, they've set out several traps for both Able and our team. They might just think we'll take more time, wait for heavier gear or come in through a much more measured response."

"Yeah. If these assholes have been stymied by us in the past, then they know we are unpredictable," James said. "We just need to figure out what they would anticipate as our moves."

"Plan-ception," McCarter mused. "Like incep—"

"Yeah, we get it." Hawkins cut him off.

McCarter scratched his chin. "They might also think

we're doing things like Able Team. After all, there's really no official roster that our enemy has for who did what to them. They might expect Carl and the boys, as they've done work in Mexico in the past."

"So've we," Encizo added.

"There's a gas station in a hundred miles," Manning pointed out. "We'll pause there, get some rest and then review."

"It'll be sunset in two hours, so when we get to the prison, it'll be dark," McCarter observed. "We'll see what Akira can pull from nonmilitary photo sources of the prison before we get there. Not that we won't recon and look ourselves."

"We'll be able to move faster without fear of overheating the engines after dark," Hawkins noted. "That means we can cut the six hours down to five or so. We get there maybe three, three and a half hours after sunset. We'll have plenty of time in the dark to recon with night vision and infrared cameras."

McCarter mulled over the situation. They had one night to get to El Calabozo sin Piedad, figure out its security measures, come up with a plan and hit it before the enemy could harden its defenses to the point where anything they tried would be tantamount to suicide.

Any delay, however, was akin to torture.

Just another impossible thing for them to accomplish.

CHAPTER TEN

Carl Lyons was pleased that no one took a potshot at them as they loaded Lao Ti into the van under the guise of the Castillo children. With Mae Ling Fu in a fallout shelter a hundred feet beneath the Yuma federal building, armed to the teeth with a crew of seething, highly trained black-suits looking to provide payback to whoever had killed their brethren, the three youths could not have been better defended. So far, it didn't look as if the Caballeros de Durango and its Los Lictors muscle wanted to move in closer on the building.

No, the Able Team van had attracted their attention. The tail was on them the moment they left the garage.

If Lyons hadn't wanted to draw the whole lot in for a brutal slaughter, he would have felt some tension. Instead, this was welcome focus. It meant that their plan was working out well.

"Gadgets," he growled. The van had built-in gear that would make it immune to external eavesdropping, even from laser microphones or bugs. Schwarz's electronics genius, coupled with the skills of the cyber crew and the other technologically minded Stony Man staff, had made certain that the three warriors of Able Team had at least one area of complete operational security. "How're the kids?"

"I'm going over the area. So far, things are pretty good," Schwarz answered. "May has some decent backup with her, including Baby Iron."

"I thought Aspen died," Lyons returned.

"No. This is Dave Kowalski," Schwarz clarified. "The one who went berserker mode on one of those two bastards who hospitalized you at Dulles."

Lyons nodded. "Right. He and Orlando Wazdi also pulled some duty with Mack in North Africa."

"Ski and Wazdi are there together," Schwarz said. "We also have Khalid, Toro and Graham Benjamin."

"Did you pick those guys because Accion Obrar has white supremacist muscle on our cases?" Blancanales asked from the driver's seat. Riding shotgun, Lyons saw the grin on his friend's face.

"A Jew, an Arab, a big Dominican, a half Arab/half Black and a Pollack. All of whom show zero concern about blowing a goose-stepping asshole in two." Schwarz chuckled. "Nah. Just coincidence."

Lyons could feel the wink in Schwarz's voice as he said that. "Great. Couldn't happen to a better bunch of baby-murdering bastards if they make a run at them."

"And what about us?" Domingo Perez asked.

"'Us' will engage in harassment and mass murder of anyone even remotely related to Accion Obrar," Lyons answered. "Starting now."

Perez tilted his head. "Now?"

"One of the hitters from the first wave around the building in Yuma was an Iranian convert to the Truth of Pinchas ministry," Lyons elaborated. "At first, I'd thought that they'd called in some Middle Eastern muscle, but instead, they're an all-American hate group."

"Pincharites. I remember you mentioned them," Perez said. He sneered. "I was born and raised Roman Catholic, and though I might not go to church every Sunday and curse like a sailor, I take enormous offense at these so-called Christian fanatics. How do they not get called a terrorist organization?"

"The Southern Poverty Law Center lists them. The thing is, the big news agencies don't cover them because their violence takes the form of bank robberies and gang fights under the aegis of drug turf wars. In this case, meth and other hard drugs." Lyons paused.

"So when are we going to pay these thugs a visit?" Perez asked.

"Fifteen minutes and counting down," Lyons answered, nodded toward the windshield.

Perez leaned over Lyons's shoulder to look through the windshield at the Pincharite temple. "You're kidding me."

Lyons shook his head.

Blancanales leaned over. "We're going to lean on this group and make an example of them. And, look, they already know we're coming!"

Perez could see the gates of the Pincharite compound. There was a fence, with razor wire coiled around the top, securing prefabricated buildings, both Quonset huts and steel storage buildings. There was a church in the middle of it all, but scattered among the grounds were burly men dressed in camouflage and carrying either an assault rifle or a shotgun. Hate flags flapped in the wind, and Perez could feel the anger and animosity throbbing off the compound walls.

"How many you figure?" Lyons asked.

"Don't ask a stupid question," Blancanales chided. "We already scoped this joint out and know they've got forty men on hand. And the rumors about their receipt of a shipment of heavy firepower are pretty dead-on."

"We're really going to roll in there and start asking questions?" Perez asked.

Lyons shook his head. "No. Pol, Gadgets and I are going to make their acquaintances. The van stays out here. Stay on the wheel. Lao…"

"I've got vehicle security, right," Lao Ti said. She took

out an update of one of her favorite long-arms, a 9 mm MAC-10 variant. This one, however, was engineered for reliability and accuracy, as well as to fit her small hands. She didn't seem to mind at all.

Perez could feel an infectious energy in the van's interior.

"If our tails get too close to the van, the jig might be up," Lyons continued. "So you need to stay on babysitting duty. I'm not supposed to be in the van, but if the cover gets blown..."

"Don't worry," Perez said. "You were telling me the escape-and-evade plan."

"We'll call you when we need a pickup. And don't worry, the van is mostly bulletproof," Lyons added.

"Mostly," Perez repeated as Lyons geared up and Blancanales pulled the van to a halt.

It was nearing sunset and Perez watched the long shadows of gunmen scramble for positions on the grounds below. The van was on a hillock overlooking the compound from far away, and Perez was able to get a better look at the scene thanks to a high-definition monitor built into the dash. Telescopic cameras hidden on the hull of the Able Team van allowed the team to see the enemy without giving away their position.

Still, the Pincharites were given a heads-up by the tails, either from members of their own crew following the team or perhaps sent down from above.

Either way, Perez didn't envy their position. No matter how much advanced intel the extremists in the compound received, no one looked prepared for the trio of commandos currently sneaking through the underbrush.

"We wait." Lao Ti spoke up. She did have a tinge of yearning to be alongside the three men as they launched their attack, but for now, the plan didn't include her presence on the front lines.

HERMANN "GADGETS" SCHWARZ was not a vicious man, not
by birth, not by age and cynicism, but the actions of Los
Lictors and the Pincharites had made him unconcerned
with any dignity for their demise. He was here to kill and
to end the threat of a group of heavily armed racist maniacs. He'd fought them around the world, and this bunch,
working alongside a Mexican cartel, were among the very
worst. They had government ties, as well, meaning that
any nuggets of information Able Team could knock loose
would also be beneficial to finding out who was on the
warpath to put the Farm on the chopping block.

It could have been a coincidence that a deniable CIA
interpreter was hooked to the mercenaries hired by the
Caballeros Cartel to continue the stateside attack on Able
Team, drawing them out by threatening the Castillo children. But Schwarz and his brothers in blood hadn't survived so many deadly missions by ignoring coincidence.
This smelled like a twisted, brutal skein of corruption
that had threads infesting American and Mexican governments.

Naturally, blowing holes in groups of bigoted thugs
improved every mission. Few creatures were more repre-
hensible than bigots of any sort who utilized some "ism"
to justify their need to destroy those they felt threatened
by. How many of these men, from African Janjaweed mi-
litiamen to neo-Nazis, were otherwise unmotivated slugs
drawn into a mindless power fantasy, engaging in violence
and passing off their failures on uninvolved innocents?

The three men of Able Team moved silently, with the
grace of jungle cats slithering through the scrub and brush.
Each of them approached the Pincharite compound as part
of a plan that they'd worked on before loading Perez and
Lao Ti into the van. The actual assault was one the three
had practiced and rehearsed on countless occasions; the
only thing different this time was the layout.

Even then, the Truth of Pinchas ministry had built their compound on a tried-and-true pattern used by similar groups across the decades. The perimeter fence, the guard towers and other security layout specifics were nothing new to the Able Team experts. However, just because the enemy base was familiar, as were the thugs and maniacs present, that didn't mean the trio of professionals could approach this carelessly.

The order of battle was one composed of audacity, surprise and all-around dirty tricks.

Schwarz took a knee and set down his contribution to confusion and mayhem. It was an electronic transmitter, and since the enemy was composed of apologists for racism and cruelty, it was set to blast out angry rebel rap and other urban tunes, filling every communication frequency across the area with that righteous revolution. Schwarz was a fan of jive and funk, and the music it evolved into, so he had a good arsenal devoted to pissing off the Pincharites.

Anyone with a radio, the minute they tried to communicate, would instead find the airwaves plugged with the fighting music. Cut off from each other, the base would be unable to respond to calls for help or to inform others of an incoming attack. A second transmitter was set up close to it to do the same thing, except it would penetrate their wireless computer networks, as well.

The two devices were set on a countdown so that Schwarz could maneuver into his combat position. The transmitters were low to the ground, hidden within thickets of long grass and scrub to keep them from enemy notice.

Lyons and Blancanales transmitted that they were in position with signal clicks over their encrypted com sets. The encryption on the Able Team coms would not only keep others from listening in, but would also shield the Stony Man force from the scrambler onslaught that Schwarz had set up.

He moved closer to the fence line then brought up a pair of infrared binoculars, sweeping the compound.

There were forty armed men down there, as well as plenty of women and unarmed men. As much as Schwarz would have loved to have scoured the Pincharite base from the surface of the planet, there were noncombatants down there. Able Team was avengers, not wanton murderers. Nothing less than precision and skill would do for this encounter.

If any of the women or noncombatant men took up arms, even so much as a knife, then neither Schwarz nor the others would hesitate to defend themselves with lethal force. Too many cops and soldiers had died at the hands of women and children with knives. As it was, he wasn't keen on simply raining hell upon them when they appeared as harmless bystanders.

Finally in position, Schwarz brought his rifle down from its sling across his shoulders. It was a full-size M16 A-4, in standard 5.56 mm NATO. Schwarz and Blancanales had been in far too many firefights with the M16 to regard it as a "puny .22," no matter how much Lyons derided it. Indeed, the Phoenix Force leader had a respect for the M16 in close quarters.

Mounted under the barrel was a 40 mm M203 grenade launcher, but considering the potential of noncombatants in the area, Schwarz, Blancanales and Lyons had less-lethal ordnance in their bandoliers. When it came to killing, it was going to be a concentrated, aimed burst of rifle fire. CS-CN riot control gas and flash-bangs were to keep the enemy forces scattered and confused, as well as to drive those without weapons to cover and out of the path of gunfire.

Schwarz clicked his throat mike, signaling that he was ready for action, as well.

Off to one side of the facility, Blancanales was the only

one with high-explosive shells for his M203, and those were for the purpose of slashing holes through the compound's perimeter. Blancanales's Ranger training allowed him to aim, fire and space his shots so that he could hit three targets simultaneously, thanks to the parabolic arcs that the 40 mm HE grenades could be fired. With timing and proper aim, he'd cut holes for all three of the men of Able Team and then be on the move as the last shell detonated and shredded protective fencing.

The hollow thump of Blancanales's first shot reached Schwarz's ears and he brought the rifle up, looking through the night-vision optic he'd mounted on the Picatinny top rail. Lyons, on his approach, was doing the same thing, and both men were swiftly scanning for signs of recognition of the muted pops. There was plenty of activity down below, but for the time being, no one appeared to have noticed.

The second pop resounded and Schwarz swung his rifle toward the guard tower overlooking Blancanales's approach to the compound. Sure enough, someone had recognized the retort of a grenade launcher. A radio rose to lips, but Blancanales had fired after Schwarz's radio interference began.

Confusion crossed the face of Schwarz's target. The tower sentry wouldn't be confused for long, as Schwarz pulled the trigger twice. At over 3,000 feet per second, the two 5.56 mm tumblers struck the guard. Thanks to a suppressor designed by Mack Bolan and Cowboy Kissinger, the twin rifle reports were distorted and muffled enough to not sound like actual gunshots. A hundred yards downrange, however, the bullets struck with authority, obliterating the tower guard's face.

Schwarz scanned to see if any other men on the fence noticed, and saw the results of Carl Lyons's sniping.

So far, so quiet.

Almost in unison, Blancanales's trio of 40 mm grenades

struck the perimeter. Each charge produced a night-splitting thunderclap, accompanied by the force necessary to shred chain link and razor wire. Three holes were blasted through the defenses of the radical cult, and Schwarz switched to his M203, firing off a gas grenade toward one of the residential buildings on the compound.

Lyons's own gas bomb landed at the same time as Schwarz's, thick clouds spewing out to choke and blind the supremacists.

Confusion erupted.

Able Team waded in, firmly in its element.

CARL LYONS FIRED on the move. Each step, he scanned the Pincharite compound, looking for armed gunmen, and the moment he saw one and had a clear shot, he fired. A trained finger and countless hours of firearms training with the M16 allowed him to tap off a 3-round burst, even though the rate of fire on fully automatic was 800 rounds per minute.

He tapped the trigger, not mashed it. He breathed evenly. He focused on the front sight when it came time to shoot, and when he fired, he sent 231 grains of hollowpoint into cultist flesh, turning the living threats into dead bodies waiting for gravity to overcome the last impulses to their leg muscles to have them remain standing. This was surgical shooting, and his M16 was the scalpel. Among groups of people, it was neat, precise, exacting.

But when it wrought its damage, each of the 77-grain supersonic projectiles churned grisly wound paths through muscle and bone. Pulped flesh and fluid burst from bodies, and head hits invariably resulted in eyeballs popping from sockets and dangling down cheeks on rubbery optic nerves.

By the time Lyons reached the fence, he'd ended eight gunmen, not counting the man in the guard tower who'd been attracted to the sound of Blancanales's grenade launcher.

Lyons reloaded on the stalk, scanning around. Schwarz loosed a flash-bang to keep the dormitory contained. The distraction devices, aside from being stunning in close confines, also resounded with real explosions that would make anyone leery of heading out into a storm of them. In the meantime, Blancanales alternated between laying down tear gas and burning down defending cultists.

This was a complete rout, and Lyons had no qualms about looking for more targets in the compound. Every one of these thugs was at minimum involved in methamphetamine sales and, at worst, had committed violent bank and armored-car robberies.

Fresh magazine, armored load-bearing vest festooned with another six 30-round curved boxes to feed his assault rifle, and his sidearms, he was set and ready to continue tearing a hole through the opposition. Maybe the initial Able Team assault had been too effective, because if the rest of the team even did half of the damage that he'd done, there were nearly twenty corpses strewed across the Pincharite base.

A choking, dazed man stepped into the open, sputtering and gasping for breath, but the rifle in his hands showed that he was not a bystander. Lyons didn't offer him a chance to fire. He shot the man down, cutting him in two with a coring triburst of 5.56 mm fury.

Who else was there?

Schwarz and Blancanales had erected a wall of tear gas around the residential buildings. Anyone who fought their way through those clouds would be on the attack.

Lyons continued his rampage of righteous slaughter. Two more of the Pincharite fanatics lurched around a corner, one of them in the midst of tugging on a gas mask, the other leading the way, muzzle of his rifle aimed at the ground. Too bad for them; both were armed and ready for the tear gas.

Lyons focus-punched the fully masked man through center of mass. The gunman twisted and jerked violently as hollowpoints did cartwheels through his internal organs, whipping intestine, stomach and muscle into a froth. The other man let his half-donned mask sit askew across his skull, putting both hands to work in drawing his rifle up to bear in battle.

The Able Team commander killed him, too, a rapid triple burst making a fist-size, elbow-deep channel of destruction through his rib cage. Two more corpses on the ground and Lyons could tell from the lessening staccato of cultist guns and the precision bursts of his comrades that the battle was still going lopsidedly, in the favor of the Stony Man avengers.

"Drop your rifle, sir!" a voice called over a megaphone. "Unless you want to test how well women and children survive gasoline bombs built into their dormitories."

Lyons paused, his jaw set in anger.

"What makes you think we give a damn about them?" Lyons roared back.

"Because you've practically cut them off from the rest of this fight."

Lyons knew who this bastard was. Rufus Harms, the founder of the Truth of Pinchas ministry.

"I'm no fool," he returned, letting his M16 drop to the ground. He unhooked his load-bearing vest with its pouches for 40 mm grenades and magazines and set them down next to it. He could see that there were lights on in the church, in a tower just under the steeple, which would have more than enough room for the "minister's" office and a stairwell. The loudspeaker was wired on a landline, so Schwarz's electronic transmissions wouldn't interfere with it.

In some ways, the old wire-and-cable methods were still the best, Lyons decided.

"Very good," Harms responded.

Lyons stepped closer to the church. "You're the fool, Harms."

"Really? How so?" the Pincharite leader asked.

Lyons continued walking closer and closer to the church. Obviously the madman had had microphones built into his church steeple, as he could hear the ex-cop's replies. "You picked a fight that brought us to your front door."

"And yet you've got no rifle and I have innocent lives under my command to ensure your behavior," Harms taunted.

"You do?" Lyons asked. He pulled his FrankenColt from its holster then strode toward the church's side door.

"What are you doing?" Harms shouted.

Lyons didn't answer. At least not verbally. He kicked open the door to the church with brutal force, sending splinters everywhere.

CHAPTER ELEVEN

As soon as Hermann Schwarz heard the loudspeaker talking about the gasoline bombs, he immediately veered off toward the dormitory. Rosario Blancanales followed him, providing security as the electronics genius changed course to prevent a massive tragedy from striking. If the Pincharite compound burned with women and kids inside, conspiracy theorists and extreme right-wing militias would have a brand-new set of martyrs to rally behind.

The last time maniacs such as these had a "religious" movement full of scorched children's corpses, a federal building in Oklahoma was blown to hell, complete with a day-care center full of toddlers.

Blancanales took down another three of the Pincharite gunmen, shooting them with deadly marksmanship. Apparently even the announcement that Rufus Harms was holding their women and children as barter didn't keep them from moving forward to kill the other two members of Able Team.

Blancanales knew, though, that if anyone had the mental acuity and sharpness to disarm any booby trap, it would be Schwarz. Already, he was looking at the dorms for the now very essential staff.

"Pol, junction box side three!" Schwarz called out.

Without hesitation, Blancanales aimed the M16 and opened fire, blowing away the offending node of cables. In the distance, he heard Schwarz's rifle take down another juncture of wires.

Since Harms seemed to have had the wherewithal to have hardline microphones and speakers on the premises, there was a good chance that any wiring might have been the signal source for the detonation of the family quarters in the compound.

Blancanales fired until every line connected to the box had fallen away, severed completely. There could be no half measures, as a single spark could detonate those juncture boxes.

Schwarz got out his Combat PDA and activated a program.

"Full-on radio-signal suppression, from the van," Schwarz explained. "We've disconnected the dorms and the folks within."

"Positive?" Blancanales asked. "What about underground connections?"

"Already took care of that," Schwarz answered. "And with the van blasting down radio-frequency jamming, there's very little way that Harms could set the gasoline bombs off by himself."

"That leaves a fanatic inside the dorms, though," Blancanales said.

"You take the left. I've got the right," Schwarz answered.

There was very little time to waste and both men moved to the entrances of their respective Quonset huts.

Blancanales kicked through the door, looking for all the world like a nightmare in his night-vision goggles and the respirator over his mouth and nose to keep him from being stung by his own riot gas. The rest of him was festooned with weapons and armor, as well, and he didn't relish the idea of seeming like a monster when his actual purpose was to protect them. Women and children cowered from the sudden noise, mothers wrapping their arms around their sons and daughters at the sight of him.

In his NVGs, he spotted one figure tearing open a trapdoor in the flooring.

"Stop!" Blancanales ordered, voice sharp and authoritative.

The woman looked up, glaring at him, her hatred given an inhuman nature in the glowing green of the NVD imagers he wore. She reached for a handgun she'd laid on the floor beside her.

Blancanales had no hesitation. He shot her once through the middle of her face, not into her forehead. The brow was thick and protective, and there had been too many cases where even a rifle bullet didn't have the punch to go through thick skull bone. His shot went into the bridge of her nose, drilling through the thinner nasal and sinus structures and digging into the very depths of her central nervous system, 72 grains of hollowpoint moving at nearly 3,000 feet per second. Disrupted once it struck her skin, it turned into a flower of lead and copper that held together. The razor-edged blossom shattered bone and slashed apart her brain's core. The nerve junctures that held all the hardware for controlling her limbs were instantly severed.

The true believer collapsed to the floor, gravity sucking her down the trapdoor. Blancanales advanced quickly, scanning left and right.

"I'm not here to hurt you," he announced, finger off the trigger, muzzle aimed at the floorboards. The moment he reached the trapdoor he noticed that there was only the woman and a set of rigged tanks down there. Sure enough, Schwarz's severing of the ground-level junctures was right as he saw that there was another set of pipes that came in low on the ground, turning a hairpin.

Just to be certain, Blancanales picked up the dead woman's pistol and tucked it into his vest. He lowered into the trapdoor and disconnected the explosives from the canisters of gasoline. He set them onto the floor and looked around.

Women stood in a circle around the trapdoor, looking down on him.

"Is it true? She was going to set off a bomb?" one asked Blancanales.

He nodded. He tugged down his respirator and slid the goggles from his eyes. "Harms knew that nothing would give him and this cult more sympathy than you and your children dying in a fire. Just like at Waco."

"Oh, God," another breathed. "I never thought…"

"That was his effort," Blancanales said. "He gave you and your men the most direct route to profit *him*."

Now they could see his face, could see that he wasn't a monster. He was in Politician mode, and he needed them calm and cooperative.

"The bomb is disarmed," he said to console them. "And Harms is going to pay for trying to murder you under our watch."

There were silent nods from the stunned, frightened women standing around the entrance to the bomb chamber. Blancanales climbed out and closed the door, putting a solid barrier between the detonation charge and the accelerants below. He also didn't need these women seeing one of their own laying dead among the tanks. Sure, she'd tried to kill them, but sooner or later, they'd realize that she had been one of them.

Closing that door kept these people on his side for the time being.

"Gadgets, you clear on your side?" he said into his throat mike.

"Completely," Schwarz answered. "Had to pop someone, but everything's copacetic now."

"Same here," Blancanales answered. "Let's move these people somewhere safer, just in case."

"Already sending off a message to Arizona State Police," Schwarz explained. "They'll send troopers, ambulances, anything these families need."

"Now it's all up to Ironman," Blancanales mused.

CARL LYONS'S ENTRANCE into Harms's church was explosive, and as soon as he was inside, his FrankenColt was up and sweeping the darkness. His NVGs cut through the shadows, making out the glowing green silhouettes of two gunmen who'd taken concealment. One was behind a pew, while the other was in the apse, using the dais for his shelter.

Lyons flicked the machine pistol to burst-fire and punched out a blast of .45 slugs. The pew that hid one of the gunmen was scarcely cover, sandwiched layers of cork and plywood offering little resistance to Lyons's gunfire. The Pincharite screamed as pieces of his face and shoulder were torn away. Lyons adjusted his aim a little and fired another salvo, ending the cultist's suffering with a burst that tore into his heart.

The man at the dais poked his weapon out into the open. Lyons pivoted and fired first, as always, looking over his sights to direct the FrankenColt's deadly message. By the time the second gunman pulled the trigger, his bullets were chopping into the pews and his right arm was broken by the irresistible force of 230-grain blocks of copper and lead.

The gunman howled, his rifle dropping to the floor of the apse as he struggled to crawl into cover. The dais was not made of sturdier stuff than the backs of the pews. As soon as Lyons fired into the dais, he watched the man's legs kick out in death throes.

"Harms!" Lyons bellowed. "Your last two monkeys are dead!"

The Able Team commander wasn't about to take any

chances with whatever other opposition there was. While there was a lull in the shooting, he dumped the partially spent magazine from his high-capacity .45 and stuffed home another box of fifteen. He tucked the half-filled box into a pocket, in case he'd need it later.

"Those were warriors for the cause." Harms's voice crackled over the speakers. "Men who believed—"

"Who were stupid enough to swallow your bullshit." Lyons cut him off. "I've read your treatises, and anyone with half an understanding of the context of the Bible would see through the smear of crud you've painted on the wall."

Lyons heard movement on the stairs behind the altar. The steeple was at the front of the church, so that Harms wouldn't have far to go to return to his elevated office. He heard the familiar wisp of shotgun shells sliding into a magazine.

"You loading that 12-gauge I'm going to shove down your throat, con man?" Lyons asked.

There was sudden silence.

The Able Team leader wanted to take this man alive. He had questions for the charlatan. That was why he was glad that he had a precision weapon in his hands. According to the NVG scan of the church, Harms was alone in his office. The only bodyguards he had were the dead men in the apse.

Lyons aimed and held his fire. He had a good line of sight on the stairs, and the moment that Harms put his foot there, he was ready to go. Waiting for the gun-toting minister to step fully into view, where he could see a shotgun, was asking to get shot, even if Lyons was in the shadows. The other gunmen had been armed with night-vision goggles, so it was likely Harms could see just as well in this murk as Lyons.

Harms might have been anticipating some form of laser

sights on the guns used by Able Team, but nothing beat a good old alignment of dots on blades.

Harms's right foot crept down onto the step, right into view.

Lyons flicked the FrankenColt to single shot and pulled the trigger.

Instantly 230 grains of lead and copper tore through tarsal and metatarsal bones, destroying the only means of support Rufus Harms could maintain while coming down the stairs. In the next instant, he screamed and toppled, crashing down the last eight steps. His shotgun roared, blasting a hole in the floor next to Lyons's position. Had he not moved the instant he'd fired, he might have caught a stray buckshot pellet in the arm.

Now he was whole and healthy, with fifteen rounds of .45 ACP ready to take the rest of the fight out of Harms.

Fortunately the shotgun's recoil tore it from Harms's frightened hands as he flailed for a hold to stop his fall. Unarmed and helpless, Rufus Harms was now at the mercy of six feet of cold-eyed rage.

"I'm bleeding!"

"Don't worry, Rufus. It's far from that shriveled sack of bile you call a heart," Lyons told him. He squatted, removing his goggles so that the downed minister could see into the crazed countenance of the Ironman. "Allow me to introduce myself."

"You have to call an ambulance. I won't talk until…"

Lyons put his finger to Harms's lips. It was such a gentle touch that Harms was completely mentally disarmed.

"I don't have to do jack," Lyons told him in a soft, singsong voice. "Like I said, let me introduce myself."

"Who… What…" Harms stammered.

"You see, you've been talking crap in order to make your wallet fat. In the meantime, you've supplemented the earnings of your ministry with bank robbery, gun smuggling and methamphetamine dealing," Lyons said.

Harms's bulging eyes rolled around in their sockets. The religious con man had no idea where this badass commando was going, especially after tearing a deadly swath of fire and death through his best muscle.

"God probably doesn't like men like you twisting His words," Lyons continued. "But since He's trying to save electricity, I was sent to set you straight."

"Straight…right…straight and narrow. No more lawbreaking. I can't run from the cops any—"

Lyons clucked his tongue and put his finger to Harms's lips once more. The false minister grew silent.

In a flash of movement, a ribbon of silver flickered in front of Harms's eyes, the impact of a knife point ramming into hardwood floor just millimeters from his ear sounding louder than a gunshot. Harms's cheek was warm where the edge of the blade had scraped it.

Suddenly the soft, gentle voice was gone.

"Who asked you to send your thugs?" Lyons demanded.

"They'll kill me," Harms responded.

Lyons tilted his head. Then he cupped Harms's chin and turned *his* head so that the sharp cutting edge of the fighting knife sank hotly into his cheek, drawing blood. "Really? You're going to worry about them?"

"You're crazy," Harms said.

"No. Practical. See, the people who asked you to attack us and those we're charged with protecting are not on my best side. I'm not exactly sure who they are, but you might have a clue. You might give me a link and I will go after them," Lyons said. "You saw what happened to your little religious commune."

"Yes," Harms answered.

"Do you honestly feel that I will leave any one of them alive when you tell me who hired you?" Lyons asked.

"I don't know. I—I mean, these are bad people," Harms stammered.

Lyons's eyes and nostrils flared. Harms picked up on that and he began to choke and sputter.

"They might have some power. They might not have a single ethical bone in their body. But me, I'm not good cop. I'm not bad cop. I'm the leader of the Death Squad reborn," he growled. "I killed your protectors here and killed the dozens you sent to ambush us in Yuma. I'm splitting your cheek open with a knife I'm not even holding in my hand, and I will not think twice about taking your damaged foot and feeding it to you."

The minister's bladder released. Lyons could smell the hot wash of potassium. Tears flowed down the pretender's cheeks.

"You think they are bad. Well, I'm a different kind of bad. I gorge myself on their entrails. I devour them alive and leave what's left for the cops to mop up," Lyons continued.

Harms let go. There was no more that the man could stand, and the dam that had bottled up his vow of secrecy crumbled like blocks of talc ground under boot heels.

The man above him didn't need torture. He had become the living embodiment of terror, a force of nature that swept away his resistance like a tornado erased a trailer park.

Harms likely found it ironic, that for all the bluster and thunder he conjured, speaking of the face and intents of Satan, that this man did not merely invoke thoughts of the King of Hell, but convincingly became the incarnation of the Lord of Torment. So Harms wailed; he cried for mercy between each sentence of his confession, begging a God he had not actually believed in for mercy.

All the while, Lyons listened. He did more than listen; he used the CPDA microphone to record everything that blubbered past Rufus Harms's spittle-soaked lips. For twenty minutes Harms gave his accounting of the deeds and the deals he'd engaged in, how he'd worked under the aegis of certain administrators of the CIA and the FBI.

Lyons hadn't been surprised by the Central Intelligence Agency connection, not when Harms had hired out a couple of his people as interpreters for their nonofficial cover operations. That those same men were also at home engaging in homicide on American soil was further proof of the charlatan's complicity in the criminal conspiracy.

The man would lose most of that foot, possibly have it amputated, but the Able Team commander didn't care. The inability to walk and the PTSD nightmares produced by this encounter were but a small price to pay for the information he required to hunt down and exterminate the forces at work.

Lyons ended the recording and stood. Outside, Arizona State troopers were on their way, sirens wailing in the distance.

"What do I tell the police?" Harms asked.

"Tell them that you're going to lose that foot. As to anything else, it's your choice. Hell, even call in your markers with your FBI and CIA friends," Lyons told him. "That way, they know that you survived our visit and that you talked to me. They might forgive you for coughing up their secrets, but it's hard to imagine that they could mobilize a kill team for you before we get to them."

Lyons took a step away. "Hard to imagine, but not impossible."

Harms's sobs followed Lyons out into the Arizona night. He and the rest of his team left through one of the holes they'd torn in the perimeter fence, wending their way back to the Able Team van.

"Did you get anything good for all that sitting around you made us do?" Blancanales asked.

"Lots of details about his links to the conspiracy," Lyons said.

CHAPTER TWELVE

Amanda Castillo had only been forced to walk two hours in the sun, barely dressed in a smattering of rags wound around her waist. Compared to the leathery back of the person marching in front of her, her skin wasn't subjected to that much damage. Barefoot on the sunbaked concrete, however, was even more painful than she'd anticipated. As the forced, circular march slowed with sunset, each touch of the soles of her feet on the ground was a storm of knives stabbing up her legs.

Better to be treated as a slave, to be put through torment and torture, than to be used as a plaything for the maniacs who lived here as if this were a home away from home.

But as to the skin damage she hadn't received, compared to the person in front of her, just before sunset the distant crack of a rifle bullet warned her. None of the others in the ring of fire march flinched from it, but the person who walked only inches ahead of her suddenly sprayed hot gore from a fresh wound.

A security guard in the yard overseeing them barked into his radio, "Not so close to the new meat. We're supposed to keep her as bait on the hook, damn it." The man cursed.

There was chatter on the other end, static crackling too much for her to make out the exact words spoken in response to the prison guard.

She knew the owner of that voice, though.

Hector Moran, her cousin.

The man who had opposed her wedding to what he called "a brown-eyed half-blood."

Moran put far too much importance on the "pure Spaniard" bloodline of their family. Amanda was unimpressed with Hector's fashion or his money, and when she'd met and eventually married Joaquin Castillo, she'd found her true calling, her true family worth.

It was that journalistic integrity and the belief that actions and aspirations were more important than genetics and money that had gotten her and her husband into this situation.

Joaquin was dead, of course. She'd heard that from Marshal Donald Burnett before he was wounded and she was captured. Her kids were all right, somewhere north of the border, still under the protection of the Justice Department and the trained agents Hal Brognola had assembled. But Joaquin was dead, and she was here in El Calabozo sin Piedad, the Dungeon without Pity.

The prison itself was a microcosm of the Mexico that Amanda, her husband and children had been exiled from. There were the rich and the powerful, criminals with "clean" bloodlines and long lines of credit that made the penitentiary just short of a spa vacation. Obviously, one of the many activities here was practicing marksmanship, especially as the prisoner marching in front of her had been killed with a clean spine shot.

Amanda heard the tinny words of her cousin over the radio.

Of course someone would be shot *very* close to Amanda. This was to be hell, and the execution of a prisoner was to drive home the point that her stay could end as quickly or as brutally as Hector Moran decided. The flash of a rifle bullet smashing the neck and unplugging her central nervous system was to show off the true worth of the people she was sentenced with.

Where the rich and powerful members of the cartel, men who obviously had paid good money to align themselves with Accion Obrar, had free reign, afternoons at the pool and telephone contact with the outside world, Amanda's fellow prisoners were those who didn't have that sort of rank and worth.

Amanda could see faces and could tell that some of them were prisoners not because of their crimes but as hostages to stay the hands of other criminal organizations. There was also a middle ground of prisoners, those who were put to work for the rich and powerful "guests of the state." Those people might have been guilty of real crimes, and were either given the choice of slavery, as Amanda had been, or were simply looking for easier treatment.

Amanda Castillo was not going to have a hand pressed against the back of her head and her throat blocked just so that she wouldn't have to endure forced marches and terrorism from her cousin Hector.

She was a married woman, not a cartel officer's sex slave.

Even as a widow, she still held Joaquin in her heart.

"All right, you've had your exercise for the day, maggots," the guard bellowed. His cheeks were flushed, having been dutifully chewed out by Moran.

"Where do we go in to sleep?" Amanda asked.

The guard's embarrassment disappeared under a peal of laughter that left Amanda's spine tingling with dread.

"We stay here," a prisoner standing close to her whispered. It was another woman, this one appearing old and frail, her hair bleached from too long in the sun, her skin hanging in inelastic folds and cracks.

"Quiet!" the guard snapped.

The old woman looked down, going silent.

Like something out of the end of a voodoo movie, the bodies around her broke from the walking circle and

picked a spot of ground for themselves. Then they laid
down, frail and bony forms moving like zombies returning to their dreamless eternal slumber.

Amanda looked at the corpse of the woman who'd
walked ahead of her in the ring, the victim of the sniper
shot that had either been fired or been ordered by Hector
Moran. She couldn't help but wonder why this poor victim had been chosen.

The old woman tugged at Amanda's hand, pulling her
from her examination of the horror at her feet.

No words were spoken by any of the walking dead here.
They each were drawn into a numbed quietness that was
indicative of a shattered spirit. Even so, there was still humanity among them, as evidenced by the gentle touch of
the frail old woman taking her to somewhere to lie.

Amanda sat and the sudden freedom from supporting
her made her feet feel as if they would explode off of the
ends of her legs. She gulped down breaths to control the
stabbing jolts pulsing on her soles.

Almost on instinct, she knew that any word that dropped
from her lips would be met with harsh punishment. She
could feel it in the mirror-shaded glare of the prison guard
looking over the exercise yard. Instead of saying a word,
she squirmed into a position that would resemble comfort.
She let her head rest on one arm, using her biceps as a pil-
low. The concrete was still warm, but she already knew
that within a few hours, the cold of the Mexican desert
night would sweep in and make her wish for something
more than a rag.

Muffled coughs sounded from around the gathered prisoners and, stuck here, naked and unable to speak, Amanda
wondered just how this situation could be salvaged.

Your children are under protection, her mind reassured
her. Hector told you that much and that they were being
watched by a small army of lawmen.

Joaquin and I were already protected by a small army, Amanda reminded herself.

She thought about what Moran also said: that she was being kept here, alive, as bait. That meant that somewhere, out in the desert, someone was on the way to help her.

They're coming into a trap.

Amanda clenched her jaw. Even that tiny shred of hope was snatched away from her, a squandered bit of tantalizing possibility rendered useless. She was bait for a rescue team, and that rescue team was not just expected, they were coming to a facility where even the inmates were armed and had run of the asylum. The guards were all in good shape, and she'd been around the drug wars enough to recognize state-of-the-art AR-15-style carbines equipped with scopes and thirty-round curved magazines.

She wondered what the rifle was that had killed the woman in front of her, especially given that she'd heard the gunshot a moment before the bullet had struck its target. Whatever the case, the Dungeon without Pity had riflemen with long-range sniper rifles.

The trip from the landing strip had evidenced that there was very little terrain that could be used by any rescuer to sneak up close to the walls.

And once at those walls, the rescuers would have thick stone, maybe even reinforced with iron rebar, to blast through. Nothing short of an artillery barrage looked as if it would be sufficient to smash open the gates. Climbing over the top would leave intruders vulnerable to snipers in guard towers, and that was even if they could get through the coiled razor wire without being sliced to ribbons.

This was an impossible place to break into.

Then again, if the cartels were this worried about an enemy, there was a chance the opposition would have access to helicopters or other means of infiltration.

Of course, American stealth helicopters breaking into

a Mexican prison would likely be the impetus for a border war or worse. That was, of course, if the Americans possessed stealth helicopters and would use them for this type of rescue.

She'd heard about the so-called silent birds that had dropped in a SEAL team to kill the most wanted terrorist in the world and knew that one of those copters had malfunctioned. Even when the crippled helicopter had been destroyed, there was more than sufficient concern in the American government that the tail boom surviving the "sanitizing" of the scene had fallen into the possession of an allied state to the US.

Amanda, lying on her side, scanned the area around her. All right, she thought. How would you get yourself out of this place?

Amanda wasn't a commando, but she'd spent plenty of time with honest members of the Mexican military in their efforts to destroy heroin and marijuana growth in the various states.

That's not the same thing, she chided silently. Those units scouted ahead and confirmed that there were crops growing in the areas we struck.

Amanda narrowed her eyes.

She'd been on a long and winding trip, and she wondered if the so-called rescue party would have known ahead of time her destination.

Of course they'd have been tipped off at the possibility. That was the whole purpose of the trap.

Amanda mentally counted down the amount of time she'd been in motion since the attack this morning. Had it really been just one day?

There have been no moments of unconsciousness, and this is the first sunset you've experienced since the attack. You've been in motion...

Amanda ran through her thoughts trying to remember

how early in the evening sunset came in Mexico. The day had been so hectic, she couldn't even think of how long she'd been made to march in a circle, or how long she'd been lying on the sun-cooked concrete. At the very least, the desert-baked stone beneath her would keep her from getting too cold for a few hours. Then the nearly naked, exposure-riddled prisoners would crawl closer together, sharing the warmth of their bodies as a means of staving off the chill of night.

That wouldn't last long, either. The moment the sun rose, the prisoners would have to separate.

Focus.

Amanda Castillo wasn't a fragile woman. Amanda Moran might have been raised in a society where women were supposed to know their place, looking good and hanging on to their husbands' arms as a trophy, but the woman she was now, the woman she was since she had been a rebellious teenager, was a smart, capable human being. Sure, she'd been captured and abused by other humans, but that was the nature of flesh, weakness and taking a few knocks here and there. What really mattered was that she still was alive and her brain still worked.

She was bait, and as such, there were people in the area who would soon be charged with her safety and welfare. Amanda half wanted to call out and tell them to avoid the trap.

Of course, since this was a ploy to get someone to come to her rescue, and several lawmen had been sacrificed as part of the ruse to get the team good and mad, and running into the jaws of this trap, Amanda had to sum up the range of abilities of this group.

For the first part, it had to be a small agency, one that made friends and contacts among the United States Marshal's Service as well as other Justice Department agencies so as to gather together the ties that would make the safe-house attack a personal incident.

A small agency, meaning there could be anything from five to ten men in Mexico looking for her and the prison. She estimated down to five, as there were also people protecting her children in Yuma, Arizona, as Moran had said.

They might have pilots, but coming in via airplane or helicopter would open up the whole of the US government to criticism over "invasion" of a sovereign nation, as had happened in Pakistan.

That meant they would have come through some other way. Marching across the border would take days; Amanda had followed immigrants taking that route, forced to carry bales of drugs or illegal weapons through the desert. No, they'd need a faster, more direct route, which meant a smuggling tunnel.

A smuggling tunnel would lead to some form of ground vehicles, not easily noticed and quick to cross the countryside.

A smuggling tunnel would also provide a modicum of supplies.

Keep focused on who is coming for you, she told herself.

Think about the people who are so spectacular that they risked a war between the US and Mexico to eliminate them. Because they picked you as bait, knowing that they'd dare one of the world's worst rumored prisons, worse than Black Dolphin in the former Soviet Union.

That was giving Amanda Castillo a feeling that there was a future out there. A group of very special men were here to get her out of this prison, and they would only be coming if they could think of a way to rescue her.

Amanda forced herself to calm down, stemming her excitement at the prospect of survival, at the thought of being reunited with her children.

Don't give up hope, but do not get ahead of yourself. Whoever is coming to Mexico may be highly skilled, but they're going up against a heavily armed security force. Depending on the approach, there's a good chance that you might catch a bullet or a thousand in the cross fire.

Fighting off both an overabundance of hope and dread cynicism was exhausting, and within a few moments, Amanda found herself growing sleepy.

She allowed herself to give in to slumber. She'd need the energy. She didn't know how long she'd be stuck in this prison, but she had this opportunity for rest, for an actual escape from this nightmare. She closed her eyes, and her husband Joaquin was there, as were her children.

This was imagination, but she clung to their images. This was her faith, keeping her steeled against the impossibility of freedom, let alone the kids again.

Whatever came, she'd need her strength, her wits, and she'd have to be rested. Sleep was a vital necessity.

After a few moments, sleep took over.

The cooling concrete faded away, the razor wire and high walls, even the thugs with guns looking over her.

Blessed darkness carried her away.

The President didn't look too happy as he sat on the sofa in his office, smoking a cigarette. It was one of the few vices that was still allowed within certain deep, private areas of the White House, and a bottle of beer marked with the area code of his home city—312—was open on the coffee table in front of him.

Hal Brognola knew that this was the result of stress. And Stony Man Farm was once more at the heart of his troubles.

"You know what gets me?" the Man asked.

Brognola shook his head, even though he knew the answer.

"There are people on cable news networks who have the audacity to claim that I haven't done a single positive thing for national security. And now that they have wind that I do have the tools at my disposal, and have been protecting this country, they want to crucify you and me for it."

The President gestured, offering Brognola a seat.

"No, thank you, sir. I've got other places to be tonight," Brognola said.

"Sorry for dumping on you, Hal," the Man apologized. He put the cigarette to his lips and inhaled. "What do you have for me?"

"We received information about a couple of administrators in Homeland Security who have been working alongside a group called the Arrangement," Brognola reported. "They've been resurrecting the Aryan Right Coalition for a long time, starting not long after Carl Lyons decapitated the Fascist International."

"Literally or figuratively?"

Brognola knew what the President meant. The leader of Able Team was a dangerous human being, and it wouldn't be outside the veil for Lyons to have taken a machete to the leadership of a terrorist organization. "Figuratively."

"And you think that this Arrangement and the Fascist International are all linked?" the President asked.

Brognola nodded. "I'm not one to pull conspiracies out of thin air, sir. So when I give evidence of one, you know I'm providing you with actual evidence."

He handed a file over to the President. "These are some of the men we are going to arrest."

"And what about the others involved in the conspiracy?"

"Those are going to be dealt with," Brognola said.

The President frowned. "Oh."

"This isn't a precedent that I care for, but we're doing what we can," Brognola stated. "We're not going to be the people who assassinate our senators because they are opposed to our group. But we are going to have their careers wrecked for the truth of their criminal dealings."

"And if that doesn't work?" the President asked.

"It will work," Brognola stated. "The men we're going after violated their oaths of office and have committed treason. That cannot be ignored."

The President nodded. "If there is one thing I've learned to trust over my term as Chief Executive, it's that if Stony Man Farm says there is a threat against our country, they will take care of it."

He managed a weak smile, then raised his bottle of beer in a salute. "Godspeed, Hal."

Brognola tipped an imaginary hat in salute to the Commander in Chief and left the President to his concerns.

CHAPTER THIRTEEN

Gary Manning saw that the terrain around sin Piedad was going to be untraversable, at least with any form of secrecy. Even so, he carefully divided the perimeter outlying grounds into grids, examining them for signs of a pathway into the prison. He also looked for spots of cover where the members of Phoenix Force could take shelter from enemy fire while retreating from the prison wall. He wasn't thrilled by the odds or by the fact that there were good sniper hides atop the taller buildings of the prison complex.

Thankfully, among the gear they'd stolen from the Caballeros Cartel's tunnel warehouse was a Barrett M82, Mexican Army issue. The big .50-caliber anti-matériel rifle was designed for long-range engagements, as well as for punching through the light armor of trucks and Jeeps. He would need every bit of range, because right now they were nearly three quarters of a mile from the nearest target.

Only one area was walled off, and there was a collection of office buildings off to the side. Sin Piedad also had a runway strip where planes could land, refuel and take off. Manning studied the airfield itself and saw that there were helicopters and airplanes on hand.

"Got to admit one thing," Manning said softly. "Accion Obrar knows how to place its fortresses."

"*Fortress* isn't even the beginning of it. It's a fully walled city," Hawkins agreed, looking through his spotter scope. They were well over a kilometer from the nearest corner of the facility, and the two Phoenix Force specialists were utilizing a sandy tarpaulin as their concealment. They'd arrived an hour ago, somewhere close to midnight by their synchronized watches, and were now looking for means to get in.

The airstrip had plenty of helicopter activity over in one corner of the small airport. There was also a highway a good stretch along. Phoenix Force had turned their small fleet of vehicles off a mile back, driving into an arroyo behind the sight of even the tallest of the prison's buildings, thanks to the walls of the short canyon and the bend of the horizon.

"We're definitely not going to get close to the place with anything short of a tank, and none of the vehicles we've grabbed are close to being cobbled into one, even if we cannibalized the others," Hawkins added. "So, our new approach is going to have to be smarts and subterfuge."

"The complex reminds me of Langley headquarters," Manning noted. "So this is not just where AO has their prison, but their main force."

"That means we're going to have to be especially careful," Hawkins mused. "Because, sure, there might be armed guards and agents who are in on the corruption of the agency, but there's also going to be hundreds of noncombatants."

"David might be as balls-to-the-wall as Carl, but there's no way we're going to shoot our way in and then turn around and blast our way out," Manning said. "Whoever set this in motion might think we would try that to get the US into worse hot water than it had been in with the SEAL mission in Pakistan."

"So, would we be that dumb?" Hawkins asked. "Or what?"

Manning pursed his lips. "We do not have the time to

dither about our plan. But that doesn't mean we can go in without a plan."

"I think we've taken enough photographs of the prison. Let's send them back to the Farm to see what they can reconstruct," Hawkins added.

Silently, the two men began their crawl, still using the tarp as their cover, back toward the small wash where Phoenix Force had set up camp.

AARON KURTZMAN LOOKED over the digital images transmitted from Mexico. They only had one direction from which they'd observed, but Gary Manning was nothing if he was not thorough and contemplative.

With only one angle, Manning had managed to map out the Mexican prison complex and the Accion Obrar headquarters to a point where Kurtzman could build a three-dimensional view of the miniature city.

"He said that it reminded him of Langley," Barbara Price said. "And you can see it, at least from the office park off to the side."

"Yes. And the prison itself looks familiar to me, too," Kurtzman added. He ran through a quick list. "Pelican Bay State Prison. Same setup."

The projected layout of sin Piedad and the California penitentiary were on his screen, side by side, each showing similar attributes, but the main prison structures were of similar design.

"Of course, Pelican Bay is a recent design, and one developed according to studies. The butterfly shape allows you to keep hostile opposing sides away from each other," Price noted. "Though, in this case, it looks as if hundreds of prisoners aren't being allowed to sleep indoors on the south end."

"Yeah. While the northern half of that 'wing' side doesn't have basketball courts so much as tennis courts…

and is that a pool?" Kurtzman queried, indignation in his voice.

"No wonder they don't want the US getting a close look at the place via satellite," Price noted.

"Maybe the guys who coughed up the money for the spa treatment are spread out into more comfy cells. That's why they're kept in the yard," Kurtzman thought out loud.

"Can we do a search for Amanda Castillo?" Price asked.

"Manning sent this one directly tagged for identification of her," Kurtzman answered, pulling up a picture of a woman with fairer skin than those around her. She was curled on the ground, her back to Manning's lens, but her blond hair was much cleaner than that of her close neighbors.

"She's not darkened from too much time in the sun, at least on her shoulders, and look at the hair," Price added. "Too flyaway. She's bathed and washed it inside the past couple of days, compared to the greasy locks of those around her."

"Sharp eye." Kurtzman complimented her. "I'm going to try to get more details out of her. They stripped her down to the waist."

"No one's wearing a top, leggings or footwear. Just a rag diaper," Price noted. "And check her foot in the picture."

Kurtzman was at once glad for the telescopic zoom of the digital camera Manning had used to survey and investigate sin Piedad and disgusted at the cruel details it brought to light. Amanda Castillo's feet were chewed and blistered. The feet of others around her were masses of calluses and didn't look as if they'd ever fit into shoes again. Some of them had melanomas forming on their sun baked flesh; all of that was apparent in the narrow frame of the digital photo.

"She's alive, and she might be able to walk," Price said. "That much is good news."

"She's not going to be running quickly anywhere," Kurtzman countered. "What can the guys hope to do with something like that?"

"We'll keep our eyes open for who might be delivering to the prison. I mean, look at it. There's no way that this is a self-sustaining facility," Price said. "The boys located the prison, so we should have a way to find threads to the outside world."

Kurtzman nodded. "Even we get a shipment of office supplies from Steel Hill Unlimited."

"Find the Mexican version of that contractor," Price stated. "If Phoenix can't para drop into the prison, then by God they'll walk in carrying paper clips and erasers."

"On it," Kurtzman responded.

Barbara Price looked at the photograph of Amanda Castillo, rendered nearly naked and forced to sleep out in the desert night's chill air. It was winter, which didn't mean much in terms of coolness during the day, but at night, it was a good means of succumbing to frostbite or hypothermia.

"We're here, and we're going to get you out of there," Price promised under her breath. "You'll get back to your children."

THE NEAREST MONTANAHIERRO facility was only an hour away from the prison, provided one put the pedal to the metal, and the roads were clear by being after midnight.

Manning and Hawkins stayed back in the arroyo overlooking Sin Piedad, sniper-scout and his spotter, watching the deadly situation that Amanda Castillo had been set into.

Calvin James, Rafael Encizo and David McCarter were in one car together, carrying only their handguns. They wanted to find their means of getting into the prison complex, and the three men didn't want to shed blood over that premise.

However, there was the possibility that they could run afoul of armed guards who were both in the employ of Accion Obrar or the prison and were willing to ruthlessly murder for their employers or beliefs. So, no, they wouldn't pack submachine guns or rifles, but they weren't going to leave behind their sidearms, knives or communicators.

Barbara Price had come through with a means to get into the sin Piedad complex, but that was all dependent on finding the right vehicle for that penetration, both figuratively and literally.

The plan was to intercept and hijack a truck loaded with office supplies for the prison. If there was one thing that even the most secret of agencies had, it was paperwork, and Montanahierro was the means by which sensitive documents were shredded and utterly destroyed, or saved for nearly eternal backup filing. Most of the time, the paperwork was destroyed, shredded and recycled. The Mexican company was a counterpart to an American version, dealing with government work, and thus was usually trusted with all but the most confidential of records.

"Since these guys are just working for a living, we'll take it easy on them," McCarter reminded his partners, even though he knew in his heart that neither James nor Encizo would murder an unarmed man.

"That'll be tough if we have to deal with guards," James said. "Because I don't think they're going to make it easy to hijack a truck shipment. He checked the Beretta 92-F he'd chosen as his personal sidearm since the team standardized on 9 mm handguns. He flicked the safety on and returned it to its holster. It was nervous busywork, but he maintained firearm safety even in this, avoiding the flagging of either of his partners with the muzzle of the handgun.

Meanwhile, Encizo left his knives and Heckler & Koch P-30 9 mm in place under his lightweight jacket. McCarter had his Browning Hi-Power in its shoulder holster, balanced by a pair of 15-round spare magazines. All three had backup pistols and blades, McCarter his Charter Arms .38, Encizo his Walther PPK in 7.65 mm and James his two-and-a-half-inch Colt Python loaded with six rounds of .357 Magnum. They were hardly poorly equipped, but they also knew the reality of handguns versus long-arms.

"There's the truck," Encizo noted. "Ready up."

"Do your magic," James charged.

McCarter revved the engine and swerved the sedan into the path of the truck. The mad-dog Englishman swung the back of the car so close to the front bumper of the Montanahierro truck that the driver came within inches of jackknifing. Air brakes popped and hissed, sizzling and snarling, tires wailing on asphalt. The truck driver, however, had a lot of skill and control with the big rig.

Instead of twisting and flipping, the driver brought the truck to a halt, keeping it under control enough to steer onto the shoulder and decelerate.

McCarter swung the car around and brought it to a halt nose to nose with the stopped truck. The driver swung open the door, his face full of anger.

"*¡Hijo de puta!*" the man snarled as he hopped down. He had a tire iron in hand, but then found himself looking down the muzzles of three 9 mm handguns.

"Talk about *mi madre* some more, sucker," James responded so the driver could understand. He had the safety on, but the terrified employee let the tire iron drop into the dust.

"What do you guys want?" the Montanahierro man asked.

McCarter waved him off to the side of the road. "A trade. Your truck for our car."

"Really?" He looked from the cab to the car, which McCarter had stolen from Nogales. "That's a hot-looking ride."

"We just need you to drive close to help. And then give us an hour," Encizo explained. "We don't want you to die out here in the middle of nowhere."

The driver stood askance from the vehicle. "This is a nice ride. Too nice for this area."

"So, not a fair trade? Ditch it within walking distance of town, then," McCarter said. "We tore out any tracking devices, if you're worried that this might be a cartel vehicle."

"It was one of theirs?" the driver asked.

"Not going to lie," Encizo added. "But they won't track it to you. It's just a step home for you."

"But don't take our giving you a way out of the desert as a reason we won't kill you if you rat us out before our deadline for you keeping quiet is up," James said. He stepped intimidatingly toward the driver. The difference in their height made the lanky, tall James seem almost gigantic in comparison.

"An hour?" the driver asked.

"Minimum," James growled.

"You can take all day," the Montanahierro driver said.

"Nah. Then you'd end up in jail. In *that* jail," James said.

"Ugh…" the driver returned.

With that, the three Phoenix Force professionals crawled into the cab of the truck and took off, bringing the big rig, complete with its trailer, up the road. They didn't want to hang around for too long, no matter what the driver promised. The thing was, the car only had enough gas to get within walking distance of the Montanahierro depot that he'd come from. It was a matter of belt-and-suspenders approach. They didn't need to be interrupted too soon.

Even as they left the spot of the hijacking, McCarter tapped off three shots into the ground, leaving casings and slugs behind to prove the event.

It took only a little bit of driving to return to the arroyo, and the five men of the team got to work opening the trailer of the delivery truck. The lock was very little effort for the skills of the team, not requiring bolt cutters to snap open. Inside, there were boxes stacked, but it was not packed to the gills. There was room for the whole team, plus extra gear and such.

Even so, the five men set quickly to work, making the storage setup in the back of the trailer more amenable to discreetly carrying four fully equipped commandos while Rafael Encizo acted as driver the rest of the way to sin Piedad.

Encizo, on the other hand, was going to be completely unarmed, except for a replacement to the original driver's tire iron and his hidden neck knife. His job, for the time being, was to get them where they needed to be. The Cuban, especially with his mastery of Mexican accents, was as close to invisible as they could get once they were inside the prison.

Meanwhile, in the back, the others continued to brace the cartons, as well as using low-velocity detonation cord to cut a small trapdoor in the bottom of the trailer. The det cord was made with a mix of gunpowder and meth-cooking chemicals brought along, and it worked quite well. Though they were in an arroyo, the duller crackle of the cord still would not have carried far. The top of the trapdoor was a hacked-off passenger door from one of Phoenix Force's stolen vehicles. It didn't have to look perfect, but it did have to be heavy enough to hold the trapdoor shut and large enough to provide a seal to prevent inspectors from noticing the new door.

"If we had an hour, we'd probably have this thing hinged," Hawkins muttered.

"But we don't," Manning returned, using some of the stolen tools in one of the cars to bolt the plate onto the car door. "Besides, don't you remember what the Italians said? 'Perfect is the enemy of good enough.'"

"It was a Texas sayin' first," Hawkins replied. He winked.

The two men situated their trapdoor so that it would sit secure, but still provided them with plenty of handholds to pick it up and move it aside.

Meanwhile, McCarter and Encizo were going over the layout of the prison together on their CPDAs. "Our best chance is for you to pause right in this loading dock. There's a man-size cover, and according to what subterranean infrared and radar have determined, there are plenty of sewer and runoff tunnels down there."

"One thing you definitely want in a desert facility is water runoff capacity," Encizo agreed. "Rain might be rare, but when it comes, it'll throw a monkey wrench into everything you've built."

"Accion Obrar might not give a crap about some of their prisoners, but they've got employees and contractors to keep happy and quiet, as well as the crooked buggers using sin Piedad as a vacation resort," McCarter said.

"Just leave everything to me," Encizo told his friend. "Now, Cal and I have to drop off my getaway car downrange."

"Make it fast—the clock's ticking," McCarter ordered.

"We'll be back by yesterday," Encizo answered.

With that, Encizo and James loaded into two of the smaller cars and tore off down the highway. Two drivers out, one driver back. The entire run was made in the space of ten minutes, and McCarter could tell that by the time of the return trip, James had run the engine nearly to the point of overheating.

That was fine, risks to be taken. They still had two more vehicles in reserve here at the arroyo and a third down the road once Encizo ditched the big rig.

Now it was time to get in and rescue a brave woman.

CHAPTER FOURTEEN

To watch David Kowalski walking down the street at 7:00 a.m. with a pizza pie in a box, one would have thought that he was some squashed version of a stoner, especially with a plastic bag full of soda bottles. He had a few days of scruff on his jaw and was sausaged into the white shirt that was drawn tight across his chest. People would never confuse him with the typical image of a rough-and-tumble, fit-and-trim Special Forces operator. He didn't look like a veteran, either, his reddish-blond beard fuzz looking more sprayed on in an attempt to avoid being carded buying alcohol.

Kowalski wasn't technically special operations, however. He was a Marine, a scout sniper who'd earned his bones in Iraq and later got a job in the United States Marshal's Service. It was there that he'd come under the recognition of first Stony Man Farm as a member of the blacksuits and then crossed paths with the SOG's founder in a brutal manhunt across the Sahara.

Carl Lyons whispered into his com set mike, activating the earbud that Kowalski wore. "I thought that if we'd pulled away, no one would still remain posted at the federal building."

"I've been wondering if all the hairy eyebrows were me looking like a Mormon missionary or from cartel goons," Kowalski subvocalized. "But my itchy neck says it's someone looking for blood to spill."

"Well, that might just be me," Lyons said.

"No, this was before you showed up, boss," Kowalski answered.

"I've been here longer than you think," Lyons returned.

Kowalski's head bobbed. "Got a point. But your murderous intent sure don't feel like the glares I've been getting from some distinctly Mexican-looking guys."

"That couldn't be a little bit of racism, could it?" Lyons asked with a chuckle.

There was a low growl on the other end of the com link.

"I'm kidding. I know you ain't a bigot," Lyons followed up. "No more than me."

"Sorry for acting like a dog," Kowalski answered. He paused at the corner. "Where are you at?"

"I'd worry about you looking at me, but you're a sniper. You won't give away my hide, even if we were watching from across the state," Lyons returned.

"Satellite or closed-circuit camera?" Kowalski asked.

"A little bit of both." Lyons answered.

The truth was that Lyons was sitting in a rental car, in one of the blind spots that the cartel's goons had left behind in the wake of Able Team's cleaning of the perimeter of the federal building. He'd made note of enemy presence as they had parked themselves in positions to watch.

Lyons wasn't lying about the closed-circuit camera or the satellite imaging, but as much as the Phoenix Force leader trusted the technical abilities of Schwarz and the Stony Man cyber wizards, he also believed in what the military called the Mark 1 Eyeball.

And what that eyeball picked up were three teams of two men following Kowalski and trading off to prevent becoming easily recognizable. It would have been good tradecraft, but Lyons could tell the young blacksuit was up to the challenge.

Of course he'd be up to it. We trained him, Lyons thought with pride.

"Happy there?" Schwarz asked over a different channel.

"As a pig in a poke. Somehow these guys aren't fooled by us taking off," Lyons returned. "Anything on their communications?"

Lyons was in the area, and Schwarz decided to make the most of having someone present around the Yuma federal building and gave him a much more powerful variant of the cell phone cloning technology than could normally be built into the Combat PDA. The suitcase-size apparatus literally was able to tap into everything for a mile radius around him as he was parked.

Lyons figured it had to do with the sheer volume of antenna that could be packed into the case, which in turn networked with the CPDA. "Breakfast pizza?"

"You're not from Chicago," Kowalski answered. "You'd never understand the joys of it."

"Is it even warm?" Lyons asked.

"We've got a mini-fridge for that purpose. Just in time for the morning shift change. And don't worry, we've got actual toast, milk, butter and jam for the kids," Kowalski continued. "So who is the mole in this operation?"

"'Mole'?" Lyons repeated. "You're fairly quick."

"Well, someone in this mess knows that the kids are still on the premises. Otherwise I wouldn't be leading the dork train around with a cold pizza," Kowalski explained himself.

"We've got clues to inside men. We're just hoping to rattle a couple more loose," Lyons responded. "And it looks like you're going to help us knock them out of place."

"Good," Kowalski said. "Just let me know if we have any shooting to do."

"If it gets to that while you're in the presence of the kids, it means we've screwed the pooch too far to recover," Lyons answered. "But don't worry, you'll get to have some fun soon."

Kowalski finally turned out of sight, entering the federal building. His pursuers had broken off when they had come within range of the office security cameras.

Lyons checked the Combat PDA, which was his interface with the briefcase "snooper," and noticed that a lot of chatter had been picked up on local cell phones. He was able, thanks to Schwarz's software, to confirm that the men shadowing Kowalski were in contact with the local FBI office or at least one of the dozens of lines assigned to said office. Schwarz's software didn't require a length of call to trace the line, as it was cloning the stalkers' cell phones and picking up precisely on the numbers they were calling. Once that was determined, they would simply use the directory of the FBI to figure out who was being called. Of course, this was no guarantee that someone wasn't utilizing someone else's phone line for this treacherous business.

Which was why Lyons felt that, despite Schwarz's and the cyber teams' wizardry with all things computer, sometimes the Mark 1 Eyeball was still one of the most important intelligence assets in the world. And the hackers and Able Team's electronics expert all agreed that it wasn't the technology; it was the brain that used said technology that was most important. Machines only processed the data and made it easier to sort. It took a human to understand the threads and correlations.

"We've homed in on the line," Schwarz said over the PDA. "And thanks to the cloning, we've got a sample of the voice being used. It's a woman's voice, but the line is assigned to a male agent."

Lyons sneered. "Do they have voice files on line for the FBI?"

"Not as far as we know, but there're three women assigned to the office," Schwarz answered. "Two are Hispanic, one is black, but there's no discernible accent. Good phone operational security on her part."

"Damn," Lyons murmured. "We'll just have to be clever."

"I've already got a program for the microphones in the PDA. Just talk to the ladies. Turn on that caveman charm," Schwarz said. "We've got one sample on record, so we have something to compare it to. The mike in the PDA will pick up their voices and make the match, sending it back to me."

"Great," Lyons returned. He started the car and drove, heading for the parking lot. "Also, we could narrow it down by just asking which female agent was present at the office this early."

He could feel Schwarz's wince on the other end.

"But your method really helps if two or more were present," Lyons added. "And it might be a woman from another office, stopping in by the FBI desks."

"Thanks for making me feel useless for only a second or two," Schwarz returned

"That's my job. Reality checks. You do the non sequiturs, I bring you back down to earth," Lyons answered with a smile.

Schwarz sputtered a raspberry response over the radio. That was Lyons's cue to park and go inside.

There was a rat to ferret out.

HAL BROGNOLA HADN'T gotten much sleep, but that didn't mean he was going into the Senate oversight hearing looking as if he were the walking dead. He'd changed shirts, combed his hair and brushed his teeth, and was feeling like a new man once more. He debated leaving the stubble on his chin and jowls, but thought against it. There was little excuse for scruffiness when being called onto the floor in front of a committee, as any sign of disrespect would only flash back upon him and the rest of the Sensitive Operations Group.

"Mr. Brognola, how do you explain this so-called black-suit program?"

"It needs little explanation. We run continuing education classes, as any other federal law enforcement training center does," Brognola answered.

A senator spoke up. "And yet there are certain blocks to disclosure on extracurricular activities."

Brognola was at the point where the rightist and the leftist were indistinguishable from each other, mirror images of the same jerkily handled meat puppet spouting someone else's ideas for money.

"No. They merely are, in addition to their time at the facility, being utilized for the protection of vital records for the government," Brognola stated. "If you will look at report 39-1980A, you'll see that—

"In an era when we have the internet, what is the logic of paper copy?" the senator persisted.

"Your assumption is that these men are protecting endless boxes of paperwork. We're also keeping electronic storage under shielded conditions. No one has ever suffered from a mass leak such as the embarrassments the State Department endured," Brognola corrected him.

"Then what is the purpose of keeping information not easily accessed?" the senator continued. "How can the American people benefit from this?"

"How can they benefit from secure information stored away from spies and disgruntled soldiers?" Brognola asked. "By having information kept safe but ready to use. And the blacksuit program, in between training shifts, keeps that under wraps."

The senator's eyes narrowed. "Then tell us about the program's founder, Colonel John Phoenix."

Brognola's face remained impassive, but deep inside

his gut was sent reeling. In the years since Mack Bolan had "died" and been once more "resurrected," the Sensitive Operations Group had done its best to obfuscate the true nature of its origins. "John Phoenix" had been a cipher put together to allow Mack Bolan government legitimacy as he traveled the world, fighting terrorism. Only moles controlled from Moscow had been able to damage Bolan's crusade, killing friends and lovers and staging a similar breach of security in the eyes of elected officials and the President himself.

Bolan had shed the Phoenix identity long ago, and though he was still in an arm's-length relationship with the Farm, the cybernetics team had done everything it could to bury the tenuous tethers between Bolan and Stony Man.

"You will have to clarify yourself," Brognola stated. "John who?"

"Colonel John Macklin Phoenix," the senator said. "Who was your partner and co-founder of this thing called the Sensitive Operations Group."

Brognola frowned. Outside, his will kept him an iron-solid masquerade of inscrutable confidence. Inside, he was as a drowning man clinging to a stone among surging waves and crashing storms. "I have never heard of a Phoenix."

"Please hand Mr. Brognola exhibit 1969F," the senator stated. "You'll find your signature next to Colonel Phoenix's."

Brognola looked down at a sheet of paper, some of the standard nondisclosure boilerplate that had been necessary for Justice Department operations. Though it was merely a photograph of the document, he could tell that it was legitimate. Brognola forced a disbelieving smirk onto his face. "In an age of Photoshop, you expect this to hold any form of weight? A photograph of a photocopy?"

The senator folded his hands. "You are being evasive. Why were American lawmen assigned to a paramilitary operation and equipped for a war?"

"The question you have to ask is why, apparently, members of a foreign criminal cartel were able to circumvent border security with firepower and high-tech aircraft." Brognola moved closer to the microphone. "Or does the senator not remember his threats to defund the Department of Homeland Security?"

"How is it that your blacksuit program seems beyond the scope of DHLS?" the senator's political counterpart interjected. "Would it not be better if everyone were under the same umbrella?"

"We are under that umbrella, sir," Brognola told him. "You have the paperwork before you regarding our FLETC requirements."

"As you said to my esteemed colleague, in this age of Photoshop…"

Brognola bit down his anger. The slam that had dug up "John Phoenix" was now being followed with a cheap shot designed to make him burst apart in rage. Thankfully, in all of his years of running the SOG and dealing with congressional hearings, Brognola had developed both some impressive emotional camouflage and quick recuperative abilities in regard to such blindside attacks.

"Sir, I respect your office, but you are engaging in false equivalency," Brognola submitted as his response. "Our Federal Law Enforcement Training Center credentials are confirmable. This secondhand copy is not. Your questions also are insulting as you appear to feel as if we did not care about the lives of our brave men and women assigned to that protection detail."

"Please have the agent's commentary stricken from the record." The first senator spoke. "He is using this podium as a means of slandering the authority of this commission."

The recorder looked to the rest of the committee, but no one seemed willing to engage one of the pair of eight-hundred-pound gorillas who were like a double-barreled shotgun aimed at Brognola and Stony Man Farm.

The chairman banged his gavel. "Let's take a recess and let heads cool down a bit, shall we?"

Neither of the bought-off senators looked pleased with this development, but they grumbled assent. They could continue their pummeling later on. What they didn't notice was that Brognola took a moment to scan the signature of Phoenix next to his on the document with his smartphone.

A few taps of the touch screen and, quietly, the proof of Mack Bolan's involvement with Stony Man Farm was forwarded to the Farm. He tagged it as a priority message and knew that it would take Kurtzman's team very little time and effort to track down the source.

Once they got hold of where the leak possibly began, the threads would take them up a chain of evidence that would give Brognola exactly what he needed to take down the two bent senators.

IT TOOK ONLY a few moments to swing the truck to the spot where Phoenix Force could enter the runoff sewers beneath the prison complex.

Gary Manning pulled aside the hatch, and his three allies dropped through, setting immediately to work on the access cover. Fortunately, it wasn't tarred over or otherwise sealed down, and utilizing tire irons, wrapped in duct tape, they were able to pull up the lid. Manning shut the hatch behind them, and the quartet of commandos was down inside. Manning's considerable strength was utilized as he was at the back of the group, lifting and settling the manhole cover with grace and silence.

With a grunt of gears shifting, Rafael Encizo started up the truck again and continued his path to the loading dock.

Phoenix Force was not enamored of the idea of being understrength by 20 percent, but the simple truth was that they didn't have the manpower or preparation to accomplish this without Encizo leaving with the delivery truck. At the same time, they did have some heart in that there was someone who could come to their rescue, as well as be their ride out.

David McCarter was at the front of the group, leading the way with his Heckler & Koch MP-7 machine pistol. All four members of the team inside the prison's underground tunnels were equipped with compact submachine guns. They'd affixed suppressors to their muzzles and utilized NVGs down here in the darkness. The tunnels were big enough to accommodate the tallest member of the team, Calvin James, in a hunch-shouldered crouch.

On the outside, Encizo would be in a position to provide overwatch utilizing the Caballeros Cartel inventory Barrett M82 in .50 caliber, giving him the range and reach to help in a hectic situation. But for now, the Phoenix pros were in stealth mode, moving quietly and carefully. It would take at least an hour for Encizo to finish his round, dispose of the Montanahierro truck and return to the arroyo to provide the kind of security only a skilled marksman could provide.

Encizo might not have been a designated sharpshooter, but he was a man who knew his way around a good number of rifles and machine guns aside from his favored Heckler & Koch family of weapons. Encizo had also been working alongside one of the finest woodsmen and sniper-scouts in the world with Manning, so McCarter couldn't feel more at ease with the stocky Cuban as his backup.

In the meantime, T. J. Hawkins was working their electronic communications with the above world, looping an antenna wire to the manhole cover to create an improvised high-powered reception dish that would provide them with solid, foolproof and fail-safe contact with the cyber team back at the Farm.

"Map's downloaded," Hawkins said softly. "We've got the layout of the tunnel system down here."

McCarter was pleased with that as the map showed up on the screen of his CPDA. "Right. Let's get to business, mates. Time's wasting."

CHAPTER FIFTEEN

Amanda Castillo's neck was cramped from how she'd slept the previous evening, and as she climbed to her feet with the rising sun, her limbs complained with the effort. At least the splash of the Mexican desert sun was a relief from the biting chill of the "winter" night. It was hot, relentless, leaning on her and mutating from a salve against the cold to a blister of torment. The group needed to walk for an hour from the first rays of dawn until "breakfast" came to them.

Having missed the evening meal the previous day, indeed, having gone an entire day without eating, her stomach grumbled and pulsed. When the meal finally came, it wasn't so much food as a slurry made from the rinsing off of plates. She could smell soap in the stew, but her mouth was so dry and parched, and the sight of tidbits and leftovers, even half-gnawed chicken bones, overcame her reluctance to take a bite.

Amanda ate what she could, slurping bits off indigestible bones and cartilage, and the churn of her stomach reversed its rotation, showing just how badly the dish soap was going to treat her digestive system. To her right, she saw an old woman breaking a drumstick bone, sucking on the marrow within.

We're reduced to vermin, Amanda thought.

The first roil of her upset stomach came as an extended belch that filled her mouth with sour bile and bubbles. Tears flowed from her eyes. If she ended up vomiting, she'd dehydrate even worse. She ground her teeth, fighting to endure the disturbance in her gut.

Inside her stomach it was a battle between digestive enzymes and her body's autonomic responses to the soap chemicals in the food she tried to digest. Convulsions slammed her; it felt like hammer blows delivered by a professional boxer, striking her just under her heart. Others were groaning, as well, struggling with their morning meals.

If they can gag this down, then so can you, Amanda told herself. She swallowed, concentrating and struggling to keep the gruel in her belly. If she emptied her stomach, then she was one day closer to death.

She absolutely did not want to imagine disgorging.

The thought came anyway, and she burped up a little more, chunks gagging in the back of her throat that she swallowed back down.

Amanda never believed that she'd be a woman who swooned, but she was doing just that right now. Keeping steadily sitting up was a torturous effort, especially as her stomach begged her to lie down once again. She didn't even dare spit the sour bile from her mouth, washing it down with the last of the sudsy gravy.

"Get up, you maggots! And toss your trays here!" a guard bellowed. He was unarmed, but he didn't need to be, not with snipers watching over the courtyard.

Amanda struggled to get to her feet again, the metal plate trembling in one hand. The edges of her vision blurred and she couldn't tell if it was because of tears flooding her eyelids or some darker, more dangerous reason. Putting one foot in front of the other, she followed the rest of the line of the marching damned.

Each impact of her foot on the concrete was another punch in the gut. Nausea rumbled and boiled, bubbling up into her brain. They were eating the stuff discarded and likely spit out by the richer, better-treated prisoners. Each thought of what they received was an assault upon her senses.

Put a bullet in my brain, please.

And with that thought, anger flared inside her.

We're not going to fail. We're not surrendering. Someone is coming, and your children need you!

Amanda staggered forward, threw her metal plate onto the pile and broke off, joining the stream of the mindless, walking damned.

Not going to swoon, she vowed. Not providing Moran that satis—

Blackness crashed down upon her and she was unconscious on the yard. Unable to consciously resist, she vomited, but, thankfully, she had collapsed facedown, so she wasn't in danger of choking, not for a little bit.

Had she been any other prisoner, they would have left her to roast in the sun, but she was important cargo to Hector Moran.

Sadly for those around her, the goon squad sent to rescue her was armed with billy clubs, and they held no qualms about breaking bones or hurling the weakened, infirm walking cadavers of the other prisoners to the ground. Blood was shed, but not on their parts.

Amanda Castillo was dragged onto a cot and ferried quickly to the infirmary.

RAFAEL ENCIZO WAS at the dump point for the Montanahierro delivery truck, having completed his unloading, and had just gotten out of the cab when his CPDA alerted him to an incoming text.

Be advised. Amanda moved from courtyard to infirmary after collapse.

Encizo grimaced at that bit of information in text form. He wouldn't have been the only one in on this, especially since he knew that the other members of Phoenix Force wouldn't have started moving far from a grating where they could contact the outside world. Inside the tunnels under the prison, reception would not be good, but utilizing the communications sequence and hookups on the CPDAs, they could turn a manhole cover or a sewer grating into an amplifier for satellite communications.

Phoenix One acknowledges receipt of message.

Encizo took a moment to text his own response, so the others wouldn't worry about his well-being. Then again, he was armed and ready for almost anything that wasn't covered in armor plate, what with his shoulder-holstered, compact MP-7 machine pistol. The little chatterbox and its 4.6 mm rounds were designed to penetrate CRISAT NATO battle helmets and vests. He'd actually tucked the gun beneath the driver's seat while he was in the cab, but once out of the prison, he'd shifted it to a shoulder harness.

He jogged over to where his car was waiting and slid in behind the wheel.

Keys in ignition, car into gear; Encizo revved the engine and tore out of the niche where he'd dumped the truck. It wouldn't matter that it'd be discovered within an hour or two. He'd also managed to obscure, ahead of time, the tire tracks from his and James's initial trip here and, with a sufficient burnout, left a good cloud to diffuse any chance of identifying who and what was present.

It wasn't much, but Phoenix Force had learned long ago that the devil hid in the details and just one moment of distraction could prove deadly. Encizo still had a scar across his hairline from where a neo-Nazi's bullet had nearly split his skull open. He also had scar tissue in the palm of one hand from when he'd been captured by terrorists who'd taken over the Vatican. Luck and skill were one thing, but constant thought and utter professionalism were all that kept him alive. Diligence was a cruel master, but as long as he thought ahead, planned, made sure every angle was covered, he would be fine.

As he drove, he was about fifteen minutes from the truck when he noted Policía Federal squad cars zooming onto the highway, right in the direction of the Montana-hierro truck.

Encizo looked to the PDA and knew that the Farm likely had its eye on the road, but he tapped the speaker function anyway.

"Barb, this is Rafe," he said.

Price was on the other end of the line, without fail. "We know. You've spotted the police racing down the highway."

"Do they know about us hijacking the rig?" Encizo asked.

"We're scanning all their radio chatter, but it's hard to tell," Price answered. "They're being evasive in their communications."

"In other words, they know they're being spied upon and don't want to let us in on that information," Encizo grumbled.

"Already texting the rest of the team with this new development," Price returned. "You're doing just a little bit over the speed limit, so it doesn't look like you're going to be noticed."

"Unless there's a BOLO for this particular car," Encizo returned. "We might have just jumped into this trap with both feet."

"Our opposition is likely hoping to catch a group of American-hired commandos on the scene," Price said. "Hal's been under heat from committee about the blacksuit program, and someone came up with a signature from Striker."

Encizo felt his cheeks prickle with fear. "Mack's been long buried, even in the deepest rumor mills."

"No. As the colonel," Price corrected Encizo.

The Cuban continued driving, not quite blasting away at breakneck, but he definitely slowed down and pulled onto the shoulder as the convoy of racing squad cars grew closer. He forced himself calm as he knew that if he acted the least bit suspicious, he'd throw all of Phoenix Force's plans into disarray, not to mention getting himself killed.

Encizo had lived a long, worthy life, fighting for all he believed in, so dying held little fear for him. Getting killed when others relied upon him, however, meant that his friends and partners would be at risk. His jaw clenched, knuckles whitening on the wheel as the first car came closer, closer, sirens wailing at maximum volume. He also thought about the arroyo and the possible consequences if the *policia* spotted their small parking-lot staging area overlooking the prison.

More tension knotted his shoulders, and he took several deep, cleansing breaths as, finally, the first two cars rushed past. A third vehicle, trailing a bit, slowed, however.

It was then that the sweat glands under Encizo's pits turned on like faucets. His brief relief at the passing of two patrol cars suddenly turned downhill, but he mentally commanded himself to remain calm. The MP-7 was concealed under his light jacket, and the car he was in didn't look hot. Of course, Phoenix Force had had the foresight to take the license plates from all of their stolen cars, cut them in two and match them with other plates. The mixture of new numbers wouldn't register on a call-in, and unless someone was right on top of them, no one would know the difference, especially with some white paint covering the seams in the center.

Encizo realized that these federal cops weren't the enemy. Though they had been mobilized against Accion Obrar, Mexico's own renegade version of Stony Man, it wasn't the Mexican government or even the rank-and-file lawmen who were the enemy. Indeed, honest cops risked their lives and dared danger in dealing with the Mexican cartels, rather than throw their lot in with the drug gangs. If a cop decided to throw down, Encizo was likely to be facing an honest man, not a cocaine cartel flunky.

Encizo rolled down the window as the third car crawled to a stop beside him. A fourth and fifth squad zipped past.

"¿Que pasa?" he asked.

The officer in the passenger seat tilted his head, scanning the inside of the vehicle for anything that seemed out of the ordinary. "We got word about a stolen truck. Did you see anything?"

Encizo decided to minimize any chance of getting caught in a lie. "I didn't see a truck, but I did see a hell of a dust cloud kicked up heading down a turnoff at mile marker…"

He paused, looking up into the roof of the car before giving the number of the side road. "It could have been an eighteen-wheeler, if that's the size of truck you're looking for."

There was a smile from the passenger. "How long ago?"

"Fifteen minutes, more or less," Encizo clarified.

The driver was already on the radio to the other cars, letting the rest of the police response know about Encizo's sighting.

"Gracias," the cop said.

Encizo nodded and tapped his forehead in slight salute to the officers. The squad car pulled away and Encizo picked up speed.

"Barb, you still there?" he asked.

"Yeah," Price answered. "Nobody is at the entrance

to the arroyo where you guys parked, and no one seems to have looked there. We've got eyes on both lots, so to speak."

"Then you know I gave them everything they needed to find the truck we nabbed. And one look into the trailer, they'd know we stole a whole team inside their prison," Encizo said. "Has it started smoking yet?"

Price paused, obviously checking the screen.

One thing that Phoenix Force anticipated was making the Montanahierro truck as hard to investigate as possible. Thanks to meth-cooking chemicals and Gary Manning's demolitions skills, they'd set a countdown in the trailer for the thing to be turned into a blazing inferno to prevent the discovery of the trapdoor they'd cut.

It wasn't a certain thing, but at this point, the Stony Man commandos were doing everything in their power to impede Mexican law enforcement's discovery of them. They hated acting as fugitives against men they'd fought beside and fought to protect before, but right now, as long as the corrupt Accion Obrar had its fingers on the pulse of the authorities, the team had to remain in full stealth mode.

At least he'd lucked out and avoided a conflict with the *policia*.

"Burning now," Price announced. "Hope you've got enough fuel in there to keep the fires burning."

"We didn't half-ass this," Encizo responded. Now the knots faded from his shoulders. In another few minutes he was at the turnoff to the small canyon. As Price had reported, no *federales* were present. That didn't mean Encizo wasn't going to take a good hard look to see if someone else might have come upon the tiny canyon.

If the enemy was thorough enough to have learned about Colonel John Phoenix, then they must have been aware that there was a small nook where intruders could set up that close to their principle prison and agency headquarters. Underestimating any foes was folly, but underestimating these men was nothing short of suicide. Not when they'd wrought so much destruction and managed to infiltrate moles into American law enforcement as well as Mexico's police community.

It didn't take more than five minutes for him to do a perimeter check of the remaining vehicles. Luckily, Phoenix had bought and used tarpaulin as camouflage for the cars that had been left behind. A close check showed that nothing had been disturbed there, either.

Phoenix Three to Phoenix One. Back at base. Truck smoking.

The text was brief; the satellite data squirt would be instantaneously sent and fully encrypted in a key that only the Combat PDAs could interpret immediately. As the CPDAs operated on line-of-sight sat com signals, the tightly focused bursts of information were next to impossible to intercept or spill over. Then again, the rest of the team was at the enemy's headquarters, where they likely had plenty of communications interception equipment.

Maybe they'd have the kind of decryption technology to even pick up on the message. On the other hand, Accion Obrar was specifically stalking the Stony Man Farm operation, so they knew of Phoenix Force and Able Team, even if only in abstract.

Encizo changed into the gillie cape and hood that he and Manning had assembled, and he brought the heavy Barrett with him, all wrapped in appropriate bandages and tarps to help it blend in with the countryside. This was the same stealth gear that had been used by Manning and Hawkins for their initial observations of the prison complex.

He moved slowly, slithering over the top of the lip overlooking the arroyo. The prison was a mere line of dots from this range, but he kept the twenty-five-pound rifle with him in its drag bag, hooked to his belt. Encizo brought up a spotting scope, a mesh of metal preventing glare from the lens, and swept the prison. He also looked along any route from the prison to the arroyo that was not the road he'd just taken.

Price and the cyber team had their orbital eyes on that approach, watching the Cuban's back as he was in position to watch the rest of Phoenix Force's back.

The CPDA was with him, too. From their orbital vantage point, they could spot trouble, spot potential enemy action, but without something more immediate, the cybernetic crew at the Farm were practically helpless. Encizo would be their firepower, and they would be his eyes.

Since the big Barrett had a two-mile range, he would have a hell of a lot of reach to enforce the cyber crew's will if necessary.

To protect his brothers in Phoenix Force, he'd move the world. Fortunately, all he needed to do was to move twenty-five pounds of thunderbolt-launching rifle, and another ten pounds of those thunderbolts loaded into 10-round magazines.

Hopefully, that would prove to be enough.

ARETHA CONNOR STEPPED into the hallway, looking at her personal cell phone. This was nothing suspicious, and she was getting as far from the FBI offices as she could. As a member of the DEA, she had every right to be on this floor, even to make use of the desk phones of various agents, but the last thing she needed was to be seen using FBI lines to call Caballeros de Durango Cartel employees.

Connor didn't feel bad about taking the Caballeros' money for information, though. After all, the cartel was a construct of Accion Obrar—a Mexican agency that was handling the war on drugs the way it *should* be handled:

no-holds-barred, no mercy. If that meant resting an executioner's blade against the neck of an enslaved gang, using its contacts and powers to spread terror among the rest of the cartels, then so be it.

Connor didn't give a damn about the men willing to murder rival criminals at a whim, and as for killing judges and reporters, who was to say that those so-called victims weren't deserving of a pop in the head with a bullet? They could have been as bent and crooked as any other cocaine peddler.

Accion Obrar gave her plenty of information to bust other scumbags here in Yuma and along the border. They were doing good over here.

And yet, she paused, looking at her reflection in the glass at the US Marshal's Service office door. Connor realized that the Durango assault had left fellow lawmen dead. She tried to look away from the USMS insignia, seeing herself in the glass behind it.

"Conscience getting to you, Agent Connor?" a grim, gravelly voice asked. The words jolted her from her momentary reflection and she turned to see the big blond guy who had arrived to watch over the kids.

"'Conscience'?" Connor repeated.

A device beeped from where it lay in the brawny man's hand.

"Voice match," Carl Lyons said. "Like I said, your conscience is bothering you."

Connor realized that with the words *voice match* they knew that she *had* used the FBI office telephone. They had her voice on tape talking with Los Lictors.

"Just to let you know…if you reach for your pistol, I will not be hindered by any bullshit about a man not being allowed to hit a woman," Lyons warned, his voice low, the creep of a barely contained demon struggling against its restraints scratching beneath the surface.

Connor looked down at the .40-caliber Glock on her hip, then up to the wide-shouldered brute standing in front of her. "If you're going to send me to jail, I'd rather die."

She started to lift her hand when a sudden flash of motion flickered across her vision. The next thing Connor realized, she was on her back, looking at ceiling tiles, her jaw hurting like hell. She tried to lift her head but couldn't. None of her mental commands were reaching her limbs but she could still feel the rest of her body, so she wasn't paralyzed with a broken neck.

Connor could even feel her Glock being pulled from her waist, complete with holster.

"You're not getting off that easy, traitor," Lyons growled. "We've got to talk."

Connor groaned as the big ex-cop hauled her to her feet and led her to the elevator.

CHAPTER SIXTEEN

Aaron Kurtzman rubbed his forehead and took a sip of coffee. Between running financial forensics on two senators *and* DEA Agent Aretha Connor, he'd delayed a rest break by about an hour.

Normally, common wisdom for staying mentally and physically healthy while working the computer was fifty minutes sitting, ten minutes standing or walking. Unfortunately a rifle bullet to the spine years ago had prevented his standing and walking. Closed eyes and rolling over to the coffee machine was his salvation.

The other members of the cyber team were deep into their work, and he was about ready to pull the foam dart gun from its holster on his wheelchair to bean a couple of them in the head as a signal to give their eyes and fingertips a rest.

Fortunately, he didn't have to start a war of spring-launched darts, as the others rolled back and away from their desks and workstations.

Hunt Wethers, the tall, lanky professor, picked up a sponge-like miniature basketball and lobbed it toward a full-size basketball rim and net hanging on the side of a post. Even with the advantage of the grapefruit-size missile, he took a couple of tries to bounce the brick into the net off of its backboard. Kurtzman chuckled, reaffirming that there was a reason why Wethers was heavily into mathematics and not sports.

On the other side of his cubicle, Akira Tokaido picked

up a stringless cutout of a guitar, slid on a second set of headphones and pressed Play. Starting slow, his fingers began moving faster and faster as he mimicked the heavy-metal masterworks of whomever he was listening to. His head began bobbing and within moments, his long black hair whipped back and forth in ebony arcs while his fingers danced and tapped on the neck of the silent guitar, his other hand moving as if to hammer out the energy put into the chords formed by the one on the neck. Kurtzman had to admit, it wasn't the kind of music or exercise that he'd be into, but Tokaido was not only clearing his mind, he was getting an intense cardio session as he transported himself to a stadium in front of a teeming crowd.

Carmen Delahunt merely walked across the computer room and joined Kurtzman at the coffee machine, stretching her long, curvy legs. She was in a knee-length skirt, and it hugged her thighs perfectly, and though she wore flat canvas shoes, her calves flexed as she moved forward on tiptoes.

"Keeping it all looking good for Gary?" Kurtzman asked.

Delahunt smirked as she poured herself a mugful from the pot that she and Price cleaned regularly. That one didn't sit, producing tar with the kind of caffeinated punch that the men were more into. A small fridge provided cool cream and a dash of sugar—not the synthetic cancer granules, but real cane sugar—went into the mug, as well. "The goal is to stretch your legs. I don't care too much for high heels, so I improvise."

Kurtzman slurped his black-tar caffeine, feeling it kick his brain like a rampant colt. "Any progress?"

"Well, the Montanahierro truck burning will slow down an investigation of who hijacked it for a long time, and no police cars or helicopters are closing in on either the arroyo where Phoenix set up camp or Rafe as he's under his sand suit," Delahunt said. "Running satellite surveillance and digging into the prison's records isn't going to be the hardest-hitting bit of this investigation."

"No, but if things run bad for you…" Kurtzman began when Delahunt's attention was drawn to a beeping of her cell phone. She pulled it out and looked at the screen.

"What is it?" Kurtzman asked.

"A couple of Mexican military helicopters are flying toward the airstrip by the prison," Delahunt answered.

The alert was one way that Delahunt could afford to step away from her station without leaving Encizo exposed and without backup. It was standard operating procedure during "wait and see" situations.

"Once the birds have landed, I'll run their registry, see who they're with," Delahunt added, taking a sip of her light and sweet coffee. "How about you?"

"Forensic accounting for senators," Kurtzman explained. "I'm kind of glad for the break with that DEA agent, at least. She has exactly one Cayman Islands account and no political action committees fronting money toward her."

"Hopefully, you can find some commonality, with all of that," Delahunt mused.

"And quickly. The sooner we find proof that we've got two senators in the back pocket of a cartel, even one sanctioned by a Mexican law enforcement agency, the better we destroy their credibility and their attacks on us," Kurtzman said.

"How about going back into the records of what the Fascist International and Unomundo had? After all, they had a huge presence in Mexico," Delahunt offered.

"The minute we saw the similarities, we began hard traces on all the old cover entities and old bank accounts of those groups. Wethers has been helping me with finding that old money and who it fell to," Kurtzman answered.

Delahunt sipped and thought. "And the endgame if we have to take down the two of them without drawing the heat of going full-on rogue and illegal?"

"We're on a fine line here, but we've dealt with bent politicians before," Kurtzman said. "And we've gotten them to pay for their crimes without raising a muzzle to one of their temples."

Delahunt nodded. "Especially with the dirt we can dig up that will turn their careers into quicksand."

Kurtzman put his mug back on the counter. "We've got evidence for all manner of convictions on both those bastards. But we need that link to the guys who are pulling their strings, so we can find out, once and for all, who is profiting from all of this mayhem."

"Once we put our minds to it, there's nothing that the four of us can't find," Delahunt confirmed.

"Yet," Kurtzman corrected her. "And the day that we fail, I worry."

Delahunt drank the last of her coffee. "Let's get back to work."

Kurtzman rolled toward his workstation. "I've already got some new ideas about where to dig."

"And who said these breaks are unproductive?" Delahunt mused aloud.

THE MEMBERS OF Phoenix Force assembled around their screens, looking at the overlay of storm drain tunnels riddling the ground beneath the surface of the Mexican prison.

"Found a path to the infirmary where they took Amanda." Gary Manning tapped his stylus on the touch screen of his PDA, where he'd traced a route for them. "We'll be under some buildings along the way, which means we'll be out of touch with the Farm."

"All the time we've had contact has been icing on the

cake," David McCarter returned. "We're big boys, and the Farm's given us every sliver of edge we've received so far. We'll carry the rest of this. Slow and steady, lads."

With that, McCarter took off in a crab-crouch walk, leading the way. *Slow and steady* was what the British Phoenix Force commander had said, but in practice they were scurrying through the tunnels with the speed and ability of rats. The hunched-over movement wasn't the most graceful seeming, but they had trained for maneuvering in such tight quarters. This was not their first run down a sewer pipe and, moving smoothly and carefully, they hoped not to make it their last.

The sound of helicopters arriving in the distance gave each of the four tunnel Phoenix Force warriors some pause, if only for the fact that it meant someone else was coming in, someone else who might have been in the form of Accion Obrar's very own action team.

The Mexican answer to Phoenix Force, or more appropriately Able Team, since this was an operation on their national soil, had been called in to bolster the security at sin Piedad. It could have merely been more prisoners in transport, or administrative personnel returning to headquarters, but Phoenix Force had not lasted this long without expecting and preparing for the worst, or underestimating the preparedness of their opposition. This prison was locked up tight, and only the most daring ploy had gotten them underneath the complex. The moments before their discovery were quickly dwindling, slithering away like mercury down a drain.

One misstep and guards backed by snipers and machine guns in armor-plated towers would rain down fire and death upon the four of them. The conspiracy that held Amanda Castillo prisoner had set up this situation to draw the team and the agency they worked for into this trap just as their attack dogs were working in congressional hearings to smear and destabilize the Justice Department and the team's boss, Hal Brognola.

With all the haste they made through the tunnels, they stopped to contact the Farm for updated information on the choppers and who might have gotten out of them.

"You know we're counting on Rafe to use the car to get us out of here," T. J. Hawkins said to McCarter through their com sets. "Were you not going to tell us about your plan to grab an aircraft?"

McCarter smirked. "Stealing one from the airstrip? I thought that would be a brilliant last-minute ace-in-the-hole example of my preparedness."

"I know this would be asking to spread us thinner, but why don't the three of us go for Amanda, and you grab us something to fly out of here?" Manning suggested. "Once we get into the infirmary with her, we'll need a hot extract."

McCarter nodded. "There are times when I wonder if Katz didn't make the wrong choice picking me to run this team."

The reference to the original commander of Phoenix Force made the two men fall silent.

"I'm usually the sniper and overwatch guy," Manning returned. "You are always in the thick of it, leading from the front. The team needs a leader, not a sage."

"Besides, with Gary as our Mr. Spock, you can go pretty far 'Kirking' it," Calvin James offered. "Just don't call me Bones."

McCarter smirked. "You know me. I can't make promises I know I can't keep."

James winked. "I'd tell you to be careful, but we don't need careful. We need a head-butting, cussin' Cockney ass kicker."

"Just like we need the Chicago Badass," McCarter added, returning the wink. "I'll hold off until you make the grab."

"That means when you hear gunshots…" Hawkins mused. "You getting this, Rafe?"

"Yes," Encizo said from his spot on overwatch. "Thanks for hooking me in to this conversation."

"We're all partners here," Hawkins replied. "Plus, you guys *are* the original three. I give your joint decision a lot of weight thanks to everything you've seen. Not that your opinion is any less valued, Cal."

"Enough chatter. Rafe, you're going to need to take out guard towers as soon as possible," McCarter said. "Enemy snipers will be a problem, but those towers could have the kind of firepower that will make flying deadly for us."

"No need to ask twice," Encizo responded. "Get to business."

The four men in the sewer put their hands in a stacked, silent goodbye-for-now.

ROSARIO BLANCANALES HAD been speaking to Aretha Connor, using all of his communications skills, his empathy, his diplomacy, the things that defined his nickname as "Politician." Though she was having some trouble enunciating with a minor fracture in her jaw, she'd melted initially from cold, terrified lady-spy reluctantly even responding to casual questions.

Able Team had spent far too many years in the field to know the difference between torture and disassembling the defenses of a reluctant prisoner.

"I mean, sure, Los Lictors aren't the kind who plays fair, but they're not doing anything we wouldn't do to keep maniacs off the streets," Connor stated. "Helping them didn't seem like it was a bad thing."

"Until you saw the kids brought in from the safe house." Blancanales's voice was warm, understanding and inviting. "Their parents…they're just so-called journalists. Muckrakers who do nothing but get in our way, then wonder why we can't keep kids from OD'ing on the streets."

Connor nodded so vehemently, Blancanales wondered if she were going into a seizure for a moment.

"Bastards every one of them," Connor murmured, surliness seeping from her words. She wasn't defensive anymore; she'd accepted Blancanales as "one of the good ones." He was concerned about her, had promised to do what he could to save her career and to get her back on the streets ending thugs.

In fact, despite the guy's graying hair, Connor felt offering *anything* and *everything* to the handsome, sultry-voiced mystery Fed wouldn't be a sacrifice at all. He had that classic Hollywood leading man appearance. Emphasis on *man*. No, he wasn't big, but neither was he tiny. He was just a hair under six feet, with sun-bronzed skin and not-quite-chiseled features or muscles, and Connor found herself wishing that he could have been an undercover case. Even when he'd shaken her hand, his grip had been firm and strong, holding a warmth that was silky on her skin.

Blancanales leaned in conspiratorially. "Listen, in this line of work, civilians just don't understand what we have to do. What we need to do to make things better."

Connor nodded her head, agreeing. "I still am not sure about ratting out that the kids are still in the building."

"How'd you guess?" Blancanales asked.

"The other guys you brought in," Connor responded, "hanging out in the basement."

She looked around. "Besides, none of you three strikes me as being good with children. I mean, that big bastard who laid me out?"

"Nah," Blancanales confirmed. "It's not as if we wanna hurt kids, but hanging around with them isn't our idea of fun."

"What is?" Connor asked, turning on the charm. "I mean, you guys have me dead to rights...so anything I can do to repay you for not screwing me over..."

Blancanales's eyebrow rose as she put emphasis on "screwing."

It couldn't hurt, Connor mused silently. Throw yourself on the mercy of the court and hope that his mercy ain't limp.

Blancanales leaned back. "We're gonna need to know more details about your contacts with the Durangos and Los Lictors here in the US."

Pronouncing the Spanish names allowed him to give a rolling treble to his tone. In English, he had an alluring voice, but when he went back to what must have been his native tongue, his words were like melted butter, smooth and tasty-sounding.

The gravity of his personality threatened to swallow her whole, even as he seemed to undress her with his sparkling eyes. Connor bit her full lower lip. "Anything you want," she said.

Blancanales slid over a yellow legal pad and she began writing down names and numbers. "A lot of these might be burners. If they even have a hint that you made me..."

"For them to do that, they'd need eyes inside the building, and as far as I know, you're the only one, right?" Blancanales offered.

Connor looked around. "Well..."

"Someone else?" Blancanales asked.

"It does sound like they've got more than just me," Connor responded. "And, naturally, they would want to keep us in the dark about each other."

"Do you have any hints?" Blancanales asked. "Because, if we have that one...well, we only need one sacrificial lamb for internal affairs to slaughter."

Connor smiled. "Why do you think I'm even saying

something? I didn't think that I'd be able to stay off the radar forever."

Blancanales prodded. "So you did a little digging?"

Connor did her best to contain her excitement. "Why do you think I used the telephone I did?"

"Really?" Blancanales asked. He accepted the legal pad back, complete with names and burner cell numbers.

"I'm glad he wasn't around when your guy busted me," Connor mused. "I'd hate for you to lose your lead…"

"Or for you to be fingered by the Durangos as the one who wrecked their operation." Blancanales nodded, as if they had been friends all of their lives.

Connor smiled at him. "Thank you for understanding."

Blancanales took her hand in both of his. His touch was electric and soothing all at once. His grasp was one of comfort, and maybe a little something more. "You are certain Baxter is the other leak?"

"I'd bet my life on it," Connor returned.

The door was suddenly kick-slammed open. It was the blond guy, his eyes burning with cold blue murder. Connor's spine tingled at the sight of the dent he'd kicked into the door panel. These doors were made of steel, she knew, and the fact that he'd done some damage to it was a sign that she was in the line of fire of a muscular maniac.

"You are betting your life on it!"

His bestial bellow only drove home his sheer power and menace.

Connor's mind flashed to the instances of "good cop, bad cop," but Blancanales was too into her, too damned decent and affectionate to be the good cop. Likewise, she doubted that any supervisor would put up with a "bad cop" that smashed locks and damaged doors in displays of rage. The look in this man's eyes was a weapon, a searing beam of hatred that made her skin want to sizzle under it. Connor was suddenly the ant under the magnifying glass.

"Listen. It's Baxter. It's Baxter for sure!" Connor begged, "Don't let him hurt me…"

Lyons scowled, trembling with rage, his big fists clenched, each one the size of a ham. The six-foot brute didn't have a gun in his holster, a safety precaution to keep cops and Feds from getting shot with their own pistols, but no one could disarm the blond man-monster of those crushing weapons. Another two men rushed in, grabbing at his corded arms, holding him back.

"Please…believe me," Connor whimpered. Tears flushed her eyes in a way that she never thought would come. She'd always considered women who cried out of fear to be something of an embarrassment of thousands of years of sexual equality. And now here she was, not just her eyes but her nostrils full and leaking down her face. She grabbed Blancanales so hard, her nails dug into his forearm. She could feel the hard muscles' strength in the limb, as well as see the lifetime of scars crisscrossed into his skin.

Blancanales's warmth disappeared. She didn't see what he did to his face, but those eyes were no longer filled with passion and promises of seduction. They were the empty dullness of a predator sizing up a carcass on the plains, nose wrinkled in disdain for a pitiful offering.

At the same moment the lion himself calmed. All of that unfettered rage boiling within him drained, the blond berserker standing as if he'd walked into the room and forgotten what he'd entered for.

"Who are you people?" Connor asked.

Blancanales pulled his arm out of her clutches. "We're the people you should never have messed with."

With that, the two men, and the other pair, turned and left her alone in the interview room.

She looked down at the table. The legal pad was still there.

You're not going to jail. But anyone who survives our visit to Durango will know that. Baxter's not going to jail, either. We knew about him already, and he knew who you were, too. And no one is going to believe you about mysterious super-Feds who break the rules. You're laundry hanging on the line.

Her Glock was atop the legal pad.

Basically, run!

Connor shuddered. These guys weren't going to execute her, but rather leave her out in the wilderness, branded a traitor. She only had one thing to protect her, the handgun in front of her.

And she had nowhere safe to go.

CHAPTER SEVENTEEN

As a veteran of the Navy SEALs and San Francisco SWAT, stacking up with trusted brother warriors at his back before entering a heavily defended enemy building wouldn't have been new even if this was Calvin James's first mission with Phoenix Force. Instead, the black hard case born in Chicago had been with the top secret Stony Man action team since their fourteenth major mission.

With all of that experience, his adrenaline still kicked it up a notch, his heartbeat throbbing through his veins and against his brain, but not so hard and loud that it was a distraction. Excitement or fear, whichever was the cause of this biochemical rush, it still held the same final result. His senses were now sharper, his reflexes were faster, his mind keener.

A gentle push, after Gary Manning's det cord burned away the lock, had allowed them to lift the lid into the basement of the infirmary. The only sound that would have given them away was the hiss of the putty-like chemical sizzling as it detonated along its entire length, destroying the locking mechanism that prevented them from slipping through the unprotected underbelly of the infirmary.

Even though it didn't seem as if there were any alarms attached to the drain-tunnel access lid, T. J. Hawkins worked painstakingly with the CPDA sensors, looking for wired or wireless signals running through the metal. Now, with the slight nudge of the manhole cover, he ran a probe up through the slight crack. It was an antenna that would pick up infrared or ultrasound motion detectors. There were no such invisible electric eyes watching this basement, so with a surge, Manning hefted the manhole cover and moved it aside. James gave Hawkins a lift then slithered up into the basement himself. Hawkins and James both reached down and hauled Manning up finally.

All three deployed their machine pistols as James took the lead, heading up the steps. He paused at the door leading into the building proper, listening for sounds of people walking beyond. Once again, the three members of Phoenix Force were limited in their ability to respond. If there were nothing but nurses and doctors beyond, then they wouldn't be able to use their guns.

Hawkins, however, had a stubby M203 loaded with a "sting ball" grenade, part of the gear that Phoenix Force had brought with them across the border. The sting balls were rubber, yielding projectiles launched as a form of less-than-lethal shrapnel by a light explosive charge. There was the possibility that the 40 mm shell could cause a fatality, but at least this was an effort to minimize the danger to noncombatants. The only trouble with it was that it would be loud.

Once the launcher was brought into play, any further pretense of stealth was gone.

Manning had a much less noisy option: a canister of tear gas. When it went off, it actually vomited clouds of burning chemical smoke.

Of course, that could lead to panic.

Unfortunately, there was very little that James could do to minimize the harm to security guards who responded to their intrusion. If they had guns and came in shooting, he and the others would have to respond with deadly force in all but the most fortuitous of circumstances. He would have liked it better if they could have blasted their way through the prisoners spending their time here as if they were at a five-star hotel. At least those were known guilty criminals who had paid off the authorities to get out of hard jail time.

Here, however, there would always be that shadow of doubt as to whether the men they would be forced to kill were unfortunates merely doing their civic duty or were in the knowing employ of a bloodthirsty, cocaine-profiteering agency.

No movement on the other side of the door panel allowed James to open it and step into the hallway, peering back and forth. "Clear."

Hawkins and Manning were hot on his heels.

"This place seems too damn quiet for a hospital," James said into his throat mike.

Manning and Hawkins both nodded in quiet agreement. Though they weren't aware of the exact pace of activity in this facility, they had been around enough hospitals to know that things were far too calm and silent.

"It could be a trap." Manning voiced his point over their com sets. "T.J., see if—"

"It looks like we're being jammed all around." Hawkins cut him off. "PDA's gone dead. They're not hijacking our line, but they're scrambling all signals in or out. Hands-free are spitting static, so that means Rafe and David are on their own, too."

"This is where she was brought," James said. "Until they let the trap jaws snap on us, let's look for Amanda."

"We can take a page from Carl's book, though," Hawkins interjected, referring to the leader of Able Team. "When we're surrounded, we finally know which way we can shoot."

James paused, distracted by a thought. He moved back toward the stairway door to the basement.

"What's wrong?"

"Who's to say that this is a trap?" James asked. "For all we know, they're still waiting for us to show up."

"Not with the cops racing after the truck. Encizo said he was going to play the cooperative traveler," Manning returned.

"Hear that from the basement?" James seemingly changed the subject.

Manning could hear the throb of turbines. "Why would they have all the air pumping in the basement? Not on the roof like any other hospital?"

"Because what's one thing that hospitals have that would be beneficial for a meth-cooking super lab?" James continued to press.

"Negative air pressure in the rooms," Manning returned. "We don't smell anything. Not even standard medicine or food for patients."

"The air is being scrubbed and filtered, probably using the sand or dirt beneath the building as part of the detoxification process," James explained. "Another problem. If this place is being used to cook, we've got to watch what we're doing if and when we shoot."

"We've hit enough meth labs to know what a spark can do. But we've also tested the MP-7s and their suppressors. They won't ignite the flammables in the air," Manning added.

Hawkins looked at his Combat PDA. "So it's not a jamming device. All of the construction material designed to contain a meth lab fire is what's blocking our signals. All right, I'm heading toward the front door ASAP to keep the others from panicking."

"Good idea," Manning noted. "Move, and keep your head on a swivel. We're going to find Amanda."

Hawkins put his forefinger to his brow in a tight, short salute and then headed out.

"I'll lead," James offered, taking point as they moved through the corridors.

Now James was feeling much less apprehensive about encountering people in this building. Not when this was a meth-cooking facility that happened to have had one of its rooms converted to infirmary purposes. As it was also running in full operation with the vents and filters, that meant that there was product cooking in the building.

That would limit the kind of response the enemy would bring to bear. They'd lose thousands, maybe even millions, of dollars by opening fire on the lab complex, not to mention the costs of equipment and construction. Even with this knowledge, James and Manning were cautious as they looked through windows in doors into labs, avoiding the attention of those within. Only about one in three of the laboratories were staffed as they made their way through. Yet, so far, none was being used for anything other than mixing and cooking the chemical poisons that made methamphetamine.

"Once we get Amanda, we're going to have to level this place," James mused softly. "Got something for that?"

"If we secure her, I can get back to the basement and introduce a spark to the ventilation system," Manning replied.

James had lost members of his family to the ravages of heroin, but he held a special amount of animosity for all manner of drug labs. These were the kitchens in which millions of dreams were destroyed, crushed by addiction-fed greed. Durango had started out with Mexican heroin, but had graduated as the tastes of the junkies to the north evolved into cocaine and then now into meth, and never letting the other markets and their victims fall into obsolescence.

"No if…" James said, peering through one final doorway. "Found her. I'll keep guard here. You run into T.J., send him up here."

Manning peered through the glass. He gave a soft clap to James's shoulder, then turned and returned the way they had come.

Amanda lay on a bed in the corner, textured windows obscuring the world outside but allowing plenty of light into the room. Closer to James, seated around a table, were three guards who were playing cards. It might have been a cliché, but considering that their charge was an unconscious, dehydrated woman with very little strength, they needed something to occupy their attention. They hadn't noticed the former SEAL's observation of them via a small hand mirror.

James scanned around, because if there were three who were not alert, that meant there was someone else who was on their toes. He spotted a shape in a chair next to Amanda Castillo, but with a partially drawn curtain, James couldn't quite be certain if it was a man with a rifle in his lap or simply the rifle of a man laid across the arms of a bedside chair.

Looking back down the corridor, he knew that impatience was not the best of strategies, but time was of the essence. On a whim, he keyed his throat mike. "T.J.?"

"I read ya, hoss," Hawkins returned. "Chompin' at the bit?"

"Yeah," James answered. "There're four guards in her room. I shouldn't feel itchy…"

"But we've got two brothers out there, their asses hanging in the wind," Hawkins replied. "Almost to you."

James continued, as low in profile as possible, to assess where each of the men was positioned in the room. He then took a marker and scribbled out the positions on the hand mirror to show to Hawkins.

The Texan scrambled down the hall and paused, letting James show him the map and layout of the room. Using hand signals, they determined that the taller James would go high, while Hawkins would sweep in low. The two of them had done this thousands of times in practice and had also accomplished this kind of hit-and-clear in reality. That itch for action was James's adrenaline surge and he didn't want it to fade. However, the moment that Hawkins reached for the doorknob, James's mind and body reached a state of calm.

James's old martial arts instructor, and sometime ninja ally of Phoenix Force, John Trent, had called it the state of Zen awareness. Trent described it as an immersion in the moment when the mind was not focused on any one thing, but aware of all the various eddies and currents of the universe, and when the mind was that unfettered by distraction, the body followed in smooth, swift response.

Hawkins had the door open and James was through and moving toward the curtain, clearing in front of Hawkins as he stayed put and sniped from the jamb. The Texan's MP-7 stuttered suppressed 4.6 mm rounds at high velocity, and his trained trigger kept the bursts short. Through the can on his SMG, the crackle of the tribursts sounded like polite applause and Hawkins had downed two of the cardplayers before the third even realized they were under attack.

James, on the other hand, surged toward the curtain, slashing it open with one outstretched arm, the stock of the machine pistol wedged tightly between his elbow and ribs. Even as the curtain fluttered and he saw that it was merely an assault rifle laid across the arms of a chair, the adrenaline-charged awareness of the Chicago badass picked up movement to his right.

With lightning speed, James whirled to face the on-rushing foe, hands already reached out, snagging the extra length of suppressor hanging off the end of the Phoenix Force warrior's machine pistol. This wasn't a cartel soldier; this was a professional soldier who had only allowed himself a moment away from his weapon. James could already feel the enemy gaining leverage on the MP-7, despite his grasp.

Instead of wrestling for control of the weapon, potentially riddling Amanda Castillo with lead, he released the chatterbox. With his hand full of curtain, James pulled hard, wrapping the cloth around his foe's head. It was the only other weapon immediately available, and now it was blinding and snagging on the former Mexican special operations soldier. Now the guard was torn between continuing to control James's MP-7 and wrestling with the shroud covering his eyes.

As his enemy was stuck in the midst of those decisions, Calvin James had a window of opportunity. He kicked the Mexican hard, knee plunging between his legs. James's fiberglass knee guard mashed the sentry's testicles, folding the Mexican down. The Chicagoan followed up with a knuckle punch into the hollow of the soldier's throat. James could feel the rigid windpipe and larynx crunch under the impact.

The machine pistol was now hanging free on James's sling; he took a step back, orienting, aiming and firing. The bullets were a quick end to the enemy trooper's life, if he wasn't already dying from a crushed trachea. A burst went into his chest, then into the curtain-wrapped head, turning the white, sterile-seeming cloth deep red.

Hawkins had finished off the third of the cardplayers with a final burst only a moment before that head shot, and he entered the room. He closed the door, and the two Phoenix pros waited to hear the sound of alarms. Their machine pistols were silenced, but that didn't mean that they hadn't produced noise. The impulse of gunfire was changed from loud banging to the rustle of clapping.

Those who'd know the sound would be aware of something going wrong.

"Gary? Can you read us?" Hawkins whispered softly into his throat mike.

"Yes," the Canadian responded.

"Any alarms going off?" Hawkins returned. "Any sign of guards moving around?"

"Nothing audible from the first floor. Why?" Manning asked.

Hawkins let a breath out. "We just secured Amanda Castillo. Four guards down."

"I've got two of the air filtration units set to blow on a timer," Manning advised. "We've got fifteen minutes to move."

James, listening in on the conversation, looked over the unconscious woman. Her pulse was strong, and there was an IV replacing her lost hydration with saline solution. He brought down the bag and used cloth tape to fasten it to her upper arm. It was standard saline solution, no drugs in it, but he noticed a small vial of sedative and a spare needle. That was what had kept her asleep during the sudden flurry of activity that had lasted only fifteen seconds, if that.

"We radio McCarter when we reach the roof access door," James said. "The last thing we need is to alert guard tower snipers that we're in here."

"No movement yet. I'm going to confirm where the roof access is," Hawkins noted. "Can you handle her?"

James nodded. "I'm just going over her vitals. Don't take too long or draw any attention."

Hawkins slid into the corridor. Reminders weren't a problem for him. Humans were fallible creatures, even the most highly skilled and constantly trained of special operations troopers.

Besides, it was better than just saying "be careful."

James checked to make certain that nothing was broken or damaged on the woman. She'd taken a beating on the way here; that much was evident in the bruises covering her, and she was half-naked. Her skin looked baked from being left too long in the sun, and the IV saline had only just rehydrated her so that her lips weren't cracked anymore. He opened one of her eyes, and there was no sign of head trauma.

"Can you wake up, Amanda?" James asked softly.

Her lips moved lazily, trying to form words. It was the sedative at work. James was tempted to bring her around with a countering agent to the injection, but given the abuse she'd been subject to, and the potential damage she'd incur on the trip out of this place, he decided to leave her out of it. He wrapped her in the bedsheet then scooped her gently into his arms, testing her weight. She was a slender, petite woman, so he didn't have an issue with carrying her.

Of course, this would mean his hands were full and he wouldn't be able to shoot to defend them.

Gary Manning was at the door and James motioned with his head. The Canadian entered.

"They're still busy in the various labs, cooking," Manning stated. "With the protective gear, and the kind of seals on each of the rooms, it's not a wonder that they didn't hear you take these men down."

"She's sedated," James said. "And I don't think we should wake her."

"Good plan. I'll carry her," Manning offered.

"Really?" James asked. "She's not that heavy."

"Then it'll be the easiest mule work I've ever done," Manning returned. "Besides, we might need you to tend to her, and you can't hold and nurse her at the same time."

James nodded. "Good point."

Hawkins was back. He opened the door and waved to

his two partners. "I stepped outside and called David and Rafe. The boss is in motion and Rafe's ready to shoot anyone shooting at us."

"What are we waiting for?" James asked, handing Amanda Castillo off to Manning.

Hawkins took his M203 stand-alone launcher from his harness and gave it to James. "To put this in the hands of the guy who can do the most damage with it."

James accepted the bandolier of 40 mm shells that came with it.

Hawkins picked up the Lictor enforcer's assault rifle. "We're going to need more range than the MP-7 can handle."

"Fair plan," James said. "We came in and needed silence, but the minute David takes off with the helicopter, we're not going to need quiet and close quarters."

The Phoenix warriors moved into the hallway and, with each step, they were closer to escape, but they also knew that they were closer to a firefight when the sin Piedad staff discovered their presence.

And when that happened, and Los Lictors went head-to-head with Phoenix Force, there wouldn't be the element of surprise and aggression aiding the Stony Man operators.

CHAPTER EIGHTEEN

"Package secure" were the words that spurred David Mc-Carter forward and the Briton exploded into action.

For the past couple of minutes Phoenix Force's commander and pilot had slithered through the runoff tunnels to get to the airstrip. He'd lost contact with his three partners the moment they'd entered the infirmary building, but that was not due to a communications shutdown, as Hawkins explained when he'd called from the doorway of the building. The infirmary was more correctly identified as a meth-cooking laboratory, a series of rooms spread across several floors. That explained the uncommonly flat and unadorned roof of the so-called infirmary, given the venting systems had been placed in the basement.

With air scrubbers on top of the building, the reek of the cooking would be noticeable to anyone on the premises. Pumping the chemical garbage into the ground, however, after processing it through air cleaners, provided enough redundancy to maintain the small infirmary as just that and not a meth super lab.

So far, McCarter had only needed to bring down one guard, and he'd done that with swiftness and a sleeper hold. To make certain that nothing came back to bite him on the ass, the Phoenix pro had gagged the man and bound his wrists and ankles. A shove out of sight and there was little chance that he'd have killed an innocent Mexican government employee, but also would not be betrayed by the discovery of a corpse.

However, now the Briton could see that there was a pair of men who wore the insignia of the enforcers of both the Caballeros de Durango Cartel and Accion Obrar—Los Lictors.

They were armed and alert. Only McCarter's hiding spot allowed him an ability to observe them and stay out of their lines of sight. When Hawkins announced the package had been secured, the SAS veteran and Olympic pistol champ moved swiftly. He utilized the MP-7 with razor-sharp precision, a skill earned in countless hours of shooting and training, both with this machine pistol and its stylistic ancestor, the Ingram MAC-10.

A flash of movement was all that one of the helicopter guards noticed out of the corner of his eye before a 3-round burst of high-velocity armor-piercing lead cored through his head. Gore and brain matter vomited out the far side of his skull as 4.6 mm steel-jacketed rounds defeated bone on both sides of his head. As the MP-7's round was designed to punch through modern combat helmets, the Lictor's head was a ripe melon to be crushed open.

The cartel commando's partner looked up in shock and horror as the first man toppled, missing major chunks of his skull. His reflexes were good enough that he brought his rifle up. He was looking directly at McCarter when the Briton hammered him into oblivion with a second sound-suppressed salvo of machine pistol fire. The Lictor gunman collapsed in a boneless heap, most of his facial features being imploded where McCarter put his bullets.

The Briton crossed the distance to the helicopter with a few strides of his long legs, and whereas inside the infirmary-lab no alerts were raised, a cry of recognition rose from other members of the Lictors contingent. McCarter's machine pistol might have been suppressed, but the Mexican former Special Forces commandos knew the sound of such a weapon. Fortunately, the nature of the suppressor disguised the sound so that it was difficult for them to figure out where those shots had came from, and the bodies of the dead guards were hidden by the bulk of the teardrop-shaped MD-600 NOTAR.

Of course, running through the power-up procedure for the helicopter was going to make it perfectly clear just where the disturbance had came from.

Luckily, as the bird was to be launched on a standby basis, the machine was mostly warmed up. McCarter hit the last of the controls to get the helicopter's engine fired up. The rotors began their slow acceleration to form the lift surface that enabled it to fly. McCarter looked out of the cockpit and saw that a group of the gunmen had come out into the open to find their aircraft was about to be taken.

There was a moment of pause for the group. They had weapons with them and could easily have opened fire on the chopper, but this was not an enemy aircraft. It was their own vehicle. Riddling it with bullets would mean losing some of their transportation and air support, especially since the helicopter was equipped with side-mounted rocket launchers.

That brief instance of reluctance gave McCarter the time to build up the rpm's for the helicopter. The bird popped up a few feet and, with a tap of the stick, McCarter swung the nose of the bulbous gunship toward the men. With two barrels, each loaded with twelve high-velocity artillery rockets, aimed at them, Los Lictors realized that they were stuck out in the open. McCarter taped the trigger and a 2.75-inch missile flared from the side launcher, skimming only inches above the ground.

The Mexican enforcers were already scrambling before the rocket launch, and now several of them threw themselves to the ground to avoid the detonation of nearly a kilogram of high explosives. The rocket finally struck the ground, triggering the warhead, but it was fifty yards past the clot of gunmen. Even so, the thunderbolt shook the ground, hurling chunks of asphalt and concrete skyward.

The blast wave didn't produce shrapnel that flew far enough to do more than pester the direct-action forces. McCarter was tempted to launch a second rocket, but there was movement and activity elsewhere. A guard tower off to one side let hatches drop open, the muzzles of machine guns probing outward.

"Rafe, anytime now," McCarter murmured into his com set. Twisting the MD-600N around and loosing artillery rockets against the towers would take much too long. By the time he was able to start shooting, the enemy machine guns, weapons throwing big and heavy bullets designed to tear through aircraft, would have perforated the helicopter and McCarter dozens of times over.

Each moment that he didn't feel the rocking impact of an enemy bullet was icing on the cake as he pulled the chopper into a hard climb, swinging it toward the infirmary.

A lanky figure exited from the roof access. McCarter had seen that silhouette enough times to recognize Calvin James even at this distance. There was the flash of a muzzle in the man's hands and the guard tower festooned with machine gun barrels suddenly found itself rocked by a blast. The Phoenix Force commander grinned, knowing exactly what happened.

Rather than potentially killing innocent prison guards, James had defused the nest of heavy weapons with a flashbang grenade. The hammer blow of the high-pressure round, especially against the armored confined space of the tower, staggered the men inside. It was akin to ringing a cloister bell with their heads within. The protective slits, which allowed mobility and aiming with the machine guns, might have been hard to slip bullets through, but the power of the flash-bang didn't need a direct impact;

it dealt with a crush of sound and overpressure. To those forces, even the smallest crack ajar was a wide-open highway to travel through.

McCarter got the MD-600N to rooftop level and other guard towers were working their sniper deployments. Nothing came from the next closest tower, however.

"Cover fire supplied, as per your request," Encizo relayed through McCarter's earbud. "Some .50-caliber armor-piercing is letting the towers know that they are not safe, even in their metal turrets."

"You are a swarthy little angel, Rafe," McCarter responded. He couldn't hear the sound of Encizo's Barrett through his hearing protection or over the throb of the helicopter's engine and rotor slap, but as long as no one thought to shoot at him, it meant that the stocky Cuban was laying down plenty of high-velocity, long-range hate. He may not have hit anyone inside those turrets, but the effect of those big rounds would be felt and keep the enemy guns from knocking him out of the sky.

The light-utility chopper began taking hits from the ground. Los Lictors, having nearly been caught on the receiving end of their own air support's weaponry, decided that discretion was the better part of saving money on replacing their fleet of helicopters. So far, it was handguns and 5.56 mm rifles, none of which was up to the task of piercing the fuselage of the McDonnell Douglas 600N, but it would only be a matter of moments before heavier weapons were brought to bear.

"Cal!"

"I hear them," James responded. "T.J. has a message for 'em, too."

"A rat-tat-tat rap," Hawkins added.

Another figure was visible atop the super lab, and the muzzle-flash of an assault rifle flickered in his hands. At 800 rounds per minute, the average 30-round magazine for an AR-15 would only last a few seconds, but Hawkins was not the kind of man to blaze from the hip on full-auto. The Texan had his weapon shouldered, and he was firing on semiauto, using the optics mounted on the top rail to acquire individual targets and kill or wound them with a single shot before turning his attention to another. The speed at which he was sweeping Los Lictors made it merely look as if he was firing on automatic.

No, Hawkins wasn't going to give Gary Manning a run for his money in terms of sniping, but with targets only a few hundred feet away, standing in the open and their attention fixed on McCarter and his helicopter, he was reaping a whirlwind of death among the enforcers.

James had planted another 40 mm flash-bang in proximity to a guard turret and, having scrambled the group, fed the M203 with another round, rushing to join Hawkins in his work against the Lictors.

This time, it wasn't less-lethal grenades that the Chicago badass brought to bear. These 40 mm rounds, thrown right into the laps of the Durango enforcers, were high-explosive fragmentation bombs, and when the first one detonated amid a clot of the riflemen, their bodies were shredded asunder. McCarter could no more hear the screams of the men down below as their lives were wrenched from their carcasses than he could have heard even the heaviest of gunfire rattling across the prison complex, but it didn't matter. For years, McCarter had counted on James's expert hand and steady aim with the M203 to even the odds against overwhelming opposition. In the Chicagoan's hands, the grenade launcher was precision artillery.

McCarter flared out with the MD-600N, swinging it low over the roof of the infirmary. With a bump, he had the chopper down and idling. He saw Gary Manning with a limp form in his brawny arms, running forward. McCarter continued scanning for threats, knowing that it was

Amanda Castillo he carried. The purpose of their covert invasion of Mexico was finished.

"All aboard!" McCarter called out over his throat mike. "Next stop, home!"

"I don't think this is the 500C, which has the 375-mile operational range," Manning said, putting Amanda into the seat in the back of the cabin.

"No, it's the 600N, with about 411 miles, but I don't think we've got enough fuel for more than 220 to 250 miles in it right now," McCarter countered. "But we've got room for all of us inside."

"Hear that? Room for all of you!" McCarter shouted to Hawkins and James. The former Ranger and the ex-SEAL had switched to their MP-7 machine pistols, blazing away after removing the suppressors on the little chatterboxes. He watched Hawkins drop a 40-round curved magazine to the ground and load in another one.

"Let's not stick around!" he prompted.

"Not sticking around," James answered, turning to jog back to the chopper. Hawkins paused, reluctant to break off the engagement, but he was right on his partner's heels. "Just wanted to give them something to remember us by."

"Till now, I never was one for long g'byes," Hawkins drawled.

"It's a wonderful sentiment, but Rafe's feelin' lonely," McCarter replied as the last two Farm operatives inside the compound climbed into the cabin.

With a push of the throttle, McCarter pulled up at a full ten meters a second, clearing into the sky above El Calabozo sin Piedad.

Building altitude, he was beyond the range of conventional small arms. All while Encizo continued to make certain that the heavier gunners in the guard towers were discouraged. McCarter swung around to stay out of the Cuban's line of fire. He was concerned that the machine-gun firepower in the guard towers could be the same armor-piercing lead Encizo was putting out. A single .50 BMG round could burst the bubble-shaped windscreen of the MD-600N and kill him, either fired from the Cuban's Barrett or the Mexican prison's own Browning Fifties.

That was when the infirmary behind them went to pieces in a vomitus blossom of fire and hurtling debris. The shock wave was more than sufficient to rattle McCarter on the stick, meaning that whatever chemical badness was inside the super meth lab had ignited with near MOAB force.

"Looks like the mother-of-all-bombs cook pot boiled over," Manning grunted as he held on to the rear bench and the slumbering Amanda Castillo.

McCarter checked the distance; they were five hundred yards from ground zero. Looking back, he noticed that the cloud of debris had risen into the air like a plump mushroom, while the complex at ground level was choked with dust. El Calabozo sin Piedad was now in an intense fog; no one on the ground or even as high as the guard towers was able to see more than a few inches in front of their faces thanks to the churned detritus. With those below thoroughly shaken by the shock wave and now blinded, McCarter and Phoenix Force were free of enemy fire for at least a minute.

The helicopter landed beside Rafael Encizo, who ditched the gillie cape and the Barrett rifle, most of its ammunition expended anyway. Another short hop and the team loaded a supply of spare gasoline snagged on their way from the border at Nogales. Some of it was poured directly into the tank while the rest was packed in storage.

Phoenix Force worked as a bucket brigade on the refueling, knowing that 411 miles would be a long stretch.

The fuel canisters, however, would help. McCarter had little intention of impeding Amanda Castillo's reunion with her children if he could help it. The team had fought too hard to allow any delays. They'd left a mark on Accion Obrar and Los Lictors that would be hard for them to ignore. Even with that knowledge, there was still the sore thumb of that Durango cartel-owned prison sitting behind them.

"We're coming back," McCarter said as he throttled up in speed. He was tempted to go all-out, but he didn't want to overload the engines and waste more fuel than he had to. Besides, cruising at 155 miles per hour, they'd reach the border soon enough. "And we're closing down the prison and the agency."

Encizo, who'd climbed into the seat beside McCarter, nodded in grim agreement. "I've been watching them abuse those poor bastards in the prison yard. All while true sacks of murderous shit watch them and gloat. We definitely need to clean house."

"With the hell we dumped on them, there's a good possibility that they'll have to dig into some of those primping prima donnas for extra security," Hawkins interjected. "I'd love that instead of worrying about who might be just an office worker or an honest cop in a crappy position."

"We won't leave this half-done," McCarter vowed. "In fact, I'm going to make a call home. It'll take four hours to get to Nogales…"

Even as he said this, he looked in the mirror, catching sight of Amanda Castillo, battered, wrapped in a bedsheet, delirious and receiving fluids from an IV.

He hoped that when they got back to America, Lyons and the others would have made certain her children were safe and ready to receive their mother.

"T.J., call Barb. We're not giving them even half a day to recover from this attack."

CARL LYONS HEARD the gunfire erupt inside the locker room. The building had almost totally been emptied by now, reg-

ular Feds confined to their desks and nonessential support
staff sent home for an "institution day." He walked calmly
through the hallways toward the ready room and saw two
figures sprawled on the floor. One was Aretha Connor,
clutching her stomach as one hand was painted shiny crimson by bubbling blood, the other filled with a smoking
Glock pistol. The other was FBI Agent—and traitor—Fran-
cis Baxter, part of his head chewed out by the impact of a
.40-caliber slug on his right cheek.

"We told you to run," Lyons said to Connor, who was
slumped against the wall. The woman glanced up at him,
but it appeared the only thing she had enough strength or
blood pressure for was to look at something. "Tried," she
rasped. She blinked then her eyes went down to the Glock
in her hand. "Him…"

Lyons plucked the pistol easily from her grasp.

From the brightness of the blood that Connor was barely
able to stem from her belly, Lyons could tell that she'd
been struck in the aorta, and with that massive blood ves-
sel ruptured by Baxter's bullet, her life span could now be
measured in seconds.

"Stopped hurtin'," Connor burbled. Blood flecked on
her lips as she looked up at Lyons. "Sorry."

"We'll tell your family that you died stopping a traitor," Lyons promised.

Her lips twitched, as if she was about to smile, but then
the light and life emptied from her gaze.

That last, final breath was all too familiar to Lyons, and
he lowered his head. He didn't think that he'd have been
so upset at her demise, not when she was feeding intel to
the men trying to murder three children, but then, she'd
only been a victim of a vigilante mind-set, one not so different from his own when he was in the LAPD or FBI,
giving Mack Bolan assistance when he could.

Then again, the Executioner had never allowed children to become targets in the crossfire.

That reality allowed the Ironman to stand up and dismiss the corpse on the floor of the locker room.

He got on the radio to Blancanales. "Both snitches are dead. Time to send the rest of our Feds home. Do not pass go —or the locker room. Do not collect two hundred dollars."

"They're not going to like that," Blancanales returned.

"This is the sound of me not giving a damn," Lyons grumbled. "Get them out of this building. I want this place clear of anyone except us and the blacksuits."

"And hope that they take the bait," Blancanales concluded.

"Damn straight. I'm getting sick of babysitting," Lyons growled. "We're getting our death squad on, gang."

CHAPTER NINETEEN

Hector Moran looked over the wreckage wrought by the invasion of the mystery commandos. He was aware that there was a group associated with the Stony Man Farm in the Blue Ridge Mountains that had interfered with the plans of creating a cleansed economic superpower from a pure nation succored by pure European blood and a permanent slave caste of the brown-skinned. It had come close to enacting those changes, trying to flush South America and North America of its muddy-blooded influences, but at seemingly every corner, they were stymied.

The meth factory was a crater, not a single stone left standing. Whoever they were, they knew enough of chemicals and of demolitions to transform the entire building into a bomb, one that covered the escape of a helicopter with his cousin. Moran thought about losing touch with that sweet blonde creature cradled in the belly of the aircraft, hurtling away from El Calabozo sin Piedad.

"Ah, Amanda, it's a shame I won't get to make you a part of the bloodline of our grand Mexican Reich," he said aloud.

Colonel Mendoza appeared through the dusty fog still settling in the wake of the lab's atomization. Mendoza was the founder of Los Lictors, members of Mexico's elite special forces who'd decided to become the officers, the magistrates, of this land.

"Sir," Mendoza said. No salute. He'd been military, but now was no longer. Not when he received paychecks from both Accion Obrar and the Caballeros de Durango Cartel. Maybe the salute wasn't warranted because Moran himself was not *currently* military, but it was more likely that things were far too hectic at the moment.

"What's the damage?" Moran asked.

Mendoza frowned. "Twenty of my men are dead. Gunned down and blown to hell by grenades."

Moran sighed. "I didn't intend to throw them away like that. They were here to make it harder for the Americans to get in here, and to break out."

"I know what the plan was," Mendoza told him. "But we were not expecting them in this manner. I mean, we anticipated that they might have entered via one of the delivery trucks, but they disappeared immediately."

Moran nodded. "Probably found their way into the utility tunnels underneath the prison."

"We figured that after the fact," Mendoza clarified. "It did us little good. I had hoped that we could have waylaid the truck and taken them out while they were all trapped in the container."

"No good plan ever survives enemy action," Moran mused.

Mendoza looked at the crater. "I had one man in there, backing up some of the cartel thugs who were sitting with Castillo. Apparently the Americans struck so fast, he didn't have the opportunity to even raise the alarm. And to add insult to injury, it looks as if my other soldiers were attacked with his assault rifle."

Moran kicked a chunk of rubble the size of a golf ball into the explosively excavated remnants of the meth lab's foundation. It took a moment for the rock to impact and the sound to echo back to his ears. "You want a second crack at them?"

"With every fiber of my being," Mendoza returned.

"Call in everything you've got in the region," Moran

said. "They saw what we have here, who we have here. And they saw our guests, the ones sitting poolside, and the ones doing the Auschwitz march. They'll want another piece of us."

"What about our crew in Yuma?" Mendoza asked.

"No. I want them to level that building. I want the world to see what happens when they mess with true warriors," Moran said. "They're gonna wish we were just another crackpot like McVeigh."

Mendoza smirked. "Oh, we'll bring that other crew down. And we'll have the Pincharites to take the heat off us for that in the public eye."

Moran was starting to feel better. Certainly, they'd lost about forty million dollars in the meth lab structure, but they had two senators hammering away at the other end of the line, destroying the one covert group that had consistently stopped the Knights of Durango's true masters in the past.

They had their fingers in American law enforcement, but of late, those fingers were being found out and cut off. Almost as if someone was actually putting their own spin on infiltrating the US government, sowing the seeds of honesty and credibility. Moran frowned as he realized exactly what the blacksuit program was doing. It was enabling and empowering a generation of clean cops and Feds, ones who were above corruption.

Moran could tell that his predecessor had fallen into slim pickings for bent Feds and operatives.

His phone beeped.

Baxter and Connor were dead. But this was a message from Connor's phone. He saw the digital photos of the lifeless pair in the locker room. It appeared as if they'd opened fire on each other.

No deposit, no return was the message attached to the pictures.

Moran showed Mendoza the pictures of their Feds inside the system in Arizona. It was merely two, but the sheer fact that someone had managed to get this message directly to Moran's phone meant several things.

First, the enemy agency had finally narrowed down some of the players in Accion Obrar, of which Moran was a part.

Second, the fact that the shooting of two federal agents wasn't news, at least in Arizona, meant that their opposing force had the whole area on lockdown.

Third, they now knew where Accion Obrar had its headquarters. And this agency was never one to not finish the job.

Moran looked to Mendoza. "I don't know whether to have your men wait until they get back to Arizona or to send your forces in right now."

Mendoza folded his arms, eyes narrowing in concentration. "You want to get back at your cousin. Even if you can't get her, taking her children, knowing she missed seeing them one last time by a few hours…"

Moran smirked. "Good. Good. I like that. What about shoring up the defenses here?"

"We've got more than enough armaments for our prisoners and their bodyguards," Mendoza said. "What about the nonessentials here?"

"We'll keep them on the premises. Kill them all if we're attacked," Moran answered. "After all, they're here because they find themselves somehow morally superior to us. We make this a Pyrrhic victory for those bastards, if they can somehow overcome what we can throw at them."

"And what about the administration of this group? They know where you are, and we know where they are…" Mendoza began.

Moran wasn't fazed. "Our lackeys in Washington—the elected, the appointed, the bent Feds in our pocket—will make certain we can root out the group, once we make Brognola cough up the list of his blacksuits."

"This is a full-court press, isn't it?"

"We lost far too many American resources when we tried to get the US and Japan into a war over whaling, including my uncle, Stewart Crowmass," Moran said. He took a deep breath. "Without him, our Balkanization of America is stalling."

"Why the hostility toward this group?"

"Because of my father," Moran answered. "Miguel Moran...but the world knew him by another name. Unomundo. A man named Karl Stone killed him. And Stone was part of that organization. He's in Yuma, protecting my cousin's mewling half-breed pups...the observers have confirmed it."

Mendoza took a deep breath. "He'll be dead. We're not going to leave a stone standing if we can."

"Good," Moran said. "Keep me posted."

HAL BROGNOLA SAW the two men who had been laying siege to the Sensitive Operations Group's cover—the blacksuit program—together at the bar. Both white-haired men considered themselves the sages of partisan politics, but were more than partially responsible for the transformation of Washington politics from a committee of rivals working together for the common good into feces flinging spats between tribes of apes. Rudeness to presidents of either's opposing parties was not censured, and constant threats of shutdowns and filibusters made any change of law or effort at creating a budget impossible except in the most token of senses. Of course the atmosphere of partisan animosity they fomented didn't keep the two-faced rats from fraternizing together over Scotch and cigars in a private club.

Brognola was in his natural look now: rumpled clothing from working such long hours that he often slept on the sofa in his office. His tie was loosened so that it hung inches below the unbuttoned top, and his five-o'clock shadow had kicked in big-time. However, he felt refreshed, and his eyes were clear, and in his pocket were two thumb drives. Though he was not expecting a gun battle, Brognola had brought along his Justice Department–issued Glock 23 and his personal backup pistol, a Charter Arms .44 Bulldog Pug. To feel fully at home, he had the stub of an unlit cigar clenched in the corner of his mouth. He paused briefly and, as the senators looked up from their laughing and drinking, lit it.

He puffed on it then blew a smoke ring into the air. Confidence settled over his shoulders.

"Mr. Brognola!" the left-aisler declared. "To what do we owe the honor?"

"No honor," Brognola answered, moving closer to them. "Not for you."

The right-wing senator frowned. "I'll have you know that you have your job at our pleasure."

Brognola squinted, rolling the stub of his cigar around in between his lips. Still, even here in their private club, they wore the masks of their righteousness and clung to them without fail. He tugged a chair out for himself and plopped down, facing them both, and yet, inwardly he chuckled at the irony of doing so with men who had more than one face.

"Then you're going to be highly disappointed, distinguished gentlemen." Brognola sneered as he pronounced the final two words. He reached into his pocket and tossed the thumb drives onto the table between them. "And I'm using the terms *distinguished* and *gentlemen* so loosely, I can call this bar a church of alcoholic abstinence with the same accuracy."

The senators looked down at the little objects on the table and then back to Brognola.

"What do you have on those?" the leftist asked.

The conservative scowled. "What do you think, idiot?"

"Mick..."

"Shut up, Reed."

"You had to have realized that this kind of a coordinated assault on our agency would turn the heat back toward you," Brognola stated. "And I have a team of the very finest minds in forensic accounting and records diving at my disposal. The minute you two started using your committee to look at the Farm, we went to work. Cui bono, gentlemen. 'Who profits,' if either of you have failed Latin."

"To whose benefit," the liberal said. "If you're going to be—"

His counterpart slapped his hand across his brow. "Reed..."

"We already knew that your congressional dog-and-pony show had been to the benefit of Stewart Crowmass's various news outlets, wars fought in large print on front pages while the two of you sit here boasting to each other about the aides you've molested," Brognola returned.

Now it was the Republican's turn to lean forward. "You sniveling little bureaucrat..."

"Mick!"

"'Bureaucrat,'" Brognola repeated. "I am with the Department of Justice. It is my job to locate and uncover corruption. Bureaucrats keep machinery, even rotten, malfunctioning machinery, running. Like you two, who've been reelected so many times it's as if you had lifelong appointments made. I, however, actually try to do something to improve the system. And that means removing the chips and debris that keep the cogs from turning."

"Are you saying that your little assassination organization is going to remove us?" the leftist asked.

Brognola remained silent for a moment. "That you said

that only proves how deep you are in the pocket of Accion Obrar. And how truly out of touch you are with what we do."

"You end up harming patriots as well as the Islamists," the right winger said.

Brognola sneered at him. "Patriots? You mean violent bigots who think nothing of trampling the ideals of the Constitution and the Bill of Rights. But that's okay, I've been in Washington long enough to know how badly traitors like you stretch and mutilate the English language."

"Now listen here—"

"No. You listen." Brognola cut him off. "We're going to enter a new age. And it's one that you can either quietly retire from or see yourselves planted on pikes to display your sins for the world to see. And, trust me, thanks to the cable news cycle the two of you have fomented, you'll be good and truly exposed."

Reed cringed at the thought. Mick, however, turned beet red. Brognola had anticipated this and placed a bottle of aspirin on the table between them.

"No heart attacks yet," Brognola said. "The two of you have some phone calls to make. And then you're going after the actual corrupt law enforcement officials with your committee."

Brognola rattled off the AO patsies in the FBI, DHS and other agencies. "Those men are going to be uprooted, crucified in your kangaroo court and sent packing."

Mick chewed on a mouthful of tablets, washing them down with a shot of whiskey. "Bastard."

"Anthony or Leon? Oh, wait! You were calling me that, not talking about one of your illegitimates," Brognola returned.

Mick's eyes were wide, his redness faded to ashen gray.

"Blackmail is illegal," Reed said.

"This isn't blackmail. This is you undoing your mutilation of American law enforcement. The Knights of Durango and their pet agency are going to burn to the ground, but the rotten parts they implanted on our side of the border still require removal," Brognola stated. "You will be our scalpel for that, removing those tumors without causing damage to the infrastructure of these agencies. There are millions of good Feds out there, doing their job to protect this nation."

Reed flushed. "But you operate outside of the law…"

"Not for profit…not to harm ourselves or any nation," Brognola returned. "But you wouldn't know anything about expediting around red tape or acting in selfless abandon to preserve peace and uphold justice. I've buried far too many good men to have to explain myself to the likes of you bribe-eating parasites."

"We still have influence." Mick spoke up, but his words were empty. Brognola had broken them.

The big Fed stood, straightened his tie and blew one last smoke ring. "The files on those thumb drives are backed up and ready to smear you across news channels as the mountebanks you are. There is also a folder with the documentation necessary to clean up your messes. Use them."

He turned and left.

The real battle, however, had yet to be fought on the ground. He thought of what he'd spoken of: burying far too many of his men. Men assumed that they were expendable creatures, sent out as cannon fodder for the sake of gaining some tactical advantage. Able Team and Phoenix Force were his second family, as much his sons and brothers as his own blood relations.

He wanted to get back to the Farm so that he could watch over those brave men as they went into battle. It may have been an exercise in impotence, as he personally could not help them, but he wanted to provide as much moral support as he could.

DAVID MCCARTER REALIZED that not only would the journey to the US-Mexico border provide a half day of preparation for the Durangos and their minions for a subsequent assault, but it would also be exhausting for him and the rest of Phoenix Force. Hawkins had been burning up their satellite linkage to Stony Man Farm, and they had flown two hundred miles out of their way, landing at a small airfield.

One thing that the blacksuit program provided was contacts with other friendly governments. More often than not, that included well vetted and truly honest Mexican federal police. The landing strip that McCarter had chosen was one that had been seized by a team of such elite officers.

Getting out of the helicopter, Phoenix Force and Amanda Castillo were greeted by a group of rough-and-ready men, each of them dressed casually beneath police vests.

Their leader was a man named Roberto Panga, the last person one expected to be trusted by one of America's most covert agencies. His face showed a trail of years that stretched seemingly back to the dawn of time, wrinkles and scars providing him with a mask that none could consider young. It looked out of place, however, on a stocky, well-toned body. If seeing him from the neck down, one would assume that this was a man in his twenties, with sun-bronzed flesh and lean, ropy musculature. The only signs of age beneath his chin were hands that were as rough and weathered as his craggy countenance.

"David," Panga greeted. Despite the miles of gravel in his voice, his welcome was warm and friendly, arms spread wide for a welcoming *abrazzo*, a manly hug between old friends.

"Berto!" McCarter returned. "You should really invest in some face cream, mate."

Panga flicked his long curls. "I spent almost seventy

years making this face interesting. I'm not going to throw that away."

McCarter chuckled. "These boys can be trusted?"

Panga nodded, his good humor falling away. "We got the message from the Farm, and I got as many of my best boys together as I could."

His dark eyes locked on to Amanda Castillo. She'd come around, but was still shaken, bags sagging under her eyes. She was wound in bed linen wrapped in a toga-like set of folds.

"I know we trained you for more than babysitting, Berto," McCarter offered.

"De nada," Panga responded. "Protecting fair maidens is the least I can do for you blokes."

McCarter's smile returned. "Great. And what about the helicopter?"

"You guys rest. We will load her up with what you requested," Panga returned. "We've borrowed some stuff, the same as we've borrowed this airfield."

"Hopefully, we can keep you out of this," McCarter offered.

Panga shook his head. "The Lictors are an insult to us, *hermano*. There's outside of the law and then there's being straight-out evil. If you had room on there, I'd have loved to hitch a ride."

Panga patted his hip where a big chrome-shiny Colt .45 automatic with engraved but well-worn and tarnished silver grips was attached, as if to emphasize his readiness to come down hard on sin Piedad. "The Dungeon without Pity is a blight on my country's honor."

McCarter frowned. "You have a pilot?"

Panga's brown eyes sparkled. *"¡Sobrino, ándale!"*

A man in his forties ran up. He was taller than his uncle, but he looked as far from a rookie as the title "nephew" immediately evoked in McCarter's imagination. "I'm Daniel Rodriguez. But you can call me Rod."

"As in Hot Rod?" McCarter asked, sizing up the pilot. He was tall, with a face that easily could have made him ten years younger, and his shoulders were broad. Rod's eyes glittered with intelligence and competence.

"I haven't met a speed limit or performance spec I couldn't break," Rod returned.

Panga shrugged. "Light speed."

Rod grinned. "Someday, *tio*."

McCarter cracked his knuckles. "Good. I'd have hated to miss out on some ground action."

With that, the Stony Man warriors and the Mexican blacksuits retreated to a hut to plan.

CHAPTER TWENTY

The streets of Yuma were quiet as the sun crawled toward afternoon. The explosions and gunfire from earlier had been covered up with other stories, and because of reports of gas leaks, the citizens of the city were told to avoid the area around the federal building. There didn't need to be any police perimeter, one that would have provided easy targets for Los Lictors and what allies they'd assembled.

The stage was prepared for this battle. Carl Lyons, backed by his brothers in arms, Hermann Schwarz and Rosario Blancanales, and reunited with Dr. Lao Ti, felt a peace roll through him. It was a lull, but Lyons could feel the reservoirs of rage and indignation rumbling, ready to turn into cleansing fire the moment the enemy lit the first spark. To help that cleansing fire focus and burn those who needed such flame, Lyons had his arsenal with him.

Everyone on the team was equipped with their favorite weapons or their most modern updates. Lao Ti had been a fan of the MAC-11 machine pistol back when she'd first accompanied Able Team. Now, however, she'd upgraded, if not in bullet size then powder charge. A .380 didn't have much punch, though, while the MP-7 she chose was designed to go through NATO-standard body armor. A 40-round magazine and a completely collapsible buttstock were drastic improvements over the old chatterbox. She'd also upgraded from her old Colt Mustang .380 pistol by going to a SIG-Sauer P-938. It, too, held seven rounds of roughly the same caliber, but it was small enough for her tiny hands and fired a much faster, heavier bullet than the old Colt.

Then again, his friends always looked askance at him for looking down on the .380 when his own .357 Magnum had the same bore diameter as said pocket pistol. Ballistics, however, was more than just a matter of caliber. Even his favored 12- gauge shotgun generally was loaded with 00 Buck, which meant that each pellet was .36 inches in diameter. But its power came from disgorging an ounce of those pellets in one tight wad. And while Kissinger did his best to standardize the team with updates of Andrzej Konzaki's—the Farm's first weaponsmith—FrankenColts, Lyons kept turning away from the .45 automatic to his first love, the Magnum revolver.

Able Team was all decked out in their combat armor, as well. Sandwiched layers of Kevlar and chain mail were combined to provide maximum protection, and to limit the toll of weight, the chain mail was formed of carbon fiber. The force necessary to cut through these load-bearing vests would exceed the ability for a human's rib cage to resist collapse.

Lao Ti was sitting beside Lyons, and she, too, was in a state of Zen calm, her mind open and processing incoming information. While Lyons and Lao Ti were on opposite ends of the spectrum in size and temperament, they were also close friends, practically brother and sister due to their several missions together and continuing relationship over the years. As well, they both practiced the martial arts with the same intensity and had been sparring partners for every opportunity available.

She'd also been Able Team's West Coast wizardry closet. If there weren't the electronics ready-made for a mission, Schwarz was always welcome in Lao Ti's labs to whip something up. Some of the gear that Schwarz and Lao Ti had put together in her tech firm provided patents that kept Stony Man relatively independent from American taxpayers, as well as the company being one of many where the SOG could launder the loot the teams would acquire from criminal and terrorist organizations after their defeat.

Neither Lyons nor Lao Ti was truly meditating right now. They were perched together in a hide where they could observe the federal building, giving them the ability to respond and ambush any attack intended for the team and their blacksuit support. Though their gear was predominantly close quarters, both of the Able Team vets could take out opponents out to 100 meters with the shotgun or the machine pistol. Lyons's Pythons could reach even farther. And both team members had grenades that could be used to herd and channel enemy forces.

Lyons wanted to make damned certain that when Los Lictors attacked, the Mexican magistrates and their American added muscle were pulverized in a brutal spasm of counterviolence.

The hiding spot was in plain sight—a newsstand whose proprietor had been evacuated over the threat of gas leaks that had emptied out the rest of this area of town. Breezes fluttered at the corners of various periodicals, weighted down to keep them from being blown away in the wind, and the two were hidden behind a curtain of dark mesh that hung over the counter. They could see through the fine cloth, but given the sunlight and shadows in the day, it looked as if all that was present in the kiosk was inky blackness. It was simple camouflage, but it didn't look to a casual observer as if someone was actively hiding something. In the meantime, the gauzy fabric would provide little hindrance to gunfire that they'd start out with. A few heavy steel plates set up beneath the counter would give them a modicum of protection from incoming bullets, but neither intended to stick around for too long.

Lyons and Lao Ti anticipated that when the enemy arrived, they would be bringing every ounce of firepower that they could muster, and that meant they intended to collapse the federal building, if not with a truck bomb, then shoulder-fired rocket launchers.

No amount of steel plate on a newsstand kiosk could negate the detonation of an RPG-7 warhead.

"Movement coming in," Schwarz called over the com link. "We've got them coming from four directions. Pinwheel approach, counterclockwise from east."

"Copy," Lyons returned. He hefted his Atchisson. The big, battle shotgun was designed to be fed from quickly replaced box magazines or rotary drums, and the twenty-first-century version had lightened the cannon with polymer and fiberglass parts instead of stamped metal and aluminum.

The barrel was twelve inches for the sake of maneuverability and mobility in the kiosk and out of vehicles. Despite the abbreviated barrel, it was also equipped with a durable Aimpoint red-dot optic on top. Those who said that shotguns didn't need to be aimed were generally fools. Precision with any firearm was paramount, and the concept of a shotgun sweeping a two-yard-wide arc of death was naive and contrary to the laws of physics. Even so, with slugs and grenade rounds, a shotgun could be something akin to a sniper rifle. The last adjustment was that the Auto Assault 12 was already designed to handle 3-inch, 12-gauge Magnum shells; hence the current load was a 20-round drum of FRAG-12 shells, turning the shotgun into a true cannon. The explosive slugs were designed to knock out engine blocks and penetrate quarter-inch-thick light armor even at 200 meters.

"They *would* encroach our perimeter in a swastika formation," Lao Ti mentioned.

"As if there was any mistake that they were neo-Nazi scumbags," Lyons returned. A grim, humorless smile bared his teeth. "Let them come. I'm getting bored sitting and thinking and talking about taking them out of the equation. I want to actually put them away."

"Then get ready to sort some laundry," Lao Ti said. "Enemy in sight."

Lyons maintained his veneer of patience, but the anger and disgust as the violence committed by Los Lictors and their American allies was there, on tap like a burst of nitrous for a drag racer. From zero to battle mode in the space of a few moments, yet he kept the reins on himself held tightly. If he opened up too soon, the enemy could bolt or outmaneuver him. He needed them committed to their attack and task, which required restraint.

This time, not a single one of his enemies would leave the scene of this battle.

"We've got a hundred of them," Schwarz added to his battlefield assessment. "Split up into various vehicles. They've got shoulder-fired rocket launchers according to drone imagery."

"No doubt they brought enough to level FBI headquarters," Lao Ti added softly.

"All the better reason to blow them away. Besides, this is the glazier's son breaking a shopkeeper's window. A benefit to the city in construction jobs as they rebuild," Lyons returned. "But don't mistake me for a Keynesian."

"Never," Lao Ti replied. She was tensed with her MP-7 hanging on a sling around her neck. The slender, modular grips of a Milkor multishot grenade launcher were clutched in her small hands. Easy for her to grip, but putting out a hell of a lot more punch than Lyons's FRAG-12 shotgun grenades.

There were four pickups on the spear heading in from the north, and three cars and two Jeeps from the east. Lyons and Lao Ti chose their lines of fire based on the new approach information.

One of the pickups from the north flared and spat out

a spear riding on a trail of cottony rocket exhaust. The first grenade shell slammed into one of the upper floors of the federal building, blowing out dozens of windows and smashing out a man-size section of wall. Other RPGs roared to life, sizzling from street level and impacting on other sides of the structure. The building shook and rocked, hammered from four directions and from the backs of a dozen vehicles.

The cacophony of the combined assault was a sure sign that the Mexican drug gang enforcers bore little sign of subtlety at this point. Their efforts to contain and capture the children of Amanda Castillo had been blunted twice, and the Pincharites were still sore and hurting from Able Team's attack on their headquarters. Lyons, watching through the optics mounted on his shotgun, could see the symbols of a dozen Aryan and Nazi-allied gangs among the attackers.

He didn't want to open fire until the farthest vehicle back was within range of the explosive shells in his 20-round drum.

Able Team had built a kill box to trap the enemy force and, true to form, a supposedly unstoppable, heavily armed company of mechanized troops showed up. After all, what could a handful of federal agents do in the face of light machine guns and shoulder-fired rocket launchers? With their portable artillery, they had done an outstanding job of crumbling the facade of the building.

"Drop the hammer," Lyons growled once he was certain the attack force was totally committed. He pulled the trigger, and from various positions around the plaza, he heard the distant pops of grenade launchers. Lyons kept his focus on the rearmost of his target line of pickups. While the AA-12 had the potential for fully automatic fire, he wanted his rounds to do the most damage possible. That meant single-shot, aimed and shoulder-fired.

Lyons's first FRAG-12 detonated downrange against the rib cage of an RPG gunner standing in the bed of one of the farthest pickups. Upon connecting with a solid target, the rocketeer's torso disintegrated in a cloud of crimson, spattering all around him with hot gore and gooey, pulverized tissue.

Lyons aimed at the windshield and the driver of that same vehicle and fired a second round. The safety glass turned white for an instant, then imploded into the cab of the pickup, creating a bloodbath as jagged cubes turned into shrapnel. The driver still had control over his body, though he was lacerated brutally, and he started to back his vehicle away from where he assumed fire came from.

Lyons cut short that escape, his third high-explosive shell striking the driver in the face. Nothing remained of the man's head except for flopping flower petals of skin peeled raggedly back from where a skull used to exist. The pickup, out of control, backed into a concrete pylon, momentum throwing the gunners in its bed to the asphalt with bruising, disarming force.

Lyons spared those men on foot to send some hell toward the closer trucks. The one only twenty-five yards from the newsstand kiosk received a trio of rapid FRAG-12s in its grille, the grenades smashing its engine block into useless junk before Lyons pumped two rounds into the cab. One explosive shell tore open a fist-size hole in the driver's upper chest, the other tearing away the shoulder and left arm of the man in his passenger seat. Both attackers were dead, the explosive dismemberment shredding brachial arteries and inducing murderous shock. Lyons fired a third round into the cab and blew out the back window, turning the glass and the FRAG-12's own shrapnel into a wave of flying razors that tore through the legs of that transport's gunmen. Screams filled the air while explosions continued rumbling, both from flying RPG shells and arcing 40 mm grenades hammering the rocketeers.

The streets of Yuma became a battle of man-portable artillery, and Los Lictors and their American allies were only just starting to realize that they'd come under assault. It was time to move, but Lyons hung around just a moment more, sweeping a trail of the ten remaining explosive-shot shells from his cannon across the second closest pickup. His first FRAG-12s smashed the fender and engine even as the gunners in the back turned their attention toward the newsstand.

The muzzle blast of the AA-12 was bright and noticeable, and several rifles had swiveled toward Lyons. Unfortunately for them, he turned his hose of shotgun grenades on them, and the 19 mm fists removed body parts and smashed guns where they struck.

Outside, Lao Ti was in full action mode. She'd left the Milkor behind, having crushed the rear and lead vehicles of her convoy, blocking the street. Her remaining grenades had sowed chaos among the strike force, and she was in mop-up with her MP-7. In close quarters to a hundred yards, she was able to direct concise precision fire into the opposition, rattled and confused by 40 mm grenades that rained hard on them. Stock firm to the shoulder, optic framing targets, the Vietnamese computer expert slashed through half a dozen men in the space of a few moments.

Lyons could see that Lao Ti was heading toward a concrete divider that had been placed for cover. It was sheltered in a heavy Kevlar tarpaulin to provide enhanced firearms protection for her so she had an excellent turret position.

Lyons let the empty drum fall from his Atchisson and he pushed a 10-round stick into the gaping magazine well. This time, his battle load out was high-pressure Magnum buckshot. He stripped the top round into the chamber and fired at one of the assault team. A fist-size swarm of pellets struck a dazed gunman in his neck and jaw, tearing it to bloody pieces.

He targeted another of the strike force. They were wearing personal body armor, as well, which meant head or leg shots. Fortunately, part of the effectiveness of 12-gauge buck was its mass and ability to tear wide wounds. Lyons blasted the thigh of another Lictor, producing a fountain of femoral arterial blood squirting bright crimson clear across the street to the nearest sidewalk. The force of the impact broke the enemy's femur and collapsed him into a battered mess on the asphalt.

Lyons fired the shotgun as fast as he could pull the trigger to get rid of the buck rounds in the magazine, but he made sure to destroy pelvises and thighs if he couldn't core hearts or hit faces under helmets. Seven of the attackers on the federal building were down, groins and legs ravaged by high-speed buck.

Once empty, he dumped the box mag and pulled out a stick of tungsten-cored saboted slugs, slamming it home. With a pull of the trigger, Lyons blasted the heart of a Lictor, a Mexican man in professional black military gear, complete with a state-of-the-art Heckler & Koch MP-7 sidearm. The sabot, a chunk of diamond-hard metal, discarded its plastic sleeve petals to protect the barrel of the AA-12 instants before parting Kevlar, ceramic trauma plate, breastbone, heart and spine in one relentless juggernaut charge. The enemy commando folded in death, crashing headfirst into the street.

Lyons fired a second round into another fully clad Lictor, the tungsten slug obliterating the man's face and brain pan, tearing his helmet away from the ragged remains of his head. The grenade fire had died down and was replaced by ARs and other small arms. So-called American patriots and Mexican white supremacist commandos had been set to rout, and it was all over except for the mop-up, but even so, the Ironman was glad for the backup in the form of the group of blacksuits, Lao Ti and May Ling Fu and Domingo Perez.

Lyons could see the deputy marshal's position down the road; he was doing work with an M16/M203. Perez didn't clamp the M16 to his hip and hold down the trigger. He was aiming down sights, loosing short bursts, making sure every round hit instead of spraying like an 80s action hero. As with every trained blacksuit and military veteran of America's Iraq and Afghanistan wars, he knew the key to making the bad guys fall down, and that was precise application of firepower. Perez moved from cover to cover, avoiding most of the enemy's incoming fire.

Lyons also recognized the Mexican magistrates as they, too, were firing and maneuvering, moving from protected position to protected position, shouldering their rifles in a lightning-quick motion before unleashing their return fire.

Los Lictors were good at their marksmanship. More than a few bursts had struck Lyons in his body armor, and he'd be nursing bruises all up and down his torso if he survived. The Able Team commander stayed on the move himself, but when he pulled the trigger, there was no doubt that his target went down as an ounce of fat tungsten smashed body armor, bone, muscle and organ, creating a tunnel of carnage through his targets.

This was never the time to get cocky, especially as he'd seen too many brothers in arms fall under enemy gunfire at the last minute, some put out of action for months and others slain brutally. Images of Flor Trujillo, one of his loves, in the cabin of a helicopter that was burning and crashing to the desert flashed as a reminder in his mind.

Lyons's AA-12 ran dry and there were still targets standing. One of his big Magnums leaped into his hand, and he continued killing the "patriots" and their Mexican masters. The big R-8 Magnum spoke, blowing faces off, crushing hips, ending the fight in both American and Mexican bigots.

And as quickly as the explosions began, the gunfire died out. Lyons saw that his sleeves were covered in blood from near misses that had grazed his shoulders and forearms. He wondered what his face looked like, given he could feel the sting of sweat in minor scrapes on his forehead and cheeks now that his adrenaline had run out in his bloodstream.

Yet, even as he looked at the carnage strewed across his latest battlefield, he knew there were still some loose ends that needed clipping. He reloaded his AA-12 and the 8-shot Colt and went to work, policing the area, looking to see if any of the armed maniacs who'd initiated this bloodbath in the center of an American city were still alive and playing possum.

Once this was cleaned up, he knew there were a few more visits to be made.

CHAPTER TWENTY-ONE

Daniel "Hot Rod" Rodriguez, a Mexican blacksuit who had also been in the Stony Man program, was a steady hand on the stick of the MD-600N as he swung the whirlybird over the desert, staying low to remain off the radar. In the back, Rod's uncle, Berto Panga, sat at the controls of one of two M134 Dillon Aero miniguns mounted in the cabin of the helicopter.

Miguel Pena, another of the Mexican blacksuits, was on the other rapid-firing Gatling. Three honest, courageous Mexican federal agents had been assembled from a larger pool of operatives to man the state-of-the-art helicopter laden with weaponry. Their job, however, was secondary, acting as air support for the Phoenix Force warriors, who were loaded into the cabin, ready to fast-rope.

Another small army had been left behind to protect the recently rescued Amanda Castillo, a ring of courage and firepower designed to keep her from falling into the hands of the corrupt Accion Obrar, Caballeros de Durango and Los Lictors, the three-headed bestial organization that had been responsible for countless murders on both sides of the border and a sweeping wave of corruption and horror in Mexico itself. Leaving all those skilled operators behind wasn't a sign of distrust; it was simply the way of Phoenix Force.

The five-man team would be on the ground, in close quarters with the enemy, making certain the targets that needed elimination were put down hard. Chief among the list was Hector Moran, Amanda's cousin and a high-ranking official in the enemy agency. There were also the many ranking members of the Durango Cartel who were hiding in plain sight in the security of what was supposed to be a super max-level penitentiary, but were actually enjoying an easy life in accommodations that made some Cancun resorts seem like seedy dives. David McCarter planned to go hard against those who found the blanket of authority as protection and camouflage from justice.

At maximum speed, 175 miles an hour, Rod kept the chopper skimming the tall grasses. They would be on the premises within a matter of moments. Phoenix Force was armed to the toenails, all pretense of stealth thrown to the wind.

Each of the five was armed with his favorite flavor of close-quarters battle carbine or assault rifle. Calvin James had replaced his "Kitty" with a full-length M16/M203, while Rafael Encizo mirrored James's rifle/portable artillery load with a Heckler & Koch IAR M27, the H&K 320 single-shot grenade launcher beneath. No stun or tear-gas grenades for this attack, either; they were going with HEAP rounds, 40 mm of high-explosive antipersonnel capable of killing everyone in a ten-foot radius. The only concession made to fighting ability was that the two AR gunners had changed from normal 5.56 mm NATO to .300 Blackout "uppers" to increase the punch of their rifles without limiting the capacity of their magazines.

T. J. Hawkins, also a fan of the M16 platform, swapped out his Kitty's 5.56 mm barrel and action to chamber the same ammunition as his brothers in arms. Instead of subsonic lead for suppressed kills, they were using armor-piercing ammunition loaded to supersonic velocities. They'd received word that Los Lictors had hit Yuma wearing body armor and were using shoulder-fired rocket launchers and trucks as "technicals."

Gary Manning didn't have to replace his OSW based on the classic FN FAL battle rifle, and McCarter found himself drawn to the heavy-caliber, compact blaster. It didn't hurt that McCarter had cut his teeth in the British military with the FAL, thanks to the finicky nature of the L-85 bull-pup assault rifle. The SAS avoided that particular issue rifle, preferring to either stay with FAL battle rifles or M16s when they needed something heavier than an MP5 submachine gun. However, McCarter decided to add to Phoenix Force's available portable artillery, affixing a grenade launcher to the Picatinny rail under the barrel of the Offensive Special Weapon.

Each of the team had a sidearm, spare magazines and munitions attached to his battle vest, and was decked out in battle armor, as well. This was going to be a do-or-die assault.

"Panga, amigo, when you drop us off, blow an escape route for the raggedy mob," McCarter ordered.

"I'm not sure they can make much of a run, but they'll at least have an escape route to get out of the way," Panga answered. "Stay aggressive down there."

"Aggressive is my middle name," McCarter returned with a smirk.

"Really? I thought it was Mac," Panga quipped. He leaned into the Dillon Aero electric Gatling gun, looking for targets.

In a flurry, the chopper was over the edge of the wash where the Phoenix commandos had made their base camp for the rescue of Amanda Castillo. El Calabozo sin Piedad was in plain sight.

"Hose 'em, Pena!" Encizo called, stuffing a 40 mm shell into the breech of his grenade launcher.

As one, the Mexican federal agents hung out the sides of the speeding helicopter, pulling the triggers on their electric-powered Gatling guns. At 3,000 rounds per minute, the M134s were hoses of death and destruction, and as they closed to within 1500 yards, Panga and Pena sprayed streams from their multi-barreled guns at a rate that tore through two separate guard towers, 7.62 mm NATO armor-piercing turning steel walls into ragged cheesecloth. The soft flesh and blood of the sentries within fared little better; bodies torn open by savage rakes of high-velocity rounds.

As McCarter had been in contact with Stony Man Farm, and the cyber crew had slaved a satellite and several drones to observe the compound of sin Piedad, they were fully aware of the evacuation of the prison. Even so, the two gunners and Rod had to be careful, because while civilians had been allegedly evacuated, thermal scans showed that the population of the prison had only changed slightly.

Indeed, there was a convoy of buses making its way to the road, which looked suspicious. The only reason Panga and Pena were weapons-free to fire on the guard towers was that there were gunmen inside actively shooting in the direction of the helicopter. Down below, McCarter's instincts warned him that it was likely Accion Obrar had set a trap for Phoenix Force.

"Barb, can the drones tell if the bus convoy has armed escort?" McCarter asked through his com link, knowing she was listening.

"Akira's swinging one down on them to check," Price said. "That's a confirm!"

"Rod, drop us off and hit those buses," McCarter bellowed. "They're evacuating the cartel bosses that they had in custody."

"We get to clean up the convoy, but what about you?" Pena asked.

"We'll be puttin' boot to crooked ass, partner," Hawkins answered. "Stay safe!"

Rodriguez blasted open a couple of perimeter gates

to the outer courtyards with the artillery rockets on the helicopter, then swung up short. Panga and Pena laid down 7.62 mm hatred at 3,000 rounds per minute, slashing through enemy guard towers with brutal efficiency, keeping Phoenix Force covered as the team disgorged from the cabin.

Hitting the ground, James, Encizo and McCarter braced, taking a knee and targeting guard towers that had not been eliminated by the helicopter gunners with sailing 40 mm grenades. Thunderclap blasts cut through the air, providing protection and cover for their Mexican allies to leave and handle the escaping column of drug bosses.

Dozens of ragged humans looked on in pure horror, all dressed in tatters, at the sight of the five men who landed in their courtyard.

"Stay down!" Encizo ordered in Spanish, feeding another high-explosive shell into the breech of his launcher.

Hawkins and Manning swept their carbines across visible rooftops, keeping a sharp eye out for enemy marksmen poised on them. Manning caught one gunman in the open and milked a precision round into the man's nose area, a high-velocity NATO slug smashing through facial bones, brain matter, skull and vertebrae. The enemy sniper dropped off the parapet like a marionette whose strings had been severed, crashing to the ground thirty feet down.

Hawkins swatted another rooftop pest with a controlled burst from his .300 Blackout, stitching steel-cored bullets through the torso of one of the Lictors and dropping him backward out of sight. Accion Obrar and their allies had learned the lesson of losing a couple of their men out in the open when Hawkins and James had cut loose on them before, but most of the rooftoppers had taken cover when the guard towers had taken slashing Gatling fire from the helicopter.

Barbara Price was present in their coms, pointing out

concentrations of cartel and renegade *federale* gunmen on rooftops so that Phoenix Force knew where and when to place their counterambush.

In a battle such as this, there was no such thing as an unfair advantage, so when the enemy was staying out of sight to avoid direct fire, James, Encizo and McCarter made use of the indirect nature of their collective grenade launchers. This was another case where the best defense was a good offense because the HEAP shells they dropped on top of cartel gun thugs and corrupt military officials disrupted any effort to shoot back as 40 mm packets of high explosive and shrapnel detonated over their heads. Air-burst blasts peppered enemy soldiers and gangsters alike with supersonic notched wire and shell fragments.

The rain of deadly steel made certain that Phoenix Force had created a good window through which Hawkins could take over propelling the half-starved and frightened prisoners toward a safer environment between the perimeter walls. The Texan and his mastery of Spanish enabled him to urge the prisoners to their feet, the stronger ones helping the more feeble, even as Hawkins returned his attention to scanning for snipers.

Scores of the "lower class" prisoners moved at a painfully slow rate, making it seem like an eternity as Phoenix Force held the line with long-range marksmanship and grenade attacks. Hawkins knew that his comrades had the benefit of aerial intelligence, drones scanning from on high, looking for rooftop adversaries. In the meantime, the Stony Man warriors were doing what they did best: forming the wall between savageries and the victimized. Tearing holes through the flesh of the monsters with bullets and explosive shrapnel was merely the icing on the cake as they eliminated the minions who enforced the will of the true masterminds.

"Top floors cleared of gunners," Price announced

through their earbuds. "But we have movement from the other quadrants of the prison. Men on foot and heavily armed."

"Getting close and personal," McCarter mused. "T.J.!"

"I'm moving them along," Hawkins returned. "They're not gonna make any fifty-yard dashes."

"Ah, we're going to have to hold on," Encizo returned. A rocket sizzled over the group's head, one of the cartel gunners cutting loose with an RPG. The Cuban shouldered his rifle and returned fire, cutting down the man trying to help the rocket shooter reload. He shifted his aim and put a burst into the killer with the rocket launcher himself. Outnumbered and surrounded as they were, there was no way he was going to allow that man to hammer Phoenix Force or the frightened political prisoners held by Accion Obrar.

Hawkins kept waving the group along, the Texan moving to help those who stumbled, pausing every so often to whirl and crack off precision shots to protect the evacuating throng. Fortunately, the members of the Stony Man team managed to find plenty of hard cover in the form of rocket-burst wall fragments. Crouched behind the stone, they were able to return fire, harrying the cartel goon squads with streams of rapid fire as James and Encizo dropped high-explosive shells in the midst of the enemy group. RPG shells smashed the ground behind the last of Hawkins's charges, and he followed the smoke trail of the rocket grenade back to its shooter. The scope on his Blackout helped Hawkins kill the thug who'd sprayed the rearmost of the group, those strong and hearty enough to have taken up the task of carrying the wounded, with gravel and flying pebbles.

That rocketeer had intended to murder those brave Mexicans, and only Phoenix Force's superior marksmanship and the thunderbolt blasts of their grenade launchers had kept his shell from slamming on target and killing dozens. As it was, Hawkins noticed that his shoulder was bleeding from a shrapnel fragment spat out by the shell's detonation. He gave his arm a shrug, testing to see if any bone or joint damage had been inflicted, but though it hurt, he was able to self-diagnose no major injury. The blood was dark, so it had avoided arteries, and the fragment had been held back by the ballistic nylon of his tunic. He wrenched the piece loose and his arm's discomfort lessened as he moved it. To keep from losing too much blood, he improvised a bandage using a length of duct tape with a square of gauze in the center and sealed the cut.

This bit of self first-aid was a stopgap. Hawkins still had plenty of targets to take down, but for now, except for a few fallen prisoners, most of the "concentration camp" victims were safe between a pair of walls. Now he could turn his anger and disgust over the brutally ended lives of the weakened, starved and sickly Mexicans toward fueling his body's need for adrenaline. Tortured and deprived, those people had been given a bare subsistence while being taunted by the almost resort-like airs of their much more guilty, but much wealthier and corrupt opponents across the fence. Now the muscle-heads and itchy trigger fingers in their employ were doing their best to advance upon Phoenix Force, and in cutting through the team, eliminating the relative innocents who'd been tormented by law without justice and power without mercy.

Now this assemblage of lawmen and soldiers known as Phoenix Force was striking back, showing how ineffective their corrupt might was in the face of trained, focused strength employed in the *protection* of the weak and helpless, and the avenging of the fallen, the murdered and the tortured. The charge of the drug thugs had been blunted and the gunfire issuing from their corner had abated, the force retreating even as Hawkins joined his brothers in arms, shooting down enemies in retreat.

As outnumbered as they were, Phoenix Force's best option to survive was to keep the broken crew from re-assembling their forces in any level of strength.

"Rodriguez!" McCarter's voice crackled across the com. "How are you doing with that convoy?"

"The chopper took a hit from an RPG!" Rodriguez answered. "My uncle's down and hurting."

"Can you still fly?" McCarter said, his voice filled with concern. "We need the chopper to watch the perimeter."

"I don't want to let them get away," Rodriguez said.

"If Berto is injured, we have one of the best medics around," McCarter countered. "We can hunt them down later. They're on the run."

"And half of them are dead," Miguel Pena added. Hawkins could hear the buzz of the Gatling gun on the other end. "Let's not add Panga to the list of the fallen."

There was a croak of indecision on the other end then the sound of the MD-600 shuddering as the last of its artillery rockets lanced outward.

"On my way back," Rodriguez advised. "I may not have finished them off, but I sure as hell made a dent."

"Good man," McCarter said.

Hawkins understood the necessity for even a landed helicopter. Calvin James raced to Hawkins's side, and the two men traded rifles. James was going to be busy putting his corpsman skills to use on both Panga and the rest of the wounded Mexicans, at least for a little while.

That meant that the Texan was going to step in as the third member of the artillery line, and he grabbed the bandolier of 40 mm shells from James.

"One in the breech," James returned.

Hawkins nodded in understanding and looked for extant threats, but for now, the scene had grown quiet. He looked into the bandolier bag and saw that there were only a handful of shells left. In clearing rooftops of snipers and turning back the drug soldier charge, they'd expended a lot of the firepower that had enabled five men to fight like five hundred. He shouldered the bandolier and glanced back at James, who was hard at work dealing with injuries among the prisoners.

There were corpses in the wake of the escaping throng of "innocent" prisoners, men and women shot down by snipers, slaughtered for the sin of only being in opposition to corrupt government or brutal drug gangs.

"Damn," Hawkins cursed, looking at the fallen.

A hand clapped on his shoulder. It was McCarter, the team's leader. "We'll have time to mourn for them later. We still have the living to protect."

"I hear you, boss," Hawkins returned. "I'm just putting somethin' in the bank for when we're after the top bastards."

"Yeah. The two waves we've dealt with here were softening us up, making us expend ammo," McCarter agreed.

"But then they made the mistake of murdering helpless people," Hawkins grumbled. He dumped the magazine on the Blackout and was satisfied it was topped off. He returned it to place, scanning toward the office tower.

"Infrared tells the Farm that the upper three floors are swarming with people," McCarter noted. "I'd wager that if we get up there, we'll encounter near-impossible resistance."

"Near," Hawkins repeated. "So we've got a sliver of odds on our side."

McCarter smiled. "I knew there was a reason I liked you."

The helicopter appeared, swinging wide of the prison campus, trailing smoke. From one side of the aircraft, Pena opened fire, sweeping the tower, as the same information sent to McCarter had been transmitted to the Mexican blacksuit. McCarter and Hawkins swung their optics toward where the minigun struck the building.

Even at 3,000 rounds per minute and 3,000 feet per second, the storm of high-velocity lead had done nothing to the glass on the outside of the building. If anything, one panel broke away, revealing that the mirrored glass was simply a patina covering a steel shell.

"They armored that place," McCarter breathed, lowering the scope on his rifle. "We might have gotten through the armor if we had artillery rockets."

"But the bus convoy and cutting a hole in the perimeter took care of that," Hawkins replied. He sighed. "I don't think our 40 mm shells could do much."

"We have to go inside," McCarter said. "Though we could take a few shots with some RPGs from the gangster gunners. See how reinforced those upper floors are."

Hawkins frowned. "Wait…if infrared is seeing a massed group on the upper floors and they're armored enough to withstand…"

McCarter grimaced. "It's a trap. Everybody…heads on swivels!"

Rodriguez was bringing the helicopter in when it shuddered again. A rocket had lanced toward it, but the Mexican pilot's reflexes were good enough that he was able to turn a direct hit into a glancing blow. The aircraft whirled as the deflected RPG-7 shell detonated away from its hull. Even so, the rotors and engine took damage, and he found himself fighting to autogiro the bird in to a landing.

The chopper landed on its skids. Not gently, but it landed, and Rodriguez and Pena leaped out, pulling the wounded Panga from the back.

"RPG gunners on the ground, able to hit an aircraft," McCarter noted as he and Hawkins rushed to aid their Mexican allies. "Los Lictors are out and on the move."

"Well, that's who we're here to wipe out, ain't it?" Hawkins asked, thickening his drawl.

"Mighty neighborly of them to make themselves easier to find," McCarter replied, echoing his friend's tone.

"Mighty," Hawkins repeated with a smile he didn't fully feel.

If Phoenix Force fell in their engagement with Los Lictors, hundreds of lives would be at stake, not to mention the propaganda coup that Accion Obrar's true masters would have with the bodies of five American operatives on Mexican soil, with the bodies of slaughtered *federales* all around them.

Now was the point when Phoenix Force rose from the ashes and flew or became a flaming ember crashing to the ground.

CHAPTER TWENTY-TWO

Barbara Price looked over the battle scene as one by one, their drones were transmitting static and fuzz, no longer clarifying intel electronically. She frowned, realizing that the enemy had given them just enough information to commit Phoenix Force to an action that they could regret. The office tower had showed a large concentration of people inside hidden behind what seemed to be rocket- and bulletproof shielding. And then the logic hit, just as radio and sensor interference struck and drones started dropping like flies.

Sin Piedad was suddenly surrounded in a field of radio interference, cutting them off from Phoenix Force in the field, but the sight of an RPG sizzling into the sky to take out one of the drones gave Stony Man Farm's mission controller hope that the five commandos on the ground knew that this was a trap and distraction. The enemy had tried to fool them into attacking a false front, but if Price had seen rocket fire launched from the ground and that the tower was heavily fortified, then so did they.

"Get some eyes on Yuma! How's Able Team holding up?" Price called out.

"We've got static emanating from downtown, where the gang is busy on street cleaning," Kurtzman answered. "Looks like the enemy just pulled the same maneuver as they did in sin Piedad."

"Draw them out, make them expend strength and ammunition, and then move in when they think the fight's done," Price said. "Damn…"

"Don't worry. Our boys are smart and on their toes," Kurtzman promised. "And they already realized that this enemy is gunning for them and are as tricky as they are."

Price gnawed her upper lip, looking at the blackouts where her field teams were stuck in the open, facing off with organized and well-equipped enemy forces intent on exterminating them. They'd been outnumbered before and assailed by military entities that had both targeted them for Stony Man's interference in their machinations and sent as the best of the best to eliminate them.

This time, however, the Caballeros de Durango Cartel and Accion Obrar—or rather, the mind behind them, Hector Moran, son of Stewart Crowmass—had set things up so that the warriors had expended a substantial amount of energy and ammunition in dealing with cannon fodder, not their elites.

It was a stratagem that the Stony Men teams had engaged in before, running their opposition ragged and confused. The prison break, the attacks on the federal building, all of it was meant to keep Able Team and Phoenix Force moving continually between the offensive and the defensive, hardly giving them time to relax and think.

Her hope, however, waxed on the fact that the men that were handpicked and vetted by Bolan and Brognola had not just been selected for their planning skills and speed on the trigger. The eight warriors, and to a lesser extent the blacksuits and their allies, had been chosen for their ability to adapt, improvise and overcome in the space of a few moments.

"Do us proud," Price murmured, knowing that there'd never been an instance where, even in death or failure, the heroes of the Stony Man action teams didn't give their all. It was, however, that all that meant another brave warrior's blood had been spent in the protection of freedom and justice. Too many brave men and women had died in this struggle.

"An eye for an eye eventually leads to everyone going blind," Price mused softly. She shook off that thought. The Sensitive Operations Group was first and foremost out to stop violent thugs and governments from imposing tyranny on others. A tool of that effort was vengeance, but it was secondary to the primary aim: eliminating threats to freedom around the world.

Right now, all the mission controller had were traffic cameras in Yuma and the satellite peering down from orbit in Mexico.

The battles in Arizona and at sin Piedad were still raging, but she was cut off from her warriors in the field.

CARL LYONS CLOSED the cylinder on his plus-size Python, eight fresh pills ready to blast away under the hammer; 158-grain flat-faced hollowpoints that could tear and render flesh and shatter bone. His com set was silent, which could only mean that the enemy jammed them. He glanced and saw that the yellow stoplight was flashing akin to an alarm Klaxon, something so out of the ordinary that he immediately recognized it as a signal from the Farm. They were without drone coverage, but there were traffic cameras, and through those links, the cyber guys back at Stony Man were letting him know that they weren't completely out of touch.

He gave the closest traffic camera a thumbs-up then fed another magazine into his AA-12. *We're ready*, he mouthed for the guys back home. No, they weren't as ready as they'd have liked to have been. After all, they'd expended most of their anti-vehicular firepower against the wave of cannon fodder that had left the Yuma building a smoldering mess. But the men of Able Team, Lao Ti, May Ling Fu, Domingo Perez and the blacksuits were all ready.

David Kowalski rode toward Lyons and Lao Ti on a four-wheeler ATV. Its fat tires allowed it to navigate the broken concrete, wreckage of vehicles and bits of corpses strewed across the street. A basket on the back of the chunky quad bike carried a duffel bag loaded with ammunition to replenish what the two Able Team members had exhausted. Kowalski himself was loaded with his own personal weaponry to aid in the final pitch against Los Lictors' professional killers and assassins present in Arizona.

Lyons had been impressed with the younger man in earlier encounters, especially his transformation from a slob packing a pizza to a hard-faced warrior, complete with a tomahawk sheathed on one hip. Under his right shoulder—indicating that Kowalski was a southpaw—the kid had an unusual looking 1911 variant. The magazine looked far too long to be a normal .45. "That the new production Coonan?"

Kowalski glanced down to his sidearm. "Yes, it is the Coonan .357 Magnum automatic, sir."

"Don't call me sir. I work for a living," Lyons replied immediately. "Smaller and sleeker than Gary's old Desert Eagle…"

"If we make it through this, I'll let you wring it out," Kowalski answered.

"No ifs," Lyons told him. "We fight to win. Even if we're on what looks to be a losing side. We fight and never give up. That's the Able way."

Kowalski nodded, giving the big blond ex-cop a sharp salute.

"I said I… Never mind," Lyons began, then gave up. Kowalski apparently aspired to the role model that the Able Team commander never realized he was. "Get ready. Trouble's gonna hit fast and hard."

"Just for once, I'd rather enemies hit us soft and slow," Lao Ti and Kowalski answered, almost in unison. Lyons smiled. The two of them still had their spirits up and were ready for more battle, no matter how tired they seemed.

"You're free to use marshmallows and molasses on them," Lyons countered. "I prefer another way myself."

"We'll make those bastards bounce," Kowalski said.

Lyons nodded. "Good."

The throb of a helicopter zooming into the airspace around them brought their attention to the arrival of Los Lictors.

Lyons was glad he had another box of FRAG-12 grenades in his AA-12 as one of the enemy's MD-600s whipped over a rooftop into view. It was loaded with gunmen and had weapons bristling through the open side doors. He aimed and triggered, playing skeet with helicopters and a high-tech, grenade-spitting shotgun. This was a case where the clays could shoot back if he wasn't swift and ruthless on the draw.

FRAG shells slammed into the armored belly of the bird, sparking and bursting with considerable force, but Lyons was hoping to get the door gunners. Fragmentation blasts peppered the men inside, but they were shielded from the shrapnel by flak jackets and helmets.

He'd require a direct hit on one such jacket or helmet to penetrate with the high-explosive shells.

The MD-600 shuddered, however, struck by one of Lao Ti's 40 mm grenade bursts smashing into the open doorway. With a vastly larger payload of explosives and shrapnel, her Milkor's antipersonnel round caused a bit more mayhem.

At the same time, Kowalski had drawn his Coonan .357, apparently not having the kind of armor-punching grenade power in any of his personal weapons. The Magnum automatic spat its rounds but there was little attendant spark and ring of ricochets, meaning that Kowalski'd had the foresight to put some high-penetration ammo in the automatic, likely steel-cored slugs atop a fearsome power charge given the muzzle blast. Lyons had similar horsepower in his Python Plus revolvers and let his Atchisson drop on its sling, pulling the converted Colt Anaconda.

Between Magnum precision and Lao Ti's 40 mm onslaught, the helicopter and its crew was sent veering wildly into the facade of the crumbling federal building, erupting into flame as its fuel burst and sprayed all over. One enemy bird was already down, but the beat and grunt of other helicopters and other door-mounted machine guns told Lyons that the battle was not finished by a long shot.

"Cover!" Lyons bellowed as a fresh aircraft swung into line of sight. High-velocity artillery rockets rippled out of the firing tubes mounted on the sides of the next MD-600. Shooting back was not an option as 2.75-inch missiles smacked the street, blowing craters in asphalt and concrete. Blast waves washed across Lyons's back as he pushed his two partners ahead of him and around the corner from the bulk of the explosive devastation wrought by the enemy war bird. Chunks of stone impacted on him, but the armor meant to preserve his life against enemy gunfire served him well against raining rubble, as well.

The chopper roared past, leaving Lyons, Lao Ti and Kowalski in its wake, covered by a smoke screen of detritus kicked up and still raining in the form of dust. The clouds had given Able Team and its allies aid in the form of obfuscation, though Lyons knew he'd be a mass of bruises come morning. Without communications, however, there was little way that he could get his team coordinated with the blacksuits.

Of course, if anyone could adapt, improvise and overcome, it was Blancanales and Schwarz.

"Get to it fast, guys," Lyons growled.

Some messages, Schwarz always explained, tapping his metaphysical theorems, could get through amid even the heaviest of interference and blackouts. Lyons figured, given they had become as brothers over their many years of battle, shoulder to shoulder, that they could know what each other thought, usually when they thought it simply through familiarity. Either way, he continued pressing his will in the hope that some telepathic contact could be made.

CALVIN JAMES FINISHED cleaning the shrapnel bits out of Berto Panga's face. The man didn't suffer any crippling harm, his goggles having protected his eyes, but the man would have more lines and scar tissue on his already craggy features. The shock wave accompanying the debris had been mitigated some by the same helmet that had kept Panga's head from being turned into a colander, though James could see the signs of a concussion in the man's eyes.

James hated that Panga would have to get back on his feet and into battle before that concussion could be dealt with. Unfortunately, right now, with Los Lictors forces amassing and ready for a final push against Phoenix Force and the freed prisoners, they needed everyone that they could get.

"*Gracias*, amigo." Panga's gravelly voice crackled.

James dug out a spare helmet for the veteran officer. "Keep your head protected. We're going to get a lot of heat coming in the next few minutes."

Panga nodded gingerly, and James could see that he was still suffering from the shock waves that had struck him when that RPG air-burst close to the helicopter. Right now, the Mexican warrior chewed and swallowed aspirin tablets to maintain any swelling in his brain tissues as well as to deal with the aches.

Panga limped and got back on the controls of the Dillon

Aero minigun, which the members of Phoenix Force, Hot Rod Rodriguez and Miguel Pena had repositioned, taking them off the crashed helicopter. The two guns were anchored on broken sections of wall, which allowed them large angles of fire both from inside the prison and possibly from the outside if the Lictor enforcers were savvy enough to attempt a flanking maneuver on the survivors of captivity. It was a strong possibility, especially since coming through the former prisoners would force the Stony Man warriors to hold their fire in case they hit a bystander.

Rodriguez would be a more mobile operative, armed with an M4 carbine with a grenade launcher, picked up from one of the enemy dead as members of Phoenix Force raided them for replenishment of ammunition and arms. In addition to the emplaced guns, the honest Mexican lawmen had their personal sidearms and the rifles with which they'd come to the airstrip. There was no shortage of firepower available; these lawmen used the same ammunition in their rifles as the gangsters employed by Accion Obrar, and even the same mechanisms of each gun.

The huge .500 Smith & Wesson on Panga's hip was the only weapon that didn't have a battlefield source to resupply its hungry cylinder, but Panga was pragmatic. "This only holds five shots at a time. And I've got three speed loaders for it. If I can't finish the fight with twenty of these bad boys, it's a fight I never should have entered."

"I can feel that." Gary Manning spoke up. For this final thrust, the burly Canadian had brought out his most favorite combat handgun in the world, the Desert Eagle in .357 Magnum. Its bullets didn't have the size and mass of Bolan's .44 Magnum, nor the huge diameter of the .50 Action Express, but with a load of nine in each magazine and one in the pipe, there was plenty of firepower with solid, deadly anchoring hits that had been putting bad guys and dangerous animals down since 1935.

James managed to scrounge a battlefield pickup piece for himself, a Colt Combat Commander—just like his preferred weapon when he'd first joined Phoenix Force. The gangsters who made the previous attack were believers in .45 Auto, just as the San Francisco SWAT team from which James had been recruited. Having the locked-and-cocked Colt on hand felt good for him. Of course, if the battle got down to handguns, that meant they'd been overwhelmed and it would be a desperation shoot-out anyway. James had his rifle and grenade launcher combo to go through first, just as the Mexican lawmen had their mounted machine guns.

"You don't have to act like *mi madre*," Panga admonished James.

The Phoenix Force medic smirked. "It's a professional hazard. I just want to be sure you don't fall over."

"I'll likely be knocked over by incoming fire," Panga answered.

"That's why we've got armor," Manning continued as James finished attending to Panga's concussion and injuries.

"Armor chips away," Panga offered. "But you know that."

Manning nodded solemnly. James himself had seen far too many battlefield injuries to believe that getting shot at *any* time was a good thing. Eventually bullets made their way through Kevlar vests and trauma plates, or found gaps in that protection, slipping between seams or finding that lucky angle that allowed them into the vital organs the wearer had sought to shield. Luck and skill only provided so much protection. The only way to ensure that you didn't die in a gunfight was to avoid it completely. The second best way, however, was the only option to Phoenix Force and their allies. Attack and overwhelm your attackers before they had the chance to kill you. It wasn't a perfect strategy, but it was better than sitting and waiting for the enemy to pour pounds of lead into your body.

There was something in the tower, though, and James didn't like that Phoenix Force was going to have to divide in two. There must have been someone in the building's upper floors that the renegade agency wanted the strike team to attack and destroy. It could have been records, hostages or something much worse. Either way, someone had to go inside to deal with it.

James and Encizo volunteered to stay back with the prisoners and the Mexican federal agents to repel Los Lictors. That left Manning, Hawkins and their leader, David McCarter, to make the assault inside.

Those three stalked off, but they were going to still be in a position to fall back and shatter the spine of the trained commando assault if necessary. They moved quickly, keeping out of sight and to cover. Sunset was coming, and the shadows stretched to provide concealment for them. Unfortunately, the same shadows gave Los Lictors their own shelter from observation. Night-vision goggles were useless until the sun actually was down past the horizon, making the dusk a danger zone. Splitting their forces was risky, but the mystery of the tower was something that could not be ignored.

Not when there were lives potentially at stake. If nothing, then at least Manning would have a higher vantage point from which to apply his marksmanship skills against ground assaulting enemies.

"Es del tiempo," Rafael Encizo said in Spanish for all present; the former prisoners of sin Piedad, the three local lawmen and James, who had learned it to the point of fluency in his friendship with the Cuban.

The ragtag survivors huddled behind segments of wall and in shallow foxholes to protect themselves from enemy cross fire, while the federal agents made last-moment adjustments to their aim and weapons. Encizo and James took to the shadows, slithering out to where they could watch over their allies while retaining the option to flank and ambush enemy forces.

As such, the two men moved not with their rifles at the ready, but with knives clutched in fists, because their blades were the only truly silent weapons that they had available. Certainly, both men had suppressors for their handguns, but carrying them in holsters was problematic, and cutting loose at 100 decibels, they still produced a loud report rather than the hushed whisper spits one heard in movies or on television. And while there were holsters optimized for carrying a suppressed handgun, neither James nor Encizo, who'd been packing plenty of artillery through Mexico, had the room or inclination to go with all of that on their hips. It was one thing for sling-mounted, collapsible machine pistols like the MP-7s, but a nearly two-foot-long handgun was never easy to maneuver while on the run.

So it was that James and Encizo, moving parallel to each other, blended in with the long shadows of encroaching sunset, the former SEAL fighting off worries about the fates of his friends and the condition of things back home in America. James cursed himself for allowing irrelevant concerns to overwhelm his awareness of the moment when a figure lunged at him, brawny arms lashing to seize him. Out of the corner of his eye, he noticed that Encizo was similarly under attack, and now the two Phoenix Force pros were in hand-to-hand conflict with two members of a corrupt agency's answer to Stony Man's commandos.

The flicker of metal gleamed out of the corner of James's eye, impelling him out of stunned surprise and into deadly action.

CHAPTER TWENTY-THREE

Powerful hands erupted from the shadows at Rafael Encizo. One was clawed, seeking to seize the Cuban in blunt, hooked fingers with battle-chipped and broken nails, and the other was clenched tightly around the handle of a deadly fighting knife, its point plunging toward his shoulder and neck junction.

With the reflexes of a cat, Encizo surged forward. While his upper body was broad and heavily muscled due to his life on the ocean, rowing and rigging ropes, his thinner legs were no slouch, either, spring-steely and lean from countless hours of scuba diving. He leaped out of the path of the dropping blade with a breath's distance to spare and brought his Cold Steel Tanto knife up. The attacking Mexican's grappling arm proved little resistance to Encizo's razor-sharp blade, BDU, skin and muscle parting until the edge chipped into forearm bone.

The blade was stopped from cleaving through the Lictor's arm, but it wasn't trapped. With a wicked twist, Encizo yanked the edge free, producing a bright spray of crimson and a growl of agony as he pulled back for another attack.

The Mexican enforcer pulled his arm in toward himself, his knife hand hovering between lashing out to keep the Cuban away from him or dropping the weapon to clamp his injured forearm. That brief instant of dithering gave the Phoenix Force pro all the opening he needed to plunge the Tanto through his opponent's ribs and deep into his heart. Encizo's free hand knocked the Mexican's other limb away, holding it at arm's length to keep from being filleted by his enemy.

In the meantime, Encizo worked his own knife like the stick shift on a race car, bones crunching and tissue parting under the brutal assault, cleaving his foe's heart in two. It wasn't precision or pretty, especially since the spine of the knife was blunt, but the trauma Encizo inflicted was more than sufficient to end this fight in the space of a few moments.

It was just in time as a second of the crooked Mexican magistrates launched his assault. Encizo let go of the knife that was temporarily snagged on his first ambusher's rib bones, and took a hop backward to avoid the spearing lunge of the newcomer. There was zero time to waste, but instinct warned him that if James hadn't interceded by now, he was stuck and busy fighting off his own set of attackers.

The Cuban brought up his boot, kicking toward the back swing of his opponent. He missed the man's arm, barely, but the steel toe crashed brutally into the outside of the man's thigh just above his knee. Spastic reflex knocked the attacker off balance and crashing into the dirt, buying Encizo the precious moments he needed to draw his neck knife and drop atop the stunned man. Sharp steel tore into the Mexican's throat, backed by all of Encizo's weight and muscle, carving open the man's neck to the point where the Cuban could hear the grind of steel on bone.

With a wrenching pull, he had the knife free from his foe's neck and glanced across to where James stalked in the shadows parallel to Encizo. He couldn't see anything, but he could hear the grunts of effort between at least two men, and that meant the Cuban was not alone in peril.

"Cal! *Shita!*" Encizo shouted. His hand dropped to a pouch on his belt, instinct kicking in to swiftly pull his throwing stars. The Cuban had cried out in Japanese, something both men had familiarity with, James from his time learning martial arts under Japanese-American John Trent, and Encizo having been a close friend with deceased Phoenix Force comrade Keio Ohara. As it was unlikely that their counterparts here in Mexico would have a relatively intimate understanding of the Asian language, they'd be confused by the sudden warning, but James would know exactly what his friend meant.

Encizo's eyes adjusted to the dimness of the shadows that James had hidden in, and he saw two figures still standing, confused as the lanky silhouette of James dropped to his belly on Encizo's command. In quick succession, Encizo had his throwing stars out and hurled them with deadly accuracy and great force. The aforementioned Keio Ohara had been Encizo's teacher in *shurukenjutsu*, the art of combat with the razor-tined throwing blades. Encizo had utilized this skill many times over his career in Phoenix Force to save his own or others' lives.

Encizo's initial star cracked into the cheekbone of one of Los Lictors, causing him to cry out in pain. He fell in a spiral pirouette to the ground, clutching his perforated face, but the other managed to avoid injury, steel points rebounding off the commando's helmet.

Unfortunately for the crooked Mexican commando, the impact and surprise were more than sufficient to distract him from James on the ground. The black badass from Chicago came up swinging, and what he swung was his G-96 Jet Aer knife, its razor edge running along the curvature of his opponent's groin armor. The wicked blade carved through muscle and femoral artery in one brutal slash, creating a deadly wound that fountained bright crimson. James took a shower in arterial blood that gushed from the mortal wound then swung toward the one that Encizo had stunned with the *shuriken*.

Though half blinded and in pain, the Mexican reached for his gun, knife fallen away in the melee and the attack on his face. The renegade magistrate's wrist was carved brutally by James's fighting blade, handgun tumbling from numbed fingers as nerves and muscles slashed asunder. James flipped the blade point down and plunged it into the hollow of his opponent's throat, puncturing his windpipe and cutting off his air supply.

James withdrew from the dying pair and gave a nod of acknowledgment and thanks to his Cuban partner.

Encizo smiled, retrieving his fighting knives. The two men had encountered the flanking force that had been sent against the prisoners and Phoenix Force's allies. The grunts and cries of pain might have been enough of a warning for the Mexican lawmen, but just to make sure, Encizo pulled his Heckler & Koch P-30 and fired two shots into the ground. The reports were a clear signal that the enemy was on the move.

"So much for stealth," James stated in a stage whisper. The ex-SEAL drew his rifle and scanned the maze of the prison complex for more opponents he knew were on the way. The dull whump of a grenade launcher in the distance reached Encizo's ears as well as his partners', and the two Phoenix Force warriors turned their attention toward the source of the initial attack.

Encizo was quicker on the draw, firing his 40 mm round in the direction of the enemy launch. Experience and training set Encizo into motion, moving away from his launch site in an instant, even as his shell arched in flight toward the target. The enemy's initial grenade burst close to where the refugees were hiding, but Phoenix Force had anticipated the potential of Los Lictors using man-portable artillery against their former prisoners. Sand bags and foxholes had been set up, so a ground blast would only cause limited injuries.

That didn't mean that Encizo was going to allow the Mexican renegades to rain down hell upon helpless victims. As it was, the Cuban feared for the victims of the outlaw agency and how many could have been injured by the attack.

James's rifle cracked an instant later, informing Encizo that his friend had more hostiles in visual contact. Without radio communications, thanks to Los Lictors' jamming, he couldn't be certain where the enemy was coming from, but he shifted to cover and scanned for the opposition.

Shadows moved like wraiths, heads visible for only moments before ducking out of sight and taking aim. Encizo figured their position in relation to James then let out some sharp whistles, giving the mystery figures' direction in a code the enemy wouldn't know right away.

The signal was immediately acted upon by the ex-SEAL.

Encizo knew that the opposition was using cover effectively, so rifle fire would not be sufficient to root them out, but James's M203 thumped quickly. The High Explosive Dual Purpose grenade round dropped from on high. The detonation was much more distinctive and loud in comparison to the launch, and Encizo saw an arm cartwheel through the air as the result of a close impact.

The blast sent a couple of the enemy commandos into the open, where Encizo was waiting, rifle shouldered. He swiveled his sights onto them, tapping off short, precision bursts for each of the staggered men who sought out new cover. A flurry of 5.56 mm NATO rounds ripped through flesh and bone, the Cuban Phoenix Force pro burning down members of the Lictors force that had the bad fortune to be staggered by the grenade assault.

Gunfire erupted from those who'd not been showered by shrapnel or stunned by explosive shock waves. The blaze of muzzle-flashes was elongated from Encizo's point of view, stretching out and pointing like arrows toward Calvin James. If the opposition was firing toward him, the flares from their muzzles would have been more circular, and so far, no one had noticed him as he swiveled away from where he'd gunned down the Mexican troopers. He saw a couple of teardrop lances of fire, the telltale sign of bullets slashing where Encizo had been a moment before.

These killers were skilled, and had they been of any better level of ethics, they might have made it as part of Stony Man's blacksuit program. As it was, they had sold their skills to the cartels and the highest bidder. They'd murdered for the sake of profit, acting in the interests of racist politicians and drug dealers. As such, Encizo felt very little regret at flanking the Mexican gunmen and hosing them down with precise, deadly bursts of autofire.

Los Lictors immediately retreated, those who survived the initial contact with the Cuban, and found themselves steered into the path of James's own rifle fire. The Chicago badass caught them in their brand-new blind spot, their attention turned toward Encizo's muzzle-flash and thus, not seeing him ambush them. Caught in the cross fire, the brutal enforcers found themselves shredded and cut down in a blaze of high-velocity projectiles.

In the distance, thanks to the warning via gunfire, twin Gatling guns joined the fracas, the unmistakable buzz of the high-speed weapons creating tremulous roars that shook the air.

"Keep hammering them," Encizo whispered, knowing they wouldn't be able to hear.

Pena's rifle and grenade launcher spoke, as well; a single man opening combat with a 40 mm shrapnel shell, then cleaning up with his rifle's rapid, precision bursts. Encizo gave a whistle to James, indicating he was heading to back up the Mexican lawman. James was going to take a more roundabout course to reinforce Panga and his comrades.

The whole goal was to avoid crossing each other's fields of fire while making life miserable for their assailants.

All the while, the two men of Phoenix Force knew that their three brothers in arms were heading into the den of Los Lictors to find out what was in the office tower they so wanted destroyed.

DAVID MCCARTER PAUSED at the base of the tower. He heard the roar of grenades and automatic rifles, including the ripping snarl of the high-velocity M134 miniguns used by the Mexican blacksuits.

"Gary?" McCarter called.

"Looks like our boys have them surrounded," Manning returned. He'd paused and scurried up a lamppost using a belt to get a vantage on the enemy battlefield. With his weight and the leverage of the strap, he was able to advance the height of the pole as if he were a monkey. He also had a good view of the rest of the area, and no one else seemed to be making an approach to reinforce the protections in the tower. Granted, for a moment, he was an easily spotted target, but it was worth it to at least keep tabs on the battlefield. Without drones and communications, they were otherwise blind.

Manning slackened the tension on the belt and skidded down the pole, back with his allies, not wishing to remain in his improvised crow's nest as a tempting target any longer than necessary.

Besides, it was time to get into the main office tower. The upper floors had been armored, but marked for targeting and destruction by its builders, an unholy amalgamation of Mexican agency Accion Obrar and the Caballeros Cartel, a double-headed entity that had, for the most part, legitimized government corruption in the nation and taken over the lion's share of the drug trade. Through murder of both officers of the court and criminals, through torture and intimidation of the Mexican free press and large sums of money to corrupt American lawmakers and lawmen, this union had been providing support for narco-terrorism and the subversion of justice across the Americas to the point of near ruin for so many governments and economies.

McCarter took point, using one of Manning's prepacked breaching charges on the doors to the tower. High-velocity detonation cord and concentrated pockets of plastic explosive smashed the first barrier to entry to the building. At this point, stealth was not an option. McCarter also hoped to bring Los Lictors, the amalgam's enforcement magistrates, toward them in the office building and away from assaulting the recently liberated prisoners in the dungeons of sin Piedad.

Hawkins ran through the breached entrance, having sidelined his shoulder-slung MP-7 for a 12-gauge shotgun, an ideal weapon for both clearing a narrow corridor or blowing away the hinges and locks on a door. Hawkins moved so swiftly on the heels of the door-smashing explosion that he both outran the expectations of the two guards within the maintenance entrance, but also had the sheathing concealment of flowing, swirling smoke. He burst out of the cloud, the muzzle of his shotgun tracking and cutting loose on one of the two surprised sentries.

The frangible slugs designed to obliterate dead-bolt locks and reinforced door hinges also worked pretty well against body armor. Hawkins gored the man with his first shot, the epoxied chunk of iron filings hitting nothing hard enough to shatter it until it struck the guard's spinal column, and even then, the slug only snapped in two after pulverizing backbone.

The other gunman was frozen in shock for an instant, stunned by the sight of his partner being almost cut in two by the lethal shotgun slug. However, reflexive response elicited a burst from the sentry's machine pistol. Bullets sizzled over Hawkins's head, and only the surprise and recoil kept a stream of bullets from slashing his head from his shoulders. Even so, he could feel the pummeling of supersonic slugs pelting his cheek with their passage. The Texan rushed even closer, diving into the gunman's blind spot before he could regain control of his weapon.

David McCarter entered the fray, focusing on the flash of the remaining guard's weapon. He shouldered his Heckler & Koch and ripped off three short bursts toward the enemy gunman, spacing them carefully to make certain that he could at least target the opposition through the smoke.

"Clear! Good shootin'," Hawkins called out.

McCarter and Manning advanced through the clearing smoke, spotting two corpses draped over the railing of the stairwell, slumped where they'd been shattered by the marksmanship of Phoenix Force.

McCarter paused for a moment, replacing the ammo he'd spent. As they passed the bodies, he snagged magazines from the fallen foes to up his ammunition reservoir. This was going to be a long, intensive fight, and he meant to stay in it for as long as possible. That was why Phoenix Force had come south of the border with Mexican military-issue weapons and magazines.

They were in the heart of their enemy's territory, so they might as well load up with easily replenished equipment. Even so, Manning still had prepared a load of specialty gadgets while they were at the airfield where they'd dropped the rescued Amanda Castillo. These included flare bombs and discus grenades—miniature disks that burst out a guillotine of force and shrapnel, the flat, circular shape allowing it to be hurled even farther than normal grenades. McCarter palmed one of the far-flying bombs as he made the stairwell door. It was unlocked and he stopped cold. If he barreled through the door, there was a good chance that there was a reception committee on the other side ready to pour down a monsoon of bullets on any who entered.

Two guards at a relatively easily breached doorway was a sure sign that this was a sucker play.

McCarter pointed to his eyes, then upward, signing for Manning to use one of his extra-strength flares.

Manning borrowed Hawkins's shotgun, fed a shell-loaded flasher into the breech, then waited for McCarter to crack the door ajar.

With a pull of the trigger, McCarter winced at the sudden blaze of bright white light that erupted in the stairwell. Any troops on the steps who were looking down, waiting for Phoenix to roll into their field of fire, were looking at a miniature magnesium sun, their retinas seared by the glare.

McCarter swooped in and looked upward, the brilliant flare having dimmed to a mere fraction of its original blast. Hawkins was right at his shoulder. There were a dozen sets of heads and shoulders. Los Lictors caught in the open. Their visors and helmets might have protected them from most of a standard flash-bang, but Manning's chemical and pyrotechnic knowledge enabled him to produce an air-burst flare that could overwhelm even that. There was not much sound from the high-candlepower weapon, but as most people were vision-oriented, and all eyes were on the bottom of the staircase, Manning had bought them precious seconds.

Together, McCarter and Hawkins raked the silhouettes poking over the rails, and automatic weapons tumbled from lifeless fingers as the two Phoenix Force pros swept the gunmen positioned above them. A burst of 4.6 mm projectiles swarmed upward, spearing into faces at supersonic speed, the slender slivers of high-velocity metal upset by sudden interaction with elastic skin and unyielding facial bones. With their streamlined forms suddenly deprived of air as a medium to go through, the bullets smashed through cheeks and occipitals, cartwheeling as their momentum kept them going despite the disruption of form. The resultant carnage wrought burst eyeballs and brains whipped to froth.

Manning swung into the stairwell and hurled two of his discus grenades in rapid tandem, his powerful wrists stretching the range of the explosive disks to the upper floors of the staircase. Explosions rumbled, and anyone not raked by a wave of pressure and shrapnel was left stunned by the roar of the loud blasts. Phoenix Force's hearing protection filtered out most of the sonic pressure, keeping them up and still active in the fight, but Los Lictors had their strength sapped.

Phoenix Force was here to administer justice, and the only mercy on hand was a swift bullet to the head of a wounded, suffering opponent.

The enemy had chosen its position, its final battleground, and the Stony Man warriors were too outnumbered, too outgunned, to leave a single capable opposing gunman standing in their wake. If their methods seemed cruel, then those who judged were grossly unaware of the realities of combat. Also, leaving men to suffer after horrible injuries was far from the style of the men of Phoenix Force.

Whatever mystery awaited on the top floors was likely to have even more hard-core defenders, and after defeating two layers of them, McCarter was certain that this would be a war to the knife, if not down to tooth and nail.

Unflinching, McCarter and his team stacked up to breach the top floors, ready to fly once more into the fray.

CHAPTER TWENTY-FOUR

Hermann Schwarz saw that Lyons and his buddies had just taken down one of the helicopters brought in to hammer the heart of Yuma, Arizona. While Rosario Blancanales and Lao Ti used their rifles to harry and hinder the other two birds, keeping to the cover of concrete barriers, Schwarz was busy assembling his weaponry to deal with the enemy aircraft.

"Hustle with that, Gadgets!" Blancanales called out. "The guns on those things are chopping our cover to pieces!"

Schwarz had his specially designed gear mostly disassembled in a duffel, if only for the fact that it had prove too unwieldy to move with. He slipped the wings onto the body of what looked to be an oversize toy airplane. Indeed, its shell and wing system was made from traditional hobby store gliders. This, however, had a couple of improvements over the hand-thrown toys. He'd fitted it with adapters, simple rods that could be put down the barrel of a shotgun and fired with either a blank or a live shell with minimal damage to the weapon. He laid out three of them, loading a fourth onto his Remington 870 MCS. The shotgun was packed with blanks to provide the propulsion for the searing gliders with reinforced wing spars to handle the rapid speed, and of course, the shells of the gliders were stuffed with sufficient high explosives to tear through a light tank's armor.

Indeed, in the initial assault by the Durango's allies,

Schwarz had used two duffels with another eight of these brutal missiles to turn trucks and cars into heaps of slag with roasted human meat in the core. Now he was down to just four, and he had little hope of being able to knock a helicopter out of the sky until it slowed to a hover to dig a pest out of a well-protected position.

As if answering Schwarz's wishes, one of the helicopters swung toward Blancanales's position, and in the side of the flying beast was a pintle-mounted machine gun belching flame and lead with more than enough power to chew through reinforced concrete. Only the density of the walls and rubble Blancanales hid behind kept him from being slashed to ribbons by the enemy gunfire.

Schwarz took aim and fired the explosive glider at the enemy bird. The blank's ignition also set off conventional combustion rocket motors stacked in the shotgun adapter, and the broad-winged missile hadn't even hit its maximum speed before it crossed the two hundred yards and impacted with the MD-600 gunship. A blasting cap design in the nose, as well as a copper funnel bought from a grocery store, turned a model airplane into an antitank-worthy warhead, and with the detonation of the explosives Schwarz had stuffed aboard, the fiberglass shell erupted, producing a lance of heated, deadly copper. The jet of molten metal carved through the pilot and copilot, while the concussive burst of the model and the needle-like shrapnel formed from its splintered fiberglass hull left the door gunner rattled and bloody.

An aircraft full of screaming Lictors swerved and spiraled crazily from the sky, spinning and smashing into the street where rotors snapped apart and flames belched from burst fuel lines. If there were any survivors on board, Blancanales ended their suffering with the pop of a 40 mm grenade from his rifle, sailing it into the shattered windscreen of the burning, bent hulk. Without the incessant rattle of the helicopter's machine gun, Blancanales had been able to target a weakened portion of the craft.

That left just one aircraft, which rapidly gained altitude, realizing that it had lost two of its squadron to enemy ground fire

As if to reinforce the idea that the battle at the Yuma federal building was over, the radio coms crackled back to life, signals coming through Schwarz's earbud.

"That last bird is burning out of here like someone lit the fires of hell under it," Lyons said. "Good work."

"But that last one is still on the run, with a belly full of bad guys," Blancanales countered.

"We'll catch up with them," Lyons growled. "No one's getting away. You watching this, Barb?"

The satellite link on their communicators sparked as Price's voice cut across the airwaves for the first time since the helicopters had made their approach. "Satellites are tracking them right now back to home base. We didn't notice them coming in because the pilots were good enough to fly nap of the Earth. They stayed off the radar, but they can't get away from a formation of surveillance satellites over a clear-sky desert."

"So we think, after all, they hid an entire prison and agency headquarters campus from us," Schwarz mentioned.

Price paused for a moment. "But they had time to get that all set up, in the desert. Just like we did when Mack and Hal started this business years ago. A selected blind spot, built off the radar."

"Which means this has been going on for years and years," Blancanales offered. "No surprise, given the history of the Mexican drug cartels' violence and its upswing over the past two decades. We've taken on Mexico's renegade lawmen as often as we've bumped heads with crooked cops and Feds over the years."

"This is probably the same strain we've been smacking

around all the while," Schwarz added. "They just decided to go to war with us."

"Too bad they didn't think out their exit strategy from this battle," Lyons said. "Because there's no way they're getting untangled from this fight without complete extermination. Can we get a pickup?"

"Jack's coming in with the new *Dragonslayer*," Price responded. "So the chase is on."

"We're finishing with them now," Lyons swore.

HECTOR MORAN HAD heard the thunderous rumble of detonations accompanied by the crackle of autofire coming from the stairwell. He'd suited up for war, his head encased in polycarbonate Kevlar and thick, bullet-resistant Lexan, his torso wound in trauma plates and even more ballistic nylon. He clutched his assault rifle complete with a double-drum magazine, a Beta-C in which the *C* was the Roman numeral for 100. He wasn't going to go down before he'd put out or at least inundated the Americans—or whomever they sent—with a storm of sizzling lead. Very little on Moran was exposed and vulnerable to such a return salvo of gunfire, but he'd been a part of the Caballeros de Durango Cartel and the head of Accion Obrar for too long to realize that any armor was only bullet resistant, not invulnerable to harm.

Colonel Alonzo Mendoza, the founder of Los Lictors, was similarly adorned with armor, spare magazines and weaponry. Even through the tinted visor on Mendoza's helmet, Moran could see a scowl forming on his features.

"My men have been broken outside," the head magistrate of the outlaw cartel agency said grimly. "Our opposition has not destroyed them all, but as a fighting unit, they've been scattered, and morale has been shattered."

"How many survivors?" Moran asked.

Mendoza's eyes flashed with lightning rage. "Ten men

out of the group we sent to the prison walls to deal with our intruders. Of them, only six remain healthy enough to continue fighting. If they still had the willpower."

Moran glanced toward the stairwell. "We have some hope…"

The thunder and clatter of gunfire and battle in the stairwell ebbed. Right now, members of a mysterious paramilitary team were several floors above them, primed to penetrate what they thought was the ultimate fortress of Accion Obrar. The trap was multilayered and an effort to get Phoenix Force into a killing box and catch them unaware. The guard force in the stairwell added to the allure of that bait.

Their enemy was known to value the lives of bystanders and noncombatants and would assume, rightly so, that the top floors were where hostages were imprisoned. Moran had indeed ordered a group of office and support staff to the top of the tower, counting on his foes to rush to the rescue, just as they had fought to protect the former "honest" prisoners of sin Piedad.

As soon as the enemy commandos were inside that killing box, instincts to protect taking over for the men and women Moran had ordered wounded, Los Lictors would ascend the steps and plunge at them, guns blazing. Caught with no place to hide and innocents to defend, Moran and the enforcers would slaughter everyone inside the building. Anyone coming to their rescue would run into a second ambush.

Down here, at least the Mexican renegade magistrates had a back door for escape, so if their foes tried to turn the tables, they wouldn't have the same effect as stuffing Phoenix Force into a death chamber. Moran and his buddies weren't trapped and cornered.

Mendoza frowned.

"No breaching charges," he muttered. "And whatever

those men used to clear the stairwell took down our audio and video feeds."

"They're coming down at us," Moran said. He sneered. "They must have figured out that we were railroading them. But it doesn't matter."

Mendoza nodded. "You lead the flank attack. We'll stay here and become a meat grinder for them."

Moran looked to both entrances to the basement.

"You're not retreating, you're going on the attack," Mendoza said. "In fact, if you don't swing around behind them, we're completely screwed."

Moran snapped his fingers. His personal troupe of bodyguards grabbed their weaponry and followed their armor-clad leader. Breaking the back of the Phoenix Force counterambush would be just as good, just as satisfying, as pulverizing them inside the killing box on the top floor. Moran's machismo wouldn't allow him to fight from the rear, but to attack from the front. "Leave something for me to crush."

"No promises," Mendoza returned. He and his team huddled behind "Jersey" barriers that had been reinforced with bomb-squad blankets of heavy Kevlar and trauma plates, adding to the protection of concrete lattice-skeletoned with wrought-iron rebar. With their helmets and body armor, they would be able to stand their ground against all but direct rocket fire if necessary. And while they were concentrating on that Maginot line defense, Moran and his cadre would swoop in behind them.

Things were looking up. He had expected to have trouble in eliminating the Americans and their commandos, and while the losses were enormous, at least once he cleared the way, he could rebuild with impunity. The Caballeros Cartel and Accion Obrar's supporters in Mexico City would provide the means to rejuvenate the collaboration. The Durangos enjoyed legitimate support, and the

Mexican government saw Accion Obrar's pruning of the Durangos' competition as good propaganda, as well as lucrative in terms of kickbacks.

All it would take would be a pull of the trigger, and several hundred rounds with which to pulverize the American goon squad that had attacked and assailed Moran's family and American connections for so long…

The sky was dark as he pushed open the hatch that led out of the basement. All the better. He and his men turned on their infrared illuminators, swinging down the night-vision goggles attached to their helmets. The mounted, heavy units were a headache to wear, but to gain the element of surprise, Moran considered them as valuable as a massage from a large-breasted whore.

Even though he had the cover of darkness and shadow, he'd risen from the hatch quietly. Moran and his bodyguards were professionals, and the AO chief had trained under Mendoza and with other special operations soldiers.

They slithered with stealth and caution, fingers off the trigger, but ready to unload lightning and thunder from their assault rifles at a moment's reflex.

Slipping around the perimeter of the tower, his muscles tense, he saw people limping and struggling their way from the front lobby. Moran paused and activated the zoom on his night-vision optics.

The hostages from the top floor were free, and they were moving away from the tower as quickly as they could.

He whispered into his headset mike. "Mendoza…" He paused to listen and suddenly a spike of noise pierced his eardrum, his brain reeling as if a bullet had crashed into his helmet. Moran staggered, clumsily ripping the cord from his communicator. With a glance back, he saw that his squad of commandos were all doing the same thing, having received a burst of sonic agony on the same radio frequencies.

"What now?" one of his men whispered. "They've cut our radios…"

"Just like we did to them," Moran murmured. He winced, his ears still aching from the shrill howl of radio interference. "Payback's a bitch."

"Yeah," another bodyguard grumbled. "Do we take the wounded?"

"No. We need to close off the enemy and take them down. Unarmed and injured assholes can be taken down at leisure," Moran growled. "Mendoza's counting on us."

"Great," another of his gunman said. "Let's roll."

Moran grinned. His boys were badass warriors, and they were ready to unleash hell upon his command. Moran was still the general. Sure, his family and the Crowmass clan in America had provided the money and influence to get him up this far, but he'd still had to fight and claw his way up to ensure he kept his promotions. There was plenty of blood on his hands, nothing he'd ever regretted, but he'd torn his way through whoever challenged him or destroyed everything he was told to accomplish.

He scanned through the scope of his assault rifle. The Beta-C drum hanging off the weapon made it heavy as hell, but Moran wasn't a soft bureaucrat. He could let the gun hang once he lightened it by the weight of 100 rounds of 5.56 mm NATO. Movement abated toward the entrance as the last of the walking wounded moved along. They were headed to where the helicopter had crashed, and Moran's former enemies were now freed. They were mostly soft people, reporters and politicians or snitches, so none of them had the strength from starvation rations and death marches to do more than huddle. If any of them had enough muscle remaining to lift so much as a handgun, they probably wouldn't be able to aim due to lack of training or infirmity and sickness.

The way that the helicopter came in and its lack of provision of air support meant that the crew of that ship was grounded and likely had wounded aboard, as well. From what Moran knew, there were two teams, totaling about eight men in all, sometimes nine. There were at least four enemy commandos on the grounds and, given the troubles they'd encountered so far, it was a fair bet that it was the five-man mystery team. He wasn't certain of how many were making the assault and were inside the tower, but given the kind of mayhem wrought on the hunter-killer squad sent to the helicopter, the odds were most likely two left behind and three inside. That would be a problem, but once they took out the majority of the enemy force, it would make the final dribbles of opposition easier to mop up.

A man clad in black and festooned with weapons waited for a moment in the doorway to the lobby, obviously watching over the recently released prisoners of the tower. Moran focused his sights on him; the stranger was barrel-chested, brawny but proportional. Moran couldn't see his eyes behind his protective goggles, but it was as if the enemy trooper was glaring right back at him through the scope.

Moran glanced over his shoulder. If his communications were jammed, then it was a good chance that this guy was in contact with his friends, both at the perimeter of the prison and back in the States where they got their intelligence support. His own bodyguards, however, were posted, each covering the other, eyes and ears sharp for threats in the shadows. The skies were still bright purple, tinted by the last reflections of the sun, which dipped beneath the horizon. It was dark enough, though, to have shadows where enemies could hide and to make the night-vision goggles necessary.

He focused once more on the stranger when the screen blazed a sheet of glowing green-white, meaning that the light-sensitive optics were suddenly overloaded. Moran pushed the goggles from in front of his eyes, but the hanging afterimage remained, blanking out the center of his vision. His wasn't the only set of NVDs affected.

The bodyguards behind him were grunting and struggling with their own visual aids, meaning that someone had found a way to overload all of the Starlight-style goggles. All of this came to him at lightning speed, even as the first crackle of autofire filled the air.

Just as Los Lictors had sought to pull Phoenix Force into a trap, the five warriors from Stony Man Farm had done the same. Bullets hammered into Moran's armor, pinging off his helmet and body armor, giving him a few precious moments to dive to the ground. Others did the same, but not all were so fortunate. Two bodies toppled to the ground in dead, mangled heaps, high-powered bullets either punching through armor or finding weaknesses and openings within it.

The image of the gunman in the lobby flickered in his mind's eye and Moran focused on the weapon he held.

The stranger, while providing overwatch for the rescued hostages, had been armed with a G-3 rifle or a compatible facsimile, complete with all manner of optics and other rail attachments. Precision marksmanship had been a hallmark of at least one group of the enemies Moran was aware of, and two dead out of the eight he'd brought with him was livid, vibrant testimony to that. He turned and looked at the lifeless forms on the ground. The death-shots had been upper arm or underarm hits, which crushed through flesh and muscle, circumventing body armor by going through sleeve holes in their vests.

From ambushing to pinned down, Moran cursed his

luck. Well, they had grenades and could engage in non-direct fire warfare, as well as the…

Moran remembered his foes' grenade launchers as a parachute flare flashed to life above them.

"¡Dios!"

CHAPTER TWENTY-FIVE

"This is too damned pat and easy," McCarter said as he, Manning and Hawkins stacked to penetrate the upper floor of the tower. The outside had been heavily armored, to make it seem like an attractive, tempting target for destruction by missile salvo. Then the logic of such a fortified set of offices at the top of the building changed, reminding both Phoenix Force and the control team at the Farm of the efforts of Accion Obrar and Los Lictors to undermine the Sensitive Operations Group, especially the attempts to spotlight the covert agency in the congressional hearings.

"Make a quiet cut," McCarter whispered. "They want us to make noise going into this."

Manning nodded. "I don't see any back ways out of this place. They're gonna slam us in this hole."

"So why fuss with quietly getting inside?" Hawkins asked.

"Because normally, we'd turn if there was no need to stay here," McCarter answered.

"Bait. As in wounded hostages," Hawkins surmised.

McCarter tapped his nose, indicating that the Texan was on the same page. With its dead bolts carved out by a high-temperature incendiary, the door swung open, revealing an empty floor, no cubicles, no walls, barely even supports for the roof. The floor was crowded with frightened people, many of them injured, wide, fearful eyes cast upon the three newly arrived men.

"Lo siento, mis amigos." Hawkins started out with

somewhat of an apology, speaking softly and calmly to the group. He continued rolling on in Spanish. "We're only here to help you, but we need you to remain quiet."

A flurry of murmurs arose, but Hawkins's facility with the language and his calming tone had been enough for them to remain soft-spoken.

McCarter's Spanish was less adept, less naturally native, but he still could get his messages across clearly. "Those who can walk, help those who can't. We need you out of here as soon as possible."

In the meantime, Manning checked around for more booby traps, not wanting to be blown up at the last possible moment. He doubted that there would be anything truly fatal to a man fitted in Kevlar and battle equipment, but none of the battered Mexican workers trapped in here were so fortunate to have that protection.

"They must have wanted scalps," Manning said. "Nothing here that would have taken us out in a single shot."

"Machismo," McCarter replied. "At least Moran and his thugs have that much as a positive trait."

"Positive?" Hawkins asked. He pointed to four of the hostages who had bled out in the time they'd waited up here as bait for the three of them. "They just want to prove themselves as badasses, but the truly tough and strong don't mutilate people and leave them to slowly die."

McCarter sneered, looking at the fallen. Los Lictors were unmistakably savages, the kind of heartless, cruel terrorists whom all of Phoenix Force had been recruited to battle. Four more innocents had been added to the red ledger, lost lives taken unnecessarily. What made it worse was that they suffered their injuries in the name of keeping the three of them occupied in assisting wounded noncombatants. That would have provided time for Moran and his enforcers to swing up and slaughter everyone in this abattoir.

Vowing justice for these murdered victims, and for the suffering of those who yet lived, McCarter turned to assist Manning and Hawkins in providing aid to the hostages.

There were yelps and whimpers as the former prisoners looked at the shattered remains of Hector Moran's guards, corpses scattered and spilling down the steps. More than a couple of times, people slipped as they endeavored to avoid stepping in a puddle of blood, but other than a few bruises, and thanks to the quick reflexes of the men of Phoenix Force, no one turned an ankle or worse. There was more than enough injury to go around without adding to the mix.

The throng of noncombatants would be slow enough in getting out of this battlefield without adding another limping escapee to the line.

McCarter paused as they reached the lobby. Hawkins at the lead of the group had held them up, noting that it was dark outside.

"Perfect place for an ambush," McCarter mused. "You guys have that gun light that Gadgets built for us?"

"The one that can overwhelm IR-based night vision?" Hawkins returned.

McCarter nodded. "Mount them up. There's a good chance the enemy is waiting out there to catch a piece of us. Or trap us if we go downstairs, where we assume the enemy is waiting for us."

"We have coms back again," Hawkins noted.

McCarter activated his mike. "Cal? Rafe? Things quieted down for you?"

"Search and destroy isn't quite complete," James answered.

"Well, we destroyed enough of them. Some are still evading our search, but it looks like they're making tracks for the next county," Encizo added. "You need us there?"

"We need you to look for a group that might have

slipped out a back entrance and is closing in on the tower," McCarter returned. "We figured out their trap, but they have a backup plan. Something that's not going to make it easy for us to finish this mess off."

"They go for a hammer-and-anvil play, we turn it back on them," Encizo responded. "Barb, you getting that?"

"We can steer you. Drones are back online." The mission controller cued in, only moments of delay away at light speed thanks to satellite communications. "Scanning the area for enemy troops and we've got nine heat signatures popping up in a tight mass. Probably coming out of an escape hatch."

"Gary, make sure you don't get blindsided in the lobby here," McCarter ordered as the position of the enemy was noted on his Combat PDA. He began to unsnap his armored vest and peel out of it. "You'll be our overwatch out there."

"What's with the striptease?" Hawkins asked.

"I don't want to show up as a target as we go out with the prisoners," McCarter explained. He stuffed his Browning Hi-Power into his belt after removing all of the harnesses that would have made him stand out as different from the support staff they'd just released.

Hawkins began doing the same.

"I'm not ordering you to risk your life the same as me," McCarter told the Texan.

"Yeah, well, screw that," Hawkins returned. "You ain't going out there alone."

McCarter smiled and the two shared a fist bump. They slid spare extended magazines for their handguns and the compact MP-7 submachine guns into cargo and side pockets on their BDU trousers. They then undid their BDU tops and slung the chatterboxes underneath the loose, untucked shirts. There was enough slack in the slings on the guns that they could extend them to firing, easily snapping down the foregrip and shoulder stock if necessary, yet keeping them hidden within the folds of the oversize tops.

"If things get too hot, we're going to catch a ton of lead," Hawkins mused.

"Now you have doubts?" McCarter asked.

"Not doubts, expectations and impetus to get 'er done quick," Hawkins answered.

Hawkins and McCarter blended into the crowd, lending their strength and shoulders to those who couldn't walk, using the bodies and shadows of those they aided to further obfuscate their personal arsenals. It wouldn't provide much, but the two men moved swiftly, even as Manning hastily erected a series of trip mines to guard him from ambush from behind.

"Set?" McCarter asked.

Manning nodded. The big man had his rifle ready to unleash long-range precision death. "Anyone armed who isn't 'family' gets canceled."

"Let's do this," Hawkins said.

So far, McCarter's hunches had been correct as he and Hawkins exited the lobby among the noncombatants. Though he was engaging in the same kind of camouflage as terrorists who hid in civilian areas, there was a difference, he realized. He was armed and among the former hostages as a further means of protecting them. If they were fired upon, he and Hawkins would immediately spring to the defense of the unarmed throng, putting themselves between certain death and those who could not fight on their own. It was a fine line, and one he would feel uncomfortable with had there not been an actual team of cold-blooded murderers assembled out here.

Murderers who were responsible for the bruises, lacerations and gunshot wounds on these and the four left behind. Protecting these victims from them meant that they had to end the murderers, because there was little doubt that Los Lictors would silence every witness to their crimes at El Calabozo sin Piedad. While it was likely that they could open fire and finish the job, McCarter counted on their desire to destroy Phoenix Force and Stony Man, thus holding their fire to take the three of them by surprise.

"In position," James and Encizo whispered over their mikes, words coming through clearly to the Phoenix commander through his com set.

"The enemy is scrambled now, using similar interference to what they used on us," Price added.

"Fair payback for that headache," McCarter mused.

"I see them. Your four o'clock," Manning added. "When do we attack?"

"Peel off," McCarter whispered to Hawkins. The two men handed off their civilians then crouched into the shadows, using the building's architecture and foliage to their advantage. They took the path most hidden from the group placed at Manning's callout. Quickly, they drew their MP-7s from beneath their untucked, unbuttoned shirts, attaching their IR illuminators on forward rails.

"Blind 'em!" McCarter ordered.

It was a quiet, almost anticlimactic act, the activation of a light switch, but downrange, McCarter could hear the grunts and slaps of discomfort as goggles were pulled or pivoted away from flashed eyeballs. He knew the opposition would be seeing afterglare for several moments, but felt that not quite enough of their night vision had been destroyed. "Gimme a parachute flare."

From as far back as the helicopter, one of their allied federal agents launched such a flare skyward. In twenty seconds, it would arc and blaze to life, a tiny sun hanging from a handkerchief-size chute, and would take at least a minute to finish burning and hit the ground.

"Burn the bastards," McCarter snapped as he poked his head up from behind his concealment and swept two of the enemy gunmen with his MP-7, high-velocity 4.6 mm rounds whipping toward the crouched opposition.

Hawkins's Heckler & Koch spoke, as well, and while he saw that he was making direct hits on the silhouetted enforcers, they were scrambling and reacting to the gunfire as if unimpressed by the hits.

"Of course not, they've got armor," McCarter grumbled.

Manning provided the solution to that, his G-3 chugging loudly. Two of the enemy figures stiffened and toppled, poleaxed by 7.62 mm NATO through weak points in their vests.

The parachute flare came to life, shining down like the flashlight of the gods and casting Lictors in stark contrast to their surrounding terrain. The Mexican gangster commandos were huddled and crouched, using benches and trash cans to make themselves less obvious targets, at least to the Phoenix Force sniper.

McCarter aimed low toward one of the armored paramilitary thugs and struck the ground just in front of the belly-crawler. His bullets ricocheted off the concrete walkway and up into the chin and throat of the helmeted enemy, bypassing the heavy polycarbonate head shell and its thick visor. The man screamed in horror, his jaw torn asunder by the bouncing projectiles. As he rolled, clutching his shattered, torn face, McCarter followed with a second burst, raking across his forearms, tearing muscles and breaking bone. Heavy plates protecting the gunman's elbows managed to protect those joints, but the ex-SAS man had ruined any hope that the gunman could use his weapons again.

To his right, a brilliant fireball erupted.

Hawkins drew his backup .357 Magnum revolver and fired it. The enemy's armor might have had the ability to stop even a supersonic steel-cored bullet, but Phoenix Force had thought and planned ahead. Hawkins's tiny backup Magnum was loaded with a larger version of the diminutive cartridge, and moving at 1,500 feet per second, the Texan's six-gun punched through the Lexan face plate on another of the Mexican gunmen. Clear plastic shattered brutally, and the deformed, steel-cored slug crushed his target's nose, digging through into the base of his brain.

On cue, a pair of 40 mm shells landed amid the group. The HEDP shells were meant to penetrate light vehicle armor, and at least one of the grenades scored a direct impact. The shaped charge at the tip lanced molten steel through Kevlar and trauma plates like a hot chain saw through tissue paper. Other men screamed as they were whipped with broken wire and steel casing splinters, arms, legs and exposed jaws covered with dozens of fresh razor slices. The grenades weren't lethal, but James and Encizo had ended one more of the opposition and were eating away at the morale of the enemy group as a whole.

"No mercy," McCarter growled. He reloaded and advanced. Satellite imaging had showed that nine men had approached the tower, circling in the hope to cut off Phoenix Force's means of escape. Five were dead, and it appeared that three more were wounded.

There was no sign of number nine.

"Eyes open! One of them ghosted!" McCarter called out.

A series of explosions detonated from the tower's lobby.

"Phase two is attacking from below," Manning reported.

"Get outside," McCarter ordered. "Cal and Rafe, pelt the building with everything you have left. T.J., on me."

Moments later more grenades erupted in the lobby of the tower. Manning, however, was out of the line of friendly fire from personal artillery.

There was a dangerous gunman on the loose and unaccounted for. Even as McCarter and Hawkins hosed down the remaining trio of Lictors, his instincts warned him that a fanatical foe was still on the loose.

Amid the blaze of an artificial sun and the thunder of grenades and rifle fire, he had to bring down this enemy if they had any hope to walk out of here.

HUNDREDS OF MILES AWAY, Carl Lyons was in hot pursuit of an opponent. He and the rest of Able Team were in a helicopter piloted by Jack Grimaldi, a familiar old friend from back in the days when Lyons was part of a task force hunting down a violent vigilante and Grimaldi was said fugitive's personal pilot and informant inside organized crime.

Right now they were in *Dragonslayer*—a modified helicopter commissioned and assembled by the SOG for the purposes of combating organized crime and terrorism. The sleek, deadly bird was only a few miles behind an enemy helicopter utilized by the forces employed by Hector Moran, the Caballeros Cartel and the Accion Obrar. Whether these were hired mercenaries or actual core troops in the Lictors organization was unknown at this moment.

The helicopter, however, was full of bad men who'd hit a small area of Yuma, Arizona, with heavy machine guns and rockets in an effort to eliminate Able Team.

Lyons knew they were in full escape mode, which meant they were heading somewhere that might have the last dregs of the conspiracy that had threatened the Justice Department and every administration since the founding of Stony Man Farm. The men buoying those in the fleeing aircraft were responsible for riddling American law enforcement and government with moles, patsies, bought politicians and sundry scum.

So far, Brognola had taken actions against two fully corrupt senators, setting things in play so that their influence would further be defanged. Even so, there were others out there that had Caballeros Cartel or Accion Obrar fingers slipping bribes into their pockets. Lyons's goal was to bring down hell so hard that no one would dare come close to the crooked politicians, and vice versa.

Hermann Schwarz leaned over, his CPDA in hand. Schwarz's compact little tablet computer was as far advanced and more durable than the ones assigned to the rest of Stony Man operatives simply because Schwarz had designed the unit and was constantly tinkering and testing out cutting-edge programming and electronics within it.

"I've been figuring the course of the enemy bird, given its make and range, versus the maps we have," Schwarz announced. "There's only one logical location where the helicopter could land."

Lyons glanced at the screen. "Isn't that the mansion of former governor—"

Schwarz nodded, cutting him off. "The same moron who claimed that stretches of desert were littered with decapitated corpses."

Lyons sneered. "*Are* these idiots going there?"

Schwarz tapped a button on his screen.

Barbara Price's live-feed image appeared. "Schwarz sent us likely destinations for your quarry, and we've been running all manner of financials."

"Forensic accounting going that quickly?" Lyons asked. He smirked. "Looking for the same earmarks that showed up in the paper trail to bring down any of our already investigated subjects."

"On the nose," Price told him. "And former Governor Florence Brady seems to have truly come into a large amount of money."

"Of course," Lyons growled. "She raised enough concerns that the DEA increased its eyes into the area, upping the prices and profits for the cartels she claimed she was against."

"Preliminary and, mind you, sketchy satellite scans show a lot of activity at her estate," Price added.

"Preliminary scans," Lyons murmured. "Meaning no high-resolution imagery, but we can count the infrared dots to tell there are a lot of men on the premises."

"Count of around forty," Price confirmed. "No idea of weaponry, but there's at least four hot engines, meaning trucks or cars are idling."

Lyons nodded, frowning. "We have an idea of the fire-power present. After all, we got a preview of it when they came at us in Yuma."

Lyons looked at the AA-12 combat shotgun at his feet. He had it loaded, having replenished its magazines. This time, he made do with standard buckshot loadings, if entirely brass-cased 3-inch Magnum 00 Buck could be considered standard. The all-brass cartridges were designed not to melt, unlike normal plastic shells, meaning that Lyons could run the AA-12 as fast and hot as it needed to be without choking on ammunition stuck in the chamber.

Forty enemy bogies meant that he was going to lean hot and heavy on the trigger of the battle shotgun, revving it up to its full 300 rounds per minute, and with each brass shell holding fifteen .33-caliber slugs in its wad, he was going to be firing at rates of fire that only mounted, electric-motored Gatling guns could match or exceed. And unlike in movies, the spread on a good shotgun within 25 yards meant a group of around twelve to twenty inches, which meant that all the pellets would likely land on a human torso 75 feet distant.

Fifteen wound channels, pellets moving as fast as a 9 mm bullet at 1,250 feet per second, was the equivalent of emptying half of an Uzi into an opponent, but all the bullets struck at the same instant. *That* was the killing element of even a single-shot 12-gauge. Sure, the weight of the charge was significant, but all of those wounds meant much more crushed flesh and broken bone than singular gunshot wounds. At practically 4,500 projectiles a minute, Lyons intended to scythe his way through the opposition.

And if a certain lying former governor stood in his way, she'd be put down, too. Her compliance with the cartels made her as responsible for overdoses and murders over drug territory disputes as the lords of Durango themselves.

The mansion and estate weren't far ahead. He looked through a pair of binoculars and saw that the enemy helicopter had landed. His mind ticked off a list as to Able Team's modus operandi.

Seek. Locate. Destroy.

Seek and locate: accomplished.

His bellow was loud and clear, audible even over the roar of *Dragonslayer*'s engines and the hearing protection everyone wore as the side door was open. "Load up! It's killing time!"

CHAPTER TWENTY-SIX

Former Governor Florence Brady hadn't felt her life was over once she'd finished her tour in charge of Arizona. Certainly she'd been a controversial figure, but her efforts against illegal immigration and the drug trade had gained her enormous support—most especially from the Mexican cartels themselves. Long in need of mules, and always interested in a reason to hike the prices of cocaine and heroin moving across the border, the Caballeros Cartel had been especially generous, money siphoned through countless cover corporations and Cayman Islands bank accounts to keep her sparkling clean.

Brady felt she was as worthy of making a run at the presidency, and in the polls, she fared as the most attractive of candidates, both in beliefs and in regard of being on the cover of *Best Beach Bodies Over 40*.

However, no amount of showing her bronzed, still-fit form in tasteful swimwear could get her out of the mouth of this fresh hell she'd descended into.

Around her mansion were dozens of heavily armed men, and not just the buff, young US military dropouts that she'd handpicked to be on her protective payroll. These were the very men of whom she spoke. The paramilitary-trained Mexican drug soldiers she claimed committed acts of atrocity miles across the border from Mexico, the enemy at the gates that forced the immigration issue to the forefront of politics, just as Mick and Reed had asked her to.

Now not one but two helicopters were approaching her

estate, and from the reaction of the Mexicans, one of the two was not one of the three that had taken off from her personal helipad.

"What's going on?" Brady asked several times before she laid eyes upon the leader of the contingent of imported guns. His name was Evan Earl, the son of a former Grand Dragon of the Ku Klux Klan who'd attempted to run for President. The son had taken on the rank of major.

Major Earl regarded Brady with cold, grim eyes as she questioned him.

"If it's not obvious by now, then you're even more useless than I thought," Earl growled. "Our attack failed, and the idiot pilot is bringing back hot pursuit."

Brady's shoulders slumped.

"You've got two choices," Earl said, handing her a pistol, butt-first. "Shoot yourself or fight alongside us."

"But—" Brady began.

"They'll either kill you or arrest you," Earl interrupted her. "So, you can spare yourself time in a prison cell, or you can keep them off. It's so simple, even a tool like you can understand."

Brady looked down at the pistol, frowning. Before she could give an answer, Earl was gone.

Shoulder-fired missiles pierced the sky from the security wall of the estate, and Brady's jaw dropped. The lead helicopter exploded into a mass of flame and splintering metal while the second aircraft spat out streaks of hot, white fire and smoke. A moment later the enemy helicopter wasn't blowing up prematurely, because the blazing spears launched by the ground troops curved away from the sleek transport, following a line of flares. Warheads detonated harmlessly, far from its vitals and passengers.

"Oh, God," Brady prayed, her stomach flopping inside.

More streaks of fire and smoke erupted from the helicopter, but these were sharply directed to the courtyard where the rocket shooters rapidly fought to reload. Gunmen around them shouldered weapons of various sizes, pulling triggers to spit tongues of light toward the incoming aircraft. In the darkness, the larger projectiles produced visible trails, even with the floodlights blazing all around her mansion.

She'd expected the weapons coming down from the attacking ship to detonate loud and violently and braced herself for shock waves that never came. Instead, chemical smoke gouged into the air, spreading and obscuring vision all around. She caught a whiff of the acrid smoke, but she didn't feel the accompanying nausea or burning associated with riot-control fumes. This was merely, literally, a smoke screen.

Brady felt a surge of relief as the attackers weren't out to level her mansion.

Then a small figure burst from the haze. It was a woman, barely five feet tall by Brady's judgment. The former governor began to raise her handgun, but the woman in black moved with the speed of a serpent.

Dr. Lao Ti slapped Brady's handgun to one side with a chop that turned the woman's fingers numb. Lao Ti had caused several small fractures in the woman's wrist, rendering that hand useless for holding anything heavier than a plastic spoon thanks to a precision application of Shotokan karate. Though the Vietnamese woman had the firepower and justification to cut loose with full-automatic fire, the politician was someone to arrest and grill for more information.

Lao Ti knew a high-value target when she saw one. Brady's arrest and public humiliation would go a long way toward exposing the kind of duplicity and dishonesty of her particular wing of her political party. Florence Brady would go from rich and powerful to a flag-waved warning to those who saw their elected seat as a means to profit through criminal malfeasance.

She rammed her tiny but weathered fist into Brady's ribs, feeling them crack under the impact, even through the steel caps protecting her knuckles. Another punch blew even more air from the woman's lungs, and Lao Ti swept her off her feet with a kick to the ankles.

Bodyguards rushed to their boss's rescue, stunned by the suddenness of Lao Ti's attack. Her swift actions had disarmed the former governor in the space of seconds, so when the burly men she'd hired finally got their wits about them, the Able Team alumnus whipped up her H&K machine pistol and pulled the trigger. PDW rounds ripped through the body armor of one of the buff protectors and, despite their diminutive .46 mm caliber, produced horrendous wound channels through his torso. His headlong charge to protect Brady turned into a lifeless crash to the ground. The second man paused, startled by the loss of his partner.

Lao Ti didn't have the time or range to attempt to disarm this goon, either. The military washout didn't have the kind of experience as a true combatant, so when someone died close to him, his attention was taken away from battle. When his focus would return in the space of a millisecond, he would do his best to gun down Lao Ti. She beat him to the punch, ripping most of his face off with a snarl of slugs at 800 rounds per minute.

Having bought herself some space, and with the spread of the smoke cloud giving her further concealment, Lao Ti knelt and restrained Brady with nylon cable ties. "All hands, we've got cargo," she announced through her com set.

"Well, Hal can make use of her," Carl Lyons growled in return. His grunt of disdain disappeared in the thunder of the AA-12 shotgun as it opened fire.

Already ahead of the game in terms of prisoner count, Able Team was in final knockout mode.

DOMINGO PEREZ HOPED that he wouldn't let Able Team down in their final assault as he descended into the smoke. He was one of five fast-roping in from the sleek high-tech helicopter piloted by Stony Man ace Jack Grimaldi.

He had a 12-gauge Auto Assault shotgun, much like Carl Lyons's Atchisson, but his was loaded with a 7-round magazine with one in the chamber. Perez was fairly tall and in good shape, but he wasn't a football-playing powerhouse like Lyons, who could be festooned with 20-round drums and still move with nimble grace on the battlefield. Even so, having a rapid reload for a shotgun, firing on semiautomatic only, he had enormous firepower at his fingertips.

Perez spotted one of the American mercenaries on the Brady estate through the hazy smoke screen vomited by *Dragonslayer.*

The guard pulled on a gas mask, his light squad automatic weapon hanging around his neck as he strapped into the self-contained breather. Once he was finished, he'd pick up the SAW and fire at Lyons. Despite the thick chemical fog, the Able Team leader was quite visible as the AA-12 shotgun lit up the smoke as if it were a strobe light. Lyons made himself an enormous target no matter how much obfuscation was around him.

Luckily, Perez was in a position to do something about that. He shouldered the AA-12 and pulled the trigger twice. The first load of Magnum buck destroyed the guard's gas mask, turning the heavy plastic into shards of flesh-slashing shrapnel that peeled the skin and muscle from his bones. Perez's second blast was a little lower as he was leaning into the shotgun, and this fist of fifteen .33-caliber slugs tore off his jaw and scooped out his throat with deadly abandon.

Another enemy gunman spotted Perez's entry into the battle and was caught flat-footed, wondering which target he should take down first. Perez absolved him of his indecision with a shotgun blast to the pelvis, shattering the man's hips. Suddenly without anything to stand on, his hands flew outward in an effort to remain upright. He lost his gun, but Perez's follow-up shot to the face ended his suffering as more than an ounce of metal drilled a cavern through his skull.

Hermann Schwarz rushed up to Perez, grabbed him by the epaulet handle on his battle vest and yanked hard. As the world around Perez jerked to the right, the heat and wind of a sniper's bullet lashed his cheek. Instantly, Perez realized that had not Schwarz torn him off balance, the slug would have smashed his own brain and severed his spine, killing him instantly.

Schwarz held on to Perez's epaulet so he wouldn't tumble and fall. At the same time, he had his H&K M7 stiff-armed, firing so fast, its stream of slugs sounded like tearing canvas. Gadgets had some form of optic that enabled him to see through the smoke, because he was aiming to strike something on an upper-floor window of the mansion. He fired three extended bursts from the compact hammer-shaped machine pistol then looked around for more opposition.

"You okay? Were you hit?" Schwarz asked Perez.

The deputy marshal shook his head. "No, I'm good."

"Outstanding. Keep blazing away," Schwarz replied before disappearing into the swirling mists.

All around him, the thunder and chatter of heavy weaponry shook the very air. Punctuating the bang and boom of all of this gunfire were screams of dying men and those suffering horrendous injuries. Perez added to the cacophony of the slaughter ground with his own shotgun, swatting down any unfamiliar figure that appeared through the mists.

The deputy marshal grunted as a swathe of lead smashed into his body armor. He could feel the pinprick knives of pain seething in his chest, indicating that his ribs had fractured, even with the protective layers of Kevlar and sandwiched chain mail he wore. Pain wheeled him backward, but another strong hand snaked from out of nowhere, hooked him under his armpit and lowered him to the ground.

A flash of salt-and-pepper hair and the thump of an M203 grenade launcher identified his rescuer as Rosario Blancanales. The Puerto Rican Able Team veteran got both hands back on his rifle-launcher and cut loose with a spray of 5.56 mm ammo to follow up the 40 mm shell he'd just fired. By now, the smoke screen had faded to the point where he could see the flickers of burning fires and bodies slumped against walls.

In a matter of moments, Perez had gone through two magazines of 12-gauge for his AA-12. There had been more than three dozen enemies on these grounds, but things had grown coldly quiet.

"Are you all right?" Blancanales asked.

Perez grimaced. "Chest feels hot. Maybe cracked some ribs."

Blancanales glanced around. "Gadgets! Ti! Cover us!"

"We've got you," Lao Ti called out. The tiny woman was hauling a form, larger than she was, and yet she moved along with speed belying her size.

Of course, she's a member of this crew, Perez told himself. She's going to be better trained and stronger than any man her size.

"Any tangos still active?" Blancanales asked, checking Perez's pupils for signs of shock and feeling his pulse.

"Everyone but us, and I presume the governor, is approaching ambient air temperature," Schwarz returned.

"I picked up two figures on *Dragonslayer*'s thermals," Grimaldi's voice came over his earbud. "Running away from the main grounds."

"Carl's nowhere to be seen," Lao Ti noted.

"Yup, the second one has a Stony Man IFF on him," Grimaldi reported.

Perez coughed, and the spasm sent a new wave of prickling aches through his chest. "I guess he was serious."

"About killing them all?" Blancanales asked. "When Lyons says he's burning everyone to the ground, he brings gasoline and matches with him."

Perez didn't doubt that, after all of the carnage that Able Team had wrought through Arizona.

There was at least one last bastard who was going to be added to that pile of corpses.

For now, Perez's fight was done; his injuries needed tending.

CARL LYONS RECOGNIZED the leader of this force, Major Evan Earl, of White Aegis. While he spoke politically of white separatism and small government, putting forth a "respectable" face, the man was merely a bully and terrorist. He raised his guns to protect meth shipments or to rob armored cars. His "protests" were vicious beatings of minorities or same-sex couples.

And sure enough, at the first sign of concentrated, violent resistance to his own brutality, Earl turned and ran like the moral coward he was. Lyons couldn't let a piece of racist filth like him escape. The trouble was, Earl had some good running speed, and he was just outside the range of his AA-12 shotgun.

The Able Team leader grimaced, realizing that he'd been so intent on catching up to Earl that he'd forgotten about his Colt Python Plus in its holster. The son of a Klan dragon could have been 200 yards away and he could still get precision hits on the thug.

He let the big auto shotgun bounce on its sling, fingers pulling the tacky rubber grips of his big Magnum revolver. All of this was done as he slowed to a standstill. His second hand wrapped around his other, locking the weapon in place, one arm slightly bent to absorb recoil like a pistol spring, pushing against the stabilizing pressure of the other's pull. If Earl got away, he had guns on him. He could carjack an innocent family, and he'd seek out new animals to employ him to engage in more senseless violence.

The Kissinger-tuned, double-action trigger was smooth as glass, and the Able Team leader's sights didn't wobble from the Klansman mercenary as the hammer cycled back and tripped loose.

Lyons hit Earl in the shoulder, his body armor taking the heavy, steel-cored slug.

Distance and ceramic trauma plates turned a crippling impact into something that merely spun Earl off his feet.

"Now it's a fight," Lyons growled. Gunfire whipped blisteringly close to the Ironman's cheeks, and he pulled the trigger again, spearing out a second armor-piercing Magnum slug.

On his belly, Earl fired short bursts from his assault rifle. As a gunman, he did have some small talent, but Lyons's body armor protected him from the rounds that hit his torso. His shoulders and upper arms were nicked and cut by glancing impacts. It was that incoming fire that pushed his aim off course, forcing Lyons to miss his next three shots directed at Earl's forehead and face.

The enemy rifleman knew that he wasn't having much of an effect by firing at chest level at Lyons, so he threw himself aside, rolling to the protection of a knoll of dirt.

Lyons watched as he blew a clot of sod from that bit of Brady's estate, the bullet stopping inside his opponent's fresh cover.

"Damnation," Lyons grumbled, continuing to fire until his 8-shot converted Anaconda ran dry.

Now that Earl was cowering behind a berm of earth, he was no longer firing upon Lyons, giving him a chance to advance.

"How about we make a deal?" Major Earl called out. "You look like someone who would fit in with my men."

"Blond and blue-eyed? You're as stupid about whites as you are blacks," Lyons snarled. He sidestepped. In the shadows, he was able to get a better angle on the mercenary boss. He shouldered his AA-12, fully loaded and ready to fire. "Just because I resemble one of your damned Aryan wet dreams doesn't mean I tolerate your garbage."

"So what? You're good with a gun. It's not like I'm any great shakes. I'm working for Mexicans, for hell's sake!" Earl shouted back.

Lyons was silent now. He advanced, but Earl was gone from the spot where he'd crawled.

Cat and mouse.

No, that implied Lyons had a physical or firepower advantage on Earl.

This was mongoose and cobra. Both were swift, dangerous predators, and both had deadly weaponry.

True to this analogy, Earl rose up, striking like a cobra. The Klansman mercenary had discarded his rifle, all of its ammunition likely expended in trying to stop the advancing juggernaut that was Carl Lyons.

The Able Team commander winced as .45-caliber slugs glanced off his shoulder and chest, whirling swiftly in an effort to protect his arm and head, tucking himself behind the turtle shell of his body armor's back panel. However, this was a momentary measure.

Lyons bent and fired his auto shotgun through the gap between his legs. He had little control given the weapon wasn't shouldered and, despite demonstration videos, he seriously feared that he would induce a jam in the AA-12, but his initial salvo of almost fifty projectiles was on target. Lyons tore flesh and bone away from Earl's feet, even through the leather and Kevlar of his combat boots.

Earl let out a howl of agony. No longer capable of standing, he dumped to the ground.

Lyons turned to see that at least the enemy mercenary had physical courage and strength; he was struggling to reload his handgun.

It was just his dishonesty that made him a coward. Lyons didn't care about the nature of his twisted politics and beliefs. He just cared that Evan Earl used them to legitimize his violence against others.

He pulled his snub-nosed backup from its holster.

"You're never going to stop us. America is ready for another civil war, and this time we'll clean this nation," Earl sputtered. "We're going to make this nation just as God and the founding fathers intended…"

Lyons kicked the gun from Earl's fingers. It sailed, spiraling to the ground. He sneered down at the son of bigotry incarnate. A smirk crossed his lips as he realized he'd come here on a helicopter named *Dragonslayer* and Earl was the son of a "Grand Dragon."

"Kill me, you create a martyr—"

"No, I won't," Lyons said. "Because the world's only going to see you as aiding in the illegal immigration pipeline. You'll be a slaver and bastard to those you oppose, and you'll be a race traitor to your fellow thugs."

Earl sputtered, eyes widening.

"You're done, Major," Lyons growled.

One .357 slug was enough. The rest of the cylinder was

merely bleeding off his anger at those who would inevitably follow in Earl's footsteps.

He reloaded the nubby.

"Let them come. I'm not going anywhere," Lyons challenged the universe under his breath.

CHAPTER TWENTY-SEVEN

As the other members of Phoenix Force unleashed a storm of destruction and death against the remnants of Accion Obrar's commando forces, David McCarter and Thomas Jefferson Hawkins were in hot pursuit of one man who had escaped the ambush shattered by the Stony Man warriors.

From McCarter's observations, he'd noted that the ambush team had deferred to a very specific leader, and after Phoenix Force had surrounded and annihilated them, that the leader had gone without a trace. No corpse, no pieces of body, just a pile of brass indicative of one more shooter than they'd found remains.

The Briton knew that the leader of such a strike team was a dangerous human being, as every member of Los Lictors was a veteran of special operations missions and training, as well as a proven killer several times over. Said leader would likely have connections with other drug cartels not in direct conflict with either Accion Obrar or the Caballeros de Durango Cartel, giving him a place to start over.

Those connections and his awareness of Stony Man's existence made this escapee a true threat to the Sensitive Operations Group and national security.

According to what the cyber crew had learned and what Amanda Castillo had relayed of the hierarchy between the Caballeros Cartel and the renegade Mexican agency, Hector Moran was a big shot in both groups.

Positions of power in the Caballeros de Durango were only achieved through hands-on bloodshed and violence. At the same time, Moran was also a veteran of Mexican special operations, where he'd undoubtedly honed the deadly skills that had advanced him in the cartel. A similar meteoric rise through the ranks of a Mexican agency, especially one as corrupt as Accion Obrar, couldn't be explained merely by muscle and fighting skill, even as a combat machine. It was status and money that bought officer ranks, which dovetailed nicely with his cruelty and machismo.

Moran's odious racist prejudices and international arms and drug smuggling ties had earned him allies north of the border. He was a minor celebrity among such groups as evidenced by the bigoted fanatics whom Able Team battled to a standstill in Arizona. If Moran couldn't find refuge in Mexico or Colombia, then he'd easily find support and shelter among any one of a dozen so-called "militias" from Yuma to Albany.

McCarter's instincts told him that Moran was the very prey that he and Hawkins pursued from the failed flanking maneuver.

Hawkins hand signaled McCarter. The Texan may not have been the woodsman that Canadian Gary Manning had been, but he was still a very good hunter and tracker, especially with the assistance of a thermal-imaging camera. He'd picked up the tracks of their quarry. As Moran's goal was distance, not stealth, he'd kicked up a lot of dirt as he'd run to escape.

"He slipped into the sewer runoff," McCarter mused softly. "Same way we invaded this place."

"He'll also have no qualms about putting his night-vision goggles back on. We blinded him once before, but now that he's ahead of us, he'll see us coming when we turn on our illuminators in the tunnel," Hawkins warned.

McCarter opened the already loose grating and slithered into the tunnel. "He knows we're onto him already. Every moment we worry about him spotting us—"

Hawkins cut him off. "Let's get him. I'm just letting you know what we're up against."

"I know what we're up against," McCarter grumbled.

He spoke louder. "And we're not sneaking after you, Moran! We're coming for you!"

The two men left their illuminators off, for all of the bluster of not sneaking up on the renegade Mexican official, they still needed to locate him. The tactic worked extremely well, they could see the glow of their quarry through their goggles, faint and distant, but it still allowed them a direction to follow in the maze of underground tunnels. The scuffle of Moran's boots also provided an indication of how quickly he moved through the culverts.

Here in the desert beneath the prison complex, Hawkins's thermal scanner picked up the warmth of their prey's footprints. The tunnels had little moisture in them, and were cool for being out of the baking Mexican sun, so Moran's trail was bright and clear.

McCarter advanced quickly, Hawkins striding to keep up with the longer-legged Briton. The boots made enough racket to drown out Moran's retreat, but with the thermal imager, neither had to slow for fear of losing track of him.

The Phoenix Force commander kept his weapon welded tightly to his cheek and shoulder, a hand on each grip to make the submachine gun as stable as possible. The minute they had a clear target, his goal was to pepper it with a swarm of high-velocity, copper-jacketed lead.

"I've got a range of about 150 yards," Hawkins announced in a low tone.

McCarter grimaced. While the MP-7's bullets were rated to penetrate a Kevlar helmet or a trauma plate at 218 yards, putting a hole in armor was different from a fight-ending injury.

A sudden burst of gunfire erupted downrange and Mc-Carter watched as Hawkins, slammed backward, clutched his hammered chest.

"T.J.?" McCarter prompted.

"Armor and spare magazines took the brunt of it," Hawkins growled with a grimace.

McCarter lowered his winged comrade to the ground, both of them hugging the bottom of the culvert. More bursts ripped over their heads, the crackles loud and angry.

"Let me see," McCarter said.

Hawkins grabbed McCarter's hand and guided it to where dented magazine and frayed nylon pocket shells indicated where the Texan had been hit.

McCarter felt around and beneath the vest. There was no dampness beneath.

"I'm fine," Hawkins returned. "Get the fucker."

McCarter nodded then pulled a deformed projectile from the magazine pocket it had stopped within. Moran was using 4.6 mm slugs, just like the MP-7 machine pistol that McCarter had brought. Since Hawkins had been at an extreme range for the penetrative abilities of the round, he'd been all right.

McCarter took aim downrange. The thermal imager was a victim of the incoming fire and had been just the thing that had kept Hawkins's fingers together and on his hand instead of being blown off. Getting a direct shot on the opposition was going to be difficult, but he saw the distant flicker of gunfire as Moran put out another burst.

The Phoenix Force commander aimed low and raked his target at knee and shin level.

The suppressor and McCarter's electronic earplugs combined well to protect his hearing from what would have been the normal muzzle blast of the Heckler & Koch, as well as smothering the flash and flare of the gasses erupting from the barrel. Moran wouldn't see or hear the incoming fire at a football field and a half away.

McCarter's return fire couldn't be noticed by Moran until his rounds struck home, but as soon as the 4.6 mm bullets struck at rifle-like speeds, he was aware.

Moran's shattered knee and lower leg caused the cartel boss to cry out in agony. The weight he put on the leg served only to snap splintered bone, and he crashed to the ground in a fit of suffering.

McCarter fired again and again, homing in on his opponent. Slowly killing Moran was not a thing that he'd ever relish, but he was certain that if he didn't pound the gangster relentlessly, the man would continue to be a danger to himself and, most of all, McCarter's injured partner.

Truth be told, McCarter didn't worry much about his own safety or health, but Hawkins suffered from broken ribs, at least. He could also have a lacerated lung from the high-velocity impacts, which could be even more life threatening. As the leader of Phoenix Force, McCarter felt responsible for all of his team, easily giving himself up for their sakes.

By the time the Briton had burned through half of a second magazine, he was certain Moran was either dead or too crippled to put up a fight. He looked at Hawkins, who waved him on. The Texan was tough, but McCarter had been struck by enough incoming fire to know that even body armor wasn't much comfort in such an instance.

He got to his feet and checked his com set. "Cal, if you're free, T.J. took a hit," McCarter said into the throat mike. "Armor stopped most of it…"

"I read you," the Phoenix Force medic responded. There was static on the transceiver, but not so much that he couldn't understand what was being said. "How about you?"

"Unhurt. Checking on our last opponent down here," McCarter said as he reloaded, wanting a full magazine when he closed with his wounded prey. "All done up there?"

"The butchery is complete," James answered, voice weary. The job of killing the enemy was not one that the warriors of Phoenix Force or Able Team loathed, but after all the battles over the past few days, sometimes even the hardest of men grew nauseated with slaughter.

McCarter knew he had enough to put down one more rabid animal, and he scanned Moran's prone form with his night-vision and the IR illuminator. Moran's twitching and groaning was audible through the electronic pickups that amplified soft sounds but filtered out gunfire. McCarter kept the muzzle of his suppressed machine pistol trained on the fallen Mexican.

"Why...draw it out?" Moran rasped, blood flecking on his lips.

"I'm being careful so you don't hurt my man any more," McCarter growled in response as he was within ten yards of the injured gangster. "Also looking for any more of your mates down here."

"You walked over 120 meters while I'm bleeding, and nobody came..." Moran coughed. Black rivulets streamed from his nostrils and the corner of his mouth. McCarter knew that it was really blood, just from the flow and his knowledge of how gore looked, a shimmery dark mass in the green-haze filter of his NVGs.

McCarter flicked the illuminator on his shoulder from IR to white light and looked down on the blood-smeared face of his opponent. The streams from his nose and mouth were bright arterial red, meaning that his final moments were dwindling rapidly. He drew his CPDA and photographed the dying man. As soon as the digital image was put into the system, it was on its way back to the Farm at the speed of light.

"You are Moran, right?" McCarter asked.

"Sí," the dying criminal confirmed. "You're British? I thought it was an all-American...team."

"The only nationality that matters to us is pro-human or pro-barbarian," McCarter growled. "Skin color and country of origin don't matter."

The CPDA beeped. Identity confirmed. Hector Moran.

"You destroyed so much of our organization, but there will be others to come," Moran rasped. "Maybe not Mexicans, maybe it'll be Muslims. And I hear the Soviets are getting their act back together..."

McCarter looked down on his target. "To destroy America, or just to take me and mine out?"

"You know, it doesn't matter, *pendejo*," Moran said. "You've killed all the family that matters to me..."

McCarter nodded. He folded away his MP-7, slinging it over his shoulder before kneeling beside the injured gun thug. Moran's arms had been shattered, fingers blasted off in the rain of 4.6 mm lead the Briton had unleashed.

"So, you want us to suffer. And if that means America rots from within...?"

"It's already rotting," Moran growled. "But you bastards are cutting out the bad bits and allowing the US to heal."

McCarter smirked. "And when you came after us, you served up a load of that rot on a silver platter. Honest cops in America and Mexico are hunting down all the leaks and all the parasites. I'm not saying we'll get rid of corruption anytime soon, or even in the next ten years, but every little bit helps."

"All that you've probably seen…and you still have optimism?" Moran asked.

McCarter nodded. He pulled his Browning Hi-Power from its holster and flicked down its thumb safety. "Because we see the up-and-coming generations, Hector. As much disenfranchised trash that appears, there are just as many, if not more, out there ready and willing to fight for a better world. You might appeal to the greedy, the hate-filled, but Hemingway said it best…"

Moran sneered. But when he spoke, his quote was dead-on. "'The world is a fine place and worth fighting for.'"

Moran spat out a glob of blood. "Just get it over with. You've got confirmation of who I—"

McCarter obliged Moran, ending his suffering mid-sentence.

Rising, he tucked the Hi-Power away and turned around.

Several days of combat and exertion caught up with McCarter as he walked back toward Hawkins. He could already see James, with his shoulder illuminator on bright white light, examining the Texan's injuries.

"A black man shining light on the injuries of a white," McCarter mused softly. "Literally on Mexico's soil. Tending to each other as brothers."

McCarter took a deep breath. That was what Phoenix Force was all about. Men—and women, he added as he remembered his beloved Mei as well as other allies—united by righteousness, not nationality or politics, helping those who needed it, shining light on what was wrong and working to fix it. Fighting for peace might have seemed a contradiction, but it was one that McCarter could live with.

They'd ended the threat of Los Lictors and, sure, there'd be other threats out there in the future.

But Stony Man would still be there to take them all on.

For now, it was time to clean up the mess, to send the former prisoners home and to close the books on this threat.

Going home was all the exit strategy Phoenix Force would need now.

* * * * *

UPCOMING TITLES FROM

KILL SQUAD
Available March 2016
Nine million dollars goes missing from a Vegas casino, and an accountant threatens to spill to the Feds. But with the mob on his back, the moneyman skips town. Bolan must race across the country to secure the fugitive before the guy's bosses shut him up—forever.

DEATH GAME
Available June 2016
Two American scientists are kidnapped just as North Korea makes a play for Cold War–era ballistic missiles. Determined to save the scientists and prevent a world war, Bolan learns he's not the only one with his sights set on retrieving the missiles…

TERRORIST DISPATCH
Available September 2016
Atrocities continue in the Ukraine and the adjoining Crimean Peninsula, annexed by Russia in March 2014. With no end in sight, a plan is hatched to force American involvement by sending Ukrainian militants to strike Washington, DC, killing civilians and seizing the Lincoln Memorial as protest against their homeland's threat from Russia. Can Bolan bring the war home to the plotters' doorstep?

COMBAT MACHINES
Available December 2016
What began in a Romanian orphanage twenty years earlier, when a man walked away with ten children and disappeared, leads Mack Bolan and a team of Interpol agents to fend off a group of "invisible" assassins carving their way across Europe…toward the USA.

THE EXECUTIONER

THE DON PENDLETON'S EXECUTIONER.

Check out this sneak preview of
KILL SQUAD
by **Don Pendleton!**

"This is crazy," Sherman said.

His words were ignored as Bolan assessed their position. In the confines of the rail car, there was no chance they could conceal themselves. They were in the open, with armed men facing them. Once the shooters decided to push their way through, it would become a turkey shoot. If Bolan had been on his own, he might have considered resisting. But he had Sherman to consider, plus the burden of the other passengers. If he put up a fight, any retaliatory gunfire could overlap and cause injury to the innocent. That was something Bolan refused to allow.

He and Sherman were in line for the hostile fire. Bolan accepted that—with reservations where Sherman was concerned. The man was making an attempt to right wrongs, and he didn't deserve to become a victim himself.

The only way out was for Bolan and Sherman to remove themselves from the situation, which was easier to consider than to achieve. The soldier glanced at the window. The landscape slid by, an area of undulating terrain, wide and empty.

Another burst of autofire drove slugs against the connecting door. This time a couple of slugs broke through.

Bolan had already considered what he knew to be his

and Sherman's only option. He made his decision. He triggered a triburst through the connecting door to force the opposition back, even if it was only a brief distraction.

"Harry, let's go," he said. "Stay low and head for the other door."

"What…?"

"Do it, Harry, before those guys come our way."

Bolan fired off another triburst. Crouching, they made for the connecting door at the far end of the car. Bolan flung it open and hustled Sherman through. They paused on the swaying, open platform between the two cars, the rattle and rumble of the train loud in their ears.

The ground swept by, a spread of green below the slope that bordered the track.

Bolan glanced back through the connecting door and saw armed men moving into view. This time he held the Beretta in both hands and fired. Glass shattered. Bolan saw one man fall and the others pull aside. The delay would only last for seconds. He holstered the 93-R and zipped up his jacket.

"Have you ever jumped from a moving train?"

Don't miss
KILL SQUAD by Don Pendleton,
available March 2016 wherever
Gold Eagle® books and ebooks are sold.

GEXEXP446

STONY MAN®

"As the President's extralegal arm, Stony Man employs high-tech ordnance and weaponry to annihilate threats to the USA and to defenseless populations everywhere."

This larger format series, with a more high-tech focus than the other two Bolan series, features the ultracovert Stony Man Farm facility situated in the Blue Ridge Mountains of Virginia. It serves as the operations center for a team of dedicated cybernetic experts who provide mission control guidance and backup for the Able Team and Phoenix Force commandos, including ace pilot Jack Grimaldi, in the field.

Available wherever Gold Eagle® books and ebooks are sold.

GOLD EAGLE®

DON PENDLETON'S MACK BOLAN®

"Sanctioned by the Oval Office, Mack Bolan's mandate is to defuse threats against Americans and to protect the innocent and powerless anywhere in the world."

This longer format series features Mack Bolan and presents action/adventure storylines with an epic sweep that includes subplots. Bolan is supported by the Stony Man Farm teams, and can elicit assistance from allies that he encounters while on mission.

Available wherever Gold Eagle® books and ebooks are sold.

GOLD EAGLE®